WHILE PARIS DANCED

Also by Patricia Wright

THE STORMS OF FATE
HEART OF THE STORM
SHADOW OF THE ROCK
JOURNEY INTO FIRE
A SPACE OF THE HEART

WHILE PARIS DANCED

Patricia *Wright*

DOUBLEDAY & COMPANY, INC.
GARDEN CITY, NEW YORK
1982

Library of Congress Cataloging in Publication Data
Wright, Patricia, 1932–
    While Paris danced.
    I. Title.
PR6073.R54W5 1982   823'.914   AACR2
ISBN: 0-385-17898-0
Library of Congress Catalog Card Number 81-43376

WHILE PARIS DANCED

PROLOGUE

Today it would be over.

After four earthquake years which destroyed the world ten million men had died to preserve, only fifteen minutes remained of the war to end wars.

Fourteen minutes. Thirteen. Then armistice would come, the guns fall silent and those still living escape from hell. Escape quickly, half believing, disbelieving they had survived.

Ten minutes.

Second Lieutenant Charles Wyville was just eighteen years old and very far from being a survivor of past battles. He had reached the British front line near Mons only hours before, after a hurried course on Salisbury Plain and a week's embarkation leave, hustled to France as British casualties mounted during the offensive of 1918. Now he had arrived to find the war within minutes of ending. He looked at his watch: nine minutes, to be exact. In fact, around Mons the guns were already silent. The night before, this place where British troops fought their first battle of the war had been recaptured and the Germans had pulled out fast enough for all contact to be lost. Now Canadian pipers were fingering chanters and breathing into tartan bags, preparing for a celebration entry into the town the moment armistice came, at eleven o'clock precisely. Around them, British and Canadian troops waited quietly, not cheering, not speaking, the silence too strange for speech.

Charles Wyville swore and stamped his feet in cold mud. His nose ran and he sneezed explosively, making everyone jump. A cold in the head would remain his sole experience of the Great War. About four hundred yards away, he could see a ruined village, the church tower snapped off, an unmilked cow moaning somewhere close. When he arrived, last night, German snipers had still been posted there, but they had not fired for hours and must have been withdrawn once it became clear that here the enemy would wait out the last hours of the war. With close to a million British dead and three times that number maimed, this was no time for heroics. On the other hand, it would be a splendid time to capture a village for himself, Charles Wyville thought.

He moved cautiously to where a destroyed section of trench allowed some view over the sodden landscape; the village was nearer than he had thought, and Charles's hand moved to the holster at his belt. After all his efforts to become part of the greatest war man had seen, he must at least fire a shot. He kicked a toehold in mud and levered himself higher, heart thumping.

"Best keep down, sir. It's a bloody stupid time to get killed," a sergeant called.

Charles caught the man's tone of contemptuous indulgence, and straightened angrily. Why the devil should his platoon skulk out these last minutes of the war? He never felt the bullet that took him through the bridge of his nose and blew his brains into the sergeant's lap.

Five minutes now.

Around Mons the land was ruined but not utterly destroyed; farther south destruction was complete. Where towns had once stood were rubbish piles of broken bricks shoveled aside to allow military transport to pass. Villages had vanished, topsoil was blasted; blackened tree stumps, shredded clothing, bleached bones and putrefied flesh were set into a framework of mud and shell holes which denied any connection with the earth men knew before they came here—as those who now inhabited this land were set apart from the men they once had been, from men who did not know this place. They thought they would forget because now it was nearly over they wanted passionately to forget; instead they would remember, be haunted and driven by remembrance of shelling and untended wounds, the stench and squalor and fear, the terror of friends who vanished without trace, the friends who died in agony, unaided, a few paces out of reach. Survivors would scream and tremble fifty years later, when chance swept recollection back.

Outside Sedan, artillery and machine guns had been firing all through the last night of the war, bludgeoning belief that it soon would end. The French had taken a few houses in the suburbs, the Germans still held the rest of the town. When dawn came, a mist settled over the valley of the Meuse, hiding everything more than twenty paces distant, though shells and bullets still tore through murk as both sides watched the seconds tick away.

A burst of machine-gun fire overhead, close enough to make the men of the 121st Regiment of Chasseurs burrow into earth. A few of them had lived long enough to have fought at Verdun; one survived from 1914 but was no longer sane. His fellows treated him as a mascot and pushed and pulled him with them from rest area to trench and back again, from shell hole to tumbledown billet. They were not cruel, since nothing remained for him except a memory of comradeship, all life beyond the trenches menacing and strange. After four years in which the French Army had been ground down, rebuilt, and then ground down again, few long-serving frontline poilus were entirely sane.

Commandant Guy Saulx stared at filth beneath his face and thought about the hands of his watch. He lay where a man had died an unknown time ago but was beyond the point where he recoiled from any man's suffering, least of all his own. Into shock and beyond, into the terror where a wound is welcome, into the void where feeling dies. And then beyond again. How would he live when this was done, how gather up the rough pieces of his life again?

Behind him, his sergeant shifted and swore; Commandant Saulx's boots were almost in his face. Damn the Commandant's boots, and damn the Boches, who kept firing three minutes before armistice. Sergeant Bertrand Joubaire possessed an unerring sense of opportunity, as well as conviction that he was born to take advantage of whatever came along: he had succeeded in spending most of the war in base areas and had been outraged when France's desperate situation in 1918 resulted in his being posted to a frontline unit. But see how even that is working for the best, he thought complacently. *Il faut faire contre mauvais fortune bonne coeur.* One must make the best of a bad job; two minutes more and the war would be over without a scratch on his hide to show for it, and if his plans were successful, then the Commandant would provide his way into a prosperous future. Others died in the trenches; Sergeant Bertrand Joubaire had found even better opportunities for profit there than he had in base stores.

Joubaire swore again, but good-naturedly this time. Only one machine gun still firing, and he was cold to the backbone. Be silent, Boches! I, Sergeant Joubaire, command it. Go home like beaten dogs, because you have lost this war. I wish to stand up like a man instead of wallowing in mud, embark on the business of providing myself with the good things of life. The machine gun stopped, and he laughed.

On the flank of the 121st Chasseurs lay the American Army. Although they had fought hard these past few months, they were newcomers to war as Europe had come to understand it. Strong, healthy, and rash; convinced that their coming, rather than the murderous years before, had destroyed the German Army, and anxious to cram this belief down the throats of their allies before it was too late.

So on the American front there was a dawn attack on November 11, and by ten o'clock they were advancing, the blare of battle as loud as ever. Rick Dwyer, reporting for the Washington *Times,* went forward with the second wave of the attack—to go with the first would be foolhardy, to wait for the third, cowardly. Rick was the kind of reporter who never glossed the truth as he saw it; a cynic sometimes made gloomy by his own prophecies of disaster. He was also as truculent, energetic and self-confident as the American Expeditionary Force itself, and had written several trenchant dispatches about the need for America to impress her allies with the fact of her supremacy. Let others argue over who came out on the winning side, America was the undisputed victor in this war.

A boy from Iowa was shot through the throat at Rick's side, and despite his belief that this last offensive was necessary, the hands of his watch seemed to move with tantalizing slowness. The Germans were fighting with stubborn bitterness here, finding pleasure in pouring steel into the all-enveloping power which had swamped them these past months.

Rick remembered the Iowa boy sitting with his buddies the night before and how he had heard him agree that the best way to leave fear behind was to go forward all the time.

Well, the boy was bleeding to death now, and Rick was lying in a shell hole beside him, not going forward and very scared. His own sweat stank on the leather lining of his British helmet; the U. S. Army had not thought helmets important when it sent men overseas, and was still so short of suitable equipment that its battles were fought with British guns and French aircraft. He turned to look at the tense faces sharing the shell hole with him, made a rude gesture and winked at them. He was not a combatant, but they were just country boys and he felt obliged to encourage them.

He looked at his watch again. Two full minutes to go.

The others looked too, and one grinned. "What do you say to us firing the last shot of the war?"

Another lifted his head from the curve of his arm; there was blood on his face. "So long as we do it from here. How long, Rick?"

Rick turned his wrist; they needed to shout at each other above the din. He was conscious of relief that these three would live; that he would live, when there wasn't enough time for him to feel he ought to lead them out of here.

"I got creased on the last day, so I guess I've earned the right to fire the last shot too," said the one with blood on his face.

"The hell you have! You were nearly a dead loser, so what right's that give?"

"The last shot of the war, that sure as hell would be something to tell the folks! I'll flip you for it."

It would be something. Not to tell or write about, but to remember for himself, thought Rick. He picked up the rifle the Iowa boy had dropped. "There's room for four fingers on the trigger. We'll pull it together."

They slithered over toward him. Bullets still ripped at the lip of their shell hole, the mist trapping smoke in eye-stinging layers against the earth. Ten seconds left, and fewer bullets now, no shells. Rick pushed the rifle over the lip of the crater, four hands locked together around the stock, all their eyes glued to his watch. The hand moved past the hour and started unhurriedly on its downward sweep again. Convulsively four fingers tightened, and since it was not securely held, the rifle recoiled over their heads and spun into the mud. The shot cracked out and they solemnly shook hands; five seconds past eleven o'clock on the eleventh day of the eleventh month, 1918, and they had fired the last shot of the war.

There were cheers and colored signal flares from the American trenches, from the French and British mostly a strange quiet. But everywhere the same gladness, the deep delight which showed on faces and the way men marched. It was over, and those who remained would live.

Three hundred yards from where the Americans cheered, Hauptmann Hugo von Kobis heard the single rifle shot an instant after he gave the order to cease firing. Months of bombardment had blunted his hearing, but he had become absurdly sensitized to anything which might affect his own safety: the extra frontline senses without which few survived for more than days in the trenches.

"Stay under cover until we're certain they are obeying the cease-fire," he said to his men. His words came out as a shout and everyone jumped in alarm, so strange was silence.

The convulsed earth was still, and they had lost.

Hugo had seen defeat coming, because he had been a diplomat in the distant time when Germany had need for diplomats. That time was past: in 1916 his deferred status had been canceled and he had exchanged the red plush of the German Foreign Office, at 76 Wilhelmstrasse, for a reserve officers' retraining school. Only three weeks later he was drafted to the front, was wounded within the day, and after convalescence redrafted there early in 1918. Compared to some, he had had a short war, but during that time had lost more men's lives than he cared to remember. He was a conscientious but not a good officer, since he possessed the kind of courage which counted odds and lacked the dash which might snatch a petty victory out of the confusion of battle. On the other hand, a few men lived because Hugo von Kobis had sometimes defied authority when it ordered his company into foolishness.

If the morning of November 11 had been gray and wet, the afternoon became grayer and wetter.

Hugo looked at his watch; two hours had passed since armistice, and everything remained silent. His men were just beginning to take silence for granted: they were also fiercely, impatiently hungry.

No supplies had come up for two days, nor had the wounded been evacuated. Even if supplies had arrived, the bitter coffee would have been nearly undrinkable, the food stomach-churning, paper bandages almost immediately disintegrated by rain and blood. The German Army had been reduced to such a state of exhaustion that it could neither accept battle nor refuse it, only take punishment.

His men watched while Hugo stood, head over trench parapet, motionless; still there was no sound. It was difficult to grasp that a man could stand and not have his head blown off, and they were only mildly curious anyway. Nobody cared whether the captain lived or died. He was less imperious and less brave than most officers and they liked him for it, but liking was no longer significant. He and his fellows had led them into this, and lost them everything at the end of it. They were weary and bitter, set adrift in a way they could not comprehend.

"Time to go," said Hugo, turning. "Back to the assembly point and start marching. We have fifteen days to take the whole Army out of France."

They climbed from their trench, blinking as if the light were strong: a pallid handful close to starvation, glad it was over but nursing the spark of anger which would glow brighter as they came home in defeat. They plodded slowly back across mud they had died to win, tripping over torn wire, so the last German wounds came from their own defenses. Shoulders bowed, gray landscape, gray cloth, thin boots weighed down with mud. Most wore uniforms which were far too big for the children and old men recruited in this last year of the war to fill empty ranks. Peter Lehr was an exception, a solidly built Berliner, a skilled printer accustomed to good wages until newsprint became so scarce he was drafted into the Army. He couldn't wait to be warm and dry again but realized he had a long way to go. Once safely back in Germany he would sell his rifle, beat up the first officer he met for the pleasure of it, and be off. He glanced at his comrades consideringly; like him, today they were simply glad to be alive and remembered the many who were not. Tomorrow he would begin teaching them how to take payment for all they had suffered.

Hugo von Kobis walked ahead of his men. He was so tired that, now the war was over, he would gladly have risked drowning in a ditch if only he could sleep undisturbed. He went ahead because he was weeping and lacked the will to stop tears from pouring down his face. A flicker of pride remained, so he did not want his men to see their captain weep; all other emotions were lost in anguish for his defeated homeland.

From his days in the Wilhelmstrasse, Hugo knew precisely why Germany had fought, and why she had been defeated. Yet nothing explained how senseless everything written, thought, and done about this war must be when a whole generation foolishly and innocently had crucified each other. A month ago he had returned from leave, understanding very well that unless peace came soon, there would be a revolution in Germany, believing also that whether peace came or not, revolution could scarcely be avoided. He could sense already how each pace nearer home switched his men's thoughts to a different kind of battle, and this time one they might easily win. Tears dried, and instead his spine felt cold. Alone in mist with these his comrades, his frontline senses told Hugo von Kobis that he was not safe.

He turned. "Two kilometers farther and then we rest for the night. Tomorrow we march again and the day after reach our railhead." Let them realize that only he knew their part of the evacuation plan.

"And after that there won't be any more marching, Herr Hauptmann?" asked Lehr, already spokesman for the rest.

"No more marching, at least until you're out of France."

"Then we march home whatever the Hauptmann says," muttered Lehr.

Hugo pretended not to hear. He owed them the journey home, and no more. I really am not a good officer, he thought wryly. Home. Even in defeat, the word offered its own comfort.

After all, he was alive. It was worth something, to be alive.

PART I

The *Wild Drummer*

See, the Conquering hero comes!
Sound the trumpets, beat the drums!
Thomas Morell

CHAPTER 1

The trains which ran from Bois-Chauvert to Rheims never arrived on time, nor left without some crisis. Steam hissed against the station roof, stretchers had to be left behind and porters rushed about, as hundreds of soldiers attempted to cram themselves into inadequate spaces.

It was wet, dark and very cold that December of 1918; France lacked everything except the spirit of victory, and even that could become very trying, Eve Ottoway thought. She had stood for nearly four hours waiting for a train, with the prospect of another wait in Rheims for a Paris connection, all the time buffeted by mobs of exultant soldiers on their first peacetime leave. They surged this way and that, singing, stamping, drinking too much wine, smoking cigarettes which made her feel sick. They wanted her to join in, kissed her and offered bread, dry sausage and acid wine, unwilling to accept refusal.

She was happy for them, but eventually could not bear it any longer. There seemed no prospect of a train and she was colder than she could remember being since she had come to France, which was saying something, since she had been freezing the whole time. The American military hospital near Bois-Chauvert, to which Eve was attached as a volunteer Red Cross worker, occupied a sprawling château through which icy gales blew so powerfully that the carpets flapped, and the only heating came from porcelain stoves in the principal salons, a wilderness of passages away from where Eve worked.

She went out to the station yard, shivering and pulling her Red Cross cloak closer about her shoulders. She'd have to flag down a truck returning to Bois-Chauvert and think again tomorrow about how to reach Paris. Of course she had been a fool to rush off almost without reflection, hoping to reach Paris on a forty-eight-hour furlough, but she hadn't been able to think what else to do. Eve Ottoway had been told for years that impetuosity would be her downfall: she agreed with her critics and promised next time to reckon the disadvantages before she acted, but somehow she never did. Each time, the situation seemed different and she quite certain of what she ought to do to remedy it.

Like being here in France, when if she'd stayed in Maine she could have married Jake Rideau by now, all muscular six feet of him. But she'd wanted to come to France; not just wanted to but thought it was right to come, so she'd spent six months arguing objections into the ground and not letting anyone rest until here she was. And unless she reached Paris fast she'd be back in Maine for Christmas, feeling thoroughly defrauded while everyone else laughed.

If Eve hadn't been strictly brought up, she would have sworn into the rain and wind. The road past the station was as empty as the railroad track, except for the same drunken soldiers shouting at her to join them. No lights, no face she recognized from Bois-Chauvert, nowhere to go.

Eventually, her mother's punishments for unladylike conduct became too irrelevant to matter, when set beside such wet desolation. "Damn," she said quietly. "Goddam this place to hell."

She felt guiltily triumphant when a truck immediately appeared, rain like wire mesh in its dim headlights; as if by defying puritan inhibitions a whole new world of exciting possibilities was immediately opened to her. Female staff from Bois-Chauvert were forbidden to solicit or accept lifts in off-base vehicles.

The truck was going toward Rheims, when she had only just decided she'd have to return to Bois-Chauvert, but she waved it down anyway. There was an American hostel in Rheims, and probably a train in the morning direct for Paris.

The truck ran past her with a howl of worn brakes, and a man stuck his head out of the flapping canvas side. "*Où c'est-y que vous voulez aller?*"

French, thought Eve, her buoyant sense of good fortune fading. Most trucks here were American, although the junction of the two armies was very close. "*Je m'excuse de vous déranger, m'sieu.* If you are going to Rheims. . . ."

He backed the truck in a shower of mud, further soaking her skirts, which were regulation Red Cross jersey, four inches off the ground and guaranteed to soak up mud from rutted French roads. "A woman, eh? Then, certainly a ride to Rheims would be my pleasure, mademoiselle."

She disliked the look of him but didn't feel able to refuse a lift now he had stopped; anyway she needed to reach Rheims and couldn't stand soaking in the road much longer without catching pneumonia. Eve scrambled into the high-sided truck and discovered with relief that another Frenchman was sitting beside the driver; there was safety in numbers. Without speaking, he moved over to make room for her on the steel bench-seat, the atmosphere unwelcoming, his clothes wet too, the cab full of drafts.

"American?" shouted the driver above the clatter of the engine.

"Yes, from the hospital at Bois-Chauvert."

"Yet you speak our language, even though *vous vous y prenez d'une façon curieuse.*"

Eve was immediately angry, although normally she wouldn't have minded such a comment in the least; acute discomfort did not make for tolerance. So she set about the language in an odd way, did she? "And just how good is your English, m'sieu?"

"One day, when I take my chances, it will be very good." If he was disconcerted he did not show it. His accent was rough and vaguely southern: I know French well enough to tell that, she thought viciously.

It was more than an hour before they ran into the outskirts of Rheims, to find the streets deserted. France was so short of fuel that cafés had to shut by half past nine, and without light or heat nearly everyone went to bed early.

The truck slithered to a halt and the driver leaned out, swearing, to rub half an onion over the fogged-up windshield. There was no other way of clearing it, and most French Army vehicles gave the impression of having been kept going for years by not much more than faith and kicks. "Where is it you want to go?"

"I'm not sure. There's an American hostel somewhere; they won't turn me away on a night like this even if they're full, and I'll try again for Paris in the morning."

"Paris? That's where you are going?"

She nodded. "I waited four hours for the local train."

"In the name of God, why? There are any number of trucks going to Rheims in daytime." His contempt for such incompetence was obvious.

"Because we're forbidden to accept lifts, and I am on my way to Paris because I want to avoid being sent back to the States immediately, now the war is over. A disciplinary action would not exactly assist my purpose. Good night, and thank you, Sergeant." She had seen his sleeve markings in headlights reflected by the rain.

"Ah, now I understand perfectly. This disciplinary action no longer mattered once it was dark and you could not be seen. Mademoiselle, allow me to offer you transport as far as Paris; we are driving through the night to reach there by morning."

Eve wanted very much to refuse. Although he had been helpful, the sergeant's overfamiliar manner grated on her; and the other, completely silent Frenchman was positively spooky. But Rheims was large, ruined, and very uninviting in pouring rain, while the hostel would certainly report her irregular arrival to the matron at Bois-Chauvert, who was unyielding on matters of conduct.

So Eve accepted, and spent the next few miles bitterly regretting her decision. The road was atrocious, the weather unrelenting, the countryside so devoid of life that there was no possibility of changing her mind. She was not surprised they saw no other vehicles; it was more remarkable that anyone should attempt such a journey in this antique truck.

The sergeant introduced himself as Bertrand Joubaire, of the Chasseurs, and continued to talk in a half-joking, half-insolent way. Eve wished she could pretend she did not understand French, but though she might speak oddly, it was too late to disguise her grasp of the language.

Then there was the man next to her. She was glad of his presence, because she would have been afraid of Joubaire alone, but such silence was unnatural. He jolted and suffered as she and Joubaire did, occasionally saving himself with a grab at the bodywork; otherwise he did not react to anything. Feet square on the floor in mud-caked boots, he made no attempt to cushion her from the punishment of the journey. When they were thrown together, Eve could feel the muscles of his arm quivering, giving the impression that if she touched him anywhere, then he would be strung like piano wire there, too.

He was uncanny.

Eve could not sleep, it was so cold. Her clothes remained sodden, the cab plank-roofed but no more than flapping canvas at the sides; soon her shudders became convulsive spasms. How could men have endured nights like this exposed in open trenches, year after year?

"You see, mademoiselle, we are going to Paris on an errand too," Joubaire was saying. "An errand of importance now this accursed war is over and a man can plan for himself."

"Yes," said Eve at random. "Yes, I suppose so. How far now to Paris?"

He lifted his hands from the steering wheel in a gesture to the uncertainties of life. "We reach there before daylight, or so we planned it." He glanced at her and laughed; he enjoyed hinting at some hidden excitement she could not comprehend.

Before daylight; why, that must be hours away, thought Eve dismayed. She would not have been interested if Joubaire had told her that President Wilson was hiding in the back of the truck. Warmth, a bed, something to make her shivering stop—that was all she could think about.

"Stop, Bertrand," said the man beside her quietly.

"*Oui, mon commandant.*" Joubaire's reply was automatic, before surprise had time to register. "But—we haven't time to stop. Already we are much later than we hoped."

The other did not reply, and reluctantly Joubaire halted the truck, allowing her neighbor to climb down and disappear into the dark. After a moment, she heard him rummaging about in the back of the truck. "Is your commandant always so silent?" she asked, curiosity stirring even while her teeth chattered on the words.

Joubaire lit one of the horsehair-smelling French cigarettes she disliked so much, match flaring, so she glimpsed full lips, black hair and fleshy, predatory nose. His thigh pressed against hers, his hand on her knee, the moment they were alone. "What is there to interest Commandant Saulx in the likes of us, mademoiselle? War forces all kinds together, but we don't have to like each other. He gives orders, but I only remember him speaking six or seven other sentences since my last bath. It is enough."

Eve tried to shift away from him, but his hand tightened and began to move up the inside of her thigh, his stench sour in her nostrils. He had good reason to date events from his last bath, she thought, annoyed. Not that trench stink was his fault, nor was it her concern if Commandant Saulx thought himself too grand even for the courtesy of greeting.

All the same, she was relieved when Saulx almost immediately reappeared; she had become resistant to groping hands these past weeks, but disliked them all the same. He could not see much in such darkness but seemed to sense something wrong. "If you would move where I have been sitting, perhaps you would be warmer."

Joubaire's hand lingered sensuously for a moment, but as soon as Eve moved, Saulx wrapped some kind of velvet material around her. Velvet. Now, that's odd, she thought, feeling it experimentally. Rich, lined velvet in a military truck on its way to Paris in the pouring rain; she did not say anything though, when these men seemed far more unpredictable than any load they carried.

She dozed a little after that, her covering thick enough to give a little warmth, but she woke quite soon, skin clammy-cold, her bones fragmented by the torture of that truck. It was still raining, Saulx driving, Joubaire snoring against her shoulder.

She put her head in her hands; she felt worse than before, not just exhausted but definitely ill. "How much farther?"

"Two hours, perhaps less. You have friends in Paris who will take you in?"

"No."

"No one, Mlle. Ottoway? You cannot descend alone on the pavements of Paris, wrapped in a velvet curtain."

Saulx was speaking English, Eve realized with a jolt. Precise, awkward English, but English nevertheless. He had also been listening sufficiently closely earlier to remember her name. She sneezed, hoping it was dust from the velvet which made her nose and throat feel inflamed. "I mean to call on someone I hope might help me dodge the draft back to the States, but he is lodged at the Crillon and I don't suppose curtains are *de rigueur* there, either."

Unexpectedly, he laughed. An odd sound, bitten off almost at once, and the truck swerved in response to the strangeness of it. A long silence fell, during which Eve became aware of his breathing: long, rasping breaths, as though talking had been an insupportable physical effort. I suppose he's tired, she thought muzzily. God knows, so am I.

Dawn came slowly, in long, gray waves, like nausea. Potholes and ruts changed into uneven pavé. The truck had solid tires, the noise and jolting quite appalling. Eve was no longer cold; instead, her body was burning hot, and thought slid as she moved. On a Paris sidewalk, wrapped in velvet drapes and all alone, she thought, and giggled. Somehow she must harness fevered mind and aching body long enough to crawl away somewhere warm to recover. Were there American hospitals in Paris? She did not think so, since the American Expeditionary Force was based in Tours, and certainly she had no idea where to start looking. She turned her head, and something in her brain failed to make the movement with her eyes: after that, reality became mixed with nightmare.

The same streets with implacably shut shops seemed to reel past again and again. Only cafés had some lights burning, chairs stacked on tables while kneeling women swabbed identical floors. Men were drinking coffee behind steamy windows; skidding, hooting traffic made her head ache worse than ever. Sour early-morning faces, bare trees and peeling, shuttered houses: somehow she had expected Paris to be joyous.

Eve next became aware of loud-voiced, petulant argument, then heard Saulx say: "Not far now."

"I'm sorry, but I think I'm going to be sick." Eve needed to shape each word separately as fever and humiliation reacted on each other.

"So am I, after a journey like that," he replied cheerfully. "But not yet. No one's ever been sick in the Champs-Élysées; it's an unwritten law of Paris."

She tried to laugh, and the spark of amusement flowed through the next space of time until the truck pulled up before a pillared portico. A gray, forbidding house, shutters firmly closed, a bell jangling somewhere very distant. A footman in a striped vest looking outraged, a floor tiled in patterns which slithered when Eve tried to focus on them. An icy room where she could not imagine a fire ever being lit.

Quarrels; distant, and then closer. She sat on hard, stuffed satin and lost hold on what was happening.

CHAPTER 2

Eve dreamed she was back in New Moose, Maine. The trees flamed orange and the lake was blue, the grass a bright, fierce green. White houses nestled among the hills, and crops filled square New England barns. She clapped her hands in joy at the color and plenty of it, beginning to run on misted earth. And as she ran, the color faded, the fields of her childhood became unfamiliar. Wire appeared and divided her off from them: in her dream she called for help and tore at the coils with her hands. Then she peered closer and saw her own delusion. The houses were burned-out shells, the fields churned mud, the trees a furnace blaze which left them black and dead. The lake was not the ruffled blue she knew but choked with the horizon-bleu bodies of France's dead. She realized that she dreamed, knew how she cried and twisted, trying to escape, but her dream pursued her. Down the years and through the foreign, hooting streets of Paris, faster and faster, until it caught her. The peace and plenty of Maine all lost, while she drowned in the suffering land of France.

Consciousness strengthened, slipped a little, strengthened again. She was propped up in bed and made to sip herb tea which tasted of ancient mold. Over the edge of a thick china cup she watched a maid in a pleated cap straightening her bed.

"Where am I?" Her voice was a whisper.

"Why, at the Hôtel Daunay, mademoiselle, where else?" The maid clucked disapprovingly when she saw that Eve had not finished her drink, and drew curtains on both sides of her bed in a rattle of wooden rings.

Eve felt her mind dulling again as she stared at an elegantly molded ceiling. She was warm and comfortable but too tired to cope with it all.

She slept again, stirring once in the dark and again in the light; then woke remembering everything. Or nearly everything; recent time was hazy, but she remembered Bois-Chauvert and her decision to come to Paris when matron said that all Red Cross volunteers would soon be ordered back to the States. By now she must have lost most of the time she had intended to use to make officialdom change its mind.

Sunlight flooded through long windows and across the waxed parquet floor, highlighting old and beautiful hangings on gilt-swagged walls. Her pillow smelled of lavender and was edged with lace. Eve lay staring around her, trying to piece together the rest of her memory: the French truck and its unusual occupants, relentless rain and Paris in the dawn.

She wanted to look out. She would not have believed she could feel so weak, never having been ill or idle in her life before, but needed to hold on to curtains and elegant, spindle-legged chairs in order to reach the window.

Outside, bare branches were a filigree against the winter sky, a low wall and pavé courtyard dividing the house from a broad walk where nursemaids pushed wicker baby carriages. Little girls in high-collared coats rolled hoops under the trees, horse-drawn cabs and motor taxis jostling in the roadway just beyond. By craning her neck, Eve could see grass edging a wide crossing, the lights of a restaurant among the trees. A group of men strolled away from it, talking, well fed and elegantly dressed, none of them in uniform. A girl linked arms with two of them, drawing their heads down to listen to what she said, making them laugh the gusty belly laughs of the luxuriously entertained.

Beyond them a huge gray arch bulked against the sky, and Eve stared at it, fascinated. The Champs-Élysées. She was lodged in the exclusive heart of Paris, her earlier, unfriendly image of the city banished. Paris, PARIS, *PARIS*. This was where she had dreamed of coming all the way from New Moose; just the same, she would have liked to understand the how and why a little better.

Over the next two days, a few of her questions were answered. Two *bonnes* looked after her, scolding her often, and darting about on felt-slippered feet. They enjoyed gossiping, and gossiped all the time.

At first Eve was more bewildered than ever, they spoke of so many people all of whom seemed to be related. Then she gathered that this was a *hôtel particulier*, or private mansion, and not at all the sort of hotel she had imagined, and matters became more logical. M. Daunay, who owned it, allowed all kinds of relatives to live there, which the *bonnes* accepted as a natural thing to do, so of course when Commandant Saulx brought her ill to the doorstep he had not turned her away. Especially a lady like herself, who had crossed the Atlantic to come to France's aid.

Eve asked them to thank M. Daunay for her, though she remembered a great deal of quarreling when she arrived, which suggested she might not be exactly welcome here. "Perhaps you would also convey my apologies and say I will leave as soon as possible," she added.

"But no, mademoiselle! You have suffered *la grippe*, which this winter has killed thousands! My sister, she was ill as you were and nearly well again; then, one day, she tired herself and died in the night."

Eve thought of the flu cases at Bois-Chauvert, where nearly a quarter of all the strong young men who caught the disease died: infection was sweeping Europe, harvesting what war had left. "A day or two longer, then, if M. Daunay will permit. Perhaps— perhaps you would also present my compliments to Mme. Daunay?" She knew something of the formalities dear to the French heart.

"Assuredly, mademoiselle, and to Mme. Gabrielle, too. Now I will bring you *poulet pressé* and you will feel much recovered."

Eve lay back on her pillows, her brain busy now. Gabrielle. She recalled a starched black bosom and imperious voice: whoever she was, Gabrielle counted for more than Mme. Daunay.

Two days later the calm outside her window disappeared, as the Champs-Élysées filled with a yelling, densely packed throng, trampling exclusive elegance underfoot. Eve had dressed and sat by the window, watching, completely astonished: the crowd was too good-humored for a riot, too emotional for mere celebration. There were decorations, too —red, white and blue hung on gas brackets and worn as *boutonnières*, the crowd waving flags which, surprisingly, often were American. The French Republic has become the next state of the union, she thought, amused. Just a little alarmed, too, when people started scrambling over the wall, their tear-stained faces and gaping mouths communicating hysteria. The noise was overwhelming, and her head began to ache again.

There was a knock on her door, and a different maid entered, starched strings fluttering from her cap and apron. "Mademoiselle, as you are dressed but not yet fully recovered, Mme. Gabrielle sends to inquire whether you would prefer to retire from such a tumult to the small salon which overlooks the garden."

"Oh, yes," said Eve gratefully. "Whatever is going on?"

"It is the entry of your President Wilson into Paris. He has said that governments will not trick us any longer, and instead give everyone what they want." Her eyes sparkled, as if President Wilson were about to appear at the Hôtel Daunay, carrying her share of life's spoils.

"A just peace. A just peace is what he promised." Eve realized how lame her words sounded, when the house shook to the passionate hopes of people who had never before attempted to express such longings.

"Ah, yes, mademoiselle. Justice will give us everything. It is a good feeling, is it not? I, too, should like to be on the streets today." She stood back to let Eve pass.

The small salon was enormous and ran the length of the house, tall, cold windows looking out over a formal garden.

"You are fully recovered, Mlle. Ottoway?"

Eve spun around; she had not seen the woman standing in a dazzle of light by one of the windows. "Yes, thank you, madame. I am very grateful for the hospitality I have received here. Am— am I speaking to Mme. Daunay?"

"You are not. I am Gabrielle Benoit. Tell me, is it not usual in America for a young—a very young lady, I am persuaded—to curtsy to her elders?"

Eve was taken aback, but answered with her usual direct candor. "Perhaps in Boston, madame. Not where I come from, once a girl is grown."

"*Tiens!*" She inspected Eve with a kind of meditative interest. "And the way you speak French, is that usual too, in these United States?"

"No, madame. Most Americans do not think it necessary to speak French at all." Eve regretted her retort as soon as it was out. Let the French be rude if they wished; she owed this household a debt of gratitude.

Gabrielle Benoit was faultlessly dressed in black silk trimmed with lace, her hair piled on top of a finely sculptured face. She had elegant hands, and wore an intimidating quantity of pearls. Her appearance was unimportant, though; it was her will which made an immediate, almost masculine impact, while gesture, poise and vanity remained delicately feminine.

The two women stared at each other as if both were aware of another personality worthy of respect, before convention forced them back to the refuge of words.

"I speak old French," said Eve. "Where I come from there are several families descended from French Huguenots, who have continued to speak the language among themselves for almost two hundred years. New Moose, our village is called now, but this is a corruption of La Meuse. I was strictly chaperoned there, but when the American Army came to fight along the Meuse, my family eventually agreed that it was only natural I should want to come as well." This had been the most telling of the many arguments she had used.

Madame Benoit inclined her head. "Thank you for the explanation. I am happy that, in a way, France called you home."

"The United States is my home. It was just that I have only been over here three weeks, and Red Cross volunteers are alerted to await transportation home! I hope I'm not too late to try and talk myself into a transfer."

"The war is over. It took your United States three years to arrive here, but doubtless three months will be sufficient for a return across the Atlantic." She flicked her fingers. "By which time this Wilson believes he will have taught us all our business."

"So your maid thinks . . . and hopes." Eve could not resist the dig. Impulse again, she thought; after all the years of restraint and punishment surely I ought to have learned to hold my tongue by now.

Madame Benoit froze instantly again. "So all the world thinks, except for the few who know different. Which means that soon a great many disappointed people will join the brew of discontent we already have, n'est-ce pas?"

Eve shrugged. The gesture was useful, and catching. "I am sure that whatever arguments you employ, they will sound more convincing than mine, madame."

The other eyed her maliciously. "But you would not agree with them, nevertheless? We dine en famille tonight, because of the state of the streets. I should be happy for you to join us."

"I'm afraid—"

"It would give me pleasure, mademoiselle." She did not say that Eve owed whatever recompense she chose to claim, but her tone was final.

Eve couldn't see any polite way to phrase refusal. "I understood that Mme. Daunay was my hostess; whatever will she say if I come down without her invitation?"

"My sister, Hortense, will do as she is told. It is understood, then? Seven o'clock in the grand salon; I will send my femme de chambre to conduct you there."

The grand salon, thought Eve, dismayed, when she had regained her own room. If that enormous room was a small salon, what on earth will a grand one be like? She possessed only her Red Cross wool skirt, and army regulations said that on all formal occasions she must wear her undertaker's lid hat. Well, she mightn't know much, but certainly she couldn't turn up in Mme. Daunay's salon wearing an army-issue undertaker's lid.

Eve rested as best she could through the rest of the day. She was far from recovered, and as seven o'clock approached wanted very much to send a message to say she felt too unwell to appear at dinner. But however far away from home she might be, the categorical opinions of New Moose remained like judge and jury in her mind; if she stayed in her room tonight, she would show lack of gumption—or backbone, which was worse. The harsh Maine climate bred people who lacked sympathy with the weaknesses of others.

So she would go, but felt ridiculously frightened as seven o'clock struck. There was a pier glass in one corner of her room, and she studied her appearance with dissatisfaction. Illness had thinned her face, in some subtle way robbing her of vitality, which normally was one of her greatest assets. She was fair, and there were reddish and darkish shadings in her hair, which usually gleamed from much brushing and good health. Tonight it merely looked streaky, her face shadowed. Her nose was lightly freckled, her mouth too wide; no one who studied each feature objectively would ever call Eve Ottoway beautiful. Her charm lay elsewhere, and gave her something more important than beauty: an uncomplicated warmth and radiance. Expressive green eyes were set under well marked, tilted eyebrows and missed few chances for laughter, compassion or indignation; her body was tenderly curved and she moved lightly, though she was strongly built, having been raised on a farm. The hardworking life of an only child on an isolated farmstead had also taught her courage, and although a rigid tradition of uprightness and honesty could have confined her so completely that hypocrisy would be the only escape, her nature was quite simply incapable of confinement. She was too generous, too adventurous, too concerned with everything around her for the cage of other men's ideas ever to snap shut on her; and yet, three weeks in France was still too short a time for her truly to find herself. Which was a dangerous tally of vulnerabilities to take with her to Mme. Daunay's salon.

Eve turned away from the mirror as she heard a knock on the door. The Red Cross uniform was a disaster, devoid of chic or even common feminine allure, bulky jacket buckled at her slim waist, the hem uneven from her soaking on the Rheims road.

A mood of fatalism settled on her as the maid led her through high-ceilinged passages and down a staircase so beautifully proportioned it seemed to float about her in daggers of light thrown by a chandelier. Downstairs, the floors and walls were of marble, cold, unwelcoming and stark. Bronze lamps shaped like serpents crawled across the ceiling; spindle-legged gilt chairs were arranged in such a way that no one would ever feel tempted to sit on them. Wrought-iron gates.

Wrought-iron gates! Inside! thought Eve incredulously, her flat-heeled brogues making such a noise on marble she wanted to carry them in her hand. A music room with huge instruments draped in cloth; a billiard room so vast its farther reaches were lost in gloom; two splendidly decorated but empty reception rooms. In the midst of such immensities of vacant space, Eve felt as if she and the maid were trapped between revolving walls.

At last Eve heard social chatter, and she was ushered into a salon of not too terrifying size, double doors open to a farther room where a dining table was lit by candelabra. She immediately received an overwhelming impression of confident backs talking to other confident backs, as if being together was the greatest pleasure these people could imagine.

For a moment, no one noticed her and Eve hesitated, wanting to hide behind the curtains, anything rather than stand ignored in a doorway.

Then a white-haired, square-faced man with tight lips and clever eyes pushed through a group and bowed over her hand. "I am happy to welcome you, Mlle. Ottoway. I trust you are fully recovered from your grippe?"

"Yes, indeed, and thank you for your hospitality to me, M. Daunay!" Eve hazarded a guess at his identity and saw him smile at the interrogation in her voice.

"Quite correct, mademoiselle. Allow me to introduce myself, and then some of our company." He bowed again, formally. "Georges Daunay."

Eve curtsied, remembering Gabrielle, and blushed when she caught her ironic stare resting on her from across the room. "Eve Ottoway."

"Yes, I know. Even Guy was able to tell us that when he arrived with a fainting woman in his arms. He should be here, but I expect he has been delayed by the crowds greeting your President." Better disguised than with Gabrielle earlier, but the same resentment was in his voice too.

Slowly, they did the rounds of the room. It seemed odd to Eve that her hostess left such a duty to her husband, which in New England would have been thought distinctly improper, but that puzzle was solved when she met Mme. Daunay. Immensely fat, she reclined on a couch, wearing a dress so long out of date that Eve wondered whether she had changed it in twenty years. Hortense will do as she is told, Eve remembered Gabrielle saying. Yes, probably, providing it cost her no effort.

Madame Benoit. Gabrielle inclined her head to the introduction, expression cold, her east-wind personality more obvious than ever. M. Benoit; a small, apologetic man wearing a velvet smoking jacket and skullcap. He responded uncertainly to Eve's smile, and she thought there was something forlorn about him, as if he knew he was superfluous beside his wife's capabilities. A gaggle of people who apparently lived close by and had not been able to contemplate an evening spent alone; dinner *en famille* at the Hôtel Daunay did not mean quite what Eve had expected.

"And this is my son, Pierre, whom we are fortunate to have back with us at last." Daunay had seemed an urbane host, but there was an odd tone to his voice when he brought Eve over to another couch, where a young man half sat, half lay. "He has been a prisoner of war in

Germany and only returned last week. Unwell as you see, but we trust he will soon recover."

"Please don't get up," said Eve hastily, offering her hand.

"I'm not well enough to try," he replied complacently. "How pleasant to have patriotism rewarded by being able to ignore chivalry for a while."

She laughed. "Perhaps I should sit beside you instead, and you can explain to me all the things I must not do."

"Ah, in this household that would be too exhausting. I see also that dinner is announced." There was a general movement toward the door, and he stood without difficulty. He looked emaciated, but languid by choice rather than necessity. He wore an overtailored jacket, a ruffled shirt and floppy tie, as if he could not wait to reenter Bohemian life. There was something about his flaring line of eye and nostril which reminded Eve of a balky and not very trustworthy horse.

He took her in to dinner though, and talked with caustic spite about the rest of the company, so Eve was able to figure out who was who at last. They sat down, thirty-four of them, to eat their way through course after course of splendid food: dishes and wines which Eve could not name and most of France had not seen for years.

Everyone talked loudly, confidently, wittily. It did not seem to matter what they said so long as it was clever, and preferably amusing: only the shrug of boredom was social death. Reputations were dissected, friends betrayed, styles condemned; Chanel, Sorel, Diaghilev; *gigot à la bretonne*, the vintages of Pommard, a way someone had of mixing absinthe with a few drops of ink to settle the stomach; *style Louis Quinze* and the new wave of *dadaïsme*. Eve's head reeled from quick-fire responses and the scalpel touch of malice. She stayed silent and covertly studied the people Pierre identified for her. M. Daunay was apparently a financier of some importance (and he'd need to be to keep this place up, Eve thought) but the relationships of the rest of the household came through his wife, Hortense; according to Pierre, his father had climbed rapidly away from his own background and never spoke of his family. Gabrielle and her husband, Marcel Benoit, were Hortense's sister and brother-in-law, their sons both killed in the war. Eve felt more sympathetic toward Mme. Benoit now: when both your sons are killed, the very lives of the survivors could seem intolerable.

An elderly, bland-looking man at the far end of the table, whom Eve had not met, was Hortense's elder brother. "Does he live here too, or has he come simply for the evening?" she asked Pierre.

"Who? Old Anselme? He lives here too. There's a miserly streak in all the Saulx and it suits him to snap up titbits from my father's business and live here free."

"Your father maintains a very large household," observed Eve.

"Sometimes I think he fails to comprehend exactly who lives here and who doesn't. But it amuses Maman to have her family about her, and leaves him free to find his pleasures elsewhere when he chooses."

Eve dropped her eyes. She could not imagine a vigorous man like M. Daunay tied to a woman who must weigh over two hundred pounds, but infidelity, on the rare occasions when it occurred, was never discussed in New Moose.

Pierre laughed at her expression. "You will become educated in Paris, mademoiselle. Shall I tell you about matters of more interest than names? Old Saulx visits that lady sitting on my father's right every day. She is famous for her lovers and is married to that man over there. I cannot imagine what she sees in Saulx. And you see that beautiful bitch who looks as if her food stinks? She slept with my cousin Guy whenever he was in Paris during the war and can't eat for bile because he is late, above all late with my sister, Eulalie."

"Guy," said Eve, telling herself that Pierre had set out to fluster her and she must refuse to be flustered. "He is M. Saulx's son, the Commandant Saulx who brought me here?"

"No half measures about Guy," Pierre agreed. "Arrives while the *bonnes* were still in their nightclothes, complete with a half-dead woman and a truck of loot which piddled oil all over *cher papa*'s courtyard. Luckily Mlle. Bitch doesn't know the details, or she'd have your blood as well as his under her fingernails when he arrives."

"We met by chance," said Eve hastily. "I wouldn't even recognize Commandant Saulx by daylight."

Pierre looked at her sideways. "*Non?* Perhaps it's as well, or my sister, Eulalie, would be after you, too. She's thirty and Papa has ordered her into respectability, which is not easy with men so lacking in France; otherwise I'd say she was getting a bad bargain with Guy, and so I told her. Guy was always a strange type, *et maintenant il a perdu la boule* . . . he's as near crazy as makes no odds. Not that I should expect Eulalie to lie warm in any man's bed, although perhaps Guy is attempting to discover this for himself at the moment." He looked at the two empty spaces down the table.

Having spoken a variety of French all her life, Eve's vocabulary was extensive, although eccentric, but did not include fashionable crudities. She understood his meaning all the same, and to her surprise found she was beginning to enjoy herself, very much. "Is conversation in Paris always so enlightening, monsieur? I must confess I find it very strange."

He threw back his head in laughter, which swiftly changed to a paroxysm of coughing. Talk died uneasily as the attack continued, seeming to tear his frail body apart; M. Daunay was on his feet, while at Pierre's side Eve felt helpless and obscurely guilty. She was a Red Cross worker and ought to know what to do, but had no idea at all of how to cope with a man suffering from the results of privation as a prisoner.

Pierre's face was gray, his muscles twitching with exhaustion before the spasms loosened their grip. He leaned back in his chair, eyes closed, corpse-like. Eve moistened her lips. "M. Daunay, if you would help me, we could take him to the salon, and I'll sit with him awhile."

Daunay nodded, and together with a footman, they laid him on a couch. "I will call my valet."

"Not for a few minutes, if you will permit me to suggest it. He needs rest first, or exertion might upset him again."

"You are a nurse?"

"No. A volunteer; I help with matters like tracing the missing and writing letters for the wounded, but—"

"But anyone with common sense could see that rest is what he needs?" He looked at her as he might at a dubious stock issue, but apparently was reassured by what he saw. "Very well. I will return to my guests and give orders for him to be assisted to his room when you ring."

Eve sat silently beside Pierre, feeling incompetent and useless.

"I often have attacks like that. If I retain the habit, they will soon become one of the scandals of Paris." Pierre's voice was detached, but rough.

"Don't talk. You've only been back a week from Germany, haven't you? Once you're stronger, I'm sure they won't trouble you any more." She wasn't certain, herself: he seemed debilitated by more than just poor food.

He gave a grunting laugh. "A pity. Since they attract attention and break up the pleasures of others."

"You enjoy that?" Eve asked skeptically; no doubt he was simply covering up embarrassment, but she didn't see why she should pretend to believe him.

"Why not?" He seemed surprisingly serious. "You commented on our outspokenness before, and the answer to that is the same. Why shouldn't we say and do as we like, when in Paris above all, we expect to be amused? If we castrate our conversation, then it becomes like the gallantries of a eunuch, an affair without savor. And at this moment I, and a great many others like me, want to make up for lost time and be less civilized in our pleasures for a while. Just now, Paris is full of pain as well as hysterical people drunk on victory, so it is easy to be uncivilized. It will change again within a few months but be just as amusing, because it is Paris. I expect you will prefer it; I'm not sure yet about myself."

Eve considered his words carefully. He looked like a dissolute poet dying of excess, but what he said sounded like sense.

They were interrupted by footsteps echoing on marble, and the clash of wrought-iron gates. A man in French Army uniform came into the salon accompanied by a woman so eccentrically dressed that Eve stared at her dumbfounded, ignoring the man, who must be Guy Saulx, to whom she owed both thanks and apology. The woman beside him wore a skullcap of crimson velvet and a dress which succeeded in almost totally disguising her shape, being cut low over the bosom and open to the waist behind. The cold flesh thus exposed was hung with black beads, while a ribbon in the colors of the Croix de Guerre was tied around her throat. A calf-length hem, high-heeled, varnished boots, and a stick with a light in the handle completed this remarkable toilette. A strained and depraved face was thickly made up with blue powder and scarlet lipstick, petulant discontent stamped all over it.

"Ah, Eulalie, my pet, has the horrible common herd tramped all over your boots, or are you merely infuriated by Guy's *grande passion?*" Pierre demanded instantly.

"I might have known you would be disagreeable, Pierre. And you know I haven't any patience with the way you lounge about all day, so your airs are quite wasted on me. Where is everyone?"

"Eating, *chérie.*" He turned to Eve. "One person who definitely has not changed while I've been away is my sister, Eulalie. A pity, when I've always thought it an attractive name."

"Who is this?" Eulalie dug her hands into patch pockets and stood with her feet widely planted, hip thrusting in a caricature of arrogant sexuality.

Pierre waved his hand languidly. "Allow me to introduce Mlle. Eve Ottoway, an emissary from our gallant allies, the Americans, who saved France single-handed and now propose to save civilization in the same way."

There it was again, the rubbed sore of France's lost power. The envy of those bled dry for the healthy, and he really did look awfully sick, Eve thought. She stood and went over to the hearth. "I'm going to ring for your father's valet. I should think you must be ready to rest for a while now."

His face darkened. "*Mon Dieu,* how I hate good little virgins who turn the other cheek. You must learn to bite back if you want to enjoy Paris."

"So it would seem," replied Eve levelly. "Which is why I do not expect to enjoy Paris so much as I had hoped. *Bonne nuit, mademoiselle, messieurs.*"

CHAPTER 3

The Hôtel Daunay and its inhabitants fascinated Eve, so she wanted to find out more about the people she had glimpsed behind their sophisticated posturings, but of course she must go now that she was better. Go quickly, too, and find Rick Dwyer at the Crillon if she wanted to avoid being packed back to the States on the next troopship out of Bordeaux.

She lay in bed planning what she must do, her imagination filled by wanton-bodied, jeweled and extravagantly dressed women, like those she had seen downstairs. She slept only in snatches and woke unexpectedly late: she would have to hurry if she wanted to take leave of Daunay before she left. It would be unpardonably rude to go without doing so, but he had impressed her as a man unlikely to linger in a house whose inhabitants idled away most of their time.

Eve hesitated at the bottom of the stairs, then boldly began opening doors to the many rooms. In most, the shutters were still closed, but a gallery at the back of the house was in daylight, a fire burning on the marble hearth. It was empty, but Eve followed the smell of coffee and discovered a smaller salon beyond, fitted snugly under a curve of stairs, pale green paint an agreeable change from oppressive formality elsewhere. Silver coffeepots and wicker baskets of croissants made another welcome sight; less pleasant was Gabrielle Benoit seated by the window, her stiff-backed attitude calculated to demonstrate that she had finished *petit déjeuner* two hours before. By a porcelain stove, Anselme Saulx stood warming his coattails, turning to look at her when Eve pushed open the door. As she did so, it was thrust violently out of her hand, and the man she had briefly seen in uniform the night before almost knocked her over.

Automatically, he steadied her. "I beg your pardon, mademoiselle." He was white with fury, struggling to collect himself, to be polite a moment and then go.

"I think I owe you much more of an apology for the trouble I caused you. I am truly grateful you didn't put me out on the sidewalk wrapped in a velvet curtain!"

He stared at her, blank-faced. "I proposed to do that?"

"No, of course not. That is, you were teasing, trying to make me last out the remaining kilometers when I felt completely finished." Eve was startled when he seemed confused by a light response.

"Well, that's fortunate, at any event. Come in, and join our gathering. We are all in a singularly agreeable mood this morning."

"You are to be complimented on a good night's sleep." Gabrielle glanced at the clock, which said nearly ten. "Please help yourself to coffee, and whatever else you wish."

"I'm usually up early, but can't have recovered fully from the grippe," responded Eve tranquilly, sitting down. Last night, Pierre had taught her how provocation must be neutralized rather than accepted, and she meant to turn the lesson to good account. "Has M. Daunay left?"

"By eight o'clock, always. No matter how he has occupied himself the night before," Anselme replied, flapping his coattails and laughing.

"I do not in the least see what amuses you, since Georges never allows himself to be distracted from matters which are important by those which are trivial," stated Gabrielle. "You would do well to follow his example."

"But as he has just explained to us, my father has no interest in following M. Daunay's example. In fact, he is so fatigued by taking a *taximètre* to the Rue Daunou five or six times a month, that he does not intend to continue making even that small effort." Guy Saulx had been facing his father, fury blazing again, but suddenly he turned to grip the edge of the table so hard that Eve heard sinews crack. There was a long silence; when he spoke again his voice was muffled. "You have not the right. It is fraud."

"*Mon fils*, I have a perfect right, as you very well know. Le Trésor is mine—"

"On the contrary, you owe Georges and me 22 percent of the profits each," interrupted Gabrielle.

Anselme waved this aside as an irrelevance. He seemed a man grown old in the study of elegance; from pink, close-shaved cheeks to patent leather boots, it was impossible to fault him. "Georges has offered me a sound bargain, and so the matter arranges itself without difficulty."

"Not for me, it doesn't!" shouted his son.

Eve watched Guy Saulx with astonishment. So far, each time she had encountered him he had been almost menacingly silent; now he was transformed into a man beside himself. He grasped the table edge as if it were the only thing which kept him from violence.

Anselme chuckled, swaying slightly on the balls of his feet. "No, I can see that. But I do not need to regard your concerns; only mine. Alsace is French again now; you may go back to living there if you wish, *comme locotaire, naturellement.*"

"I'll never be a tenant of yours again, and without my efforts Le Trésor would have been bankrupt years ago."

"I told you that Georges had offered to make Le Trésor part of Eulalie's *dot*; your engagement can be celebrated as soon as the contract is drawn up, since we are agreed on the details."

"I do not wish to marry Eulalie Daunay for her dowry," said Guy between his teeth.

"What is that to the matter? Georges wishes to settle the girl, which is not entirely easy. Either you value Le Trésor and the Alsace domaine enough to accept a favorable offer, or you do not; and if you do not, then Georges must place the girl elsewhere, which will be expensive and inconvenient, since she is so notorious. He simply offers you first choice, even though Pierre advised against it. But whatever he proposes, that's where you are, my boy!" Anselme jabbed his thumb downward and laughed with surprising malevolence at his son's ashen face.

The gesture seemed to release Guy from the compulsion which had kept him gripping the table; with a grunting curse he launched himself at his father, seizing him by the throat.

Eve leaped to her feet, stumbling against the table in her haste, and without thought grabbed at his wrists. He did not even notice her intervention, and was too strong for her to make any impression on his fury.

Anselme's breath rattled, his face was livid, his weight hanging from his son's hands. Eve shouted, still wrenching at his grip. Nothing she did made any difference, but a second later Guy staggered back, bumped into the table and fell in a crash of crockery.

"Reason is wasted on a man in a killing rage." Gabrielle replaced the candlestick, with which she had hit Guy, on the mantelpiece. "Fetch some cognac from the salon where we dined last night, and keep a still tongue in your head."

When Eve returned, Anselme was slumped in a chair, hands to his bruised throat, his collar burst open, elegance vanished. Several gulps of neat spirit revived him, and Eve took the decanter across to Guy. He had not been completely stunned and was standing with his face against cold glass, looking out over the garden.

He drank without a word, then returned to his contemplation of wet leaves and winter sky, licking his lips occasionally and swallowing as if he expected to be sick.

Can you beat it? thought Eve. Life in a Champs-Élysées household, and then some!

Gabrielle was seated again, and turned to Eve. "As an uninvited guest in our house, I hope you feel you owe us your discretion?"

Eve immediately felt irrational sympathy with Guy, as her own calm temper uncoiled. "Of course."

"Then, I would ask you to keep the happenings of this morning to yourself, since only the gossips are served by scandal and you have understood nothing of what you have seen. Commandant Saulx"—she flicked a glance at her nephew's back—"will be returning to the rougher habits of forward troops in a day or so, and is unlikely to reenter this house until his *contrat de mariage* is signed. I am confident that Eulalie has sufficient personality to control him in their future together." She spoke as if Saulx were a child in a tantrum, and he gave no sign that he had heard.

But this man has just nearly killed his father, thought Eve, amazed. And now his family continues to plan some trickery which will force him to marry a cousin he dislikes, a girl whose brother told me that Guy Saulx was as near crazy as made no odds. "Of course I shouldn't betray your confidence, madame. But don't you . . . I was thinking—"

Gabrielle held up her hand. "I am desolated to interrupt such a useful activity, but thought is best left to those with knowledge and experience. Perhaps I might ask you to summon the good Sergeant Joubaire from the kitchen, since he is better able to take charge of Guy than I am."

Eve went out and shut the door behind her with a snap; she was through with these dreadful people. She would return this evening to take leave of M. Daunay and collect her valise; meanwhile, she could not get out fast enough.

A few minutes later, when a footman ushered her down the front steps, she was surprised and delighted to discover that the day was fine; she seemed scarcely to have seen the sun since she arrived in France. A brisk wind drove clouds scudding overhead and helped to disperse the crude unpleasantness of the scene she had just witnessed. Consequently, she was far from pleased when she came face to face with Guy Saulx as he emerged from a side door of Daunay's walled garden.

He glanced at her as if her face were unfamiliar; if he had passed without a word, Eve would have been thankful, but after a moment his expression cleared. "Mlle. Ottoway. I did not know you were leaving us."

"I'm coming back tonight to thank M. Daunay," said Eve defensively.

"I thought that perhaps I should make a hotel reservation first, but I don't want to impose on your family's hospitality now I am better."

"I can easily understand that."

Eve colored, and then laughed, "I must admit I am enjoying the air."

"May I call a *fiacre* or a *taximètre* for you? I don't think you will enjoy it for very long alone as Paris is at present, when a quarter of a million troops are on leave here."

"Surely it is safe in the Champs-Élysées, when the walk is exactly what I should enjoy?"

"Perfectly safe, but not agreeable. Where are you going?" He hesitated, the memory of his hands on his father's throat a gulf of awkwardness between them. "If you would not dislike it too much, I could accompany you until you are sufficiently tired to prefer a taxi."

Eve did not want him beside her, but now she was out of the Hôtel Daunay, curiosity had resurfaced from a confusion of other emotions. She could imagine the unexplained hatreds she had witnessed nibbling away at her for years unless someone answered a few questions before she went, and this looked like her only chance of asking them.

So she accepted Saulx's offer, hoping that he would continue to behave normally in the bracing air of the Champs-Élysées. Eve studied him surreptitiously as they walked under bare trees, traffic roaring past over fan-patterned granite blocks. He looked tired and drawn, frowning heavily and blinking his eyes as if he had a headache. He probably had, she realized; if Gabrielle Benoit hit someone with a candlestick, she would not do it halfheartedly. He was not much taller than she; indeed many Frenchmen appeared undersized compared to the American boys she was used to; and although more heavily muscled than Pierre, he was almost as skinned down, looked in fact as if he had not eaten or slept well in years. There was an intensity about his face, a disturbing sense of strain she could not place, although his features were ordinary enough: a high-bridged nose, dark hair beneath a shabby *képi*, thick eyebrows defensively puckered. Lines, perhaps of temper, about mouth and nose. Not a serene face, difficult to judge, not at all at peace. He looked forty, nearly twenty years older than herself.

His silence was becoming as unnerving as when they drove together through wet darkness, but this time Paris lay all about her, waiting to be enjoyed. None of the people at the Hôtel Daunay were her business, and the events of the past few days faded in importance as she gazed about her. The sheer unexpectedness of Paris was what delighted her most; later she would notice splendor, today it was the little things which charmed: a bird market under the trees and some old men selling dogs, their voices outshouting each other; the note of a violin drifting from a café terrace, a line of stalls where burly women invited passersby to sample oysters, chestnuts or tiny fillets of fish. A few people were dancing to a noisy band on a plank floor in the cold, and, close by, a clutch of tables huddled around a brazier smelling of coffee. Between some trees Eve glimpsed a fountain cascading speckled light.

"How wonderfully Parisians use their streets!" she exclaimed. "As if they were part of their lives, to spill out over and make their own!"

"Wait until you reach the *grands boulevards*; then you'll find the habit less endearing. It's difficult to move there, since the road is blocked hub to hub and the pavement full of hucksters."

"I think I would love it still. Why, it's like being at the spindle of the world! In just a few moments the whole of life spins by, if only one could grasp it fast enough. Oh, look! A Punch and Judy, and I've never seen one before!"

"*Théâtre de Guignol*, as we call it in France," he said, and Eve instantly towed him off to join a group of children, all of them wrapped in so many layers of cloth they looked like molting chickens and screaming with delicious fear as Polichinelle was pursued by disaster.

"I'm sorry," said Eve guiltily, recollecting herself. "There must be a great many things you ought to be doing, and I've kept you from all of them so far."

"As it happens, I'd never seen *le Guignol* before either, so perhaps my affairs deserved to wait. Would you enjoy something to warm you, and then I will call a *taximètre* for the rest of your journey? You are only a few days out of bed after the grippe."

Eve had not felt tired before, but standing by the Punch and Judy she had become aware of wind snatching at her cape, and the brittle nature of her strength. "Wouldn't you mind? I mean, will you be in trouble if you delay, or are you on furlough?"

"I no longer give a damn about any trouble the Army might land on me; the war is over." He took her arm for the first time, to steer her across the dangerous width of the Champs-Élysées, horse cabs clippety-clopping along the fringes of solidly jammed motor traffic as the day built up toward promenade time.

Loot, Eve remembered, as memory leaped at her from the night before. Pierre had said that Guy Saulx arrived in Paris with a truck full of loot, and certainly he had dug velvet out of his load to wrap her in. He would be in Paris for his own purposes and not the Army's, which was something else she did not understand. She could not help staring at his hands as he seated her by a brazier on a glassed-in café terrace and ordered for them both: they looked powerful, with stiff black hairs on the back and muscular fingers which had been fastened around his father's throat. To outward appearances he was idling pleasantly with a woman, but to Eve he seemed more like a tricky-tempered predator loosed in the postwar jungle.

"I have ordered soup and an omelette, since I do not think circumstances allowed you to eat *petit déjeuner.*" He avoided her eyes, fingers fiddling with the buttons of his uniform.

Eve nodded. Only minutes before, she had felt at ease with him; now she was aware of an irrational conviction that unless her answers pleased him, he was capable of choking what he wanted from her, too.

She felt restored after a generous bowl of hot soup, and her sense of proportion returned. She also noticed that Guy was simply messing soup with his spoon, apparently as a substitute for eating, and fluffy omelette went the same way. "Aren't you hungry?"

"No."

"In that case, it would seem a waste to order when France is so short of food," she observed.

Unexpectedly, he laughed and picked up his fork again. "I'll probably be sick; cold omelette is like wet washing."

Eve watched while he managed two mouthfuls and gagged on the third, then impulsively covered his hand with hers. "Don't, I wasn't serious. Why should you eat it if you don't want to?"

"I suppose because one has to stay alive. God knows why."

"Perhaps because you survived four years of war, when life seemed very precious?" Suddenly she wanted to reach behind the strangeness in him.

He stared at her. "*Mon Dieu,* no. It's longer than I can remember since I wanted to live. A quick death was my desire. I suppose that's why—" He broke off and pulled away from her, calling for the waiter.

Why life seems so unrecognizable, thought Eve, compassion stirring. Or did he mean that the instinct to kill and be killed was all he understood, a trifling family quarrel bringing him close to murder?

It had become much colder. After café stuffiness, the wide gray spaces of the Place de la Concorde seemed very bleak, and by the time they reached the Crillon, Eve was shivering again. Once inside, she touched familiarity at once. American smells of paint and real coffee, American voices, jokes and uniforms. Blissful American warmth: the hotel was temporarily staffed by the U. S. Navy, and they apparently regarded the heating system in the nature of a ship's boiler, which functioned best when full of steam.

Eve was in for an immediate disappointment, however: the marine on duty refused to let her past the vestibule. "Sorry, Miss Ottoway." He handed back her papers. "You need a diplomatic pass to get in here."

"I only want to talk to a friend, a Mr. Dwyer; do you know him?"

"Okay, then. If that's all. Here, I'll give you a chit for the paging clerk, but don't get yourself noticed or I'll be on a charge. What did you say his name was?"

"Dwyer. Rick Dwyer; he's a reporter."

The marine consulted a list of names, licked pencil poised over a signal pad. "Not on this list, Miss Ottoway."

"Why, he must be! I read several dispatches he wrote with a Crillon dateline."

"Sorry, he's not listed. I guess he comes to the bar sometimes, like the other reporters, but the hotel's reserved for our Peace Conference delegation. There's nothing I can do."

Eve bit her lip; Rick Dwyer had written as if he lived in the pocket of the American delegation, and it had never occurred to her that this might simply be a way of making his information sound authentic.

"Why not leave a message for your friend, asking him to call at the Hôtel Daunay?" suggested Guy. He had stayed in the background until then, a French uniform on U. S. Government territory enough to rouse the sentry's suspicions at once.

None of the peace delegations trusted each other's motives.

"I can't impose on M. Daunay any longer," objected Eve; nor did she want to spend any more time in his house.

"Then let us find a hotel where you can stay, and when we have done so I will deliver your note here for Mr. Dwyer, with your address enclosed."

It seemed the only thing to do, but Eve had relied on appealing personally to Dwyer, whom she did not know. "You see, he comes from the same place I do; we're proud of having a Washington *Times* correspondent born in New Moose," she explained. "But he's older than I am, and if I'm lucky he'll remember a kid in pigtails at meetinghouse. Probably he won't recognize more than the name."

"What is it you want him to do for you, if I may ask? Perhaps I may be of service?"

"Oh, no! I mean, that's very kind of you, but there's nothing you could do; you're French. I saw Rick's name and thought that if I introduced myself as coming from New Moose he might feel inclined to help me. There's no reason why he should, of course, except that there is a tie if you were raised in the same place, don't you think? I'd hate to be sent back to the States just as I'd arrived in France, and I thought . . . well, I thought that during the Peace Conference there might be a job for me in Paris, if Rick would help. Not many Americans speak fluent French. Even though you laugh at the way I speak it," she added defiantly. Her idea had seemed inspired at Bois-Chauvert, but madness on the cold sidewalk outside the Crillon.

"I haven't ever done so; I think you speak delightfully." Guy whistled a *taximètre*, a battered Renault with exhaust fumes leaking through the floorboards. "What kind of hotel do you want?"

"A cheap one. I'm a volunteer, and it was a sacrifice for my family to fit me out to come." She had also only accepted the minimum few dollars necessary, after so many battles to let her come.

He nodded and said something to the driver. "Money. With money I could have Le Trésor without Eulalie."

He had withdrawn from her without any warning at all; Eve could see his fingers twisting together in the taxi's smelly darkness, his shoulder turned to her as he stared out the window.

"Le Trésor?" she prompted, after a moment. "That is what you were arguing over, wasn't it?"

"Would you like to see it?" Without waiting for an answer, he tapped the driver on the shoulder. "Rue Daunou."

They drew up in front of a grubby shop, the usual mixed trades of a side street jumbled together on either side.

Eve stared about her. Everything in Paris was unfamiliar, and Guy Saulx even more unexpected than the rest. Houses with peeling gray shutters and leprous walls lined the street, although the hum of traffic was only just around the corner; every fourth or fifth shop boarded up with legends scrawled in paint: "*Fermé pour cause de mobilisation du patron*"; "*Patron et employées sont aux armées.*" Someone had crossed out the last two words of that one, and substituted "*morts.*"

Guy held her arm tightly. "That's it."

Eve looked at the unimpressive double frontage he indicated, letters on a faded fascia proclaiming that it was *Le Trésor perdu de l'Alsace*. It seemed an unlikely title for so run-down a place; or for so much quarreling, either. "This belongs to your family?" she hazarded.

His eyes narrowed. "It is ten years of my life, and perhaps more. A squalid stack of junk without a customer from one day's end to the next. So now my father decides to sell me, instead. Come inside, and see what a splendid establishment the Saulx have built."

Still held in the same tense grip, Eve was whisked at breakneck speed through an ill-lit vestibule full of broken-down furniture, into empty storerooms and across a weed-tufted courtyard to a workshop where an elderly man was polishing wood.

"*Ah, bonjour, M. Guy, vous avez emporté une cliente. Quelle chance, alors!*" He wiped his sleeve across his face and went back to his work.

"It is something, when the employees are astonished to see a customer, don't you agree?" Guy spoke with such suppressed fury that Eve was unable to think of a suitable reply, indeed was preoccupied with keeping her feet in cluttered passages as he thrust her from one damp room to the next, right up to attics full of mouse droppings.

"Well, what do you think of it?" he demanded when they were back in the vestibule.

His fingers were like wire around her arm, and Eve winced. "What do you want me to say? Then I'll say it and you can let me go, since I don't suppose you plan to throttle me, as well." She regretted the words as soon as they were spoken, embarrassment and remorse making blood burn in her face.

He dropped her arm instantly, hands gripped behind his back, eyes clouded with shock. After a moment, he turned and fumbled among dark furniture for his *képi*.

"I'm sorry." Eve felt quite exhausted by his moods; after all, she wasn't long recovered from flu herself. "Could we go now and find a hotel where I might stay?"

There was a long silence. She stared at his back, unable to believe he would not even reply, tempted simply to walk out and leave him. Yet he had tried to help her, and left his demons behind to encourage her during the last dreadful miles of the journey to Paris. "Please, M. Saulx. I didn't mean to be unkind, but I'm tired, too, and don't know what it is you want from me."

He shook his head, hands twisting white-knuckled behind his back, as she had seen them only that morning, when he had tried to hold himself from violence. And failed.

Only after another hideous length of time had passed did she realize he was weeping.

CHAPTER 4

Rick Dwyer was drunk. Not incapably so, but he had been interviewing
the British and they always produced the same effect on him: a craving
to reach the nearest bar as soon as possible. Goddam unctuous bastards,
who thought the world owed them a living, and all the more infuriating when they were too civilized to say so.

The Café des Quatre Coins suited his mood exactly, a place where
people talked and argued as well as drank, diced for *apéritifs*, and the
patron played an off-key piano; when suitably primed with Málaga, occasionally his wife would also sing. *"Comment épouser un soldat, moi
qui aime tout le régiment?"* was the only song she knew, and the words
made her maudlin, but Rick enjoyed a bar like that.

He looked around the tiny, brick-floored room with its wine-sodden
tables, and supposed he ought to go back to the Crillon. The U.S. delegation was kicking its heels there while the British and French decided
how next to keep President Wilson out of mischief: Wilson had arrived in Paris on a date he considered suitable and seemed surprised to
discover that the Peace Conference was still at the stage where clerks
argued over what color blotting paper would be appropriate. Consequently, there was good copy to be filed exposing muddle and misun-
derstanding; also, of course, the President was receiving a hysterical reception wherever he went. The French and British were furious as
popular acclaim made him the champion of Europe's masses, and had
come to fear the American President loose in Paris without a conference
to attend, so were forced to devise official tours to keep him busy, which
then turned into triumphal progresses.

Rick enjoyed explaining the irony of it all to his Washington readers;

what he did not say, but understood very well, was that Clemenceau of France and Lloyd George of Britain were using this same time to secure their personal power at home. President Wilson believed his high purpose would be debased by such maneuverings, a dangerous delusion for any politician; so the people wept and cheered wherever he went, and also believed that wanting justice was enough.

Rick swore, and smashed down his glass on the bar. "I fired the last shot in this war, goddammit, and without us you'd be into the fifth winter of hell instead of dancing in the streets. So why not trust us with the peace when you know we haven't anything to gain?" He had not meant to say it aloud, but absinthe always loosened his tongue.

"And where were you when my only son was killed at Verdun?" demanded the *patron*, affronted. "Four winters of hell, not the fifth you prevented, gives France her right to make what terms we choose against the Boche."

Rick shook his head. He admired and liked these people, and did not want a fight. "You have suffered too much."

"*Bien sûr*, we have suffered, so do not need *le bon papa* Wilson to settle our affairs! We are not children, monsieur."

Rick threw a handful of the horrible paper scraps the French used as change on the counter, metal for centimes having vanished along with the rest of France's wealth. He could not explain to a man whose only son was dead at Verdun that torment of heart itself prevented a rational approach to peace.

Fresh air made his head reel and turned his feet into balloons which floated over misted sidewalk. Perhaps he'd better leave the Crillon until tomorrow; he wouldn't like the U.S. peace delegation to cherish doubts about Rick Dwyer's discretion.

Rick had taken rooms not far from the Crillon, but it was the following evening before he dragged himself out of bed. It didn't matter: he remembered quite sufficient of his interview with Sir Maurice Wyville to file a vitriolic article on the British which would keep his editor quiet while he decided whether he dared print it.

Rick threw open the window and breathed the smells of Paris. He loved this splendid *cocotte* of a city, and hated it at the moment. Another month before the British shipped themselves across the Channel: meanwhile their quarters at the Astoria Hotel remained empty except for a small advance party led by the wooden-faced bore he had met. A kind of dummy, Rick thought him, shunted over the points each time the British wanted to make the world forget its pertinent questions. He frowned, razor in hand. As he'd forgotten a great deal he had meant to ask. Well, not exactly forgotten, but Sir Maurice Wyville, Bart., had so infuriated him that his carefully researched interrogation had gone astray.

I suppose you could say that the dummy did his job, reflected Rick ruefully.

The Crillon bar was full when he arrived; the chill of unheated Paris encouraged Americans to gather early in their own cozy surroundings.

"You believed the British? Another month before Lloyd George comes? He's surely won a dynamite victory in his election." The Chicago *Herald Tribune* stringer offered him a drink.

"Yeah, I believed the bastard I saw. A British baronet wouldn't lie on a point of fact to a representative of the lesser races. Just freeze me if I asked a question he didn't intend to answer. If I go missing one day you'll find me in the Astoria hall, stuffed, ready for the Limeys to hang their hats on." Rick exhaled smoke and killed his match with an angry flick of his thumb.

"What's eating you?"

"American boys dying on the Argonne to add another ten thousand square miles to the British Empire, I guess. The French want German guts on a washing line and don't mind putting their name to Wilson's ideals, or anything else for that matter, so long as they get them. The British distrust ideals and won't touch anything so embarrassing."

"Jesus! You going to file a story like that?"

"It's not a story . . . yet. I'm sensitive, that's all, and smell dirt before it starts to rot. Which is one reason why I'm not a stringer any more."

The *Herald Tribune* man went off, offended, and Rick eyed the bar morosely, wondering what was the matter with him.

"Mr. Dwyer?"

He turned, to find a marine at his elbow. "Yeah?"

"A note was left for you two days ago, sir. A girl called when I was on duty and I told her you weren't listed, but Sergeant Thompson pointed you out when you came in this evening."

Rick grinned. "Was she pretty?"

"Yessir, but a real nice girl." The marine sounded aggrieved. A backwoods boy, Tennessee or somewhere near, whose face still burns if a girl so much as looks at him, thought Rick, smiling.

He tossed his cigarette into a sand bucket and ripped open the note. A pretty American girl in Paris would certainly improve the evening. He read, and laughed aloud. "A damsel in distress, soldier, no less. From New Moose, Maine; a place I left for a life of sin when still wet behind the ears. Now, do you think that Miss Eve Ottoway could still be wet behind the ears?"

"I wish I'd torn that paper up, and that's God's truth . . . sir." The marine about-faced in a clash of boots and marched away, head up, chin in.

Rick laughed again; he enjoyed shocking people.

He turned the paper over. She was lodged at 4 Rue Férou, in the St.-Sulpice district: across the river, but quite near enough for an evening call. Supper first, he decided as his stomach growled; it must be twenty-four hours since he had done much except drink, and he wouldn't like a nice girl from New Moose to swoon each time he breathed.

No, on second thoughts she could take her chances with last night's absinthe; he could use some company while he ate.

The Rue Férou was dark and narrow, not far from the Luxembourg Gardens. Rick was surprised to find an American girl lodging in such an unfashionable area, almost uneasy when he discovered that number four presented a blank face to the world and was not the cheap hotel he expected. There was a light in the concierge's room, and a smell of boiled sausage seeped under the door. Rick knocked on steamed glass and waited, wondering whether he could have made a mistake.

"Which tenant are you seeking, monsieur?" The concierge wore a piece of carpet tied with string around her waist. All Paris shivered for lack of fuel.

"I'm not sure, but an American lady wrote me from this address." Rick's French was adequate after a year across the Atlantic, but left grammar strewn like rocks behind it.

"Comment? Une Américaine?" She peered at him as if the nationality was unheard of, but there was knowledge in her tone.

"Oui, madame, depuis quelques jours, je crois." Rick showed her the paper and address, putting the full force of charm he knew he possessed into his smile. In France, those whom concierges disliked stayed out in the street.

She disregarded charm but accepted the notes he offered. "Au quatrième étage, en arrière." She pressed a light switch and shuffled back into her hutch.

This would be something to syndicate for the folks back home, thought Rick mischievously. Those meetinghouse elders would bust a gut if they could see where nice Eve Ottoway chose to lodge in wicked Paree. He was halfway up bare-boarded stairs when the light went out; switches were timed so you seldom had time to find the door you wanted before they flicked off.

The house was clean, but built on a maze of levels. Rick disturbed several families before he discovered what must be the fourth floor back. One of the tenants he disturbed told him it belonged to a French Army major, a jolt to Rick's hopes of a promising evening.

An Eve from Maine living in a place like this had distinct possibilities, but detaching her from a Frog major might require more effort than she was worth.

The door opened quickly to his knock, and a woman stood holding a lamp, eyes crinkled to see him through the flare of it. Rick was immediately conscious of a ridiculous desire to apologize to the marine at the Crillon; so just what was a real nice girl doing in a joint like this? "Miss Ottoway?"

She nodded, and shook his hand with immediate friendliness. "You must be Rick Dwyer, but you won't remember me. I didn't mean you to come right over, though; just hoped to fix a time to meet you."

The lamp struck reddish-fair lights from her hair and painted shadows to highlight delicate bones. "I wasn't sure how long your note had been waiting at the Crillon, or how urgent your business was." Unusually for him, Rick felt a need to explain just why he came.

"Well, thank you, Mr. Dwyer." Her smile was politely skeptical. "I left it there two days ago, but I guess I was a mite optimistic at the time. I've just gotten around to reckoning everything up and find I've been nine days away from Bois-Chauvert on a two-day pass. No one's going to listen to anything I say when I get back."

"Do you mind?"

"Of course I do! I may only be a volunteer, but I should think they'd still list me as a deserter."

"There's hundreds of American deserters in France, and the figure's climbing all the time. I guess the M.P.'s won't worry over you."

"*I'm* worried over me," she retorted. "I had a job to do which I thought important enough to be seasick all the way across the Atlantic for."

"Say you had flu and were left with just enough strength to climb four flights of stairs in the Rue Férou," he said flippantly. "Am I invited in, or must we discuss your affairs in the passage?"

"Whatever can you think of me, after you've come all this way! As it happens, I did have flu, but I guess it won't sound too good an excuse after nine days."

Her words were warm, but Rick detected a real reluctance to invite him in. She hadn't expected him to come and was annoyed he had. It takes a while to shuck the upbringing of New Moose, he reflected wryly. Conscience is an awful thing.

The room was small and bare. Plank table, two hard chairs, some rough shelving and very little else. An alcove curtained off, and a fire of smoldering wood blocks: the room was cold, and Rick instinctively made for the grate.

"I can't get them to burn properly," said Eve apologetically. "I've tried everything, but old timber pavé is all the fuel on sale around here, and they just refuse to give out any heat."

"A few generations of horse manure soaked into them, I expect." Rick kicked the fire, which spat sulkily back at him. "What are we waiting for? You're already wearing all the clothes you've got, so let's go find some food in a heated café and talk later."

"No," said Eve, reluctantly but definitely. "I'd like to, but I can't."

"Why not?"

She hesitated and then smiled. "I could invent all kinds of reasons, but I'm not going to. I prefer the truth if you don't mind. I can't come."

Rick stared at her, nonplussed. "If you're going to stick to bare truths all your life, you'll find Paris a difficult city to survive in."

"I expect I should, if I stayed," she agreed. "Don't you ever find that deception has a way of getting out of hand too?"

"Sure, often. But then I spin some more to cover the cracks." They both laughed and Rick sat down on one of the hard chairs. "Suppose you tell me about it?"

"About what?"

He waved his hand at the stark room. "How you came to the Rue Férou instead of going back to Bois-Chauvert, for a start. Then I'll tell you whether I can help. Because we both come from New Moose, and not for any ulterior design," he added untruthfully.

"Now, that is exactly what I meant by deception getting out of hand, Mr. Dwyer," exclaimed Eve.

"Rick, please, since I remember you in pinafores. All motives strictly ulterior, then, but you could still tell me about it."

She looked at him consideringly: if she still wanted anything from him, now was the time to ask. He was intrigued, curious, relaxed. Even his glance was a caress, when she could imagine it like iron on a victim; thick hair magnificently untidy, expressive mouth and full face. A sensual man and a ruthless one, who would expect payment for favors done.

But, in spite of everything, he was a type she recognized, someone whose thought processes she could follow; born within sight of the totem pine behind the Ottoway homestead.

She took a deep breath and began explaining, or some of it at least; Rick frowned when she had finished. "Why come here, then?"

"That's another thing I'm not going to tell you, Mr. Dwyer."

"Rick."

She smiled. "Rick."

He ran his fingers through his hair. "I'm a reporter. I guess I could find out easily enough."

"I expect you could, but why care enough to try?" She was taken aback, had not expected such a notion, but hid it well.

"I don't, but no newsman swallows mysteries whole. And Daunay is quite well known: background dirt on financiers nearly always comes in useful eventually, and he has a very piebald reputation."

"Well, I couldn't tell you anything beyond the decor of his rooms," said Eve tartly. "I must report back to Bois-Chauvert soon; so long as they don't lock me up, do you know of any work I could do in Paris? You remember how our family always spoke French at home?"

"Sure, I could find you something. In our delegation there's so many darned experts on everything you could name except the French language, that all the professors would be fighting over you. Danube navigation, the minorities in the Sanjak of Novibazar—you name it and they're full of ideas with no way to express them in French, who mislay their translators whenever it suits them." Anger was back in his voice.

"That would be marvelous, Rick. Could you ask around— would you mind? Then I'd call you when I get back."

"I'll write you, since I never know where I'll be." He'd be on her doorstep once she was working for the American delegation. "Will a message here find you?"

She looked confused and unhappy, fingers pleating folds into her skirt. "Yes, it would find me."

"But you might not still be living here?" he prompted.

"I'll be around."

Her warmth had vanished, lips pressed together, back taut, but for the first time the deep gut feeling of desire came to him, so sharp it hurt. "Look, Eve, you don't have to pretend with me. I left New Moose a long time ago. You enjoying Paris doesn't shock me."

"Why should it, when you don't know anything about me and care less?" she countered instantly, defiantly.

And Rick suddenly felt exasperated with himself. He had made the same mistake before when he abandoned commercial calculation in his dealings with women, and trouble always followed. Eve Ottoway from New Moose with her green glinting eyes and friendly warmth was very different from Paris *cocottes*, which was also why he wanted her and couldn't now walk away. He possessed a nose for dirt, he had told the *Herald Tribune* stringer, and it was true; for so tough and truculent a man he was also surprisingly sensitive to emotions left unexpressed. Having obtained what she wanted from him, Eve Ottoway had no intention of offering anything in return. She wasn't going to meet him, touch him, or confide another thing; and she wanted him out of this room on skids. His scalp prickled as he grasped the reason for it. Her Frog major was here, listening. Behind one of those curtains, so still that in half an hour not even breathing had betrayed him; even now it wasn't sound which made Rick certain, but an overwhelming sense of danger. The bastard wanted his hands on Rick's throat and Eve knew it, was willing him to leave before it happened.

Rick's next impulse was to jerk those curtains back and find a throat for himself, but something in Eve's face stopped him. She was afraid, not for herself, but of some unexplained disaster which she had dreaded ever since instinctive hospitality forced her to admit him to this room. He could not precipitate a crisis against her will, when he understood so little of the web in which she had been caught.

For she had been caught, he realized, and before she returned from Bois-Chauvert he would make it his business to find out exactly how and why.

"Are you safe here?" he asked abruptly, eyes on drawn curtain.

"Why, yes. Of course." She was genuinely surprised. "It's a much nicer neighborhood to live in than you'd expect. There are market stalls in the square early, and I go shopping with a string bag like any *bonne à toute faire*, I've been learning how I must examine each potato before I buy it, and the cutest little boy from the room below helps me upstairs with the load."

"Okay, okay. It's a Paris back street, though, and you—"

Eve laughed at him, mischievous, the shadow of trouble eased. Again he felt sweet pain, which he was too experienced not to know was craving she would one day satisfy. Not here. Not tonight. Not while she was held by concern he could not name and gave him no thought at all.

The sooner he left, the better; his time would come, away from the constraint and mysteries of the Rue Férou.

CHAPTER 5

Lieutenant Bolderini, personnel officer at U. S. Army Forward Hospital No. 6, Bois-Chauvert, France, was a conscientious officer. It annoyed him that Eve Ottoway would almost certainly escape the consequences of overstaying her leave by two weeks, but circumstances defeated him. Her fellow volunteer workers had already left to await transportation back to the States, and Red Cross status made discipline a problem anyway. And now a request for her services had been received from the U. S. Peace Delegation Secretariat.

He looked up at Eve, standing in front of his desk. "You realize that I must file an unfavorable report on your military record?"

"Yes, I'm sorry."

She didn't look it, he thought. Fine figure, though; I bet she had a hot time in Paris. Pity her cap hides her hair; probably it'd come to her waist. He cleared his throat. "You are ordered to report to the U. S. Information Services in the Rue Castiglione as soon as possible. I guess you'll be in a position to stop any press release to the New England papers on the subject of the desertion of personnel."

"Perhaps," Eve replied quietly.

He shuffled her papers together, irritated by her manner. "Take these to Red Cross H.Q. in Paris and they will discharge you. Without pay," he added pointedly.

Of course without pay, Eve thought, dismayed. As a volunteer she was entitled to discharge payment on return to the States, and pocket money off base. But she wasn't returning to the States, and Lieutenant Bolderini certainly wouldn't put through the documents which might entitle her to payment in France.

At least he wrote out a pass to Paris for her, the journey this time accomplished in such comfort as overloaded, unpunctual trains allowed. Once there, Eve walked a long time in early-morning sunshine, for the sheer pleasure of it. Just for today she was off everyone's map and badly needed time to consider her situation, in some way to integrate herself again. She walked along *quais* edged by trees, the Seine, flowing briskly under its many bridges, by her side. *Bateaux mouches* and barges overtook her, the floats of patient fishermen bobbing in their wake, tugs tooting in derision. The fishermen used jointed cane poles and quill floats; they never seemed to catch anything and did not worry about the boats.

Ahead squatted the bulk of Notre-Dame on its island, which ended in a point like the prow of a ship, while bare-branched trees framed high houses either side of the river; Eve walked past Henri IV regarding it all cynically from his bronze horse, and stood on the wooden footbridge between the island and the left bank, lost in thought. Such a short time ago and life had been so simple: this country of her distant heritage waiting to be explored outside the gates of Bois-Chauvert, her days filled with uncomplicated, hard-working routine.

All finished.

An unlucky attack of flu, and her life was thrown violently off track, plunged into emotions she scarcely comprehended. She ought to admit defeat and go, before it was too late. Tell Red Cross Headquarters that, after all, she wanted transportation home; they couldn't make her stay.

She stared at intricate roof lines and intersecting light where the sun flashed through the trees. Paris was a very old city and nothing was simple here; also, she hated the idea of defeat. For just this same brief time when chance had brought her here, Paris was the center of the world: she did not want to scuttle for safety back to Maine, no matter what the risks of staying. She longed to walk the boulevards dressed in the latest fashion instead of a dowdy Red Cross uniform; she wanted to help the statesmen shape a lasting peace and speak French as Parisians spoke it, feel herself elegant and admired.

She shook her head and smiled wryly at gray Seine water: all that was a dream, since if she stayed, her life in Paris was likely to be very different. She had come to France for a labyrinth of reasons, for escape and curiosity and pity, among others. Now that she was here and felt the dreadful cost of war on every side, she couldn't simply turn her back on it and return to a land of peace and overwhelming plenty.

In everyone's life there is at least one moment, this way or that, when choice changes everything. How trite, how feeble, to choose return to a safe haven.

Eve threw back her head; lips tight, eyes a fighting, sharp-edged green. Staying on in Paris wasn't likely to be easy, but she had been raised in a tradition which expected you to fight for anything worthwhile. A different life from the even tenor of New Moose was what she wanted, so no matter what the penalties of her choice, the time for thinking about them was past.

The old St.-Sulpice bell was striking eight in the evening before she crossed the graveled walks of the Luxembourg, darkness already intense. The Place St.-Sulpice at last, the sound of its fountain pattering on stone but the lions sculptured around its base invisible when there wasn't any lighting, her hurrying footsteps loud on cobbles.

She ought not to have come here again, had meant to find some lodging of her own before she saw Guy, but the day had vanished in endless official formalities, and she had so little money, with prices rising faster than she would have thought possible. Paris was crammed with soldiers and diplomats and people taking their first holiday of the peace; if the concierge at the Rue Férou refused to let her in, then she didn't know where she could stay until she found some colleague at work who might be willing to share a room.

The concierge was full of complaints, and Eve didn't blame her. It wasn't much of a job when she was forced to live in a hutch and answer calls at any time of day or night. Her sympathy had an effect, and the concierge waited at the bottom of the stairwell to press the light switch for her a second time. *M. le Commandant* was in, she told Eve, and then as an afterthought, called up the stairs: "Very restless, mademoiselle, since you left. The couple in the third floor back complained he was pacing the boards all night, but I told them that now it is peace the Commandant has a right to his desires."

Eve heard her still cackling as she went back across the courtyard.

Guy was there but looked at her as if she was far from welcome. "I told you to keep away."

"I didn't mean to come, but tonight I haven't anywhere else to go." She told him quickly about her discharge, and Lieutenant Bolderini's satisfaction with such penalties as he could impose. "I can't blame him, when anyone except a Red Cross worker would have faced court-martial. He thought I didn't care, but—" She gave a swift, unhappy smile: it had been her first job and she disliked failing in it. Which, just possibly, had something to do with not wanting to accept defeat in Paris, too.

"Didn't you tell them you'd had grippe?"

"More than two weeks over my pass, and without notifying anyone? What are disciplinary officers like in the French Army?"

He held her then but without passion. "My fault. Again. You should have told him you were nursing the French for a change."

She thrust him away and sat down on one of the hard chairs. "It wouldn't have made any difference, and doesn't matter anyway. It's finished and I've no regrets. It's just a cut at my pride, I guess. I'll get over it."

His eyes flickered and he looked away. He looked desperately tired, fretted, drained, as he had at Le Trésor, that ugly clutter of a shop which in some odd way he visualized as a path to normal life. "Of course you are welcome here tonight or any night. Too welcome, as you know."

Eve bit her lip; she knew. Much about Guy Saulx remained a mystery, but she had come to his lodging here when nothing she did sufficed to dredge him from a spiraling attack of tears and unraveled nerves. He had clung to her then, as the still center of his sanity and nothing more. Later, he felt humiliation but still needed her.

Eve thought that Rick Dwyer had guessed there was someone else in the room, but what he could not know was how the unseen man was rigid with terror at the time, his mind shriveled by a knock on the door.

Eve had encountered shell shock at Bois-Chauvert, but never as she saw it in Guy Saulx. The longest-serving American soldier had endured nine months on the Western Front, and as in other armies, some died, others were maimed or went mad with the horror of it all. Not one could have any conception of how a man's whole being was shredded by years of animal existence; by fear beyond measure and without end, above all by the fact of his own survival when he survived only to command others to their death.

Guy Saulx was neither sane nor insane: he was the remains of a man who once had existed and now needed to struggle every moment of each day to grasp sense out of the world in which he found himself. Perhaps with peace he would improve, but just now the effort sometimes tipped exhausted mind and body back into the void; occasionally both were sufficiently bludgeoned to allow him to sleep for more than minutes at a time, otherwise he existed by trying not to sleep.

Except when she was there. That first night, when the tears would not stop, he had come to trust her, and accepted that she would wake him before the hauntings started. So sometimes when she held him, he could sleep.

"Have you arranged your posting?" she asked at last.

"I think so. Commandant of the guard for the German delegation when it arrives to sign the peace. Since that looks like a long time off, I should be able to attend to my own affairs for much of the time meanwhile."

"It wasn't as difficult as you expected?"

"No. The government of France desires to honor its veterans, nor is it averse to rubbing German noses against *brisques* which show how many of their compatriots I have killed."

Eve glanced at the badges on his sleeve which showed length of frontline service. Seven had been issued, and in all of France few men survived to wear the full number. Guy wore five, one missed because he joined the Army late in 1914, another when he was wounded and spent eight months recovering in a staff appointment.

He had told her a few unemotional facts, and she had pieced others together when she wasn't quick enough to wake him from his dreams; in the yawning gap between remained a chaos about which she dared not ask, for fear of the damage she might do.

Her mind switched abruptly. "How long before you can get out of the Army?"

He shrugged. "God knows. Perhaps one day they'll discover how I served in the German Army, and make me a prisoner of war."

Eve stared at him, staggered. "You did what?"

He rubbed his forehead. "Didn't you know? Yes, I remember telling you yesterday."

"I wasn't here yesterday."

"Certainly you were here. I remember talking . . . you were sitting on that sofa with the gilt legs I brought from Soissons."

There were only two wooden chairs in the room. Eve went over and folded her hands in his. "No. I was at Bois-Chauvert, remember? It's six days since I was here."

His fingers tightened on hers. "You're very sweet. When you were away . . . I liked to think of you here; it helped a little." His voice stumbled. "Not here really; somewhere better. One of those apartments on the Ile St.-Louis facing the river, where the old harridans who live there won't allow any traffic. You'd like it there."

"Guy, I—"

"Yes," he said quietly, no strangeness at all. "I know, *chérie*. It is a dream and the Rue Férou which is the truth. I find pleasure thinking of it, but I don't expect you to feel the same."

"Well, well," said Pierre from the doorway. "Next time the hour of the lovebirds strikes, you might remember to lock the door. My dear Mlle. Ottoway. I had no idea you were still in Paris."

"I haven't been. I just returned this evening from Rheims." Eve was annoyed, because she knew her embarrassment showed.

He smiled, glance traveling over her figure and back to her face again. "Now you are so happily returned to us, you must come to the Carnival Ball at the Opéra with me next week. All the best people buy tickets to show how charitable they are, then give them to their servants, since such occasions are no longer chic. Now me, I think a little vulgarity is entertaining. Eulalie expects you to take her, Guy."

Guy dropped Eve's hand and clasped his own behind his back in a gesture she recognized. "I never asked her."

"I always said that the courtesies which make life tolerable were not included in your makeup. She has her costume chosen, something you will find quite outrageous, I believe. Now, let me see. Cleopatra with her bosoms hanging loose, and an asp spilling from her corsage, or so she said. Go as D'Artagnan, *mon cher*, you'll need a sword when every man in the place will want to fondle so choicely visible a prize." He glanced around the bare room. "Dear me, is this really the *pied à terre* you preferred to the Hôtel Daunay when on furlough?"

"At least there was peace," said Guy wearily. "And it was mine. Eulalie . . . I never agreed to anything with her."

"Have you any choice? Mlle. Eve is charming, of course, but with Eulalie as your . . . er . . . *légitime*, the field may be played more skillfully than before, not less."

Eve knew that by coming alone to the Rue Férou she had forfeited any right to feel insulted by such taunts, but they annoyed her. Irrationally, her anger turned against Guy more than Pierre, when he offered no defense for her. He did not seem to notice Pierre's malice and went over to the dormer window, his back turned to the room. "Why did you come here?"

"To tie up your bargain for Eulalie, *mon cher*. What is it, ten days since you savaged your papa's throat and walked out? It is our family's considered opinion that you have been given long enough to sulk; the time has come for notaries and agreements."

Guy turned. "What is it you propose, exactly?"

For the first time, Pierre was disconcerted. "You know perfectly well."

"I don't remember."

"Won't remember, more like!"

"If you wish. I—" His face contorted without warning. "I hate them all," he whispered. "*Mon Dieu*, how I hate them!"

Eve went over and stood close to him. These times when she alone seemed able to reach him in his hell, when no one else even tried to reach him there, had been another reason for staying on in Paris. "Pierre has come with a proposition to discuss, but you needn't agree to anything at all. Just think about it. I suppose your father and M. Daunay are trying to arrange matters in the best way they can. Eulalie—"

Guy shook his head in a dazed way and licked his lips, but her voice drew him back again from wherever he had been. "She's like a bitch in heat. No. Not a bitch at all; the reverse, in fact. And my welfare certainly isn't my father's concern, is it, Pierre?"

"So you do remember?"

"I'm not likely to forget, when Le Trésor and every sou I'm ever likely to own is tied up in this."

"But you said just now—"

"Pierre, Guy has obtained an appointment in Paris," interrupted Eve. "Couldn't he discuss this with your father later on? I'm sure I oughtn't to listen to your family affairs."

"Why not, when you have apparently become a temporary member of it?"

Eve nearly slapped his face; instead she thrust him out of the room and slammed the door behind them. "How dare you! Whatever I've done, it's none of your business, and you have no right to speak to me in such a way!"

"Sweetheart, I like you better when you're angry." Pierre kissed her on the cheek and then thirstily on the mouth. "Very, very much better. So cousin Guy is a fool, who hasn't made the most of his opportunities?" He laughed at her expression and kissed her again, recoiling with a curse when she bit him, hard.

"You told me I'd have to learn how," Eve said coldly. "Now you just listen to me, and tell your family to stop behaving like a pack of selfish kids with Guy. Can't you see he must have peace? Months, perhaps years of life on a slack rein, of . . . I can't describe what I mean, but he mustn't look for things and find they aren't there. Then perhaps he will be able to pick up his life again. He's trying hard enough; too hard, when trying is more than he can bear, or hadn't you noticed? Or noticed only to kick him flat again?"

"He'll have life bundled and delivered for him once Eulalie is his wife," observed Pierre callously. "She'll choose his women and her own, and tell him which nights they're three in a bed. You'd better book your place if you're so concerned for him."

"What are you trying to do?" asked Eve curiously. "Make me mad again, or confirm something you're still not sure about?"

He smiled, without malice this time. "Bravo, Eve. Tell Guy to come to the Champs-Élysées and we will all be very nice to him. Preferably tomorrow; then it'll be over with. Which should free you from obligation, as you deserve. He'll suck you dry if you stay; you know that, don't you?"

Eve nodded. She feared a man whose hold on reason she might become, since she wouldn't be a woman he desired but a thing on which he might rebuild his life. And foundations were driven into darkness, designed for bearing loads and nothing else. "He wouldn't be safe, though," she said reluctantly. "He'd murder Eulalie in a month."

"Or she him, more likely. Aren't you worried ever, here alone?"

"No. He's different with me."

Pierre grinned, but the cruel edge in him was sheathed for the moment. Instead of the jibe she expected, he asked about her plans and then swore he would sit in her office until she promised to come with him to the Opéra ball.

"You can't! I'll be working my first day as junior clerk!"

"That's what I meant, Eve, *chérie*. You will come, won't you?"

"I haven't anything to wear," she protested.

"Better and better. The remaining tickets will sell at double price."

"I could come as I am," she retorted. Pierre exploited weakness and showed chivalry only toward a fellow combatant.

He surveyed her drab skirt and shirt, ready-to-wear from a Boston mail-order house. "I think that would not do you justice. But the Opéra ball is fancy-dress, you understand. There are crinolines by the dozen in our attic, I will choose one for you and send it to the Rue Castiglione." He put his fingers to her cheek and tilted her face to moonlight flooding through the passage window. "A crinoline will be exactly right: you have a nineteenth-century face. Very correct, very modest. Until someone puts a torch to tinder; although I suppose you still have something to discover about the flames in you, waiting to be lit?"

"I'm not sure," Eve said honestly.

He laughed, lips just brushing hers this time, and pattered off down the stairs, hand raised in parting. "A *bientôt, chérie.*"

Eve felt strangely reluctant to return to Guy; if she meant anything to him at all, he ought not to have left her so long alone with Pierre.

He was lying flat on his back on the bed, curtain drawn back, staring at the ceiling.

Eve dropped on her knees beside him. "Guy?"

He stirred and said something indistinguishable.

She shook him urgently. "Listen to me, Guy. You don't have to do what they say. Don't hate them when they're only trying to plan for the best, but you needn't marry Eulalie, or agree to anything else you don't want."

"No. I can lie here and rot instead." He closed his eyes but not to rest, being in the state of mind in which ease was unimaginable; nor could he stand seeing or thinking any more.

Eve lay beside him as she had before, both of them dressed and lacking any sense of intimacy. The first night she lay like this she had watched Guy Saulx and imagined his hands rousing her, his gray eyes tender instead of rolled under his lids in torment, the mask which was his face relaxed. It hadn't happened, nor even the shadow of it, and now her wish for it had gone. Compassion made her still try to reach him in his pitiless prison, but she recoiled from inhabiting it herself.

Eve lay very still while he tossed and muttered, no longer holding him as she had before. It had been a hideous mistake to come back here. She must accept defeat and go at once, before she did more harm. In fact, she ought to have left tonight even if it meant walking the pavé until dawn.

Guy's eyes flicked open suddenly. "Where's Pierre?"

"He went some time ago. He left a message that you should call at the Hôtel Daunay soon."

"I suppose I shall have to go, if only for the courtesy he says I cannot comprehend. How much have you understood of what it's all about?" His face was stripped of color and expression, but he spoke as if his mind was completely clear.

"Not a great deal," confessed Eve.

He gave the ghost of a laugh. "It's going to be a long night, so you might as well hear it all. You were surprised when I told you I'd served in the German Army, but the Saulx come from Alsace. One of the lost provinces—have you heard of them in Maine?"

"Of course. My family's French as well as American, remember?"

"Ottoway isn't a French name."

"No. My grandfather was New Plymouth puritan, but even he had to learn some French when he wanted to walk out with my grandmother. It became almost a condition of the marriage!"

Instant laughter, as instantly drained from his face. "As a race we're exact over conditions of marriage. Anyway, as I said, our family comes from Alsace. When the Germans took it in 1871, of course we became German citizens, but when my grandfather died, my father decided to get out. Paris. It wasn't *la patrie*, but the call of Paris, which lured him. His sisters, my aunts Gabrielle and Hortense, had already married Frenchmen; my grandfather saw to that. No Boche grandchildren for him. Well, my father went, leaving my grandmother and me to hold the property. Alsace was part of Germany but more or less under military rule, since the Germans knew it wasn't loyal. If a Saulx male hadn't lived there, they'd soon have found a way to take the property."

"How old were you when he left?"

"Three years old. My mother was of German blood, an unpleasant scandal in the family, that, and she'd died the year before, my grandmother when I was thirteen. After her death I lived at the domaine alone. Each year, my father milked off all the profits for the fine new business he had opened in Paris: *antiques, décor, bijouterie*. Le Trésor perdu de l'Alsace, he called it; a good idea, I suppose. Frenchmen mourned the loss of Alsace, yet could not get it back; Paris had money to spend and the name helped part them from it. In the early years, I believe my father always kept some special piece from Alsace in the window. The Rue Daunou looks second-rate but it isn't a bad position for a new man starting up, with the Rue de la Paix around the corner."

"How could he milk you of profits, if you lived in Alsace and he in Paris?" demanded Eve. "The property must have been in your name as a German citizen?"

"Yes. He tied it up cleverly, though. I owned it, he leased it, then leased it back to me year by year on whatever terms he cared to name. He needed money because he wasn't—isn't—a good businessman. Once the novelty faded, Le Trésor did not do well. He borrowed from his sisters but lived very well himself on Daunay's bounty. The war killed what was left."

"Which you began in the German Army?"

"No, although I should have. I did my conscript training in the Jaegers, and very unpleasant it was too. Elsass, they called our province and proclaimed how German it was, but the Reich High Command knew that conscripts from there weren't to be trusted in war with France. So we were scattered around all the regiments of the Army, where Prussian NCO's could have their way with us. All civil and property rights forfeited if you did not serve. So I spent two years being forced around parade grounds in order to preserve the Saulx domaine, and when I returned there was no money for stock, to repair the house, to marry the girl I desired."

He broke off and lay slack-limbed, moonlight glinting on his tunic buttons in rhythm with his breathing.

Why, there's nothing the matter with him, thought Eve, amazed. Reliving that other life which is still clear in his mind, I can see how once he was. There was no self-pity in his voice, only the truculent fury of a man who intended to right his wrongs. "So what did you do?"

"Like a fool, I spent two years laboring on the domaine, intending to challenge my father's lease in the courts as soon as I had sufficient money to fight a case. I was a time-served army reservist, a German citizen, and no longer a boy. I realized that any Reich court would dispossess a Frenchman from their border areas if they could; such a case was good propaganda for them." He turned his head on the pillow. "The case was on the court calendar for the summer of 1914, but after preliminary arguments it was stood over for judgment in the autumn. The war came in August. I had served in the German Army to preserve what was mine, but I'm French in blood and bone; I couldn't fight against France. I crossed the frontier the day before war broke out, and went to Paris to confront my father."

"What did he say?"

She felt his muscles contract in a strange gesture of revulsion. "He said that if Germany won, they'd shoot me as a deserter; if France, then a case was filed in German courts which would show that I had tried unjustifiably to dispossess a Frenchman. Le Trésor was his, and the Saulx domaine also. One day I would inherit what remained after he'd lived his life in comfort, but almost half the value already belonged to Gabrielle and Daunay."

"Guy, no! Why—"

"He'd hardly seen me since I was three years old, and hadn't loved my mother. Once in Paris, he'd been made to feel ashamed of marrying a German for her flaxen plaits, or whatever it was that caught his fancy. Well, I didn't intend to be cheated twice. I wasn't on any French Army lists so I spent the first few months of the war calling myself an official, commandeering transport and using it to buy up people's treasures cheap as they fled from the Germans. After 1914 the war settled down, but during those first weeks there was panic everywhere, even here in Paris. People wanted cash, and were willing to sell a château full of antiques in exchange for a truck, if they lived in the track of the German advance. No questions asked. I own a warehouse full of valuable stuff out at Neuilly. Through the trench years which followed, the one thing I had to hold on to was the fact I'd beaten my father; I possessed the goods he'd need to get the business going again after the war. Also, I suppose I liked the idea of earning my living by handling beautiful things after all that filth, although I know nothing about the business. Under French law a father must leave his property to his children, and I'm his only child; we could reach agreement, surely. Only, you see, my father has decided to use all he still possesses to purchase an annuity from Daunay. It's legal to part with property in your lifetime, and apparently sufficient remains to keep him in comfort if he uses it in that way, but nothing will be left for me. Daunay drove a different bargain: he wants Eulalie wed to take care of scandals she may cause, and said he'd give her the domaine in Alsace and Le Trésor as dowry if I'd marry her."

What a sordid, cruel story, Eve thought, remembering with gratitude the upright strictness of her parents, though she had thought them harsh before. "You still have a choice," she said slowly. "The furniture at Neuilly is legally yours whatever your methods of purchase may have been. Sell a few pieces and use the money to set yourself up elsewhere."

"I thought of that. I had six weeks in the upheaval of 1914 to buy whatever I could find with such money as I had: some of it is good, some not, I don't know myself what's really there. I'm a farmer and a soldier, with a year's pay banked and nothing else. French Army scales are less than half American, I suppose. Le Trésor needs a great deal of money spent on it and I should have to sell some pieces to pay for making a start there, but it's a good position, and by my reckoning ought to be rent-free even if I must share some profits later. If I went elsewhere and had to pay rent as well, I'd be forced into the back streets or have too little stock left to establish myself well. And the time is now, when Paris is bursting with people, when questions won't be asked and the profiteers are burning francs to keep warm. I suppose, too, that I simply can't bear to think it all out afresh when through the past four years starting at Le Trésor was what I thought of when I thought of peace."

"So you're going to marry Eulalie." Eve spoke flatly; she had been worried by the need to leave him when he was so obviously sick, and should have been relieved by such a practical solution to his problems; instead she felt disgusted. She had a realistic mind, and had been raised in a place where property was passionately held; she also knew that marriages were only sometimes contracted for sentiment. They were not often sought in hate, though.

He moved again, bedsprings creaking, slack ease gone. And suddenly his muscles were bar-tight, his body rigid with the eruptive force of emotions loosed by a few minutes' lowered guard. Eve shot off the bed, uncomprehending, and stood beside him, gripping his arm, shaking, shouting, anything to reach him; and when tension went at last, to soothe and gentle him.

Below, the people in the third floor back hammered on the ceiling and shouted angrily.

"*Je m'excuse,*" Guy said, voice slurred. "I'm half a man, you see, and should suit Eulalie very well, since she is also half a man. She deserves me and you don't."

He was gone when Eve woke in the morning.

CHAPTER 6

Guy could not remember when first he began to fear Sergeant Joubaire, nor could he have expressed this feeling if he had. The man was helpful, always where he was wanted, usually respectful. During the ten months he served in the 121st Chasseurs, Guy had found him invaluable. It had been a time when Commandant Saulx was so dreadfully afraid to sleep that even when the regiment was in reserve, he rested only when he collapsed. And there in darkness the demons waited for him again. He hated dependence, but came to depend on Joubaire; he relayed orders when Guy could no longer accept that each word he spoke sent men to their death; he smuggled extra wine and reminded the Commandant when he had not eaten.

As the fabric of Guy's mind tore, it was Joubaire who listened to his babblings and learned of matters Guy would have paid to keep concealed, Joubaire who forced drugs on him when army doctors became desperate to keep officers of experience functioning at any cost. Drugs he loathed and might have refused if left to himself; perhaps that was when he first feared Joubaire. Now peace had come and the man was an alien presence where once Guy Saulx's will had been: he meant to be rid of him but had not yet brought himself to face more battles.

So Joubaire was still there, and harder to dislodge than ever. It was Joubaire who had commandeered trucks to carry Guy's 1914 purchases to Neuilly, and on the worst days he continued to run the Commandant's life, days when Guy's mind spun on the edge of darkness and he failed to make up his mind about anything at all, for decision killed men and he had spent too long slaughtering others.

At least he was aware now that he feared Joubaire, which was recov-

ery of a sort, the decision to free Eve by walking out himself another
sign of reviving will. Occasionally, when he was able to avoid conten-
tion for a while, he felt quite sensible again.

Because Eve might come again to the Rue Férou he went back to
live at the Hôtel Daunay, although he hated its marble spaces and the
web of frauds which made up Georges Daunay's world. Hated above all
the way Daunay set out to buy a husband for his daughter at a bargain
price, when everyone knew that, once married, Eulalie would continue
to live exactly as she pleased.

The family sat in solemn conclave to discuss the marriage contract,
and Joubaire brought wine. He was still in uniform but continued his
habit of making himself indispensable even here, and was allowed in
when house staff were excluded from such dealings. As if everyone accepted him as his master's keeper.

Guy stared at Joubaire's red lips and face glowing with health; he had
arranged for Sergeant Joubaire to be attached with him to the German
delegation guard but decided now that the sooner Joubaire went elsewhere, the better. Then he remembered how Joubaire knew of risky
purchasings and goods stored at Neuilly, brought there by army transport. It was too late to be rid of him; he already knew too much.

Joubaire touched his shoulder, respectfully but with familiarity.
"Your wine, *mon commandant*. M. Daunay has asked for your attention."

Guy pushed the wine away, but jerked from his abstraction. My God,
yes; Eulalie. But he did not want to think of her. He put his elbows on
the table, hands shading his eyes, and his thoughts drifted again. Eve
was going to wear his grandmother's crinoline to the Opéra ball. Pierre
had been in the hall when he came in, a dressmaker's box packed ready
for delivery to the Crillon.

Pierre sat next to him now; Guy felt no hate for him, only envy sharp
as a knife. Pierre dug him in the ribs. "Your contract of marriage is
agreed, if you will take some slight interest in it, *mon vieux*."

Across the table, Eulalie met his eyes mockingly; today she wore
black flannel cut as if for a male, gold earrings cast in the shape of bullets, and a cravat of white muslin. "Hold your nose and take your medicine like a good little boy."

Daunay cleared his throat. "The matter is concluded, then?"

Guy was staring at Eulalie, mesmerized. She had a body like tropical
creeper and the face of a salacious saint. He swallowed, but the words
would not come.

"More wine, *mon commandant?*" Joubaire topped up his full glass
insinuatingly.

Guy shook his head; wine curdled a system begging for drugs he would not take now peace had come. He tried to think, but tripped over the enormous complication of saying no, when saying yes was all that remained for him to do. He had no money, no plans beyond those conceived for Le Trésor at a time when making plans had seemed a simple matter; not even a home left in Alsace, since it, too, was part of the deal with Daunay; scarcely a mind which was his own. Once he cut himself loose from everything he knew, it wouldn't be long before some doctor tied him into a padded cell and forgot him; he was afraid of doctors and wanted very much to walk joyfully in the light once more. With Eve.

He looked at Daunay, and nodded.

"*Bien*. Excellent, in fact. I am happy to welcome you as my future son-in-law," said Daunay briskly. "We will invite our acquaintance to celebrate the betrothal at a repast on Sunday; the contract will be prepared for signature by then." He went to kiss his daughter but unexpectedly drew back and patted her shoulder awkwardly instead, and he was not an awkward man.

"Embrace your affianced bride, Guy. The formalities should always be observed." Gabrielle sat completely upright, bitter voice denying the glitter on her cheek. On impulse, Guy bent and kissed her as he passed, remembering how both her sons were dead.

As soon as he touched Eulalie, Guy was conscious only of how his revulsion must not show. She coiled mouth and hard, digging fingers into him, not with desire but in exultant power: she had been given a new possession and would enjoy it for a while. Her father called for champagne with the complacent relief of one who has surmounted formidable obstacles to secure his own advantage; only Pierre refused the toast, saying that if he must drink blood he preferred to do it in a butcher's shop.

As evening came everyone went out. The upper crust of Paris society, Le Tout-Paris, as its own members called it, never stayed at home unless they were dying. In and out of restaurants and ballrooms the constant procession flowed: jeweled, witty, chasing the latest fashion. Daunay left to take his mistress to the ballet, Anselme Saulx for a restaurant where he fed through the night with like-minded *bons viveurs*. Then Pierre went, whistling and swinging his cane, looking as emaciated as when he returned from Germany but telling his mother that Paris was the medicine which suited him best. Eulalie went next, alone.

"You should escort her. The day of her engagement, and she is left to amuse herself alone! You will need to become more serious as a married man." Gabrielle had resented Guy's kiss of pity and allowed her scorn to show.

"She prefers to be alone."

"She isn't alone, she's with the pink fondant," interrupted Pierre, who had come back for a quick cognac before going up to the Butte of Montmartre.

Gabrielle compressed her lips. "All the more reason for Guy to go. He is responsible for Eulalie now."

Pierre burst out laughing. "*Nom de Jésus Christ, ma tante!* He has contracted for a niche to live in, not a female who attracts him."

"*C'est vrai qu'elle manque quelques dons naturels,*" agreed Gabrielle fair-mindedly. "But now she has agreed to live as a married woman, Guy should see that she offers at least the appearance of that state."

Pierre laughed again, and departed; Guy sat alone in his darkened bedroom until Joubaire came. "Coffee, *mon commandant.* We have a great many matters to arrange, have we not?"

The bitter liquid scalded Guy's mouth. "No."

"*Mais oui, mon commandant.* You have agreed with M. Daunay to sign the marriage contract within days, and in effect you will then control Le Trésor. And indeed, there is great need for haste. The time is now, you said, and looking around Paris I see that you were right. Money is being spent as in a madness; anyone with goods to sell can make a fortune. Le Trésor—"

"Later, Bertrand. One thing at a time."

"With respect, *mon commandant,* certainly not. Many, many things at the same time." He held up his fingers and checked them off. "Painters and carpenters. There is no time to do all that needs doing at Le Trésor, but fresh paint will cover some of it. Women to clean. Advertisements in the journals, and then you must entertain the right people to achieve the publicity we need. Mlle. Eulalie should be able to help there. Some goods brought from Neuilly, and then a grand opening night with the best piece on show to whet appetites."

"What part do you plan for yourself in all this?"

"*Chef d'atelier,*" he said, eyes flicking sideways, untruth pat on his tongue. "We share our luck as before, eh, *mon commandant?*"

"And our profit, if any?"

"But of a certainty!" The mock surprise revealed contempt he had hidden until then. "How could the Commandant manage without me?"

Guy stood, seized by a fierce, despairing rage. "Very easily. Six weeks of peace . . . if you can call it that . . . and surely I am better. Once married, I can hire what help I need."

In darkness, Guy could see the gleam of Joubaire's teeth. "You hire me, on terms I choose to make. There is no peace for you, while so many battles still remain to be fought. In the marketplace, and with Mme. Saulx, once you are wed. With me, if necessary, but certainly not with me if you look to your interests." His tone had been harsh, now it became soothing. "You need rest, *mon commandant*. Allow me to help you, and bring drops to help you sleep. In the morning the world will look good again."

Joubaire's hands were as gentle as a woman's on buckles and constricting cloth, the bed soft and very welcome when Guy had not slept at all the night before. He lay back in relief, wanting never to think again. He could not endure more quarreling and so accepted Joubaire's drops, the smell of them unsnapping craving in an instant. Saliva ran in his dry mouth; he forgot he wasn't in a trench and tipped the glass secretly between bed and wall before he could be overwhelmed by wanting.

Then he had to pretend to be sleeping and so heard Joubaire laugh in derision before he left. "Sleep well, *mon cocu*. I, Bertrand, will grasp thy fortune for thee whilst thou stayest jellied by thy terrors."

Once Joubaire had gone, Guy lay rigid a long time, sweat on his body, mind and spirit writhing. There is no peace, you are at war again, *mon commandant*.

Late *fiacres* rattled past outside, and the beat of music drifted from the restaurant hidden among the trees close by. The giggle of a *bonne* in the passage outside; shouted, half-drunk jokes on the staircase as his father came home roistering. Guy moved convulsively, and held his hands to moonlight before his face. They were trembling. He remembered the plucked-fowl feel of his father's throat and thought, he hasn't made over my inheritance to Daunay yet. If he would only die tonight I would have something left; the papers for his annuity and my marriage are unsigned. If he died tonight our land and also Le Trésor would be mine without any need to take Eulalie as the price. How many Germans have I killed, decent men as frightened as myself? Strange how the only friend I ever had should be a German. Hugo; I suppose he's dead too. Perhaps I killed him; who knows, who ever knows these things? He would not have deserved to die, and Anselme Saulx does.

He tossed restlessly, burrowing his face away from thought, to wake shuddering from a dream in which mud filled his lungs, as it did that time a shell buried him near Rheims.

Rheims. He thought of Eve again, which for a short while was better than the terrors of drowning in a shell hole. He thought of bright hair and tip-tilted freckled nose, how with her he had dared sleep a little, trusting her to rouse him before the nightmares started. Joubaire had a way of letting him whirl into the pit of horrors before shaking him awake to swallow drops, and Eulalie would be the same.

He dragged himself out of bed and stood with his face against cold glass. Another night like all the rest, in which he dared not sleep. Yet he was so tired the room floated around him. He sagged against the window and saw Eulalie come home with her pink fondant, an overblown blonde wrapped in pink tulle and white fur. The taxi driver made a vulgar gesture at their backs as he drove off.

Georges Daunay is a lover of women, thought Guy cynically. He sensed tonight how obscene it would be to kiss his daughter. No wonder even I am welcome as his son-in-law; I could probably increase the *dot* if I refused to sign at once on Saturday.

He drifted across to the washstand and stood staring at the bottle of drops Bertrand had left there, and poured himself a double dose as Eulalie went past his door. His hands shook as he held the liquid a moment before drinking: there were some nights which would not pass without help.

Then, after the night, would be another day; in four years surely he ought to have caught a bullet somewhere which would have ended it all.

Guy scarcely saw his affianced bride during the next few days, although he stayed on at the Hôtel Daunay. He walked for miles in the wet leaves of the Bois de Boulogne by day, and failed to sleep at night. He had no military duties until the Peace Conference met, so there was plenty of time to attend to his own affairs, but he accomplished nothing. Bertrand sulked and swore and shook him savagely to prevent thought straying: no pretense at concern any more, instead relentless pressure to force decision out of paralysis and put Sergeant Joubaire on the road to prosperity at his expense. While Eulalie took her passions elsewhere, also at his expense.

On the evening of the Opéra ball, Eulalie came home early, and Guy went to her room. "I must talk to you, Eulalie."

"Why?" She did not turn, eyes scornful in the mirror.

"We have a great deal to discuss. Tell your dresser to go."

"Certainly not. There are only three hours before I must be ready, and my masseuse will be here soon." Eulalie was feminine enough to make a full-time occupation out of being herself. Chiropodists, hairdressers, manicurists, all came and went in startling profusion.

Guy jerked his head at her maid. "Wait outside until I call." After a moment, the woman scuttled out, confiding to the second-floor *bonne* that the Commandant looked so fierce she didn't dare refuse. "Hasn't it occurred to you that we ought to talk, or are you contemplating only a business relationship together?"

"Don't be a melodramatic dolt, Guy. I tell you, I'm late as it is."

"There are more important things than a costume ball," he suggested.

"Not when I'm dressing for one three hours away!" She glanced at a watch pinned to her blouse; she was less extravagantly dressed today, in white silk and a severe skirt. "Two hours and forty minutes, to be exact. Go away, Guy."

He knew he was a fool to force a scene when she was in a hurry, but chances to talk alone with Eulalie occurred rarely and it had taken him two days of walking to crystallize his mind. He went over and held her, and this time it seemed easier. "Eulalie, there are things only we can settle together. Whether you feel any interest at all in this marriage, for instance."

"Why should I agree to it, otherwise?" She threw back her head to watch him, hair soft against his hand. She liked to show off, to be outrageous, and make everyone wonder what she would do next. She was waiting for her moment now.

"Well, then. . . ." His voice faltered and for a dreadful moment awareness tilted and he was unable to remember what he was doing here. What had he meant to say, why had he come? He kissed her to gain time, fighting panic as he groped for memory.

It was as if he kissed a corpse. Mouth gaping, spittle drooling, she lolled like an unstrung puppet, only gleeful mischief in her eyes betraying her design. Recollection swept back and he dropped her, hard, before she read his intention.

She leaped at him from the floor, spitting fury.

Instinctively Guy threw up an arm to protect himself, grabbed at her with the other. She tried to bite his hand, screaming hate, until he held her so roughly her clothes tore. "Eulalie, for God's sake! I'll go, don't scream so. The household will think you're being murdered. Do you want everyone to see you like this?"

She didn't care, but ran out of breath in the end. "I hate you."

He carried her to the bed and set her down. "Haven't you ever been treated as you deserve before?"

"I don't know what you mean." Her blouse was ripped, breasts tumbled into sight.

"Oh, yes, you do. In all of your life has no one ever stopped you from having your own way?" That soft blonde she dotes on, he thought: I suppose she enjoys yielding to a stronger will, when the most timid husband would not find pleasure in it. He liked Eulalie better when she was angry and disheveled; perhaps he had not wasted his time after all.

Eulalie looked at him measuringly. "No, and Papa hasn't bought me a husband just so I can start learning now. Play with your shop and keep from tripping me up, then we may get along well enough. You won't find me possessive. There's a certain *cachet* in being pointed to as a woman who married one of our brave boys crazed in the war, but I can get you locked up fast enough if you make a nuisance of yourself."

The cell and doctors he feared, with their brown glass bottles of drugs and Eulalie jeering at him from a shell hole. The world was tilting again and this time he went with it, mercilessly cold, under the goad of desperation. Eulalie deserves me and you don't, he had told Eve. The *bonne* outside heard her mistress screech once more and sighed sentimentally to herself. A wild one, Mlle. Eulalie, she needed a man to master her.

CHAPTER 7

Paris was deliciously and elegantly mad about dancing. Poilus on their way home danced in the streets to impromptu bands, attempting *le turkey-trotting* and *le cake-walkant* in their heavy boots; sober functionaries danced to the phonograph in crammed apartments, the rich to jazz bands in the insolent luxury of the Faubourg. It became commonplace to dance in the foyer of the Casino de Paris, between tables and courses in restaurants, on Seine barges and in cafés. There had never been anything like it, and those not caught by the infection were shocked, amazed, disgusted. Everyone else danced and danced and danced, swept away by a kind of delirium. The war was over. The future could boil its head, the grieving and distraught jump in the Seine, who cared? And all the time the pace of the music grew hotter, the bands and dancers more fevered. Saxophones swerved and staggered, Negro instrumentalists became all the rage with their ragtime and blues, the new beat bludgeoning minds only too willing to lose awareness for a while. Fox-trot, black bottom, one-step; don't stop, never stop, for rhythm plays the same tricks as a juggler with his plates.

Paris, City of Light, was enjoying a barbarian wallow.

On the night of the carnival ball, the Avenue de l'Opéra was a tangle of carriages and *taximètres*, people crushed into trams and omnibuses and silhouetted against glittering shop fronts. Eve could not see enough of everything, for this was Paris as she had dreamed it would be, a city expert in letting the world slip. A city where so many lovers had been happy that tenderness was sunk into stone.

Pierre had fetched her in a *fiacre*, and slipped his arm around her while pointing out whatever took his fancy as they clopped over granite blocks. Everyone except the rich faced scarcity, but Le Tout-Paris had abandoned austerity long before the end of the war; would sadness in Paris make any difference to France's sufferings? Of course not! Would an end to *haute couture* benefit anyone except the couturiers of New York? *Certainement non!* So balls were given for charitable causes, fine dishes were christened with patriotic names, the most expensive dresses were those decorated by military-style insignia, and the dance went on.

The Opéra Carnival Ball which saw in the New Year of 1919 was dedicated to the support of military hospitals, but no one thought of that. Why distress oneself when everybody wanted to forget? And inside was sheer fantasy; Eve could not have imagined anything like it. A masked ball at the Paris Opéra was staged like a theatrical production, guests grouped together by the theme of their costumes, each making a grand entrance, applause greeting the clever or spectacular, indifferent gossip the merely expensive. Chandeliers glittered, the throng so dense it was incredible that space would be found where they could dance.

Pierre was a considerate escort, and although still too frail for battering through the mob, he used his stick to prize open a passage for Eve. "Do you know, I think I shall have to follow the respectable mamas next year, and strike this occasion from my diary?" he observed after a short time of this. "I will take you to the Comte de Beaumont's ball instead and then you will see the Paris I remembered in a prison camp."

"But I'm so glad we came! It's the most beautiful setting I have ever seen; aren't you charmed with it even a little?" Dancing was thought excessively fast in New Moose; Eve had occasionally joined a parlor hoedown when Frankie Laurier played his fiddle but had never been allowed to attend a subscription dance.

"In your company, yes. Do you care to dance if we can find a square centimeter on which to put our feet?"

Eve agreed enthusiastically. "That is if you're sure you ought?"

Pierre laughed. "I never do what I ought, *chérie*. Champagne will heal any damage afterward."

He was a good dancer, and allowed her natural grace to disguise her inexperience, but he tired quickly and began to cough, until Eve insisted on finding a place for him to rest. Every cranny was full of amorous, drunken couples; and disregarding his gasped protests, she went alone in search of somewhere quieter. It was so stuffy that some men had already stripped off coats and masks, and a woman dressed as a powder puff was reduced to a single transparent layer of tulle.

Eve eventually found a couch almost lost behind crimson curtains and began to force her way back to Pierre through offers lacking any pretense at subtlety. She refused to allow herself to be disconcerted and continued to watch everything with eager interest; in her wildest imaginings she could never have pictured such a scene. A man with a girl in his arms came reeling past, hiccuping with laughter, his gladiator's tunic torn and vine leaves scattering as he ran. The girl was shrieking like a steam engine. He laid her carefully in an ornamental pool full of fairy lights, and the girl burst into a storm of abuse as she crawled over the edge of the basin, draggled and dripping.

There was one man Eve could not shake off. He was dressed as a lion tamer and very drunk: she reckoned he clung to her as much for support as with desire, whatever he said. That didn't make him any less annoying as a capering crowd of his friends gathered around, one clutching a real and terrified lion cub. In the scuffle it scrambled out of his arms and shinned up a pole holding lamps and flower baskets, hot oil spraying in every direction. Eve seized her chance and escaped, blowing a kiss toward the snarling cub as she passed; her mask had gone, and the flounce of her crinoline was torn.

"Hey, Eve! You're not alone here?"

She turned swiftly. "Rick! Why, if you weren't there in front of my eyes I'd say it was impossible to meet anyone I knew in such a crush! And no, of course not, I'm with Pierre Daunay, but he's only recently back from prison camp in Germany and shouldn't really have come. I've been to scout out somewhere for him to rest a few minutes."

"Daunay, eh?" He flashed her a swift, speculative glance, then introduced the girl beside him. "Sarah Wyville, she's English and like you enjoying her first look at Paris. Sarah, this is Eve Ottoway, from my home state and the U. S. Red Cross."

"Not any more, as you well know, Rick Dwyer," retorted Eve. The English girl was far too young for Rick, with a piquant rather than a pretty face, and looked as self-willed as a mule. Not Rick's type at all, thought Eve; I bet she's the key to some information he's tracking down.

"I've been away from Paris and wasn't sure. So our peace delegation has a new clerk to help win over the French to President Wilson's view of peace and justice?"

"It has. The French are quite charming about it, and change the subject every time."

Rick laughed. "I'd bet the whole Crillon to a dead wasp what subject they turn it to when the clerk is you! Let's go, before that damned cub sets fire to everything."

The carpet was smoldering, but no one seemed to worry, beyond keeping out of the way. "Don't you think we should do something to stop it?"

"If you like," said Rick carelessly. He picked up an armful of champagne bottles and dumped them on the carpet in a shatter of glass and foam. "Come on, where's your Pierre?"

Sarah Wyville was too young to hide her annoyance over Rick's obvious pleasure at meeting Eve. "What about the cub? We can't just leave it up a pole to be singed."

"Try me, honey. It'll jump down fast enough when it wants to. At the moment, it prefers the pole to the human zoo, and I don't blame it."

"No. You get it down, or I stay here."

Rick looked exasperated, which confirmed Eve's suspicion that he had brought the girl for professional reasons, rather than for pleasure. He was quite capable of walking away from anyone who annoyed him, unless he was also cherishing a source of information. The cub was snarling and spitting, and he eyed it warily, then picked up another bottle of champagne, shook it hard and unwired the cork.

Both cork and spray caught the cub neatly under the tail and it roared with fury before leaping into the crowd, forgetting itself on the carpet as it went. A truly appalling smell made everyone shriek and hold their noses, while startled guests leaped for curtains and tables when they turned to discover what was going on and confronted a terrorized, vengeful lion cub.

"Christ," said Rick. "I hate fancy-dress balls, but I've had my revenge on this one." He propelled the two girls through the gap torn in the crush by the cub; even Sarah had forgotten her sulks in giggles.

Pierre had stopped coughing and was clearly displeased when Eve introduced Rick; part of her attraction for him was her unattached position in Paris, and Rick Dwyer's aggressive confidence was just what he did not need in the background, when he still cut such a poor figure himself. The fact that every trifling exchange had to be yelled in each other's ear made matters worse, for instead of tactfully withdrawing, Rick stayed to help Eve force a passage to the couch for Pierre.

"I assure you, monsieur, I am perfectly well. You must not allow me to distract you any longer from the charming Mlle. Wyville, or she will feel neglected and perhaps find herself another escort. Then you will have a great deal of explaining to do when you return alone to the Hôtel Astoria."

Rick took a swig of champagne from a tankard he had found. "This goddam gas, it went out with clipper ships. Why don't they serve drinks you can taste? So you've gone to balls with girls smuggled out of the staff entrance too, and recognize the signs?"

"I recognize the name," said Pierre dryly.

They were speaking French, and Eve could see that Sarah understood almost nothing; lip caught in her teeth, foot tapping, she couldn't hide her annoyance: "Rick, I want to dance. The grand unmasking comes soon, and the floor show, and—"

Pierre bowed to her with a flourish. "But certainly, mademoiselle. I should hate to detain you and your partner from enjoyment." He spoke stiff, accurate English. "Tell me, what is M. Dwyer disguised to represent?"

Her face lightened; if she chose, a little more maturity would make Sarah Wyville an entrancing and unusual young woman. "An American reporter."

"A masterpiece. A pencil behind the ear and a pad in his pocket to write down your indiscretions about your father, and his evening is complete without the slightest discomfort. At least—nearly complete. Really, M. Dwyer, such an oversight. You should have remembered *le whiskey* in your hip flask and so have avoided the—er—gas."

"Indiscretions about my father?" repeated Sarah, frowning. She had thick dark eyebrows over deep blue eyes: the contrast was striking, even though any Parisienne would have plucked the eyebrows. "What do you mean?"

"*Je m'excuse, mademoiselle,* but I suggest you ask him."

"You goddam interfering swine," said Rick savagely. "What the hell business is it of yours?"

"Perhaps I dislike seeing chickens plucked when they still have down instead of feathers. I suggest you confine yourself to *les poules,* who know how these games are played." He spoke French again, softly and with venom. *Les poules,* the streetwalkers of Paris.

"Stick together, all ye aristocrats, and keep the mob out in the streets, is that it?"

"I am flattered, when the Daunays are not even Louis-Napoléon aristos, but yes. You could put it like that if you wish." He turned to Sarah. "I will escort you home, if you would prefer not to remain here with M. Dwyer."

"No, thank you. I came, and mean to enjoy myself." She eyed Eve speculatively. "If my father finds out and is very angry, I'll say you were chaperoning our party; you won't mind, will you?"

Eve burst out laughing. "I hope I don't look a suitable tabby to sit in a corner yet!"

"Well, I daresay he'd think you better than nothing," explained Sarah.

Rick dragged her away, more irritated than amused, Eve and Pierre being treated to the distant sight of an expressively fierce row between them.

Eve sat beside Pierre on the couch. "Why did you take such a dislike to Rick?"

"Who could like him?"

"I do. He was kind when I needed help, and found me a job with our peace delegation. All reporters are unscrupulous over information. Who is her father, that you recognized the name and Rick is taking the trouble to smuggle a schoolgirl to the Opéra ball?"

"Sir Maurice Wyville. At present in charge of the administrative arrangements for the British delegation, but during the Peace Conference he will be one of their five commissioners. Not the kind of man to allow his daughter to come here with a type like Dwyer. Certainly he sees her as a useful source of indiscretion."

"I shouldn't think she would be now," observed Eve. "You put a rat in the rabbit bag there."

"I don't like the British, but it was a pleasure. The latest of many this evening, *chérie*, but the best still waits for me, I hope." He leaned toward her, lips against her cheek seeking delicate half permission before moving on to her throat and mouth.

Eve had wanted him to kiss her, and knew he would at a carnival ball. In their homes, Frenchmen did not kiss even the hand of unmarried ladies, but coming here cut through propriety. Back in New Moose a few boys had snatched inexpert kisses, and social evenings at Bois-Chauvert had always been a hazard, but Pierre was utterly different, assured and taught by experts. Eve found her emotions unexpectedly out of control, heart beating against her ribs, the very completeness of his skill alarming. Instinctive response was swept away by panic, when only a short time before she had felt old compared to Sarah Wyville. A man she scarcely knew ought not to be able to rouse her body so easily, while her mind remained cold and disapproving. Eve was too inexperienced to understand why pleasure changed to recoil, but Pierre understood, and was sufficiently shrewd not to persist when persistence would harm his cause. Besides, he was tired tonight.

He leaned back, smiling, his arm only lightly around her. "Paris, city of lovers, *chérie*. I spoke about the fires in you just waiting for a match, if you remember." He touched her lips fleetingly again, and stood. "Come, we're going to dance once more. I don't think I trust myself to sit beside you much longer and be good."

Which wasn't true; Eve was sharply annoyed this time. He remained completely master of himself, but bored when instinct told him he must wait a while longer before obtaining what he wanted. "I'm not stupid, whatever you may think of Americans."

He glanced at her, surprised. "What made you think—"

"Because that's the way your mind works. If I were a Parisienne you'd have staged all sorts of elegant flirtations, be talking to me now instead of staring at the crowd trying to recognize acquaintance. You brought me here for—for . . . well, you know why you brought me. You've accomplished as much as you can, so now you're off." Usually Eve regretted her indiscretions as soon as they were spoken; this time she felt no regret at all.

He gave a choke of laughter. "Really, you cannot be surprised if we regard Americans as different. Charmingly different, I assure you. And you are mistaken; I should adore to flirt with you."

Eve felt defeated; she had thought his air of selfish cynicism was a pose, now she wasn't sure. "I would like to go home now."

He agreed amiably enough, the chaos at the Opéra reaching a fresh pitch of sound as midnight approached.

The streets were packed too, roisterers drinking champagne in the middle of the road, everyone shouting, those who did not feel like celebrating staying out of sight behind closed shutters.

"Happy New Year." Pierre kissed her again as the clocks struck, but undemandingly. "Do you know this is the first time Frenchmen have said that in four years? During the war we wished each other a peaceful year."

"It's come true at last, thank heaven." Their *fiacre* forced its way slowly through the crush, and Eve saw a group of what the French called *gueules cassées*, broken mugs, men with facial injuries so dreadful it was impossible not to shudder and look away. They were standing, arms linked about each other's shoulders and watching the frolicking crowds; it was as if the specter of war itself stood in scornful judgment over the heirs of victory.

Eve's thoughts switched abruptly. "Guy. We never saw him or Eulalie at the ball, although I suppose that's not surprising."

"Guy is in disgrace at the moment; the less said about him the better."

"Whatever happened? Did he—" Just in time, Eve remembered that Eulalie was Pierre's sister. She hoped very much that Guy had found sufficient resolution to refuse to marry Eulalie.

"I don't want to talk about it. He'll be thrown out of the Hôtel Daunay in the morning. He's more dangerous than we realized; you keep away from him."

"He's all right with me," said Eve defensively.

"He was all right with his father until the morning he tried to throttle him. And admirably cold-blooded toward Eulalie until— if I didn't know he wasn't responsible I'd be after the swine myself." There was surprising satisfaction in his voice, as if his cousin's disgrace served some unexpected purpose of his own. Pierre's sophistication seemed so much a part of the Paris Eve wanted to experience that she had accepted it and simply enjoyed his company; hearing that note of satisfaction in his voice, she found herself wondering whether she understood him at all.

Like Guy Saulx . . . no, not like Guy, whom she had come to understand sufficiently to feel anger for his broken life, as well as regret when she had not seen him again.

And now he must be completely alone with his hauntings: she thought of the *gueules cassées* watching Paris rejoice and wanted to weep, though all around her people laughed and cheered. "Will he recover, do you suppose?"

"Guy?" Pierre shrugged. "What do you think?"

No; alone, she did not think he would.

Eve had been invited to share an apartment with five other women; most of the American delegation was male, including stenographers, the few females there because of some particular skill. Eve was the youngest by twenty years, found the others agreeable but never felt any urge to confide in them. She missed the company of someone her own age with whom she could have eased her mind, and who might have helped her decide that Guy Saulx was no worry of hers.

The heat and crowds of the ball had tired her after a long day working over translations at the Crillon, but even so she lay awake after her return from the Opéra. What would Guy do, now he had not even Le Trésor to hope for any more? And since the marriage project must be ended when he was in such apparent disgrace, there wouldn't be any refuge in Alsace, either.

Eve was too busy next day to think about him, but as she labored over dull papers, the image of despair remained in her mind. She had thought that work with the U.S. peace delegation would be exciting, but until the Conference opened it was drudgery. It's a disaster to have a delegation stuffed with professors, she reflected with rising irritation, though President Wilson had thought that professors were exactly what he needed, when justice was a question of sifting evidence. So they had come in droves to France, bringing documents on every topic which might conceivably be discussed. They were excited by the prospect of remaking Europe and wanted the other delegations to share the results of their deliberations, which meant translating everything they wrote into French.

The French will never look at any of it, thought Eve. You'd need to stand over them with a gun before they'd read American scholarship on the Transylvanian question. And what, mademoiselle, is wrong with facts gathered by the academics of France? Why, when we have lived all our history with the complexities of Europe, should *ces Américains ingénus* think they can arrange matters in five minutes? Eve could hear them say it; she might not have been long in Paris but already understood some things better than lecturers fresh out of Yale.

She hated the futility of it all, snapped at the State Department clerk who shared her desk, and chose to sit at a table with strangers in the Crillon staff restaurant, sunk in gloom.

"You look as if you have a hangover. Or did sleek M. Daunay not behave himself last night?"

She looked up at Rick Dwyer. "He behaved himself."

"And good behavior depresses you?"

"It certainly doesn't! And just remember, Rick Dwyer, that I've thanked you for helping me to a job here, It doesn't entitle you to sticky finger over my affairs."

"My, you are a hellcat today. And here was I hoping you'd come to a café with me, to help soothe wounded pride."

In spite of herself, Eve chuckled. "Does your tone suggest that Sir Maurice was waiting on the steps for you?"

"Yep, it sure does, honey. I'll say one thing for an English education, it gives a man command of the language. I'm persona non grata with the British delegation all right, but it was worth a try, if only she hadn't been such a goddam annoying kid."

"Took you for a ride, did she?"

He laughed reluctantly. "Good old Uncle Rick. There was I, handling her with kid gloves and thinking about diplomatic leaks, when I ought to have realized I was on a cold trail as soon as your damned Frog set her alarm bells ringing. She twisted my tail for the rest of the evening and then made sure Daddy saw us coming home. I ought to have enjoyed myself while I had the chance. She's vinegar, that girl."

Good for Sarah, thought Eve. She must be on good terms with Sir Maurice, to walk into a row like that just to make sure Rick got his comeuppance. I'd never have chanced it with my father. "Rick, you wouldn't like to write an article about how U.S. translation clerks here are wasting taxpayers' money, would you?"

"Come out this evening, and we'll write it together," he said promptly.

"I would enjoy that, Rick. It'll be a real humdinger."

They went to the newly named Café de la Victoire, on the Boulevard des Capucines; Eve was unfamiliar with the *grands boulevards* and could not take her eyes off the fascinating life around her. A man passed pushing a roller which printed the word CINZANO on the sidewalk every five paces, young couples strolled closely embraced; vivacious Parisiennes tapped past on ridiculously high heels, all looking as if they were on the way to an assignation. A singer by the *métro* exit sang a new song again and again until the crowd gathered around him had learned the words; then they all sang it together and each gave him a few sous for teaching them the latest craze. A Gypsy band played mazurkas in the interior of the café, which served thirty kinds of hors d'oeuvres to those who could afford the price.

"Cuts off half the animals in the zoo, I expect," said Rick, subjecting the tray to a jaundiced scrutiny. "*Merci. Un cognac fine.* What about you, Eve?"

"Well, I was going to have hors d'oeuvres, but I guess I'll just make it coffee."

"How wise! Your rich Champs-Élysées friends may have okay tables, but you want to watch what you eat in cafés."

"I think I'd choke if I ate there now I've seen how scarce food is in the markets. They throw away more from one meal than a woman with a family can buy after waiting all day in line." Shops showed signs reading "*Jour sans*" more often than not, meaning a day when whatever it sold was not available, regardless of ration entitlement.

"Selfish bastards, aren't they?" He wasn't really listening. "Eve, I've been thinking. What I really want to write is a hot piece on how the U.S. is being stood up here, and we could add your grouse in as another side of the same thing. President, Secretary of State, God knows how many others, all sitting on their asses while the Europeans jeer at us like that damned girl last night with me. Another two weeks until the Conference opens! Everyone knows that in less than a month after that, Wilson has to be back in Washington. Then they'll fix everything up behind our backs."

Eve fiddled with her coffee cup. "I wish you wouldn't, Rick."

"Why not? It's good copy. Make them really howl in Washington."

"That's what I mean." She paused to choose her words carefully. "I don't know anything about reporting and I can see how you need good copy. But the rest of us, we want peace. Please, peace at last. Ever since I've been over here I've heard how you hate the British, or the French despise Americans. Don't make things worse. Peace with justice, it's a good aim if we can get it. Only, justice means one thing to Americans just over from Washington, and something quite different to Frenchmen afraid of massacre again once we've all gone home."

"I'd be a poor reporter if I didn't understand all that, but revenge and fear won't make a peace."

"I'm sorry; I know I sounded as if I was teaching you your trade, a farm girl fresh out of Maine. It's Paris, I guess." Eve nodded at lamplit phantoms etched on the steamed-up café window. "All day you see people laughing, drunk, loving. There's dancing everywhere, while behind shutters lies the wreckage of what's been done. *Gueules cassées* like gargoyles. I saw an old woman in St.-Sulpice not long ago, a countrywoman in a straw bonnet, holding on to a lamppost because she was too shaken by weeping to move. I asked her whether she was hungry or in need and she answered, 'No, I'm not in need. I am simply unhappy. My husband and three sons are dead.'"

Rick had been flipping a coin, and it fell tinkling on the marble tabletop. "Tails you win, I guess. I'm not sure you're right, though; things are usually best said instead of shoveled out of sight to rot. So let's write us a scorcher on those professors. Have 'em making suicide pacts in pits lined with manuscripts on the Transylvanian problem."

Eve laughed, but his words niggled at her. Now that Guy had been thrown out of the Hôtel Daunay, probably he had gone to the Rue Férou. He would be alone in that bare, cold room and she could not believe that much remained to bring him out again. Once he was of no more use to them, Guy's condition would simply embarrass his family and secretly they would be relieved if he killed himself, when affection seemed so lacking. *C'est la guerre*, they would say, *pour lui la mort a été une délivrance, tu sais*.

Rick was disappointed but preoccupied when she left him, quite early. Between them they had written an off-beat, satirical five-inch column which he must file for the next edition. He liked it, and thought his editor would too; tomorrow he would see Eve again and make a date to meet in a more intimate place than the Café de la Victoire. The Moulin de la Galette, in Montmartre, perhaps, where lovers left their names scrawled on the walls; yes, he decided as he escorted Eve to the door of her apartment, the Galette would do very well. Eve was young enough to enjoy romance laid on with a shovel.

As soon as Rick had gone, Eve took the *métro* for St.-Sulpice. She did not like the area at night, but now that she had decided to visit Guy, she wouldn't rest until she had.

Everything was even darker than she remembered it, and by the time she found the right turning her courage had ebbed. She wished very much that she was back in her warm bedroom near the Rue Castiglione; he's more dangerous than we realized, Pierre had said.

To me he's never shown signs of more than strangeness, she told herself firmly. It didn't help much.

The concierge looked at her oddly but admitted that Commandant Saulx was within. "Woke me in the middle of last night, looking so wild I thought he'd been attacked. But no, just suiting himself and never thinking of me, warm for the first time since I don't know when."

She did not wait by the light switch, either, and it seemed to Eve that she fumbled a long time in cold and clutter before she reached the fourth floor. She tried Guy's door, but it was bolted. No light showed nor glow from a fire when she bent to look through the keyhole, although it wasn't very late.

"Guy? It's Eve. The *métro*'s stopped and I can't get back tonight. May I stay here?" Be matter-of-fact, she had decided.

No sound, her words falling into a pit. Yet the room was not empty; she knew Guy was very close, holding his breath, willing her to go away. The sense of his presence was too strong for him to be lying in a daze of lost memory, and Eve felt her face prickle with the kind of premonition she had never felt before. She must get into that room, at once.

She could not force the door, and to batter at it might do more harm than good. "Guy. Listen, you must help me. I can't walk back from here in the middle of the night. If you won't let me in I shall have to freeze on the stairs."

She waited a long time, everything quiet around her. She wanted to go and could not go, when everything else in his life had gone. "You may not mind rats, but I do! I can hear them behind the wainscot and I'm sure they scamper up and down the stairs all night."

She heard something this time, the rustle of cloth and breath harsh in his throat. She knelt on boards and put her lips to the keyhole so she could speak softly. "*Chéri*, you've been too long alone. I won't stay if you don't want me to, but let me in now."

The bolt snapped and the door swung open too quickly for her to scramble to her feet. "Eve?" In darkness he could not see her and she felt him grope above her head. ". . . Eve?"

She came to her feet slowly so as not to alarm him. "I'm here. Again. I hope you don't mind."

His hand fastened on her arm and he pulled her into the room, slamming and rebolting the door behind them. "I'll make sure Pierre stays outside this time."

"I don't think Pierre will be coming here again." Eve's heart was thumping unpleasantly. She scarcely recognized his rough, soft voice; disembodied and walled in with her by a bolted door. She stood very still and thought what an incredible fool she'd been to come.

"He might. If he knew he could harm me by coming." Guy reached for her again, hands on her sleeve, brushing her breast, his breath against her face.

Her mouth felt almost too dry to speak. "Would you like me to light some candles?"

She felt him stiffen. "You aren't afraid of me, are you?"

And suddenly she wasn't. She did not know what he might do under compulsions she scarcely recognized, but at this moment his mind seemed clear and he was so very much alone, she flinched at his aloneness. "No, never. Would I come here in the dark if I were?"

He gave a grunt, which might have been amusement. "Yes, you would." He touched her cheek, his fingers icy.

Eve covered his hand with hers. "Let me light a fire. There's some wood shavings I brought up before, unless you've used them."

He hesitated and then moved away; a moment later she heard him fumbling for matches. It took him a long time to light a candle, but she resisted the temptation to offer help; when the wick caught, enormous shadows sprang onto ceiling and walls.

Eve stared at him and wondered only when he had last slept. The single flame disemboweled his face, features sunk into bone and shadow. But that was something she could not remedy yet, and which might be unsafe to mention. "I'm cold, and if I'm cold, you must be freezing. What have we got to burn?"

"The floorboards?" he suggested, and laughed. A strange, hiccuping laugh, but laughter all the same.

She found she could not bear to watch the effort which made him joke, as soon as he grasped that she needed reassurance. She remembered how he had forced himself out from behind his hauntings once before, and made her laugh when she nearly had not lasted through the journey from Rheims to Paris. Yet, so far as she could tell, no one had ever considered him at all, and even she had come in patronizing pity and been proud of herself for doing so. "They'd be better than nothing," she said after a pause, and brushed past him to look for wood shavings: they were still there, and dried-up food left from last time she marketed.

"The concierge makes these," said Guy, unlocking the door and bringing in what looked like rubbish from the passage.

"What are they?"

"Soaked paper, squeezed into balls and dried. They give more heat than timber pavé."

He had known they were there but in thirty-six hours of plunging temperatures had done nothing to fix himself a fire.

Eve coaxed flames out of shavings and was pleased to discover that paper bricks burned quite well; she sliced wizened vegetables and set a pan to boil, keeping her back turned to offer privacy while he became used to her presence.

Only when the pan was simmering to her satisfaction did she turn, and found him sitting on one of the hard chairs, his head in his hands. "How long since you ate?"

He shook his head; he did not know.

He ate ravenously when her soup was done, a shred of consideration left from the past making him insist that she eat too. But the moment nourishment kindled a shadow of strength in him he began roaming the room, touching walls and door, stumbling footsteps buffeting up and down.

Eve washed their bowls and stoked the fire with the last of the fuel, moving quietly, trying to make up her mind about the only remaining thing which she could do to help. It was enormously difficult coldly to decide that this was the only possible ending to what she had begun by ever coming here, when she had been raised in a place where wantonness brought hellfire and no excuses were accepted.

At last, she stood in his way, and clung to him as he passed. "Guy, come and rest."

"No."

"Why not?"

He turned away in her hands. "I can only sleep like this, or with drops."

Eve held on to him although his wish for her to go was obvious. "You can't sleep standing; no one can."

"I fall eventually and sleep the worst of it off. It's a trick I learned in the trenches. Eve . . . please, I'm best alone. I don't—" he broke off on a long, shuddering yawn, and stepped back to lean against the wall.

"You mean you don't need help?" Eve demanded. "Why be a fool when help is here?"

He gave a gasp of laughter, sufficient in such extremity to send his senses spinning. She supported him to the bed before he could recover, the fire very low by now, the room freezing again. She undressed swiftly and lay beside him under thin blankets, understanding very well that stripped-down instinct was all that remained of him. The expiation of a latecomer to the war, she thought wretchedly, when he is a *gueule cassée* of the spirit. She deceived herself: it was also her own curiosity and longing for affection after a restrictive childhood; as well as Paris, city of lovers, all around her, now she realized that Guy Saulx had once been an attractive, self-confident man who could not be more than five or six years older than herself. He had completed conscription with the German Army not long before the war, and the subconscious calculation that he was very far from being the forty she had thought him made everything seem more inevitable. It was only her upbringing which offered the excuse of how much he needed her, and fear which hid desire.

He jerked into awareness almost at once, hands clawing at coverings, throat knotted. "I told you—I can't sleep like this."

She held him, her body pressed against the length of his. "Then, perhaps you can sleep like this instead. If we share the burden it will be easier."

He drew a shuddering breath. "I don't think so."

"You don't believe it would be easier, or you don't want to share?"

He felt her lips smile against his, her hands soothing him. "I—don't want to drown you in the mud of a shell hole too."

Eve shivered, as the complex of emotions which had brought her here congealed. Too late, too late, she saw the breaking wave of disaster gathering to destroy her as well as him.

She closed her eyes and tried to think of Wayne Collister, a doctor at Bois-Chauvert, blue-eyed, lighthearted and strongly made. She could easily have loved him, if she'd stayed there longer. Her mind screamed at her to fight free while a fraction of time remained, to scramble into her clothes and run away down the cobbles of the Rue Férou. Instead she lay unnerved, feeling Guy move more urgently against her, the weight of his body shift across her.

Eulalie, she thought.

She had most carefully stopped herself from thinking about what Pierre hinted that Guy had done, but deep inside, she knew. Panic fluttered as inexperience and preachers' sermons robbed her senses of response, and the instinct which had made her hold him shriveled.

Cloth and buttons painful on her breasts; unshaven face; harsh roughness against her thighs. Boots. She was shaken by horrified revulsion; of course, he was still wearing boots.

Any remaining sense of wanting him was swept away. Boots seemed the ultimate degradation, far worse than hellfire for lust or offering herself to a sick man in place of drugs.

CHAPTER 8

During the night, Eve was forced to wake him three times out of screaming nightmares, and each time sheer animal craving lost him in her as he came half stunned from his pit of horrors. She feared it and him, lay crushed and aching as if she had been beaten; no grace, no love, no softness at all, only a man who had been shattered by exhaustion granted nearly eight hours' sleep by the ease she gave.

Eve forgot that, last night, she, too, had felt desire, and clung to the consolation of this gift she had given him. She had not thought of her fevered dream at the Hôtel Daunay since she left there, but lay thinking of it now, and how her bright vision of woods and lake had been corrupted by the suffering of war.

Guy began to thrash and moan again as grayness showed through frost-starred glass. Eve watched him, fighting her own reluctance. He lay heavily across her, cramping legs and constricting breath: at least he kept her warm. Eyes closed, his face looked carved from one of the bleaker kinds of stone and showed some of the savagery she had experienced from him during the night.

She'd done her part, and all that remained was his image distorted by disgust.

He moved sharply as she woke him, claw hands fastening on her breast, face scraping soft flesh. She forced herself to lie still and speak gently, not wanting to spoil it now when she had freely done what she had done. Surely even a soul in hell lacked strength for four times in a night. "Guy? Wake up, it's dawn and all at peace."

He recoiled from her like a spring. Torn into consciousness by shock, body instantly strung tight. Startled by his reaction, Eve sat up too, blankets sliding to the floor so her bruised skin was revealed, patterned by buttons and rucked cloth.

He stared at her, eyes wide and blank. "What have I done?"

Confused and absurdly ashamed, for a moment she could not answer.

"Oh, my God," he said wearily, and leaned to cover her again.

After such a night, the unconscious tenderness of his gesture seemed incongruous. "You did what I invited you to do," Eve said harshly. "It's not your fault."

He left the bed and went to stand in the farthest corner of the room. "Tell me."

"There's nothing to tell that you don't know, surely?" She was unexpectedly close to tears.

He went over to a wash jug, scooping water over his face in a crackle of ice before coming back to sit on the edge of the bed, absently doing up buttons. "I'm still wearing my boots."

Eve nodded, comforted that he should find that monstrous too.

"You damned little fool. Didn't you understand what you were doing?"

"Of course I understood. Not being a fool," she said, annoyed. But of course she hadn't understood how it would be at all.

He smiled faintly but looked white and sick, certainly not harsh; the face she had seen in the dawn had vanished. "I meant, know I'm the wrong man to lose your virginity with. That's right, isn't it?"

She wiped her eyes childishly on the blanket. "How did you know?"

"I'm remembering more as time passes," he replied dryly. "Another batch of guilt to add to the rest. Why did you do it? For pity?"

Some intuition warned her against a mistake which might unravel the little she had achieved. For he was better; completely lucid, a spark renewed by even so short a time of rest. "Do you care why?"

"Very much."

Well, here goes, Eve thought. If it's hellfire for harlotry, then damnation as well for lying won't make much difference. "I stayed all that time with you before and you didn't . . . wouldn't . . ." she floundered. "The girls I work with practically said there must be something wrong with me and . . . and . . . I guess I'd become fond of you. In Paris, it's someone, very soon. I wanted it to be you."

He stared at her, frowning. "You went to the Opéra ball with Pierre."

"What of it?"

"I wouldn't have expected him to resist telling you something of what happened with Eulalie at the Hôtel Daunay the night before I came back here."

"I asked how you were or he would never have mentioned—"

"But you knew something had happened," he said flatly. "And came here the next night. Why?"

"I've told you why," she said, irritated. If she had allowed herself to think more carefully, she wouldn't have come. "Now, if you'll just move off the bed, I'll get up. I must be due at work soon."

"What if I want you to stay?"

"I can't," she said, alarmed.

He bent and kissed her fingers. "You would make me very happy if you did. I'd like a chance to start with you again, the way I would have wanted it this time."

No, Eve thought in fright. Not again, ever. But whatever her other reasons, she had also come because she believed he deserved a little mercy; also her conscience rubbed harshly at her this morning. It reached out now and whispered that one night with her had brought him more relief than six weeks of struggling by himself. "All right." She almost withdrew her words as soon as they were spoken. "But—"

"But not like this, I know. Just your company to begin with, later will be for you to choose." With unexpected tact, he went to buy bread and milk while she dressed, feeling sore and wretched, longing for a hot bath instead of an ice-rimed bucket.

He came with her to the Crillon, too, making no comment at her slow pace but silent all the way, kissing her fingers when they parted. So I'm a *cocotte* now, reflected Eve bitterly. A Frenchman does not kiss the hand of a respectable young woman.

She made a great many mistakes in translation that day, relieved beyond measure when Guy was not waiting for her at the end of it. He's realized there's no way to repair what's happened, she thought, reveling in hot water at her own apartment. She stared at her body with an odd sense of disbelief, cheated that she felt so little different. She was bruised and her legs were cut by hobnails, but in herself she felt exactly the same, mind floating drowsily in warmth. It's ridiculous, she thought vaguely, all those years of being punished for so much as a snatched hand-holding by the barn; bread and water that time Willie Trevause wrote me without permission, and the day after rape I'm hesitating between eggs and steak for supper. No, not rape; let's remember honestly, at least; I asked for it; perhaps that helps a little. She grimaced at herself; she had not asked for what she had received.

Guy was waiting for her next morning, tucked her hand under his arm as any young man might when he met his girl on a sparkling January day. The streets were full of soldiers, *spahis* in baggy trousers, cowboy-hatted Americans and New Zealanders, British Tommies, Belgian carabiniers in spectacularly ill-cut uniforms, gloomy Serbs and sneezing

Brazilians. Commandant Saulx ignored salutes as if he were already out of the Army, although he was scrupulously dressed and shaved, in recompense for how he had been before. "I thought you best left alone last night, but I should be honored and delighted if you would dine with me this evening," he said at length.

Eve's heart sank. "How did you sleep last night?"

He looked surprised. "I'd slept the night before. I walked last night."

"I promised Rick Dwyer." Eve could hear the lack of hope in her own voice. "Perhaps one day next week—"

He stopped and faced her. "Don't come at all unless you believe that this time it will be different."

In the end she agreed to meet him the following night, despising herself as she did so, and then lacked the heart to keep her date with Rick at the Moulin de la Galette.

Paris, city of lovers, she thought viciously.

Guy took her to a tiny dark place called *Le Jardin de Nini*, which was scarcely a restaurant at all, in a street full of leaning houses off Montparnasse. "You only come to a place like this if you know the *patronne*," he explained. "And she will pretend we've caught her unaware, you'll see."

Eve was fascinated by Nini, obviously a retired lady of easy virtue. She greeted Guy familiarly, she noticed. "*Ah, mon p'tit*. Safe returned from the war at last, eh?" She gave Eve a considering look.

"As you see, madame, and stationed now in Paris. An improvement on the trenches until I am out of this accursed uniform at last."

"An improvement indeed." Nini returned to leisurely contemplation of Eve. "Mademoiselle has a hand in that, no doubt."

Eve flushed, but Guy interposed smoothly enough with an offer of an apéritif, before opening a discussion about food: Eve never ceased to be astonished by the seriousness with which the French regarded even mediocre food. "What are you going to give us, then, so Mademoiselle may take a good account of Nini's Garden back to America with her?"

Nini shrugged. "*Je ne sais pas.*"

Guy grinned. "Another apéritif, madame?"

"You can't eat apéritifs, *mon p'tit*." She drank it nevertheless, eyes closed above the rim of her glass, somehow managing to give the impression of someone who has forgotten how to shop or cook.

"How about an omelette? There are eggs in the market today."

"Of a certainty, there are eggs," she admitted cautiously.

"*Alors, c'est convenu. Et puis?*"

Nini puffed out her cheeks, enthusiasm suddenly roused. "*Et ma langouste avec une sauce mayonnaise à ma façon?*"

"*D'accord, madame. Une apéritif encore?*"

She drank, then waddled away, laughing. "Enjoy yourselves, my children. Give Nini time and Mademoiselle shall take a good remembrance back with her to America." She put a finger to her nose, and winked. "If M. Guy is such a fool as to let you go, eh, mademoiselle? Me, Nini, I know the signs."

"Come over to the brazier," said Guy into awkward silence. "I thought it might amuse you to come somewhere completely Parisian, but Nini's a born intriguer."

"A born something else, as people soon will say of me." Eve was surprised to find she minded insinuation so much, when if she had loved Guy she would have rejoiced in it.

Nini's Garden had secretive wooden hutches confining marble-topped tables and was well suited to assignations. Guy led her to one of these and sat down opposite, covering her hand with his. "I never apologized, did I?"

She had taken her hand away before she could recollect that she wanted to show him softness. "No, you didn't."

"I hoped you would allow me to do so in the only way which might be adequate, by coming to the Rue Férou again tonight."

"To help you sleep?"

His head went back as if she had hit him. "No. Tonight I promise not to sleep."

"Guy, what is the point?" she said wretchedly. "I'm no good to you any more. I can't keep myself from hurting you, although I don't want to. Or I think I don't want to," she added conscientiously. "Everything's so mixed up when in one way I hardly know you, in others—"

"You know me too well for comfort," he finished for her. "Eve, this isn't just an invitation to suit myself, although nothing would make me happier than for you to be in that horrible room with me again. I would like to change a memory, if I can."

Eve twisted her fingers nervously in the strap of her bag. "What makes you think you can change anything?"

The muscles of his face tightened, and he looked again as he had in yesterday's dawn. "Just once in a lifetime something has to go right."

Eve drained her glass and put it down with a crack on marble. Whether by intent or not, he had made it almost impossible for her to refuse, without inflicting the kind of hurt which might finally destroy him. And what, after all, was she making a fuss about? It couldn't be worse than before, and just possibly might be better; she looked up and nodded.

The meal was not a success. His point gained, Guy lapsed into abstraction until Nini berated him for eating *langouste* as if it were army rations. "Mademoiselle, never put up with nonsense from men. I, Nini, tell you that the best of them require the hand of an expert, in food and with their affairs, as well as in matters of the heart."

Guy smiled and stood. "My stomach has not yet accustomed itself to *langouste* after monkeymeat, Nini. We—I—will return, I promise you." He looked deathly tired.

He'll never stay awake, thought Eve. "Guy, why don't we meet another time, when— when you feel better?"

He stared at her. "You promised."

Nini snorted. "What are promises? Like absinthe, they sour the stomach. *Va chez-toi! Mais crois-moi, pas d'histoires!*"

She could not have slammed the door on escape more successfully. Promises were sacred in the Ottoway homestead, and certainly not to be broken at the urgings of a Nini. Eve walked with Guy through narrow streets full of scurrying feet; above was a showery, smoky sky, light blotted out by drizzle. Guy kept his hand on her arm, but all the long way he did not once speak.

The concierge at the Rue Férou was used to them now, sold them paper blocks for the fire and darted back inside her hutch.

"I'm not gossip here any more," said Eve. Anything to break the silence.

She did not succeed. He climbed behind her up steep stairs, his breath sounding like a saw on wet wood. Once inside his room he took her in his arms at once. "I was afraid you wouldn't come."

He was different again, and in a way she had not expected. When she was here two nights ago he had been almost beyond human contact and she had led the way for him to go, used herself as a lifeline and been punished for her efforts. Tonight he was determined on restitution, and held to it through shuddering senses and annihilating fatigue. Each step slowly, offering pleasure and waiting for her to join him: if Eve had known more she would have been astonished he could endure such restraint. Until she was needing and wanting too, this time wanting very much.

He lay quietly afterward, still holding her in his arms.

Eve kissed the hollow of his throat. "This one thing came right."

"Will you tell me truthfully now why you came before?"

"I'd sooner tell you why I might want to come again! Who knows why we do things?"

"You knew why you came two nights ago. I'd like to hear you say it."

"All right!" she said, goaded. "I came because I'd been only a few weeks in France yet felt crushed by war. You'd been four years in the trenches; I thought I owed you a good night's sleep."

He laughed and climbed out of bed, letting in a gust of icy air. "I love you, Eve."

"I thought you'd be very upset," she said, dumbfounded.

"I minded when you wouldn't tell me. Don't you feel differently now you have?"

"Yes," she said after a moment, realizing, now the excuse was spoken, that it wasn't all of the truth. The bed was cold and she wished he would come back; instead she caught the sound of cloth rustling. "Where are you going?"

"Nowhere, but it's too cold to sit naked in a chair. I'm not risking sleep tonight, remember?"

The dark was oppressive. Eve lay while the glow chilled on her body, thinking to herself: I wonder. He has unexpected ways of making me act as he wants.

She decided to wait and see what he would do, and instead fell asleep in the ease of slackened tension.

Cold woke her, much later. The clouds had gone and moonlight poured into the stark room; Eve moved sharply, then pieced thought together, hands on her body in unconscious recollection. Shadow across the room changed shape where Guy was standing by the wall, shoulders hunched, his eyes pits in the night. "What is it?"

"I'm cold. Guy, come back to bed for pity's sake. We'll both freeze alone."

"People think of Paris in the spring as a time for lovers. Perhaps we could recommend the inducement of January frost." There was faint amusement in his tone, nothing else.

Eve swallowed. "Guy, please. I'll wake you if you dream."

"But then, it isn't just my dreams you have to fear, is it?"

She went over to him, her skin luminous in the moonlight. "I never asked for the promise you gave. It will be different this time even if you sleep; I know it will. I mean something to you now." *I love you*, he had said.

He picked her up. "Back to bed."

She laughed. "Oh, Guy. Just like my great-aunt Martha. I can easily get out again if you won't join me."

He put her in the bed, folding blankets tightly about her. "Eve, I don't want it like this for you, or me, either. You with Dwyer or Pierre tomorrow, it'd drive me crazy." He checked abruptly, as if truth was too exactly spoken.

"I'm not a *cocotte* by intention." Somehow, with him, she always ended up angry.

He recovered himself with an effort. "No. But I've done what I can to drop the trap on you, haven't I? The first step with a man you don't know is the hardest, whatever your motive. Alone in Paris . . . it isn't that, though. I cannot imagine greater happiness than for you to become my wife."

With her, he was nearly again the man he could have been. With her, surely the foulnesses of war would fade. He had been thinking the long night through, fantasy and fact spinning, and decided there was no other way to keep her. Tonight she had loved him a little and might yield before daylight bred cold sense. He seemed to remember that he had managed to offer her some pleasure, and surely it would become easier if only his other self stayed locked in its cage, as without her it would not. She had not only come for pity . . . perhaps . . . he fumbled with lost images in a sweat of panic. If she would stay, perhaps . . . he was too tired to think beyond the fact that if she stayed, the rough pieces of his mind might mend.

Eve stared at the bulk of him sitting on the bed, feeling the wave of disaster curl and break. This she had brought on herself. In the end, it had been she who swept away Guy's defenses by recklessly offering herself as a lifeline, and those who offer lifelines to the helpless become murderers if they then untie the end. Suddenly, she felt immeasurably old. She had come so hopefully to France and eagerly grasped at everything she saw: the chance to help, to plunge into a new and exciting life, to take risks after long constraint.

No more.

She felt her youth die as she faced the impossibility of refusing Guy, of leaving him alone to face his terrors. He was a brave man shattered by the war and this time had been both tender and passionate; with her he could rebuild his life. Eve Ottoway came from a land where optimism was taken for granted, and New England conscience was urged on by the sharp delight she had found with Guy tonight. Yet no man whose mind was furnished with the usual clutter of scruple and convention would propose so scandalously unequal a bargain. Eve had been warned of the punishments which awaited sinners, but never against venturing into the quagmires of compassion.

"Yes," she said baldly. "Yes, I will, as soon as we can manage. Come to bed now and warm us both."

CHAPTER 9

"I could never have asked you to marry me, except that my father died the night before last," Guy said as he walked to the Crillon with her in the morning. "Today he would have signed the documents for his annuity, which were all prepared. Daunay would have had everything without needing to pay out a sou if *cher Papa* had waited another week before guzzling five dozen oysters followed by pressed duck at the Tour d'Argent, to die of heart failure after."

"Your father was dead yesterday and you never even mentioned it last night! Guy, you must have come straight from his deathbed!" Eve exclaimed in amazement.

"We were both thinking of quite different matters last night, if you remember." His lips brushed her hair. "You can set squeamishness at rest, though; last night I had come from Le Trésor and not the Champs-Élysées."

A stinging wind blew across the spaces of the Place de la Concorde, whining strangely through captured German weapons gathered there, driving purple clouds overhead, daylight pallid on gray buildings. Gray thoughts, too, since Eve found Guy's refusal to pretend even a spark of affection for his father more chilling than the weather. "Le Trésor is yours, then? After all your fears, you've got what you wanted?"

"And the title to our domaine in Alsace, once French administration is functioning there, yes. This morning I have everything I desire." He looked about him eagerly, color whipped into his face by the wind. He had slept in her arms for a while and thought he would sleep again tonight.

Eve wouldn't admit to relief when she parted from him at the corner of the Rue Castiglione, but her desk was a haven. She wanted to rest her head on it and sleep, and sleep. Apparently Guy did not remember it, but just before dawn he had jolted screaming out of broken sleep and was a stranger again, brutal and impatient.

"Hey, Eve. I've been looking all over for you." Rick arrived within minutes.

"I was late, and now that I'm here I have a great deal of work to do."

"Yeah, the Danube question."

Eve smiled. "Transylvanian."

"You have a heavy date last night?" He looked at her searchingly.

"You could say so. I became engaged to be married." Eve stabbed her pen into State Department notepaper viciously.

"You're stringing me!" Rick said incredulously.

"I'm not stringing you, so if you'd just go, then I'll tear the guts out of Transylvania."

"Uh-uh. You just tell me what damn foolery you've been up to and I'll tear the guts out of the bastard who fixed you instead." He came around the desk and hoisted her to face him. "Okay?"

Eve shook her head, eyes clear green, the time for tears past. Vivacity and laughter gone too, which had always been the secret of her charm. "No foolery, Rick. I'm marrying Guy Saulx just as soon as we can manage, only I gather that to marry in France I need parental consent even though I'm twenty-one, as well as my birth certificate. We'll have to wait for a return mail from the States."

"Who the hell is Guy Saulx?"

"He's a commandant and cousin to Pierre Daunay, who you met at the Opéra ball. He picked me up in his truck on the way from Rheims."

"I remember you saying." Rick frowned. "Eve, for God's sake. Sleep with the bastard if you must, but marry your own kind. Perhaps you think of yourself as half French, but—"

"I don't. I'm American."

"Well, you won't be when you've married Commandant Saulx."

Eve shrugged; she hadn't thought of that. Another loss, but her decision was made and she didn't intend to change it.

"Why, Eve? And don't try telling me about how much you love his bonny blue eyes."

She smiled. "Gray. Everyone keeps asking me why this and why that. Because I want to. Now, will you please go?"

He went, since nothing could be gained by staying, but instead of going to the Quai d'Orsay, where the press was invited for a briefing on the organization of the Peace Conference, he wandered up the Champs-Élysées. He had found out a little about the Daunays when he had become intrigued by Eve's story; now he intended to discover a great deal more. War profiteers were always useful copy and Rick did not look any closer into his motives than a newsman's curiosity: he changed direction and went to find drinking cronies among the set who would be acquainted with the Daunays, and perhaps with this unknown Saulx as well.

Eve felt borne away on a torrent.

The tempo of work at the Crillon increased as the time approached for the Peace Conference to open; in theory it was to be held at Versailles, but all working sessions would take place at the Quai d'Orsay, the French Foreign Office, in central Paris. There was agreement on procedure, disagreement about everything else; opinions, claims and counterclaims all had to be brought to some kind of order before negotiations could begin. And then translated; Eve became frantically busy, often forced to work late. Fortunately Guy was busy too, selling stored furniture to pay for renovation at Le Trésor, his military duties so light that reporting for them seemed a formality. To keep up appearances, which the American delegation took seriously, Eve stayed some nights in her own room, reveling in warmth and sleeping dreamlessly alone. She had written to her parents to say how happy she was, and to ask for the birth certificate, but hoped it would not arrive too soon.

Other nights, she went to the Rue Férou, and there were a few times of real enchantment, when she looked forward with delight to marrying Guy Saulx. There were also times when she was touched by fears she could not name, and others filled with misery like the first night again; this she endured because she no longer believed she had any choice.

Guy's personality remained a tangle of frayed ends: one evening he was unable to recall in which street Le Trésor lay and walked the whole night searching for it, because he was too ashamed to ask for help. He remained unpredictably violent when emotion spun out of control, tearing at her in fear when his wits were scattered by murderous half sleep. Yet he wasn't a brutal man; it might have been easier if he were. He loathed and feared his own ferocities, blotted them from recollection if he could, and so was taken unaware again.

Eve tried to live each day as it came, to enjoy the times—surely more frequent—when he was better, and joined Guy in trying to forget the others, with very indifferent success.

Pierre came to see her and they had a blazing quarrel when she told him she was to marry Guy. Eve learned some new and unpleasant names in French and did not want ever to see him again.

Rick had been temporarily ordered out of Paris, because American newspapers were complaining that while the Allies dragged their feet over peace, Germans were starving, as their ports continued to be blockaded. It was weeks since anyone had thought of Germany except as a defeated enemy to be dealt with in due course, and Rick's editor reckoned there might be good hard news to be found there if he was quick. "I'll be back soon," Rick had said before he went. "Don't marry Saulx while I'm away, will you? There are some strange stories floating around about that family, and I've set a stringer to do some digging while I'm away. Promise?"

"No." Eve rubbed her face; she always felt tired these days. "I met a woman called Nini once, who said promises lay sour on the digestion. I've decided Nini was very wise, although I didn't think so at the time."

"But you promised Saulx?"

"Yes, I did," she said evenly. "Enjoy yourself in Germany."

They had met at a reception held for the British, whose delegation had at last arrived in Paris. Eve had not wanted to go but was newly promoted as one of the translators accredited to the Conference itself, so her excuses were not accepted when there were so few female staff.

Rick hesitated; she was no concern of his. Goddam Saulx to hell; without him Rick knew he could have had a good thing going with Eve, but she wasn't even thinking of him now. Later, perhaps. Rick had wandered into Le Trésor a few days before on the excuse that he had an apartment to furnish, and had disliked what he saw of Saulx. "Eve. . . ."

She turned, ready to leave him. "I'll be in trouble if I don't go and talk nicely to the British."

"Eve, be careful. I know the French love scandal; they'd accuse their best buddy of murder so long as it made a good story, but some hints I've picked up about the Hôtel Daunay made me curious to discover more."

Eve's eyes narrowed, cat-green and watchful. "Just what are you insinuating?"

"Nothing, yet. But Le Tout-Paris finds everything about that place a delicious gossip. Daunay's daughter screaming rape one night and your precious commandant thrown down the steps, when he'd been hired to marry her; old Saulx dead after a carouse which would have flattened an elephant. Daunay himself richer than anyone can guess, when he's never said even where he came from. And Paris is a city where barefoot boys usually stay barefoot if they're honest."

Eve felt blood leave her face. "They forgot to say anything about Gabrielle."

Rick grinned. "Give them time. Eve, I mean it. I haven't told you half of what I've heard, but there's bad blood in that family: I'll have chapter and verse tagged for you by the time I get back. Meanwhile, you cherish your glamorous commandant if you must, but use any god-

dam excuse you like to put him off until I can give it to you straight."
He waved airily and disappeared into the throng.

Glamorous, thought Eve wryly. Rick didn't understand at all just
how and why she was caught. The night before had been ecstasy and
delight, until she discovered this morning how Guy had deliberately
sought agony afterward to make sure he did not sleep and spoil it for
her. He had an old injury to thigh and back which had kept him several
months out of the trenches, and if he lay awkwardly, the nerves ached
like a rotting tooth; this he had made sure he did.

Newsmen reported war and crisis, but a man sweating in self-
inflicted pain to keep himself from sleeping revealed more of the
human carnage than a double-page spread of researched facts.

Eve sighed, and went to do her duty by the British, in due course encountering Sarah Wyville.

"Why, it's Miss Ottoway, isn't it? You must hide at once; I told Father you knitted in a corner."

"Aged about sixty and wearing homespun?"

"I never go into details," said Sarah airily. "It's a mistake to let people expect them. Especially stuffy people when I'm in Paris, although I
expect I should feel exactly the same in London."

"You'll find out when you do the season." Eve felt a staid sixty compared to Sarah, although she couldn't be more than three or four years
the elder.

"Not this summer," said Sarah regretfully. "Paris doesn't count, because Father has to be here, but I'm not allowed to enjoy myself for
pleasure yet."

Eve laughed. "Only for diplomacy?"

"Silly, isn't it? My brother was killed the day the war ended, you
see."

Peel back the surface anywhere, and pain lay underneath. "What can
I say, except I'm sorry?"

"Oh, I don't mind. I think sentiment is a great mistake. Charlie and
I did everything together and I miss him terribly, but me staying home
at Stoneham for the season won't bring him back. Mother cries nearly
all the time, but I think you have to face things and beat them."

"Perhaps sometimes people lack the heart to face things any longer."
Eve no longer believed that the human predicament was simple.

"Heart and all that is old-fashioned. It's a question of resolution and
getting what you want."

"I think I must be rather old-fashioned, then," observed Eve.

"Really?" Sarah examined her with interest. "I thought Americans
were quite modern. Jazz and ambition, get up and go, baby. I told Fa-

ther that perhaps I'd like to marry an American. I do hope they're not all like you."

"I shouldn't think so," replied Eve gravely. "It's quiet where I come from."

"It's quiet where I come from too. That's why I'm enjoying Paris so much, although I love Stoneham, of course. It's also why I'm quite determined not to listen to what anyone says when they want me to behave like a well-brought-up miss all the time." She turned impatiently as a spare, long-bodied man with gray hair and an unexpressive face came up beside her. "Father, Eve quite agrees that it would be bad for me to be buried at Stoneham again after Paris."

Eve wished the floor would swallow her up. "I assure you I offered no opinion at all, Sir Maurice." The delegation staff had been carefully drilled in the intricacies of addressing the British.

His eyes flickered, and she realized too late that a casual acquaintance would not have known his name. "I am sure you did not, since Sarah rarely listens to any opinion except her own. It is a pleasure to meet even a part-time chaperone of my daughter, for I am sure you must be Miss Ottoway."

"Oh, bother," said Sarah. "I forgot I didn't want you two to meet."

"Too late, my dear. But now Miss Ottoway is better acquainted with you, I don't suppose she is in the least surprised to discover how you used her for your purposes. You have been long in Paris, Miss Ottoway?"

He moved with practiced ease into social commonplace, apparently quite content to find himself in the company of a clerk-translator instead of the Secretary of State.

"I will invite you to tea one day, so you can tell me about America," announced Sarah as they left. "You must have been at least once to New York."

"On my way to France," admitted Eve, aware that members of the American delegation were discouraged from private social relations with their allies, in case their reputation for impartiality should be challenged.

"Well, then! I'll ask Mother to invite you, it'll do her good, and then you can tell me everything I want to know. Can you dance the fox-trot? Billy Meredith was going to teach me, but I wasn't allowed a gramophone at the Astoria."

"Not very well," said Eve apologetically. "At home we don't dance, and I just learned enough over here to go with the boys in the hospital on social evenings." She saw Maurice Wyville's expression tighten and wished the words unsaid: she had recently become almost absurdly sensitized to suffering. His son would not learn the fox-trot, in hospital or out.

"Even if you manage badly, it would be a beginning," said Sarah kindly. "There's often dancing at the Astoria, but I don't want to seem a bumpkin, not knowing anything. I shall soon learn, once I can start."

Guy laughed when Eve recounted this exchange, as they sat together in front of the fire at the Rue Férou. "What we would call *une friponne*, the sort who chews through any muzzle you try to fit."

"She's unkind, though; not deliberately, I suppose, but that doesn't help when you've been hurt."

"Unlike you, *chérie*, to whom unkindness is something others do to you." He was sitting quite relaxed while she curled up on the floor, her head against his knees. They had not lit candles, but the fire was hot, since Guy brought timber left over from repairs at Le Trésor.

"I've been unkind to you, wanting to hurt. I often say things I wish unsaid the very next moment."

He bent and kissed her. "How fortunate you are human. I wouldn't like to marry a saint."

Eve crinkled her nose, and laughed. "Splintered haloes in the bed."

Firelight flickered over their two figures, his arms locked about her shoulders, brightness reflected from her hair where it rested on his lap. "My dear," his words no more than a whisper. "I love you so. If only—"

She moved and touched his lips. "Leave it at love. No if-only's now."

His hands tightened. "I wish to God I could. If you are ever able to say that you also have some shadow of love for me, then it will be enough. I shall have won my heart's desire, and healing be complete."

She jerked in his hands and tried to turn, but he held her against his knees, facing the fire. "Don't speak. Don't try, or pretend; that alone I could not bear. I know you do not love me, nor is it possible as I am now. That's part of what I meant about healing: you help me so much, yet I need to be . . . myself . . . before anything can be complete."

They sat in silence and tenuous peace, Eve thinking with shame of what she could not offer, he of what ought never to have been accepted. Their dilemma was complete: without her, he would be set adrift again, but even the beginnings of recovery had made him realize how monstrous it would be for him to marry Eve. She had watched guilt begin its assault on his fragile peace of mind and knew that unless they married soon, he would be the one to walk away.

Though Eve did not love him, she had come to admire the way he fought his weaknesses; even compassion became a kind of angry tenderness when she discovered how he lay all night in pain for her, rather than risk sleep. This Guy Saulx was not the same man for whom she had felt pity, and she refused to let him throw away the gains they had made together. The cost had been too high; the time for scruple was past, as well as the time when she could easily unravel the part of her life which she had given him. He had asked her to marry him; now she meant to hold him to it by whatever means she could.

The room grew cold, and still neither moved, but for a different reason: the dread of what they might do with the night.

Eve stirred at last, and when he held her, her body was softly wanting. "Make love to me, Guy. It's my turn to stay awake tonight."

He did not answer but knew her wanting was no sham, nor would it be so long as he was able to control what he did. But he was so tired, Christ, he was so tired. His leg ached from the pressure he had put on it to stay awake the night before; he flinched from another night of wakeful pain.

If only he could rest away from Eve, or safely rest with her. He took her swiftly, in despair.

Next day a letter from her father waited on Eve's desk. She ripped open the envelope and frowned over economically huddled lines: he was not a writing man, although he respected learning. A folded paper was enclosed, her birth certificate. The last barrier was down.

". . . I don't rightly know how to ask Preacher to pray for your happiness at Meeting as he will ask whether Mr. Saulx is catholic, and neither of you said, so I expect the worst. Your Ma is happy you are to wed a Frenchie after her folks spent two hundred years away, but I think of my daughter lost. We read Mr. Saulx's letter but he did not say how he would keep you when he is out of the army. Your Ma is surprised he said nothing about a dot, and fears he might not be respectable. I said tho' not American he sounds decent enough. The cow Bertha has dropped twins. It is very cold here. I'd admire to know the date of your wedding so I may be with you in the spirit. . . ."*

Eve folded the letter, thinking how it brought to Paris exactly the flavor of their clapboard homestead tucked under the hillside in deep snow. Which was a long way from the chic center of Paris, although it was snowing there, too.

The Peace Conference had opened at last and Eve was even busier than before, but instead of eating at midday she hurried to the Rue Daunou. The storefront was repainted, glass reset in a way Guy said he had learned from searchlights, faceted inward to focus attention on the furniture on display. Eve liked the glass but would have arranged the window differently. In fact, her fingers itched to get at Le Trésor; she knew nothing about French furniture but longed to banish fusty drapes to a distant cellar and let in light and air.

"Eve!" Guy exclaimed as soon as she came in. "What's happened?"

"I brought this, since you know how I have to go to the ball for President Wilson tonight." She handed him the certificate. "I never knew you'd written my father."

"It is usual," he said dryly, but his fingers shook on the paper. "If I can reserve a time with the Maire, would you marry me tomorrow? He's had the length of notice the law requires."

This was her last chance; she hesitated, heart changing to panic beat, then nodded.

He folded the paper and replaced it in her hand. "Eve, go out that door and don't ever come back."

She stared at him, braced for a battle she had half expected. "I want to marry you. It isn't conscience or duty or anything else." Not love, she thought, and did not say. "I want to do it, so I'm doing it."

His mouth twisted; he looked bloodless and ill after another sleepless night on a rack of pain. "So it is best done at once."

She kissed his lips, but he did not move. "Tomorrow."

He walked back with her to the Quai d'Orsay, his head bent, hands in his pockets and no part of him touching her, silence between them clamped like a box lid over Paris. "I'll send a message of the time as soon as I know it," he said at last.

"I might not. . . ." Her voice petered out. How could she say that at short notice she might not get leave to go?

"Then, just come. The Americans probably won't employ you once you're married to a Frenchman anyway. Allies are the devil." Clumsily, he was trying to make her grasp the full implications of marrying him; she would lose America and home as well.

But just at that moment she could not think past him, looking again as he had on the road from Rheims. "Guy, what did I say to upset you? I was happy when I came."

He kept his eyes on the decorative pavé of the Place Vendôme. "You intend to marry me, but don't want to. I meant what I said; go, and don't come back. Just now I forced you to face the fact of tomorrow instead of sometime in the future, and you were *épouvantée*—appalled by the thought. I spent last night thinking, and realized that but for your courage, of course you would have gone before; yet courage . . . a woman should not. . . ." He hesitated, very nearly lost again. "Bravery is for the battlefield; I don't want you to earn the Croix de Guerre by marrying me. You have brought me back to my limits and I find I have no taste for human sacrifice."

She was swept by unreasoning, illogical resentment. She might have been expecting this but hadn't endured nights brewed out of hell just for him to turn coy and self-sacrificing on her now. And for nothing, when he had taken so much from her that life was already changed. Now she had a right to decide what she wanted, and she refused to let him waste it all. It did not occur to her that when combined with the moral absolutes of her childhood, the pleasure she had also felt with him produced a volatile mixture of emotions, which could make a punitive marriage seem bleakly right. She remembered passion but did not yet believe it had happened to her. "No. You can't make me. You can't." She held his arms, shaking him so passersby smiled slyly. "You asked me and I accepted. How would you manage if I went?"

"Very badly, I don't doubt. I prefer it to us both managing badly."

"No," she said again. "You can't rid yourself of me now."

"I can and will. It takes two of us to stand in front of M. le Maire."

"And who will support my child when it is born?" asked Eve, ice-cold and trembling. "Perhaps you could recommend another occupant of an attic in the Rue Férou? I certainly can't return unmarried to New Moose, and I should think there'd be some sniggers at the Crillon, too."

His shoulders sagged; suddenly he looked utterly defeated. "You're sure?"

"Well, of course I'm sure. I've lived with you five weeks and hardly a night when you've kept your hands off me!" She could hear her voice rising like a shrew's as she hated him for forcing her into this one way left. In the middle of the Place Vendôme, too. She gave a gulp of laughter and looked up, green eyes glinting. "So we're both caught, and must simply hope for happiness together."

He bent and kissed her fingers. "*S'il plaît à Dieu*. I will send word when I have seen the Maire."

And I never did ask whether he was Catholic, thought Eve blankly when he had gone.

She went that night to the ball given by the city of Paris in honor of President Wilson, and danced until morning. Everyone, his wife, and his *cocotte* were there; once the dignitaries had retired, the bands blared nonstop; gone were the days when formal occasions meant ceremony and nothing else. One did not stand long-faced, one danced; protocol was for the *huissiers* of the Quai d'Orsay, where elderly statesmen must now face their task of remaking the map of Europe, but as for Paris, one danced, made love and forgot it all.

Eve had discovered that she loved dancing; few of her partners guessed that most of the steps were completely unfamiliar to her, since her zest and grace so easily covered any fault. She did not want to rest or sit out a single dance, because rest meant unwelcome thought and her partners were Americans untouched by war. They made no secret about what they wanted from her, and would have been incredulous if she'd said that tomorrow she would be married to a Frenchman in an attic.

These first few weeks after the war ended, in Paris everything still

easily became hysterical, and as the night continued, the ball degener-
ated into a drunken romp, so Eve was reminded of the Carnival Ball at
the Opéra. Several times she caught herself scanning the crowds in case
Rick Dwyer had returned from Germany. It's because tonight reminds
me of the Opéra, she told herself. I met him there and might easily
meet him here; nevertheless, she wasn't thinking of Pierre, who had
also been at the Opéra.

So Eve delighted her partners, but the following day she would not
have recognized any of them in the street. Rick wasn't there; yet even
his absence reminded her of how he had wanted her to promise not to
marry before he returned. And Rick was the kind of man who liked
women but seldom worried about them, which made his warning settle
like scum on the surface of her own misgivings, however hard she tried
to forget it.

Of course, he simply wanted her for himself.

As Guy had said, the first step with a man you don't know is the
hardest, which Rick was quite experienced enough to understand. Dear
God, to be alone in Paris was more complicated than she imagined, or
ever could have imagined.

She sat next morning in the crimson opulence of a Quai d'Orsay
committee room, and decided that since she understood exactly the
kind of man Rick was, then she preferred to have made up her mind
before he returned. Her head ached and the room was airlessly hot;
with the odd clarity which can come after a festive night, Eve grasped
for the first time that she did not understand all of her own motives,
nor did she care to look more closely into them. She also earned a
reprimand from her section chief for inaccurate translation.

The world was being reshaped by these black-suited, elderly men, and
it remained completely unreal. Tempers were lost and thousands of
square miles shuttled from hand to hand; then they adjourned for tea.
Damn Rick, why couldn't he be here, so niggling doubts could finally
be crushed?

"*Messieurs les délégués italiens . . .*" deftly she picked up the thread
of a rambling speech . . . damn Rick or not, it was settled. She had
used force on Guy and must stand by the consequences. If only she had
not developed flu in his truck she would have sat beside him all the way
to Paris and never even learned his name. She almost laughed at the absurdity of it, fumbled for an abstruse meaning and lost her way so completely she had to begin a whole paragraph again. And for an instant no
one minded, as gray statesmen forgot their animosities and smiled in response to soft curved lips, and tilted nose crinkled in joyful self-
derision.

Then the bickering began again.

Apparently Guy was not a Catholic, for he had arranged only the obligatory civil ceremony. He did not ask whether republican law satisfied her, and Eve said nothing, although she could not help remembering adolescent dreams of a wedding in their own parlor with its attendant excitements of shower parties and preparations. On this day of her marriage, she was taken unaware by how much she missed the textured life she had left behind.

Another wedding had just been completed, and they were immediately taken to the Maire, his *tricolore* sash adding to Eve's sense of watching a play in which she had no part. The ceremony was more than a disappointment, it was a shock. Formal questions, a few mumbled answers, the Maire's garlic-flavored kiss, signatures in a limp-covered Livret de Famille, where space was already provided to record the date of her and Guy's deaths, the births and deaths of their children. Guy's ring on her finger, a heavy band of gold, weighing her down.

"*Toutes mes félicitations, madame,*" said the Maire archly, and they were back in the freezing-cold street in less than fifteen minutes.

So there you are, madame, thought Eve cynically. *Bonne chance, alors.*

CHAPTER 10

The jaded wrangling in Quai d'Orsay committee rooms might seem unreal, but the ruin of Europe began just east of Paris and stretched to beyond its borders with Asia. The ruin of a prosperous and dynamic world whose energies had now spun out of control as the ferocious sweep of events continued unabated. At the precise moment when Eve became Madame Saulx, Rick Dwyer was standing in the main square of Hofkirchen, in the German Rhineland, watching two German officers being beaten to death.

The town was too small for an Allied occupation force to be stationed there, but as the German Army withdrew from France its streets briefly echoed to the tramp of thousands of men. The troops had maintained discipline until they were out of France, but by the time they reached Hofkirchen the field-gray masses had become a mob: angry, passionate and vengeful. Overnight, the war industries of the town had closed down and the streets were also filled with unpaid workers, most of them middle-aged or old and belonging to an immensely successful generation who regarded German triumphs as the natural framework to their hardworking lives. Defeat was unimaginable, yet it had happened; so their fury fused with that of the soldiers, and exploded.

By the time Rick reached the town, it had settled into sulky quiet, which was disappointing. He was not there by choice but because his train had been shunted onto a siding when the railroad system went on strike, but now that he was here, he meant to stay a few hours. Hamburg, Kiel, Berlin; one by one the cities of Germany had fallen into revolutionary anarchy, then were fought over as gangs of ex-officers and NCO's tried to wrest control back again, confusion so complete that even a trained observer could sort little sense from it. In Hofkirchen everything was happening on a scale that human beings could grasp.

The blood was real too: no anonymous stains in the gutters, but the smear where Johann Muller had been caught in crossfire and was stamped into cobbles in the ensuing panic; the frozen entrails on the sidewalk were those which only yesterday Rudi Lemke had found indispensable to his well-being.

Those two officers, too. They had sat in the station buffet beside Rick and shared his cigarettes, arguing over whether they should take off their epaulets before entering the town.

They were fools to chance it, Rick decided, when both had already faced mutiny from their men; Germany was finished. They ought to have melted into the landscape, changed clothes, and walked home.

He pitched away his cigarette, starved children scrambling for the half-smoked butt, and strolled across the square. He was a victor, and ought not to watch murder being done. He seized a couple of soldiers and clouted their heads together, hard; kicked another and shouldered aside an elderly man, who was leaning on a railwayman's hammer, screeching abuse. In another day and place he would be peacefully industrious, but the foundations of his world had shifted and so he screamed hate.

"Hold it!" Rick had to yell to make himself heard. "For Christ's sake, hold it!" He hadn't a gun and spoke no German.

More blood on the cobbles, one of the officers lying on his face, the other kneeling, arm thrown protectively over his head, striking out blindly with a revolver butt. A soldier leaned out from the crowd and stuck a pitchfork into the man on the ground, sensuously, all his weight on the haft. Rick shouted and plunged across to drive his fist into the man's face.

He turned, breathing heavily; he must not become one more of a crowd and be trampled too. "I'm American, a representative of the Allied forces. Get off the streets. At once!"

They stared at him, faces blank, breath coiling in cold air.

Christ, why haven't I learned even enough German to swear at them? thought Rick. He put his hand into an inside pocket and brought out his passport embossed with the American eagle, and a press card printed in the Gothic lettering which the Washington *Times* affected. He spread them in his hand. "American, see? I command here, the war is over. Now, get."

The officer who had been on his knees stood groggily, and said something in German. Feet shuffled, and indecisively the crowd began melting away. Rick wiped his face, hands unsteady. "You okay?"

"I am alive, for which I thank you." He spoke fluent English.
"Ulrich is dead, I think."

Rick knelt and slid his hand under the bloodied tunic. "Yeah, even
before the pitchfork, I guess." He went through pockets and took out
the man's papers. "I'll have to report it."

"Yes, I think you should do that," said the other sarcastically. "Next
week a patrol will come to look, and go away again."

"What the hell else should I do?" demanded Rick. "Line up the
town and shoot a couple of kids as a lesson?"

"I am sorry. Of course you can only do your best, which happened to
save my life. It is just that we are not yet accustomed to defeat, although we are learning fast." He closed his eyes, face greenish.

"You'll have to come with me, or they'll be after you the moment
my back is turned. Though why the hell you must walk through a place
like this in uniform beats me," Rick added irritably.

"It is cold for walking in underwear. I am also under orders. The
German Army has not all disintegrated, but it soon will if those who
are left run away too."

For Chrissake, thought Rick disgustedly. Why can't the goddam
squareheads get into their skulls that they've lost, they've lost, they've
lost? It doesn't matter any more if they run away. We'll fix them up a
peace, lend them some dollars and they can start beating their pickel-
haubes into automobiles.

They stopped at a horse trough for the German to wash in icy slime.
He was badly bruised and losing blood from a dirty-looking cut across
his scalp: shelter and rest were what he needed. "Do you know
whether any Allied troops are quartered nearer than Cologne? Or
would someone take you in for a while? I can't leave you like this, but
I'm a reporter on an assignment and should have been in Berlin by
now." Rick looked at his watch, suddenly impatient.

"I am under orders to reach Berlin urgently too. Hugo von Kobis, at
your service." The other fitted his cap gingerly over wet hair.

"Rick Dwyer. You are? Why are you in Hofkirchen, then?"

"For the same reason as you, Mr. Dwyer. The railway left me here.
And yes, I do know someone who would take me in; I was on my way
to our local headquarters when the rabble decided they disliked the
look of us. You had better come with me; I owe you a place in transport to Berlin."

"Whose local headquarters?" demanded Rick. "There's no German
outfit left in this part of the world."

"You will see. We are not all willing to wave red flags and cooperate
in the ruin of the Reich."

My instinct never lets me down, thought Rick. I smelled a good story in Hofkirchen, and by God I'm going to get it.

Away from the center of the town there were fewer people, but the atmosphere of hatred did not diminish. No one likes being hated, and it is deeply shocking when met face to face. Rick stared at shabby men gathered at street corners, sensed others watching from behind curtains, and shivered. These people desired nothing so much as their flesh underfoot.

Hugo glanced at him. "It is more me than you. They do not hate Americans, and trust President Wilson to keep the French from ruining them."

"It sure as hell feels like me," said Rick frankly.

"They do not know you are American, just that you won and we lost. As they also know it was officers like me who led them to defeat." His voice was bleak, and he stared straight ahead as their heels rang into hating silence.

The outer streets at last, and the first frost-hard fields. A wide highway led into a biting wind, some kind of municipal vehicle park on the left, surrounded by a wall and barbed wire: as they came closer, Rick saw that loopholes had been hastily knocked through brick.

A guard was at the gate and he saluted Von Kobis without a flicker of surprise at blood and dishevelment. More soldiers inside, drilling with small arms to the familiar bellow of an NCO. Rick concealed his astonishment, and while he waited in a guardroom was politely offered coffee. Revolutionary, defeated Germany was a hundred paces down the road and might have been the other side of the world.

Loud, military boots in the passage, the door flung open to admit a man built like a mountaineer, tall, supple, ruddy with health. The soldiers in the guardroom leaped to attention, and Rick only just stopped himself from doing the same.

"Herr Dwyer?"

Rick nodded and stood, but kept his cigarette. He needed to show independence from such an obtrusively dominating personality.

"On behalf of the Freikorps Grauber, I thank you for saving the life of Hauptmann von Kobis. He tells me you are a reporter and wish to go to Berlin?" His English was not so good as Kobis's, but good enough for Rick to feel at a disadvantage. Goddam squareheads behaving as if they were still cocks of their roost.

All the same, he did very much want to reach Berlin.

Within an hour, it was arranged. A convoy of vehicles was due to leave as soon as it was dark, and Herr Dwyer was welcome to travel with it if he wished. He did? *Jawohl*, excellent! Meanwhile here were a bed, hot water, and food. He would be roused in good time. Not at all; the Freikorps Grauber paid its debts.

Rick's last thought as he fell asleep was that he would look damned silly when Allied patrols searched their convoy at the Rhine bridges and discovered an American newsman recruited into a reborn German Army.

Nothing of the sort happened. They drove in great discomfort through the freezing night but were not stopped. Rick never discovered which way they went, but when dawn broke they were on the central German plain, their trucks making good speed over rough roads, the soldiers' strong young voices singing as they went.

"Who the hell are all these people?" Rick's bones ached from cold and all-night jolting.

Hugo sat beside him on steel benching, his head in his hands. This was no journey for a man beaten up the day before. "The Freikorps of Colonel Grauber. You met him yesterday."

"The guy like a lion tamer?"

"A good description. He has come to help tame Berlin."

Rick thought about it carefully. This was a gen-u-ine, bull's-eye scoop; play it careful and ride in on the coattails of the Freikorps Grauber, who had it in their Teutonic minds that they owed him something. He wasn't sure about Kobis, though; he wasn't the lion-tamer kind. "You playing along with them?"

Hugo rubbed his face. "If you would put it more clearly. I am stupid today."

"I'm not surprised. Are you going all the way with this outfit, storming the Reich Chancellery, or whatever else they have in mind?"

"No, Mr. Dwyer. I am not a member of their Freikorps. I have orders to report to our Foreign Office in the Wilhelmstrasse, where I worked before the war. Provided the Spartacists do not take it first, of course."

"Spartacists? the Communists, you mean?"

"Yes. There is a general strike, and revolutionaries have seized many buildings in Berlin, but not yet the great government offices, I think. I hope. There is a general movement of Freikorps on the city to drive them out before they do."

"And Freikorps are what?"

Hugo shrugged, and winced. "Those who will take orders still. Mostly officers and *Unteroffiziere*, but others, too. Sons of men who have a great deal to lose in a revolution; men who know only how to fight and kill, and think it tame simply to go home now the war is over. A few who love Germany and do not want it destroyed. They gather about a leader like Colonel Grauber and become his corps, with his badge. A skull, in this case."

Rick studied the young men singing across the truck from him; now it was light, he could see crudely stenciled skulls on their sleeves. "Where would you classify yourself? Killer, frightened capitalist, or patriot?"

He saw Hugo's knuckles whiten, but he answered levelly. "All three, surely. Since I have fought a war, come from a privileged family and try also to serve Germany."

"You're sure you are serving it? The Allies will be like jackals on a corpse at the first whiff of a new German Army."

Hugo did not answer, the buffeting of the truck excuse enough for silence, and four hours later they reached the outskirts of Berlin. The soldiers jumped down and formed into squads, Hugo watching aloofly.

"You're not going with them?"

"No, Mr. Dwyer. I told you, I am going to the Wilhelmstrasse if I can get through." His mouth twitched into the rictus of a smile. "I do not wear a skull on my uniform, you see. I prefer to remain with loyalties I understand."

Rick went with him in a beat-up requisitioned van, since he spoke no German, knew nothing of Berlin, and public services had ceased to run. Also, Hugo von Kobis struck him as exceptionally good copy; readers liked a human angle after months of reading about faceless rioters everywhere from Petrograd to Budapest. And now Berlin.

There had been a week-long strike in the city, intended as a preliminary to taking over the state, a climax to mutinies, disorder and uprisings which began even before the armistice. As they left the outer suburbs behind, the top-heavy buildings of Berlin seemed eerie in their emptiness. The industrial areas were the same: deserted, wary, densely populated by people you couldn't see.

From the distance came a crackle of firing and the smell of smoke; as they approached the center of the city, they began to see occasional running figures, mostly sailors. Then groups of unarmed workers freezing in cotton overalls and wearing red armbands. A boy shouting at no one in particular and waving a red flag from the branches of a tree. Rick felt as tense as if he were attacking German trenches; street fighting was something outside his experience, menace increased because there were no obvious sides to take.

More men now, and sharpshooters crouched behind marble statuary. Knots of people shouting and waving their fists, mostly civilians but also a scattering of military in deliberately defaced uniforms.

"Well, Mr. Dwyer, you are eight hundred meters or so from the Unter den Linden. I suggest you take the first turn right into the

Freidrichstrasse, where you will find the American Consulate. Tell anyone who accosts you that you are American; you are safer on your own from here."

"What do you intend to do?"

"Walk. I know central Berlin very well, and should be able to reach the Wilhelmstrasse mostly through back alleys."

"I hope you aren't going to be so goddam stiff-necked as to make your walk in epaulets and rank badges?"

Hugo smiled thinly. "The First Quartermaster General came to confer with the new republican government three weeks ago and wore full dress, medals and the facings of the General Staff. He crossed Berlin without being attacked, although I do not suppose he enjoyed it. Some things are best carried off with a high hand."

"He came three weeks ago. You've gotten yourselves a war here now."

"So, you have noticed it? What of your allies in Paris, when will they notice what is happening here, lift the blockade and allow us to bring in food? So long as our people starve, the mobs will be in the streets."

Standing by a bald-tired van in a Berlin side street, Rick had to admit that in Paris no one was thinking about Germany at all. About peace, yes; about security, revenge and recasting the map of Europe, but not actually about Germany. "Herbert Hoover went to argue with the French over shipping U.S. pork to Germany as relief."

"What did they reply, Mr. Dwyer? I am interested, since my call to the Wilhelmstrasse must mean that Germany needs diplomats again, and if we are to survive, then food is our first need."

Rick shifted uncomfortably; it was crazy to be debating pork products when a bullet had just ricocheted off the plump marble belly of a cherub decorating the portico where they stood. "They said the Germans would need all their gold to pay France for the damage they had done, and could not be permitted to squander it on food." He hesitated. "They also said that the U.S. had a glut of pork which our government wanted to unload on the Boche to save a loss on the support price. It was true, and didn't help Hoover any."

Hugo stared at him, unsmiling. "How pleasant to have a glut of pork. I was nearly killed yesterday because the people of Hofkirchen had lived on a thousand calories a day since last summer."

"You lost a war," said Rick bluntly. "No one is feeling reasonable right now."

A bullet smacked into the radiator of their van, and the rusty trickle of water froze before it reached a drain.

"You had better come a little farther with me, then. I don't think you will have a chance to explain you are American, how things are, and I would like you to live long enough to write about what is happening here. It is time that in Paris they finished gloating over the fact we lost, and remembered we still exist, instead."

Grudgingly at first, over the next hour Rick came to admire Hugo von Kobis. He was still sick from the effects of his beating the day before, yet he had argued rather than whined over Germany's ruin, and refused to recognize weakness as he led the way through trapped and dangerous streets.

Berlin was an unsatisfactory city in which to attempt outflanking armed revolt. It had risen in half a century from obscurity to become the center of an imperial administration; the streets were wide and straight, the obligatory buildings of a capital grouped together in open spaces. Only the damp, dark wood of the Tiergarten offered cover, and that was full of vagabonds. There were revolutionaries behind the statuary on top of the Brandenburg Gate with splendid fields of fire, and heavy firing came from the Reichstag parliament building.

"At least they haven't taken it yet," observed Hugo. He had said very little as he guided Rick from courtyard to back entrance, edging circumspectly from tree to tree in avenues they could not avoid.

Rick grunted, his face in wet leaves where they lay under bushes in the Leipziger Platz. He respected Hugo's silences, for safety and because he sensed something of what he must be feeling. How would he feel if Brooklyn and Queens seethed with revolution, blood ran in the trolley tracks of Fifth Avenue, Wall Street was under siege? No power, no food, no work; babies dying while doctors stayed at home, the city sealed off around them.

"We must run for it again. We are not far from the Ministry of War, and so long as the main offices are held, that must be the last to go."

"If you'd take off those damned epaulets we could mingle with the crowd," said Rick irritably.

"It is easy to see that the United States has not yet experienced revolution. It isn't just pride which tells me I do not look like a mutinous sailor from Kiel."

Rick realized Hugo was right. By American standards his uniform was poor quality, leather of belt and boots as scuffed as reject saddlery, but there was no mistaking that Hugo von Kobis was an officer. They crouched, waiting for a chance to move. The width of square and street was dominated by snipers and looked hideously bare. Somewhere quite close, firing briefly increased, cheers and screams blowing on a knife-edged wind.

"Now," said Hugo.

Legs pumping, head down, belly contracted, Rick sprinted across the road, jinking as forgotten football coaches had taught him. He fell into an angle of wall and sidewalk, to look around and see Hugo following much more slowly.

Shots spurted dirt at his feet. Rick shouted and stood again as Hugo stumbled, recovered, and then tripped on an upended paving slab. No cover anywhere in blowing, empty spaces; Hugo came to his feet at once, knowing it was death to lie. Rick broke cover between trees and wall, cursing aloud at the ill luck which gave the Krauts a chance to shoot at him again, after he had survived five months of war. He grasped Hugo, and together they ran back into the trees, where bullets split bark with a curious whistling sound.

"That is the second time I must thank you," said Hugo through clenched teeth. He had a bad color and was breathing heavily.

"Where are you hurt?"

"Ribs. Not bad, I think, but this is no place to look. We must get inside."

Rick heartily agreed. "Which way?"

"Back to the right and around the corner. My godmother lives in this block and the caretaker should know me."

It was very necessary that he should, when every street door was barred, shutters closed, the only movement coming from men with guns. Turning the corner, Rick ran headfirst into a hatless sailor: a woman's red ribbons fluttered from his arm, and he held an old-model, curve-edged bayonet. Both reeled from the impact, but the sailor recovered first, lunging with the bayonet. Rick dodged frantically and felt steel slither across his upper arm. No sensation, just nerve shock which made him fumble the grip he needed.

The sailor twisted free, eyes bulging, lips working. He was quite simply terrified for his life, as was Rick, so both fought like fiends when with an instant to think they would have realized that neither had a quarrel with the other.

Two figures engraved against chipped stone and great events, everything forgotten except themselves. Rick moved straight into attack; unless he came close he would be carved in pieces. He fastened one hand on the sailor's throat and snatched for his bayonet wrist but wasn't quick enough. The other broke loose and stepped back, bayonet poised across his chest.

"*Ach, jetzt . . . ,*" he said, deep in his throat, and lunged.

Rick flung himself aside, and then again when the sailor slashed upward as he turned. Breathing raucous, sweat on both faces, the sequence of disaster so fast it was only seconds since Rick had carelessly rounded the corner of a building, to fight for his life.

There is only one end to combat when an unarmed and unskilled man is forced to defend himself against a bayonet. Rick did not have time to think of it, only saw Hugo shoulder his opponent violently aside and kick his wrist as he fell. For a heartbeat there seemed no sound, then noise again was loud enough to hurt. The rattle of heavy vehicles, sharp coughs of mortars, the blast of high explosive. Shouts and screams, very close. They had heard nothing while they fought, now all three froze, Rick doubled against a wall, the sailor sprawled on the ground.

Hugo said something and the sailor stood uncertainly before running off. "This way," said Hugo. "It must be the Freikorps attack; we haven't long to get clear."

Half dazed, Rick followed him, sleeve dripping blood. Cobbles, another street, an ornamental garden; almost immediately, they had to run again. Gray figures appeared at the next corner: they made no challenge before driving a volley down the length of street they had just left. Running men appeared from nowhere and swept past: sailors and workmen mostly, mouths gaping in fear, running for their lives.

Rick followed Hugo blindly and dropped beside him when he took cover behind a horse trough. Unexpectedly, Hugo was smiling. "My epaulets. I knew that honor would be worth its passage."

Before Rick could grasp what he intended, he stripped off his greatcoat, settled his cap on his head and stood, hands held out by his sides. The noise was worsening all the time, a battlefield developing around them, while this small space was swept clear by the coming storm. Snipers could be anywhere, though. Rick wiped his face and watched as Hugo approached a thick-slabbed building where marble stairs led to a studded door protected by sandbag bunkers. The Ministry of War, thought Rick, enlightened. Only an officer's uniform might get them in there today.

Hugo turned and gestured urgently: hurry. Piecing together what he had seen, Rick reckoned the Freikorps, and therefore presumably the Ministry of War, were winning, but he was delighted not to be caught in the open while he discovered more.

He watched events for the rest of the day from behind sandbags on a balustrade. Smoke hung low over the streets, machine-gun fire and volleys telling of revolutionaries killed; sniping shots, of those who remained alive and defiant. As evening came, the firing gradually drew away toward the industrial suburbs east of the city. Squads of Freikorpsmen stood in the street below, laughing loudly together. Exaggerated shouts of greeting echoed in emptiness, campfires glowed on eager, triumphant faces, on sleeves decorated with skulls and thunderbolts and wolf heads instead of imperial eagles.

Rick went inside, icy cold. Torn flesh on his arm hurt abominably, and a field dressing stuck there had already disintegrated, since paper was all the Germans possessed for such purposes. He found that the War Ministry was full but not busy; officers stood about drinking ersatz coffee and smoking; there were more rank badges and crimson cloth than Rick had ever seen in one place before.

Hugo came over while Rick stood staring at the plush-and-marble cavern of the main hall, where an immense chandelier hung over a sandbagged emplacement housing machine guns trained on the main door. "What do you want to do now, Mr. Dwyer?"

"Write about all this, I guess, though I wouldn't do it justice in a million years. And Rick, don't you think, after the day we've had?"

"Rick," said Hugo, smiling. "But you are a journalist, surely. Why can you not describe it?"

"It's like a hallucination. Generals with monocles sitting on sandbags under a chandelier, discussing counterrevolution with their staff. How many were killed in Berlin today? Yet there's no excitement here, just a tight, professional job."

"There isn't any excitement, because it wasn't their battle. These generals know little more than you do about what has happened; they have been left aside while a new Germany is born."

"While the new Germany is killed off," said Rick sharply. "The revolutionaries lost, didn't they?"

Hugo looked at him and then away. "Something very new won, I think. I am going to the Foreign Ministry now; it is safe at the moment. You may sleep here if you wish, or come with me and add a little more to what you have already seen."

Rick groaned. "Don't soldiers ever sleep? I'm a reporter, for Chrissake; I guess I have to come if you won't wait until morning."

Hugo did not answer, his expression unexpectedly hostile. He was too polite to scream that after four years of war there was no rest anywhere to be found, or to kick smug detachment down the steps. Berlin was only the latest marker along a helter-skelter of destruction, and already he could scarcely disentangle the day's events from those of yesterday or the day before.

Once outside the Ministry of War, they found Freikorps everywhere, but Hugo had papers which took them past without difficulty. He spoke only once, when an arrogant gang of them blocked their path. They looked three quarters drunk, although on success rather than beer, and Rick did not disagree with Hugo's judgment when he stepped around them into the gutter, and said so.

Hugo shrugged. "One sees strange sights in our streets nowadays, and at this moment I have a job to do. Yet sometimes I feel that discretion is not everything; what do you think, Rick?"

"Discretion every time, when armed thugs are holding a gun on me. Tomorrow is another day."

"Perhaps. I am afraid we have tomorrow in our streets already."

"Aren't you glad the Communists lost, this time around? I wouldn't expect a Von Kobis to welcome Lenin into the Reich Chancellery."

"I am glad they lost."

"So what the hell?" Rick felt light-headed himself, with relief and loss of blood. "Enjoy walking to the Wilhelmstrasse tonight without any need to dodge bullets or a mob."

"I would like to kill you." Hugo's voice shook. "At this moment there is nothing I would like so much. This is my home, and there aren't any winners. Only losers. So you enjoy the Wilhelmstrasse tonight, and I will go alone from here."

He disappeared into the dark, leaving Rick flat-footed with astonishment. Was all Europe full of homicidal maniacs? Then he shook his head slowly: Hugo had allowed the Communist sailor to go free, when killing him was a natural response to attack.

From the distance came a single volley, which might have come from a firing squad. Might have, but it was impossible to know anything for sure tonight. Close by, the Freikorps sentries loosed off too, apparently for enjoyment. Whatever Hugo said, certainly there were winners as well as losers.

Rick swore into the wind; forever afterward he would remember Berlin for its arctic winds. No streetlights anywhere. Alone, he needed to grope his way a step at a time and did not enjoy the Wilhelmstrasse in the dark at all.

CHAPTER 11

In Paris, Germany still seemed remote. A place talked about continually and which inspired fear, envy and hopes of plunder, but set on one side, as if victory had drawn a line under its existence. Eve had been appointed as American translator to a small committee studying Germany's western borders, and it meant that suddenly her work had sprung alive. Temperamentally, she was not suited to translating; she wanted to join the argument, to tone down insult and moderate demands. Her experiences since she came to France made her loathe war with such passionate intensity that peace seemed worth almost any concession; yet at the same time she lived with France's sufferings and became too easily incensed if an American delegate dismissed French demands as vengeful greed and nothing more.

She realized that anger simply damaged the exacting business of translation; it did no good to think of meaning behind the words she spoke, nor must she fall into the error of believing the statesmen fools, when she had never heard of many places they discussed. Yet often she could not help herself. She also realized that some slackening of tension was what everyone needed, so she smiled at rancorous delegates and hoped it helped a little, slipped in a word of softness when she believed it wouldn't be noticed.

In a sense, the multiplying committees of the Peace Conference remained a shadow play, although they felt important enough. Decision lay with the Big Four statesmen: Clemenceau, Wilson, Lloyd George and Orlando, and not with minor gatherings picking over statistics.

Eve usually ate alone, needing time away from human voices for strain to slacken and her temper to cool. Sometimes she simply walked as she did today, breathing wet air into her lungs and too tensed up to eat: it still felt strange to be a fractional part of history, but rage was real as she watched how easily hope was muddied.

She sighed when church clocks jangled saying it was time to go back, and was stopped by one of the stenographers just inside the back entrance to the Quai d'Orsay used by junior staff. "Mr. McCarthy's asking for you."

"Do you know why?" McCarthy was the translation-pool supervisor.

The other shrugged. "I guess you're such a whiz of a translator he's offering you another quarter a week."

Eve laughed; the State Department was a meager payer of temporary staff. She went up the stairs two at a time, unpinning her hat as she went. She hadn't long; there was always trouble if the staff weren't in their seats before the delegates entered.

The Quai d'Orsay was bursting with people, and McCarthy was sorting reports on a windowsill. "I heard you wanted to see me," Eve said.

"Yeah. Where the hell have you been all this time? Never mind," he added irritably before she could answer. "Tell me, Mrs. Saulx, what do you think your duties here consist of?"

"Translating—"

"Translating clearly and unambiguously. Continue, Mrs. Saulx."

Eve flushed angrily. "Of course."

"Of course *what*? You were telling me about your duties."

"Yes, I was," she said levelly.

He selected a paper from a pile on the floor. "This is a report I wrote after I listened to your translation yesterday afternoon. I come around sometimes to check, or hadn't you realized?"

She nodded; the other delegations' translators checked on you too.

"But you didn't see me yesterday," he said flatly. "You're fired, Mrs. Saulx."

The shock was like gunpowder in her lungs. "Why?"

He stared at her, a professional who disliked using amateurs, a bachelor uncomfortable with women. "I just told you why. You translate fluently but inaccurately. By intention. If you just forgot a word, okay, we're short of translators. But you don't forget, you put in a different sense you think might please the French. So I've news for you, Mrs. Saulx: you were hired to serve the U.S. delegation and not the goddam French."

"I have never once altered a meaning or confused an issue," said Eve. Shock past, she was coldly furious now.

"Okay, okay, so you haven't. Instead you helped make our people think the French might be reasonable in the end, when the bastards mean to take everything, and then some more." He glanced at the paper in his hand. "I can't give you the precise tense and clause but you know what I mean, and I know what I mean. The French demand the whole of the German Rhineland to be given to them forever, and you smile sweetly and hesitate over the word ever. They talk of French garrisons in Mainz and Cologne and you do a skid on the word occupation, as if they might be thinking of something temporary."

"They are occupying the Rhineland temporarily. The rest is anger which they can't keep corked, but the decisions will be made elsewhere. Our committee is fact-finding and nothing else. Can you name any piece of evidence, true or false, I missed a single word on?"

"You just proved my point," he said with satisfaction. "Somewhere along the line it was you and not the U. S. Government who decided to slur a few ideas and drop out the insults." He slapped at paper on the windowsill. "I want everything here, and I mean everything. Not some sweetened piddle edited by a kid still wet behind the ears. Ears wet with French spit, I guess. Just let 'em call us names, when each *saligaud* and *corniaud* the President reads will make him angrier. We need an angry man if this negotiation is to succeed. Not that it's your business. You were hired to translate straight and you broke your contract, so you're fired. You can work your week's notice on translating reports in the Crillon. Dave Black has taken your place for this afternoon's session. Good day to you, Mrs. Saulx."

It seemed strange to be walking aimlessly while the rest of Paris hurried about its business; Eve's muscles felt tight, her mind scoured blank. She had tried to help and failed again. Somewhere in Washington my file will make good reading, she thought sardonically. Thrown out of the Red Cross and the State Department, all within weeks.

She threw back her head, lips tight. She had not thought in terms of risk or blame but this time understood exactly what she'd tried to do so must accept the consequences. So take the consequences, and refuse to let them matter.

It was one of those February days in Paris when spring feels close enough to touch. Several couples were dancing to a portable phonograph at one of the gravel intersections in the Luxembourg Gardens, and Eve paused to watch. Some little girls were watching too, leaping up and down, their mothers and *bonnes* indulgently critical, as if such antics made adults no different from children. It all looked so carefree, as if peace had spilled some great, unending party into the streets. Yet just beneath the surface the frame remained the same: fear, hunger, grief, and the bitter bile of revenge.

As soon as Eve resumed her walk across the Gardens toward the Rue Férou, her mind was jogged by something familiar in the walk of a woman just ahead of her. The pistol-shot impact of contemporary clothes was not quite so obvious from behind, but when she turned, Eve caught a glimpse of painted cheek and discontented mouth. It was Eulalie.

Eve hesitated, and then shrugged. She could not live forever without meeting Guy's family. "Eulalie!"

She was well ahead but heard her name, and stood waiting. She was in a black rage, eyebrows painted into flat hyphens, skin powdered mauve, a stick like an oxgoad in one gloved hand. "Is it true that you have married Guy?"

Eve blinked. "Why, yes. Didn't he send word?"

"No, Mme. Saulx, he did not. He was probably afraid to admit his folly. And yours."

"If the rest of your family is going to be as outspoken as you, then he was probably right," retorted Eve. Guy had told her not to worry, he would write to Tante Gabrielle.

"Where is it you live? Pierre said it was near here. Unless you want a wrangle in the street, we had best go there and I will tell you what a damned fool you have been." Eulalie stamped her feet and sidled into passersby like a badly broken horse.

"You needn't bother," said Eve coldly. "We've been happy while we were left alone."

"As you please, or are you ashamed to show me the sty which is all Guy can provide for his wife?"

Eve wanted to tear blood from that painted mask, when there was just enough truth in her words to make them hurtful. Instead, she turned and walked away, fast, up the street, hoping very much that Guy was not at home. She needed time alone to assimilate her furies from such a day.

He wasn't, but her angry rush up the stairs hid other sounds, and when she unlocked their door, she discovered that Eulalie was behind her. She pushed Eve into the room and stood, hands on her hips, staring about her. "*Mon Dieu,* was this the best he could do?"

Eve had been pleased with the improvements she had made; now she looked with Eulalie's supercilious eyes and saw damp plaster instead of a freshly laid grate and bright drapes. A single shabby room to set beside the salons of the Champs-Élysées. "Now you have seen what you wanted, perhaps you would go, and carry your tales with you."

Eulalie laughed, mouth pallid against paint. "When I have said what I came to say. I wondered why Pierre had been like a bear this past week or so, and then Sergeant Joubaire told me it was you that Guy had married. I thought Americans were more practical, although regret must be growing like weeds in a farmyard now. So tell me . . . cousin: how are you enjoying Guy as a husband in the Rue Férou?"

"Will you go or shall I, and leave you for Guy to find when he comes back?" Eve had to force words past stiff lips.

Eulalie laughed and flung herself into a chair. "My trick, I think. No answer is also an answer of a sort, don't you agree? How long did it take before you realized you were married to a murderer?"

Sight darkened and blood drummed in Eve's ears. She clung to the edge of the door, wanting to scream insults at Eulalie's sneering face, but was stranded nowhere instead, doing nothing.

"I should close the door if I were you. Unless you want the whole staircase to share in your affairs, that is," said Eulalie sweetly. "And no, dear Mme. Saulx, I am not going until I've made you listen to what I came to tell. One day, you might thank me for it."

"Never, since you came for spite and nothing else."

"Strangely enough, I didn't. For curiosity if you like, and to relieve boredom on a dull afternoon. You haven't told me yet, though. When did you realize, and what precautions do you take?"

Eve sat limply in the other chair. "I don't know what you're talking about."

"I think you do; if not, then it's time you faced facts. Do you mean to say you never thought just how convenient it was, the way old Anselme died the day before he signed Guy's inheritance away?"

"He ate too much."

"Yes, he did. He'd eaten and drunk too much for years. He survived in good health until he decided to provide for future indulgence by buying himself an annuity."

Eve stood again, on hollow legs. "I am going to wait for Guy in a café. Give the key to the concierge when you leave."

Eulalie uttered a faint hoot of laughter. "A perfect, loyal wife. I didn't think they were bred like that any longer. You've listened to me; he is betrayed already. But virtue is so dull, and I'd hate you to pretend to it with me by flouncing out just yet. He's violent, isn't he? Hands like hooks and you on the bed whenever he feels like it. You know what he did to me?" She smiled disagreeably when Eve stayed silent. "He raped me, sweetheart. His own cousin and fiancée, under her father's roof. You're here, alone with him in a back-street attic where no one cares what happens."

"Why tell *me* this, instead of the police?" Eve was immediately furious with herself for answering.

"And have them tramping in and out of the Hôtel Daunay, poking their noses where they're not wanted? Not likely. 'And where were you, mademoiselle, at three A.M. on the morning Anselme Saulx died? At the Club Marin? Hm. It was raided and closed the week before, *hein*? So tell us where it meets now, or there are things about this death which you alone are able to explain. In prison, naturally.'" She grinned. "Papa would have a fit. The *flics* would jump at the chance to investigate his affairs. Who cares how Anselme died? All we want is a limit set to the damage his death can do."

"And if anything happened to me, anything at all, someone might remember that old M. Saulx is recently, and very conveniently, dead?"

"Something like that." She stood, and smoothed preposterous clothes. "I'd get out if I were you." A waved hand and she was gone, heels rattling on the stairs.

Thoughts fluttered around Eve's brain like snowflakes in a blizzard. She had listened because she was unable completely to disbelieve. Eulalie was exotic and depraved, not, today, completely unkind. Perhaps she had even come partly from concern. Now that she was alone again, Eve tried to tell herself how crazy she was to have listened: Guy was not, could not be concerned in his father's death.

Then, vividly, the scene in the breakfast salon at the Hôtel Daunay returned to her mind, as it often had before. She had never seen Guy like that again but knew, as he did, how sometimes he could not answer for himself.

"No," she said aloud; but words were a mockery when she still understood so pitifully little about her husband. Had found him both understanding and savagely inconsiderate; gentle, enduring and tenderly loving; also unbalanced in rage and under the scourge of his unquiet mind. Yet beyond all doubt he was better each day that they lived in peace together. Eve shifted in her chair: he had not been better while he lived at the Hôtel Daunay.

He was also forgetful of his own irrationalities, a forgetfulness Eve encouraged. By sheer willpower she forced the bad times out of his sight, believing that from forgetfulness would come healing, offering softness again and again when sometimes she felt only uncertainty and despair. Not fear, though. Guy's emotions had been fragmented, his control demolished, but he loved her, and even in excess she had never felt threatened.

He had not loved his father, nor Eulalie.

She sat a long time in front of a cold grate, wondering what to do. A bell tolled nearby: do, don't; go, stay. Ask, don't ask, never ask, pray he has forgotten his hands on his father's throat: not once since he told her his father was dead had he ever referred to him, or to Eulalie, again.

She felt wetness on her fingers and went over to the water bucket; it would never do for Guy to find her weeping. And unexpectedly she was racked by sobs, this shock too much when added to the other, and just lately Guy had been so much better that the tangle of emotion weaving her to him had begun to form a pattern in which real affection showed.

She did not hear his tread on the stair, and was caught wailing like a baby with her face against the wall. Eve felt his arms around her, the way he held her body close to his, voice soothing against her cheek. She laid her face on horizon-bleu cloth and wept again.

"My sweet, what has distressed you so?" he asked.

Eve shook her head and sniffed desolately. "I don't . . . I never cry. I'm sorry to be so stupid."

He laughed and kissed her. "Well, you cried today. It helps sometimes, as I have discovered."

She was absurdly touched that in order to comfort her he should admit to tears, when normally he detested his own frailties. "I don't know what came over me."

He looked at her sharply, disbelieving, but also aware of something he must wait to probe. "Come and sit down; I'll light the fire. Perhaps it was the child. I'm not familiar with such matters, but I believe that even Tante Gabrielle's calm was slightly disturbed before her sons were born."

Eve was silenced. She wished passionately she had never thought to use pregnancy as a means of forcing him to take the final step into a marriage she knew he both needed and desired. What a hideous mess she had made of things! Guy talked undemandingly while he lit the fire and heated soup, but intimate domesticity unsettled her still more. She did not want to think about the many changes she had helped to make in him while Eulalie's accusations still echoed in her ears.

He stood over her until she ate, then moved quietly about the room out of her sight, not at all the restless fidgeting of his bad days. Eve sat and stared at the fire; Anselme Saulx was dead, and through her, his son had laid hold on life again. This she had given; surely it was too late for her to start raking over accusation and join the destroyers now?

"Now tell me why you wept." Guy leaned over the back of her chair, his hands caressing her breasts before linking under her chin. "Something worse than a woman's fancy upset you tonight."

Eve sat rigid, terror leaping out of nowhere. His thumbs were on the artery under her jaw, the pulse in his wrist thumping against her ear.

He moved and kissed her, fingers tightening. ". . . Eve?"

She closed her eyes, back pressed into the chair, muscles like wire. "It wasn't anything important."

"If you were upset, it is important to me."

"Guy, please! There are some things I must work out for myself."

She heard his pulse change beat, accelerating into danger. "Why?"

Her neck was sweating where his hands circled tight enough to stop breath if she moved, panic very close. "Guy, you're hurting me."

"I am?" he said softly, roughness of chin against her face.

She could not think, or move, or speak. Blood beating behind her eyes as if his thumbs already moved to finish what was begun. Please God, she must say something. Must. "I feel useless tonight. Make love to me, Guy, and later I will tell you." She brought her hands up to cover his, prized his fingers loose, slid them down to her breasts again. Her neck instantly became icy as sweat chilled and she began to shiver.

He was quite still, completely unresponsive. "If you wish."

"Why, of course I want . . ." She turned in his arms, her fears mere sick imaginings the moment she was out of that hateful chair and his hands no longer on her throat. Eulalie. It was she who had deliberately dripped poison where it would spread as if on sand.

As she had asked, Guy made love to her then, but in a way she had not known before. Neither tenderly nor in frenzy, but with efficient, exhausting thoroughness. They lay side by side when he was done at last, Eve drowsing into a kind of uneasy content. For the past hour, at least, she had not thought beyond the passion he could rouse.

She felt him move, flat on his back now and impersonal in darkness. "You have something you said you would tell me later, if you remember."

Eve wriggled closer to his warmth. "I'd forgotten, though I thought you were the one with the bad memory."

"A selectively bad memory. And along with the rest of me, it's improving as time passes. Thanks to you."

"You mustn't worry about every little thing, then," she said fretfully.

She felt him shrug. "Some kinds of bad news I prefer to face. Who is it, Eve? Who did you meet today who brought you such unhappiness? I have a right to know, even if not to feel jealousy over your affections."

Eve reached out impulsively, discovering that lying alone in darkness with her husband, she no longer believed anything Eulalie said. She would not, could not, feel so easy with him if she did. "It's nothing like you're thinking. Yes, I ran into Rick Dwyer this morning, he's just back from Germany, but—"

"What did he say?"

Rick had been horrified to discover her married to Guy Saulx. "Not much. I told you, it wasn't like that at all. In fact, I'd forgotten him until now because this afternoon I lost my job. If you remember, I said I felt useless tonight."

Guy moved then, turning toward her in darkness. "Because you have married a Frenchman?"

"Mr. McCarthy said my translations favored the French. Yes, I suppose my French nationality was the reason, really. I was locally hired so he could fire me if he wanted, and even the cooks at the Crillon are U. S. Navy while the Conference lasts."

He held her then, the feel of him quite different. It occurred to Eve that Guy Saulx possessed an unusually expressive body. "The British brought their own cooks too; they're all complaining about the food. *Chérie*, why should you mind? Translating other men's foolishness is not exciting work."

"No, but—" Whatever she pretended to herself, Eve had been minding very much as she walked home, until Eulalie swept everything except horror from her mind. Now she was minding again, because Eulalie was a liar. "I hated to feel I couldn't be trusted. Sure I dropped some insults and phrased a few things more tactfully, but that was all. McCarthy acted as though I were a package mailed over from the U.S. to France. No loyalties or principles of my own, a nothing ready to be used."

"We are all used, *chérie*. Only those who know and love us best truly want us as we are."

Eve sighed. "Don't go tonight."

"No, I won't go." Since they had married, he refused to stay beside her through the night, and lay on the floor instead. He still slept badly but said the floor was not the cause, being luxurious after trenches.

Eve was deeply asleep within minutes, while he lay painfully making sure he did not sleep at all. There was something she had not told him, he was certain. Something more than a lost job, surely, when he had never seen her weep before. He kissed soft hair on the pillow beside him as she slept: Eve, whom he loved and who might soon love him if only they were left in peace; Eve, whose greatest quality was not courage or vivacity—although she possessed both—but such a complete lack of indifference that even her disregard was something to be cherished.

When Eve woke, he was gone. She felt ravenous, and was horrified when her watch showed that it was half past ten. Half past ten! Clerical staff were expected to be at their desks by half past eight. She flew out of bed, splashed herself in icy water and dressed hastily. There were fresh croissants on a plate, a note beside them in Guy's rectangular writing. He had told her once that he wrote oddly because of German schooling in Gothic script and spoke English for similar reasons: in Alsace, English had been taught intensively, to crowd French and French literature out of children's education.

"*Since you have been dismissed, you might as well enjoy a croissant before you go.*" Eve laughed and sat to eat. Certainly, she might as well.

She stopped eating halfway through the first croissant, her throat closed on rage. "It wasn't true," she said aloud, thought crystallizing from the night before. Eulalie had come in malice, to spoil the contentment of a man she had not wanted but expected to be given. Eve was certain of it on a crisp morning when bare branches glittered against blue sky. Or nearly sure, perhaps.

She decided not to bother with going to the Crillon, and went instead to Rick's office. A pert and painted girl said he wasn't in, so Eve waited restlessly through what was left of the morning.

"I expect he'll be gone all day," said the girl, picking her teeth with a pen. "There's some fuss with Wilson and his League of Nations."

"Then, I'll wait all day." Eve felt obstinate, conscious of time running against her.

Rick came in on a gust of cold air at four o'clock. "Eve! What a sight for sore eyes after goddam endless wrangles on the League."

"Well, that doesn't sound much of a compliment," she observed. "Could we go somewhere private?"

"Sure, I could do with a drink. I must file something within the next couple of hours, though."

He had already had several drinks to while away tedium, and was in an expansive mood. With time short, Eve went straight to the point. "You said yesterday that I didn't know the half about the family I'd married into." Rick nodded. "I want you to tell me everything you know."

"Are you crazy? I'd have done it to stop you from marrying Saulx, but you jumped with your eyes closed while I was away. It's too late to help, and you'll be happier without a load of dirt to carry around the rest of your life with him." He would tell her quick enough if it helped prize her loose from Saulx, but thought the time wasn't yet. She was too softhearted and might simply feel sorrier for the bastard.

"I'm not a nice, hometown girl any longer. They're my family now, and I want to know everything you've found out."

"Yeah?" He gulped cognac. "You sure look a nice girl still to me, with those freckles on the end of your nose. Thank God you're in Paris and not Berlin, anyway; I heard the Communists took over the Chancellery yesterday. The Germans are starving, so the mob is running wild, in uniform and out of it."

"The Hôtel Daunay," said Eve firmly. "I haven't time for anything else today. The Germans lost, didn't they? There's bound to be trouble for a while."

Rick drank again. "That's what the French say."

"I am French."

He sighed. "Okay, the Saulx. You asked for it, so don't blame me if you wish afterward you hadn't." He felt a reporter's joy in a good story, but meant to edit this one.

"Start with M. Daunay," prompted Eve. "He seems straightforward enough."

"He does. A straightforward blackguard. Well tailored and an impressive manner, I grant you. He came to Paris from the Creuse country, owning nothing. That's southwest France, and the Creusots are known to other French as a hard-fisted bunch, and that's quite something in a peasant nation. He's made money out of just about everything, I guess. Pimping as a young man, and running with the *apache* gangs. In the nineties the *apaches* drew money by threats from half the slums of Paris, and Daunay rose to lead his own mob. Dud stock issues and government contracts since he became respectable, but Le Tout-Paris finds his grooms and gardeners just too, too delicious: some from his past he still finds useful for handling stuff he doesn't touch himself any longer. He married that bladder of lard for her francs when he needed them, forty years ago. Swept her off her feet at sixteen, so now lets her stuff sleeping pills to keep her from getting underfoot."

"Gabrielle," said Eve relentlessly, refusing to be shocked, to believe or not believe. At the moment, she simply wanted information.

"We'd best go back a bit. Old man Saulx; Anselme, Gabrielle and Hortense's father— he was a tiger, by all accounts. Married two sisters."

"At the same time?"

"The younger two days after the elder died. A hell of a scandal in Alsace, by all accounts. No kids by the second, who he's said to have loved, three by the first, who he certainly didn't. So he hated the kids, too. Married his daughters off to the first Frenchman who met his eye. The Germans had taken Alsace, you see, and he intended to make sure there weren't any Boche grandchildren. Gabrielle, well, I reckon she's sucked the life out of her husband. You've met him?"

Eve nodded.

"Does what he's told, and boasts he never goes anywhere that takes his feet off good-quality carpet. That sort of idleness costs money, though, and he's let himself live off Daunay."

"Why should Daunay let him, though?"

"Gabrielle's okay; Daunay likes her. Slept together in the past, I shouldn't wonder. She manages his house and doesn't criticize; the place would be uninhabitable if Hortense had the running of it."

"How on earth did you discover all this?" demanded Eve.

"And you a Frenchwoman! The Frogs don't give a damn for truth, just the pleasure of being vicious in their gossip."

"So you're only telling me malicious rumor?"

"It's scum off real dirt, all right. Where was I? Yeah, old Saulx. Well, he made a good living in Alsace; the family had land there once."

"They still have. Guy told me." Eve thought of Guy's life there, and the bitterness it had brought.

"They'll get it back now, I guess. Decorated, frontline commandant the heir and all that. Nice for you, Mme. Guy. Châtelaine of the Domaine des Saulx."

"Rick, please. Just tell me what you know and then I'll go."

"Back to Saulx. God, Eve, when I heard you'd married him I nearly challenged the bastard to a duel. They still have them sometimes in the Bois de Boulogne, and pretend the loser died of pneumonia. Which, in a way, is often true."

"Don't be ridiculous," said Eve irritably. "You're cross because I'm off the market, not in the least jealous."

He laughed, and choked on cognac. "Keep your Yankee candor, Eve, my sweetheart, and I promise I'll be jealous. In unrefined, beautiful fact, unknown to reporters, I think I am already, whatever you say."

She looked at him, and smiled. She had been watchfully intent; now warmth broke instantly from confinement, as if it refused to be locked away for long. The promise of curved, joyful lips and direct green gaze gave Rick the same gut thrust of desire he had felt with her before. "*Merci du compliment*, Rick dear. Especially now when I'm just using you. Anselme?"

"Anselme," said Rick flatly. "He got a German girl into trouble and was forced to marry her, much to his father's fury. Did you know your fine French husband was half Boche? By all accounts, the other Saulx used to puke at the sight of him. The moment old Saulx was dead, Anselme went off to Paris, and married again when his first wife died. No children, and the woman died last year. You know the rest, I guess."

Eve chilled. "What rest? I know Guy served in the German Army."

"All Alsatians did, and deserted when war came." Rick waved a dismissive hand. "Strange, really; in Germany I met a guy whose father had been in their imperial administration there. He knew Guy Saulx, was glad to hear he hadn't been killed. I said he was crazy but alive, and Hugo—"

"He isn't crazy," interrupted Eve.

"Oh, yeah? Anyway, Hugo simply said aren't we all. After Berlin I guess I agree with him." He hesitated. "Hugo just might be coming to Paris; tell Saulx."

"With the German delegation?"

Rick swirled his drink thoughtfully. "Perhaps, but I think he'll come secretly, before. In Paris no one cares, but the Germans are starving, Eve. What I saw there frightened me enough to say I'd act as a contact here if Hugo comes, and Saulx might be useful too if he and Hugo were so friendly before the war."

"For heaven's sake, Rick!" cried Eve, aghast. "Guy's a French officer. He couldn't possibly help."

"What the hell has being an officer to do with starving kids? Or being French, for that matter? Or am I just a simpleminded Yankee civilian, Mme. Saulx?"

Eve could feel her temper rising. "I'll slap your face if you call me Mme. Saulx in that kind of voice again. Starving children have nothing to do with anything except mercy. If this Hugo asked us, we'd give what we possess to buy them food, but we haven't the power to lift blockades or influence presidents. We might whisper and bribe and plot like the small fry we are, but we couldn't possibly do any good. You'd crucify Guy's loyalties all over again and the price would be his peace of mind, the service he has given France. For nothing. You can't ask it of him, and I shall see you don't."

"What if you just might do some good?"

"We couldn't. We might make good copy."

Rick flushed. "The press back home is pretty worked up about the blockade of Germany continuing so long after the armistice."

"Good. The press has power, all right."

Rick idly traced lines through brandy rings on the table. "Returning to Anselme for a moment. Your husband hated his father; so everyone says."

"He had good reason." Eve's blood seemed to stop.

"Yep, I guess he did. It was mighty convenient the way Anselme died, all the same, but perhaps your Guy was owed a break after the war he'd fought. It's a cinch that if he was just one of the small fry you were talking about, then the *police judiciaire* would have a complaint lodged with them by now. But the *beau monde* don't run to the *flics*, and Daunay surely won't. Yeah, I reckon your husband is a lucky bastard in more ways than one."

"Is that a threat?" Eve was surprised by her own calm, since she had come to Rick hoping to discover something which might contradict Eulalie's certainty.

"Nope, not yet. It's a statement of fact. If I ever decide to lean on Saulx, then there's plenty of dirt waiting to be scraped off the walls."

"Why should you want to, or have you taken Germany so much to heart that blackmail seems okay?" She knew why Rick might want to.

"Unless you don't mind a Communist state there, and perhaps another war to kill your French officer sons, then you should take it to heart as well."

Eve stared at him, softness vanished and in its place a swift, defensive anger. "I was fired from my job when I tried to help a little, but you didn't dig into the Daunay and Saulx families because Germany was on your conscience."

"Eve, I'm sorry. I ought to have given you some idea of what I'd heard before I went, but I never dreamed you'd marry while my back was turned. When Hugo said he'd known Saulx before the war, it seemed like a good opening to me: if he used the dope I'd gathered, then it would help cut you loose. I'm serious about Germany, all right, and if it helped there, too, okay; though I guess Hugo will be disappointed by how little Saulx is worth nowadays. But now that you are married. . . . I think one day you may be thankful to have that file on the Saulx to use yourself. I'd be surprised if French divorce was easy for a woman, and you don't understand yet what you've gotten yourself into. I'm afraid for you and that's the truth. I wish to God you were back in Maine."

"I don't quit," said Eve softly. "I might in the end decide to go, but I'm not a quitter. With you and this Hugo, as well as that passel of maggots in the Hôtel Daunay laying traps for him, I reckon Guy is going to need me for a while."

"You don't find just one person worth a sacrifice out of a bloodline of maggots," said Rick soberly. "Eve, come up to my office a minute. I want to give you something."

She followed him, her mind churning while he went up the stairs three at a time ahead of her. Rick agreed with Eulalie. He was a clever, unscrupulous newsman who would not skimp on effort once he decided to research an issue, and the facts he had uncovered pointed accusation back to Guy. He was afraid for her, Rick said.

I don't believe it, she thought stubbornly. Guy isn't like that, nor are the Daunays, really. Rick's found some dirt so hasn't seen what else he's dug it from.

The girl in the outer office was still picking her teeth but Rick slammed the door on her and unlocked his safe. "Give me your bag."

Eve handed it over, surprised but preoccupied. She expected him to give her some paper which perhaps incriminated Guy, but the weight in her bag when he gave it back to her did not feel like paper.

"What is it?"

"A gun. Quite small; tuck it away somewhere handy. There's a safety catch on the left of the butt; slip it forward and it's ready to fire."

"A gun!" She stared at him, staggered, then flipped open her bag and pulled it out. "Who do you expect me to shoot, for heaven's sake?"

He did not reply, but took it from her and snapped her bag shut on it again.

For a fraction of time last night the thought of a hidden gun might have been comforting; yet it would have been tragically wrong, the end of everything between them. No, Eve thought. Whatever the truth, and I mean to discover it, Guy would never harm me. It is fighting and quarreling all his life which has nearly destroyed him, and between the two of us at least, there must be peace.

She threw the gun into the Seine when no one was looking; she did not feel courageous but recognized that once trust perished, then everything else between herself and Guy perished too.

CHAPTER 12

After that first day, Eve changed her mind and worked out the rest of her last week with the American delegation. Prices were climbing rapidly and every sou was valuable, because French Army pay was scandalously low. Also, Guy was unexpectedly called back on duty, and to a staff appointment with the military section of the Peace Conference instead of commanding guards. His fluent German and close knowledge of the border areas between France and Germany was a valuable asset as France launched her bid to convince her allies that the whole German Rhineland should be annexed to France as one of the spoils of war. Consequently Guy lacked time to make Le Trésor profitable, and also the will, Eve thought. It had been the place which sucked profit from his efforts in Alsace, a symbol of his father's indifference and a means of revenge as well as life beyond the trenches: now that the shop was his he had very little idea what to do with it.

"Wouldn't it be worth your while to hire a good salesman who really knows about antiques?" Eve asked tentatively the evening after she finished at the Crillon. Incompetence exasperated her, yet she ought not to meddle with his concerns while he still struggled to organize his life again.

"Yes, it would. But I need someone good, and can't afford to pay much while the place isn't a going concern. Old Marguerite and Paul are trustworthy at least, even if only used to junk-shop dealings."

"How about Sergeant Joubaire? He never seems to have any military duties, and told me he hopes to be out of the Army soon."

"I don't want Joubaire at Le Trésor more than I can help."

"Why not, Guy? I admit I don't care for him, but I'm sure he could sell anything, and at a good price. California wine to the French, I wouldn't be surprised."

"He'd soak off the labels. I don't want Joubaire on my premises, although often I haven't any choice." He pushed back his chair and began wandering around the room, picking up objects, dropping them, leaving them lying on the boards.

Eve watched him with troubled eyes; he had woken screaming the night before, and when she tried to persuade him into bed with her, had flung out of the room half dressed and walked the streets until dawn. He had been so much better, but this past week all their fragile gains had begun slipping through their fingers again. The Peace Conference interested him, and Eve thought he was probably far more effective with staff work he understood than attempting to cope with a baffling shop full of furniture, but he tired quickly when sleep remained a luxury and the pressures were intense during the present bitter wrangles at the Quai d'Orsay. Above all, he was sufficiently sensitive, or perhaps loved Eve enough, for her preoccupation to have become a grating irritant between them. She had not again felt fear with him, nor could she accept Eulalie and Rick's accusations, yet their sour taste remained, the subjects she must not mention, the questions she must not ask.

"If you dislike Joubaire so much, why not have him reassigned?" she asked at last. "Surely the Army doesn't care who is your *ordonnance,* and now we've married he doesn't do much that's personal for you any longer."

"Leave it, please, Eve. He—"

Eve leaped to her feet as his words slurred and he turned, fumbling, toward the door. "Guy! What is it?"

"Nothing. For God's sake, let me go. Later . . . I'll be back later."

"No. If you go, I come too." She grasped him so only violence could dislodge her.

She had been prepared for a blow; instead he simply looked relieved. "Have I stopped one at last?"

"Stopped one? Guy, what is it?"

He looked around with satisfaction, a half smile on his lips. "I've escaped them. Alive from the trenches, just think of that. A few weeks in the hospital is cheap at the price, don't you think so, nurse?"

"Guy?" whispered Eve. "Guy, *chéri,* it's me, Eve."

He nodded. "You're beautiful. God, I'm tired."

He was docile as a child, and utterly unfamiliar. She had thought of him as sometimes lacking in control before, had not realized until it was gone the strength of will and artifice with which he had hidden disability. He lay when she told him, closed his eyes and slept with her hand in his. Slept the whole night through, he who seldom dozed for more than an uneasy hour at a time. Slept without moving, stunned, breath fluttering, drawn skin a mask of exhaustion.

Joubaire, thought Eve. Just let me get my hands on him. What has he done, so his name alone is enough to bring on an attack?

She could not risk waking Guy to stoke the fire, so the room became bitterly cold, her breath floating smokily among the moonbeams. I shall remember Paris for never being warm, she thought—almost as if she accepted that this was an episode which eventually must finish.

As the night wore on, she faced an idea she had evaded before: Joubaire inhabited a part of Guy's mind he wanted to seal tight. A memory perhaps of the night Anselme Saulx died, which Eulalie said began with rape and ended in murder; a night Guy might not remember, yet be afraid of remembering when he looked at Joubaire, who remembered everything.

It fitted, and would also explain why Guy had not rid himself of a man he hated. She wished to God it didn't fit.

Guy moved as dawn came, face frowning, the peace of the night gone. His hand was still in hers, and Eve bent and kissed him, cold lips to cold lips.

His eyes opened, drowned dark against parchment skin. "Eve?"

His strangeness had vanished, and she hugged him in a paroxysm of relief, trying also to hide other fears by hugging him.

"Eve, what is it? What's the matter?" He jerked upright and swung his legs to the floor in a single movement, almost tumbling her out of bed.

"Nothing's the matter, except you've just enjoyed your first twelve-hour sleep in years."

"No drops?"

She held him tightly, overwhelmed with pity. Whatever he had done, it wasn't his fault. It was the war. "No drops, my love. Never any drops since you were with me."

He did not look rested, but as if he had lost everything except the desire to be alone, to bid the sun set on his life, and die. "You're cold," he said flatly, at last.

Eve nodded. "I can hardly remember a time when I was warm."

"Or happy, or resting in content."

She bit her lip. "I am content when you are well."

There was a long silence. "Eve . . . do you know, since we married I had come to hope . . . to begin to believe that one day you might love me? I love you so much and it seemed to me . . . until just recently . . . that sometimes you were not unhappy too."

Eve sat mute, his hand in hers, both freezing. She had known that he had noticed the change in her and wanted so much to lie to him, to pretend that nothing was the matter. But it mattered very much that she could no longer be entirely sure she wasn't married to a murderer, nor was there a convenient lie to take suspicion's place.

He sighed. "Eve, what did I say? I can't remember . . . *Mon Dieu*, I didn't—"

"You didn't say or do anything. You were tired, and slept. That's all, Guy. You thought you were back in the trenches for a while. There wasn't anything else."

In her anxiety, she overdid it. He grunted, staring at the floor, shoulders bowed, obviously struggling with the raw edges of his mind. Suddenly she was petrified with fright. He mustn't remember exactly why his memory had slipped; Joubaire couldn't prove a thing by now, and even the law spared those who committed crime while their wits were scattered. Spared them to be locked up so long as their life should last. She rushed into the silence, saying the first thing which came into her mind. "Guy, I've been thinking. Now I've finished at the Crillon, why don't I come to the shop? You haven't time to see to everything now you're on duty such long hours at the Conference." And I'm not afraid of Joubaire, she thought.

He squeezed his hands together until the knuckles shone, the effort of concentration brutally hard, but at least it switched the direction of his mind. "You are what, ten weeks pregnant?"

Eve flushed; she was not yet used to French frankness on bodily functions. "I wasn't proposing to heave furniture. I feel perfectly well; I should enjoy to be some help."

"I suppose you might as well learn about Le Trésor, in case I become completely useless," he said wearily. "Oh, Eve. What a selfish fool I've been to get you into this mess! If it weren't for the child, I'd— are you sure you can't take it back with you to America?"

"Quite sure. You must know what villages are like, and New England ones are more intolerant than most."

"You could be a war widow. God knows, it would be true."

"I'm French now. Your child is French and this country certainly needs its children." Eve stifled the thought that she would very much prefer any child of hers to be raised in Maine, away from European miseries. It didn't arise, anyway, and it still seemed unthinkable to desert Guy. Horror was close and very real; yet, looking back across the chasm of this past week, she could see how he was right: there had been times when love crept closer, unobserved.

"I feel like some kind of animal," he said quietly. "Fit for sex in the sty and precious little else. Yes, come to Le Trésor. I expect you'll make a far better job of it than I have."

He dressed and shaved, talked distantly over coffee and rolls, then went to report for duty. It was impossible to avoid the impression that he was thankful to be away.

Eve was left alone. She had a dreadful feeling that she had made some fundamental mistake and lost him forever, when the simple responses of an uncluttered mind would have put them back on the path to contentment. They could not go on like this; she had to find out the truth and then face it, decide calmly whether to go or stay. She swept and tidied briskly, planning the questions she would ask. As a new member of the family, she had a right, even a duty, to call at the Hôtel Daunay, and once there would refuse to leave without hard evidence of what had happened. Not gossip or formless fears this time, but verbatim, cross-checked facts.

She set out immediately, decision hardened, knowing that terror of what she could not bear to hear would make this the worst ordeal of her life.

A footman left her in the marble hall while he went for instructions: with a shock, Eve saw that it was only just after nine o'clock.

She was ushered into the same breakfast salon she remembered, and Gabrielle greeted her characteristically from behind silver urns and pots. "Mlle. Eve? We felt chagrined to hear no more after your precipitate departure."

"I sent flowers," said Eve, dumbfounded. "Mme. Benoit, I thought you knew. I am married to Guy."

"I never attend to rumor."

"But you must have! Eulalie and Pierre knew."

Gabrielle held out a thin, heavily ringed hand. "I should like to see your *livret*."

Eve blinked; that horrible little booklet with space provided for her death. "I don't carry it with me, but I assure you we are married."

"Then, why were we not invited to the nuptial mass?"

"We didn't have one. I mean, I'm not a Catholic." She refused to expose Guy to more recrimination, although she would have preferred almost any religious ceremony to a meaningless mumble in front of the Maire.

"Our family has always been Catholic, mademoiselle. I regret that you cannot be welcomed into it without the blessing of the Church."

"Since we live under republican law, I belong to your family whether you like it or not," Eve snapped; she was not in a patient mood today. "I may be an *arriviste* but I am legally married to your nephew."

"In my day one did not arrive."

Eve remembered wryly what Rick had told her of M. Daunay's activities: if there was any truth at all in gossip, then you had to admire the sheer shamelessness of Gabrielle's arrogance. "Well, I started off from home a long time ago, and I surely have arrived somewhere."

For an instant, Gabrielle showed a spark of answering amusement as she withdrew from battle on unfavorable ground. "Very well, but I wish to see your *livret* when next you call, since Guy did not see fit to invite a witness from his family to the ceremony. Do you suppose he was ashamed?"

"I hope not," said Eve tightly.

"Not of you, child. Of himself."

"Why should he be?" Eve wanted to walk out, but of all the people inhabiting the Hôtel Daunay, Gabrielle was the one who could probably tell her everything she wanted to know. So instead of going she stripped off gloves and coat, offering notice that she meant to stay; she decided to unpin her hat next time around, if further warning should be needed.

"I have never subscribed to this household's view of Guy's character, mademoiselle. He possesses many qualities, including the desire not to disgrace himself in front of others. You, in this case."

Eve unpinned her hat. "I thought we had agreed on my status, or am I mademoiselle until you have seen my *livret* for yourself?"

Gabrielle inclined her head. "My apologies, mademoiselle. I have no reason to disbelieve you."

The door opened to admit Pierre. "Eve! I did not expect to see you here."

"Why not . . . cousin?"

He glanced at Gabrielle, but she remained impassive, bolt upright, reinforced with whalebone. "Guy has not come with you?"

"No. He's been detached to duty with Marshal Foch's staff at the Peace Conference." She refused to rise to the sneer in his voice, when they both knew that Guy was unlikely to come here again. After some of the nights she had experienced, Eve could not disbelieve the first part of Eulalie's story.

"At least we may trust the Marshal to watch over the interests of France," observed Gabrielle. "An adventurer like Clemenceau would betray anything for money."

"Politicians sell most things, but not their winnings." Pierre sat beside Eve and took her hand in his. "Eve, for God's sake, why did you do it? When you said you were *affiancée* to Guy I never dreamed you were serious, but reckoned instead that you were a little spoiled by being set loose so young in Paris and meant to play a game with me and M. Dwyer. Make us jealous, and everyone else as well, so beautiful as you looked in your first Paris clothes. When we heard you had married him— well, my father looked up the law on annulment through incapacity."

"And what did he find?" inquired Eve silkily.

"That it did not favor a woman in such a case. You must have been crazy, Eve."

"Then, by your reckoning we are well matched. As we are," she added defiantly. "We are happy when left alone, and shall be more so when Guy is fully recovered."

"And all he needs is a loving little wife. Don't pretend to me, Eve. He raped Eulalie, did you know?"

"Yes," she said steadily. "Let go of my hands."

He lifted one and then the other to his lips. "Such strong little hands, *chérie*. I enjoy holding them."

Eve sat completely still; she was damned if she would give Gabrielle the satisfaction of watching an unseemly tussle among the coffee cups. "Tante Gabrielle, would you ask your nephew to remember his manners?"

Pierre's mouth twitched into a smile which did not reach his eyes, but he stood and moved away from her. "You did not object to holding hands and a good deal else at the Opéra ball."

"I was not then Guy's wife."

"What has that to do with anything? You are being provincial, my dear. And don't try giving me claptrap about being well matched with Guy, or do you intend to go about attacking people too?"

Eve stared at him. "Sometimes I should like to."

Just for a moment, he was disconcerted. "How delightful! Any time, Eve. I should enjoy it, although I doubt whether you will find Eulalie similarly indulgent toward Guy."

"No," said Eve thoughtfully. "Although I have the strangest feeling that she shares some blame for whatever happened."

"As you will share it when you run from him, squealing for protection?" retorted Pierre unpleasantly. "I hope you find some comfort in the thought."

"I shall share it if he is driven beyond bearing by things which aren't his fault. For the moment—" She stood suddenly, her plans forgotten; she could not bear to stay another moment. "We have built something between us, which helps hold him to life. Just leave us alone. Leave him alone."

"I wasn't aware that we were interfering." Gabrielle spoke for the first time in minutes. "You came here, not us to you."

"Eulalie came to see me last week."

"Yes?"

Eve drew a deep breath. "She made some utterly unfounded accusations against Guy."

"Eulalie has always been difficult and wears atrocious clothes." Gabrielle had a way of delivering opinions as if they were the last trump.

"Perhaps you'd prefer her to dress like her pink fondant friend," said Pierre maliciously.

"This is not the time for jokes which might possibly amuse your acquaintance but do not amuse me." Gabrielle turned to Eve. "I have not been unimpressed with your manner, madame, since this cannot be easy for you. I think you deserve frankness. As a boy, Guy smelled of the farmyard and behaved like a Boche. But for the war, he would have cheated his father out of his property in Alsace—" She held up her hand as Eve interrupted. "You may question me afterward. The ownership of the property is in suspension now, but he will gain it eventually. Le Trésor, too. If this was how events had happened, then I might regard it as a proper end to a sordid episode, since Guy is said to have fought bravely; of course he may simply have been fortunate to survive. Otherwise—"

"Otherwise he was a bucolic boor, whom Le Tout-Paris massacred with their tongues whenever he visited us. Which fortunately wasn't often, since I had to take him in tow," interrupted Pierre.

"He had no chance to be anything else." As ever, Gabrielle was scrupulously fair. "When I saw him during the war, I thought that he had become a man well able to please women. Times have changed, however. He sometimes makes you happy, and sometimes the reverse. Am I right, madame?"

Eve hesitated, and then nodded.

Gabrielle looked faintly gratified. "Sometimes he may be ardent, but I do not think Guy is, or now ever will be, a suitable husband for a young girl. Eulalie is over thirty and more than capable of looking after herself. How old are you?"

"Twenty-one." Eve felt numbed by such ruthless dissection of emotions she had never attempted to analyze.

"I never approved of allowing young women to wander unchaperoned in military areas. Only harm could come of it. Certainly she had other motives, but Eulalie came to warn you. We feel some slight responsibility, you understand, and prefer the world to congratulate us on a brave and decorated relative, rather than enjoy a scandal at our expense. I am sure Eulalie spoke in a foolishly exaggerated manner, but I would urge you to open proceedings for annulment if you can."

If this was how events had happened, Gabrielle had said, leaving little doubt about her meaning: she, too, believed that violence, and not chance, had brought Guy his inheritance. Eve stared at polished parquet, where centuries of growing timber became no more than shading between her pointed toes. How insignificant life and hope could sometimes seem. "Tell me what happened the night Anselme Saulx died."

"It is several weeks too late, my child. No one knows exactly what happened."

"Eulalie knows what happened to her."

Pierre gave a hoot of laughter. "Would you like me to fetch her for questioning?"

"Yes!" said Eve fiercely. "And your father, and . . . and Mme. Daunay. M. Benoit. Sergeant Joubaire and the servants who wait on the family. I told you, I want to know. So far I have only heard accusation. No evidence, nothing. I can see of course how easy it is to blame anything you like on a man with shell shock." The truth of her own words hit her afresh: for his sanity's sake, Guy could not be questioned, nor asked to defend himself, nor even come here again. Her eyes narrowed, cat-green and dangerous. "I'm not shell shocked, and I intend to find out what happened."

"Eulalie does not believe in reticence. I am sure she will be delighted to offer any detail you want," said Pierre politely.

"Good. I've thought of a great many questions since I saw her. You haven't been very explicit in what you said either. Is Guy meant to have killed his father, or are you hinting at something quite different?"

"Really, Eve—"

"Yes, really. I want to hear you say it."

"He killed his father," said Gabrielle calmly. "I have come to admire your courage, madame, but I will say it if you wish."

Eve gripped the carved back of her chair; Gabrielle was a woman worthy of belief. "How?"

Pierre exclaimed aloud, and left the room with unexpected tact.

"Men are often surprisingly sentimental," observed Gabrielle dispassionately. "Sit down and I will tell you."

Eve sat, being incapable of standing any longer.

"Our doctor certified heart failure; Anselme had long been intemperate in his habits. He kept a decanter of cognac beside his bed, and that night drank a great deal on top of a badly chosen meal. The doctor had no doubts and the *médecin légiste* signed the certificate almost without looking. Most people do not look closely when they are consumed by envy of excesses they cannot afford. I sent the cognac to be privately analyzed, and it contained morphine, as Guy's drops do also. You know his motive, I believe."

"If he had one, yes." Be clinical; imagine yourself Sherlock Holmes and don't think how Guy's horror of his drops might mean a shadow of memory still remained from that night. Eve pulled herself up sharply.

No. If this was to be worth anything at all, then everything was evidence. "Sergeant Joubaire kept Guy's drops."

"Only if Guy took them, and slept; so as to prevent him taking too many when fuddled in the night. If he refused them, Joubaire left the bottle on the washstand in case the night became unbearable. Guy came to rely on Joubaire, although he is not a scrupulous person."

"But you don't suspect him?" said Eve slowly. "Why Guy? Anyone could have had access to those drops."

"What possible gain to Joubaire? The strongest evidence against Guy is that he wanted very much to kill his father."

Eve put her head in her hands; this was grotesquely horrible, no matter how she strove for detachment. They were talking about a man with whom she had lived for nearly three months; whom she did not love but who loved her.

"It was the night of the Opéra ball," went on Gabrielle relentlessly. "Eulalie was preparing herself when Guy went to her room and sent out her dresser. Eulalie screamed soon after, but her dresser is from the South and believes red-blooded men ought to make their women scream." She mused for a moment and then smiled. "She might possibly be right, but Eulalie's tastes are unexpected and do not include men, whether in Guy's state or not."

"Yet, knowing this, your family intended Guy to marry her," said Eve bitterly.

"It would have been a form of words, and suitable for both."

"Guy needs a great deal more than words! If only he could find peace . . . until Eulalie came he was so much better that we were often happy together."

"You are here today, are you not? Which suggests to me that all is not as well as you would like me to believe. However, to return to that night. When M. Daunay heard what had happened, he was naturally very angry. He is direct in his anger and not a man to be trifled with, I assure you. He ordered Joubaire to stay away, and then sent for two men he employs about unpleasant affairs which may occur from time to time in his business. By then there were not many left in the house, so these men went at once to Guy's room to punish him. Georges believes in an eye for an eye, and does not bother with police in such matters. As it happens, he need not have worried to send Joubaire away: Guy was ashamed of what he had done and was in a mood to welcome punishment. He fought them but without rage in his heart, you understand. The Church knows what it is about when it imposes expiation for sin, *hein?* Afterward we find it easier to forgive ourselves. You may find this strange, but a beating probably helped Guy to forget. Or do you think he still remembers?"

Eve nodded and then shook her head. Guy retained an image of horror, of what she wasn't sure. She found it difficult to believe she was sitting in a twentieth-century salon surrounded by polished elegance and listening to a woman of Gabrielle's impartial temper, a woman for whom she was beginning to feel some liking and who possibly liked her, telling how a pair of guttersnipes had been licensed to exact medieval vengeance.

Gabrielle must have read her thoughts. "My child, you may accept my judgment in this: what Georges did was right. Sometimes it is possible to be too civilized, and life is made simpler for us all if we express justified rage and then set bitterness aside. Guy was not even put into the street while he remained uncertain of himself."

"No scandal," said Eve flatly. Gabrielle might believe what she said, but to Eve it seemed that Georges Daunay had exacted a hoodlum's vengeance on a sick man: she now accepted every word Rick had told her of his past, although she had been skeptical before.

"Precisely. He was told to go in the morning and stayed alone in the house while we all went out on our diversions. We were late, but it was New Year, if you remember, and even Hortense went to lie on a sofa elsewhere. The staff were enjoying their own celebrations belowstairs, and knew nothing when I questioned them next morning."

"Even Eulalie went out?"

"Certainly. There is a club she belongs to—"

"The Club Marin?"

"She told you?"

Eve nodded. So Eulalie had scuttled off to her pink fondant, all soothing sensibility in a corner. "Anyone could have put drops in M. Saulx's cognac before they went."

"Figure for yourself, madame. Guy had been out all day, and no one knew whether or when to expect him back. If anyone planned to incriminate him, they would have hesitated to put the drops in Anselme's cognac until they knew for certain Guy would be in that night. And almost certainly they would not have conceived such an idea until the scene with Eulalie occurred. After it, Guy was seriously unbalanced. Before—" she considered. "He might have throttled his father in fury, but was capable of defending himself against accusation if anyone thought to take advantage of his state. Nor was Anselme's cognac poisoned until after he went out."

"Do you mean to say he was there all through this . . . that his own father made no attempt to keep M. Daunay's bullies from beating Guy in revenge?"

"As I told you before, it was justice; so why should he stop it? Anselme had negotiated favorable terms for his annuity and found himself humiliated by his son's behavior; he was also late for his dinner engagement. What business was it of his? He stayed in his room; no one reached the cognac until he went out."

"And you, madame? Did you stay in your room while so much happened?"

"Naturally. Eulalie would not have welcomed the advice I would have given her. I agree with you in one respect, madame: I should be surprised to discover that Guy's behavior toward her was not provoked. Eulalie has lived a long time in the *beau monde*; she made a stupid, ill-bred fuss over very little, and nearly caused a scandal. Georges slapped her face as she deserved, and managed retribution best on his own. Guy had left the house before Anselme was discovered to be dead in the morning."

"Joubaire? When did he return?"

"Late. Georges told him to stay out for the night, although he did return to sleep with a *bonne* who favored him. I questioned the *bonne*, and he was with her for what remained of the night. Anselme would have been dead by then. Joubaire could not have done it, and had no motive."

Joubaire reminded Eve of a tramp who came to New Moose each summer; he had bold eyes and a ready tongue and a reputation for being the slickest gelder in all New England. There were whispers of other, darker proficiencies he possessed, and local children were kept indoors during the days he spent in the village. Joubaire, too, would make time for wickedness if it paid him, and certainly had a motive if he intended to blackmail Guy over furniture stored at Neuilly. A victim who inherited good premises and a business was infinitely preferable to one on army pay. Eve decided to think about Joubaire later. Think about everything later; she could not, must not start thinking now. "What made you suspicious, madame? The doctor was satisfied, the servants must have thought M. Saulx's death less dramatic than the events of the night before, or one of them would have enjoyed running to the police. Yet you sent the cognac to be analyzed. Why?"

"I sent other things as well, but it was the cognac." She considered, as if that aspect of the matter had never occurred to her. "It was the way Anselme looked, I believe. He was an affable man and did not look at peace; also, I understood how very much Guy wanted his father dead."

Eve started to protest against such blatantly illogical reasoning, but Gabrielle held up her hand. "I know, madame. I may be prejudiced, but motive is still important, *hein?*"

"Yes, of course. But—"

"Spare your efforts, my child. I was merely curious to know how Guy had done it; once I discovered about the cognac I did not sit in judgment. I told Anselme many times how I disapproved of his conduct toward Guy, and that evening he was not answerable for his actions. France needs its remaining sons, and I could not pretend to judge such circumstances."

"You sent Eulalie to me." Eve felt her muscles tighten as she spoke. No, Gabrielle was right; the Daunays had kept quiet for weeks, so why send Eulalie to stir up trouble now?

"You have been making your own inquiries, have you not?"

So that was it. Eve almost laughed with relief. Laughed at the absurdity of it too, that Rick's investigations should have created enough of a ripple in the Hôtel Daunay for them to want to frighten her off.

Yet Anselme Saulx had died, and it was murder.

Gabrielle was a scrupulous woman who perhaps was glad of the opportunity to deliver a different kind of warning altogether from a simple caution against scandal, and she added, "When my husband and I returned, Guy was sitting on the stairs with an empty medicine bottle in his hands, quite incoherent. At the time, I thought nothing of it, since I understood how disturbed he was after events earlier: I simply assumed he needed more drops than Joubaire had left for him to calm himself, and felt some pity for the man he might have been. Anselme came in drunk soon after, and I did not see him alive again."

So this was what made Gabrielle so sure, and what Guy slammed his mind shut against remembering. This helped reinforce horror of his drops; he would not sit on the stairs and beg for more now, refused to have them in the room at the Rue Férou, no matter whether he slept or not. Eve rubbed her eyes and then her face. Then her eyes again. What could she, must she, ask next? "How clear was he in his mind?"

"Confused; frightened; forgetful, without being completely blank."

Eve nodded; she knew him in that mood. The very next night, she had come to him: she felt sick just thinking about it, strange to recall how only a few weeks ago she had craved to enjoy Paris and the freedoms brought by war.

Gabrielle's voice brought back reality again. "He was not drowsy; that is the point. Joubaire told me next day he'd left the bottle half full; if Guy had taken so much himself he would have been unconscious, accustomed to them as he is. His father was not used to them, and drunk besides. It would not have taken much to kill him. You were shocked that Anselme went out to enjoy himself without attempting to help his son: if it is any comfort to you, then I believe that in deep distress of spirit, that was why Guy killed his father, and not for property at all. It is perhaps easier to accept intolerable hurt over the years as a motive, rather than mere greed."

Eve shook her head; it did not seem to help at all.

"What will you do?" Each word separately spiked, like icicles on dark eaves when beyond lay frozen plain.

Eve shook her head again; she did not know, and could not speak.

She walked the streets all day, annihilated by her thoughts. The war: but for the war, Guy would have disliked his father and done nothing worse than outsmart him over property. The war unleashed violence and chopped men's minds out of the trappings of constraint. People talked of the suffering war brought and did not understand a fraction of it. As darkness fell, she was stumbling with weariness and her mind became dimmed by sheer fatigue. She had no idea where she was, no notion of where she could go. Earlier, she had thought of Rick, but probably he wouldn't be in his office, and she didn't know where he lived. At this time of night he'd probably be drinking in the Crillon bar; she cringed at the thought of bright lights and good fellowship in the Crillon bar.

A pimp slid up and laid his hand on her arm. She shook him off distractedly, without even noticing. The Rue Férou. She was in the Rue Férou. Perhaps she had been circling it for hours; like a rabbit crazed by the stink of a ferret crouched waiting in its burrow. Nowhere else for her to go, and exhaustion at last in place of thought.

CHAPTER 13

If her mind had been clear, she could never have faced Guy again.

But all she felt was him holding her, and light which hurt her eyes. He would not let her sleep without eating, and she struggled fretfully when he made her swallow soup and bread.

"We nurse each other on alternate nights," he said, and held her close. "Eve, promise me one thing."

"Mm?" she said drowsily. There was some reason why she disliked his hands on her body, but she wasn't thinking of it just now.

"Promise that when you leave, you will tell me first."

Her eyes flicked open, distended pupils fathomless. "I'm not leaving."

"God save me from it, *chérie*, but one day you will. Just . . . please . . . tell me first. I will not complain. I was afraid tonight, not knowing whether to search Paris for you or allow you the escape you deserve."

Her eyes closed. "I promise."

She slept dreamlessly, and woke to find Guy still there. "You'll be court-martialed. Whatever time is it?"

"Nearly ten, but I wanted to be here when you woke. Anyway, an anarchist shot Clemenceau yesterday; hadn't you heard? The Conference won't meet today."

Eve lay, stupid with sleep, mind scarcely ticking over, looking with fresh eyes at the fourth floor back in the Rue Férou. Yesterday's disclosures were utterly disconnected from the man who shared this room with her; they also framed a new life of uncertainty she must enter. In minutes she must get up, accept Guy's caresses, eat and market, go with him to Le Trésor and take on fresh challenge there. Let him— no, encourage him into sex with her as often as she could; for the first time, she shied from the phrase "making love," which she had used to herself before. But he was a man who needed emotional release so desperately that she would do better to walk out today if she could no longer offer it.

Eve stared at red-and-white-checked tablecloth, at brass candlesticks she had bought off a stall and polished for the mantelpiece; the cheap, laborious possessions which marked the beginnings of a home. At Guy in shirt sleeves watching her, his face oddly defensive, as if he knew he was in some way to blame for this new strangeness in her.

Her husband, to whom she had promised faith until her life's end, no matter that the bureaucratic mumble had scarcely seemed a wedding. If she could bear it she would stay with Guy while he needed her so much; somehow she must endure until she felt free in herself to go. As he had endured four years of war, and broken at the last.

Her flesh crawled as he came over. The cliché was true; her skin physically goose-pimpled with distaste, and when he turned back the cover she saw her breasts contract and chill, nipples hard before his fingers touched. Without warning there was vomit in her mouth; she dived for the bucket and hung there, shuddering.

The worst part was that he thought it a consequence of pregnancy, so understanding that Eve could have screamed. Toying with stale bread at breakfast, she wondered how quickly they could move away from the Rue Férou; without some privacy she did not think she could last long.

"Are you free for the rest of the day?" she asked abruptly. "I'd like you to take me to Le Trésor, if you are."

"Shouldn't you rest? You were exhausted last night and aren't well this morning." He had not asked why she had returned so late and distraught.

"I guess I may not feel well again tomorrow," Eve said sourly. "The sooner I get started at Le Trésor, the better. We need profits fast."

Guy drummed his fingers on the table. "As you wish."

And I wish to tarnation that just sometimes he'd lay down the law, thought Eve, irritated. If he thinks I'm sick, then tell me to stay quiet, for land's sakes. Whatever he did grated on her now, since she had been nerved for a quarrel if he tried to insist she stay in bed.

They caught a bus across central Paris, standing on the open rear platform, squeezed against railings in the crush. Paris drivers swerved at each other by habit and staged combat at each street intersection; worn tires thundering over granite, their drivers' hands continually on the horn, the green city buses were opponents to be respected. At the best times Eve found Paris traffic frightening; today she felt sweat on her nausea close again. She stared resolutely out, ignoring Guy's arm her: narrow streets flashed by, where the women were engaged in the daily ritual of shaking mats out the windows of high, gray houses. Yellow trolley cars, their black-uniformed women conductors darting out to throw over points with long iron levers: already the men were demanding that women should be dismissed now peace had come.

Their bus crossed three streams of traffic in a cacophony of horns, driver and conductor yelling defiance as they went: I expect that both the driver's hands are off the controls, thought Eve fearfully. Sleek-rumped horses were still the principal means of transportation in New Moose.

The Seine at last; Eve craned her neck, for this was a view of which she never tired. Watery sky reflected luminous Paris light and framed a vista of splendid bridges as far as the eye could see. Bare-branched trees and misty, gray stone quays; then they plunged back into ill-tempered traffic again. They left the bus at the Place de la Concorde: Eve glanced toward the Crillon and then away again. She wished that she had searched for Rick last night, and denied her conscience time to remind her of loyalty still owed to this husband who probably was a killer. Yet, which was truly worse, when once you searched through the rubble of conventional responses, the unbalanced man who had neither thought nor memory of killing, or the conscientious soldier honored for his years of slaughtering men he had never seen? How do we, ought we to judge? Or, like Gabrielle, should she simply stand aside?

A horse and wagon careered past, whipped on by a drunken reveler who must have commandeered it after an all-night carouse; Eve jerked from her unhappy reverie to realize that Guy had not spoken since they boarded the bus, and no longer held her arm. She thought back laboriously; he had held her on the bus and she had refused to respond. Unless she conquered revulsion soon, it would become too deeply rooted ever to be overcome.

She linked her arm through his. "A penny for them."

"*Comment?*"

"*A quoi pense-tu?*"

"Of Clemenceau," he said after a pause. "An assassin's bullet makes an inglorious end for the Tiger."

She followed his lead with relief, although he had not been thinking of Clemenceau, she was certain. "Why was he shot?"

"The habit of violence is hard to break." His voice was edged, a muscle jumping under his eye.

"He's dead, then?" She groped frantically for a safer subject. How could she live like this?

"No, but he's seventy-seven and shot in the lung. Foch is pleased, as he thought Clemenceau soft on the Boches."

"And was he?"

"He is very long skilled in achieving the possible. He would flatten every steelworks and military installation in Germany if he could, but he knows he can't. Foch thinks such realism is treason and tells Clemenceau so in front of the other Allied delegates. There have been some fearsome scenes recently."

"You're on Foch's staff. What do you think?"

"I? I'm not a soldier, my dear, for all the fancy uniforms they give us nowadays." Once the Conference opened, he had been issued with gabardine tunic and breeches, *fourragère* and gold-piped *képi*. "I don't think guns can prevent war, only win it if one comes. If we take too much from the Germans they will feel as we did over Alsace, and the next war wait on their convenience."

Eve was astonished. They seldom discussed the crowding crises of Europe, perhaps because she had worked for the American delegation, who bitterly resented French jeers that justice was being sold to the Boche. Perhaps she had also taken it for granted that his mind was too fragile to form opinions contrary to the popular slogans of the day; if so she was utterly mistaken. His judgment seemed more detached than that of the delegates whose words Eve had tried to soften in her translations; his weakness lay elsewhere, in the fissured labyrinth of emotion.

"So how do you accommodate your conscience with your duty to Marshal Foch?" she asked.

"I don't have to, yet. Foch values my German and English, so makes me one of his listening posts in the Conference anterooms. We all spy on each other, as you know, and soon I may be sent for a few days to our zone in Germany, where the Army is hatching its own plan for the dismemberment of our enemies. I shall use my own judgment about what to do when I have learned more of what they intend; I may still wear a uniform, but my time for blind obedience ended with the war."

"I never realized quite how much better you were," said Eve slowly. "When—"

"When I still can't even sleep safely with you, nor bear myself alone. But as you say, in some ways I am better. The night we met I shivered all the way from Rheims to Paris, unable to put words into a sentence or offer you a seat out of drafts. Now I can consider where my duty lies between Foch and Clemenceau." His tone was bleak.

"You wrapped me in a curtain, and offered your seat before the end." Eve kissed his cheek, and only afterward remembered that minutes before she needed to nerve herself to touch him.

"Yes, too late. You caught pneumonia just the same."

"Flu. And I must have had it before I saw you."

"So you must." He looked at her, a gleam in his eyes this time, his arm relaxed, where it had been strung tight. "I'll have to remember that."

They both laughed, while all around them light glowed softly on the stone façades of the Rue de la Paix. Paris is a very feminine place and responds to altered mood.

He showed her over a cleared but still cluttered Le Trésor, and told Marguerite and Paul that they were to regard her as having authority in everything. Paul shuffled back at once to his planing and polishing, interested only in his own routine; Marguerite, a middle-aged woman in felt slippers, was barely civil.

"She knows another woman won't allow her to wear slippers," observed Eve. "Nor that dreadful rusty dress. She's enjoyed working alone with men."

Guy peered into the street, edgy and distracted again. "Joubaire ought to be here soon with a load from Neuilly."

Eve took a deep breath. "Are you sure we can't be rid of him?"

"I'm sure."

Leave it, instinct warned. She alone must find some way to be rid of Sergeant Joubaire, whose very name upset his master. "You're quite sure you don't mind what I do here? I shall make a great many mistakes, since I know so little."

"Any mistake you make, I shall have made already." The door swung open with a crash, and Joubaire came in, wearing a workman's smock over uniform breeches. "Ah, Bertrand. All successful?"

"*Pour sûr, mon commandant.*" His eyes swiveled to Eve. "Have you come to estimate our hopes of fat profits, madame?

"I have come permanently, now Commandant Saulx is called back to duty."

He scowled. "It is heavy work for *une Américaine.*"

"I was raised on a farm, and you may move the furniture for me, Sergeant."

He shrugged, and turned to Guy. "The load is in the courtyard."

The two of them went out together, leaving Eve to prowl among armoires and chiffoniers, all scrupulously polished and ranked in neat rows. The place looked about as enticing as a barrack square, but excitement at the challenge of Le Trésor struck Eve like a bolt out of nowhere. She had expected Paris to whirl her off her feet and to be seduced by the charm of France, land of impossible legends woven into her childhood. Instead she was confined in an attic with a frighteningly uncertain man, although for a while reality was blurred both by her delight in some of the pleasures he could give her and in becoming a fractional part in the splendid hopes of peacemaking.

Yesterday had finally stripped off any vestige of illusion, yet Eve Ottoway's true self survived untouched: vital, undefeated, dissatisfied with routine. She was concerned for others precisely because life flowed so strongly in her: strict upbringing might have burdened her with a sensitive conscience; it had also tempered a tough and willful mind. She had not left Guy when most girls her age would have done so, but because she stayed, she badly needed an outlet away from the Rue Férou.

Le Trésor suited her exactly.

The Peace Conference in the end was probably too abstract and too exasperating to hold her interest for long: she disliked being fired but was not sorry to be rid of such unpromising drudgery.

Le Trésor was different and abandoned into her care; she felt her responses quicken even though it was filled with wares and problems about which she knew nothing. She had a vast amount to learn but somehow would master it; and if she succeeded, then this small place could become her very own Paris legend, a welcome escape from the whirlwind she had begun to reap from the moment she married Guy.

Marguerite broke into her eager dreams. "There's so much here now, I never finish polishing before it's time to begin again. Start here, go there, just run upstairs, Marguerite. I understood my work before the Commandant began bringing *camions* full of furniture from I don't know where."

"Yes, I think I must ask him not to bring any more for a while," said Eve thoughtfully. "I shall have to decide at once which pieces to keep on display, so the rest can be moved out of the way. We'll never sell anything like this."

"Move everything again? *Quelle horreur, madame!*"

"Move everything again," said Eve firmly. "But first I must think exactly what I want. No one will be pleased if I decide that armoires sent upstairs must be moved down again."

"No indeed, madame. Bertrand will be very displeased if you ask him to move anything at all, now it is here."

Eve did not reply. Certainly there was going to be trouble with Joubaire, but the day she came was too early to provoke it. Especially as the man could not be safely dismissed.

Nor could she discuss him with Guy. He was sheet-white when he returned from unloading furniture with Joubaire, and stared at her as if nothing she said made sense.

"Don't you think you should report for duty, whether the Conference meets or not?" Eve tried to keep impatience from her voice; surely if he could discuss issues of peace and war sensibly, he ought not to allow himself to be derailed by an hour in Joubaire's company.

"Are you all right, left on your own?"

"Of course, since I'm going to be here every day."

He stared at her as if the whole matter had escaped his memory, stood irresolutely by the door for a few moments, and then went out.

"You're wasting your time on him," said Joubaire.

Eve turned on him furiously. "Time is worse wasted skulking in shadows and eavesdropping on others."

"*Et puis quoi encore?* I find both habits are amusing as well as useful, madame." He came over and stood in front of her, cigarette stuck to his lower lip. "We need to come to an arrangement, you and me. The Commandant is a nothing here, as you have seen. But if you mean to make this place profitable, then you need my help, since our purposes are the same."

Eve stood very still, fingers clenched, not answering.

"Are you listening? Because if you try to play the arrogant lady with me, then there are plenty of answers I can give. Which would you most dislike, madame? For me to tell M. Daunay that your husband has been bothering his precious daughter again, or to remind the Commandant each time I see him of matters he prefers to forget?"

"As you did today," Eve said flatly.

"I only talked of the trenches, madame; surely one would expect two comrades of war to recall the past together? I think the Commandant would be even more upset if I tried to discuss recent events at the Hôtel Daunay with him."

Eve came alert like a rooster challenged in his own barnyard; she must feel her way but would fight bloody-spurred for Guy and Le Trésor if Joubaire forced her into it. "You spoke of an arrangement."

"*Oui, madame. Nous pouvons faire un compromis.* A compromise favorable to us both. I will help in whatever you require to turn this place to profit, for these are matters I do not understand." He flicked his fingers at gilt and polished wood. "Why should men pay more for fragile uselessness than for the well-built cupboards and chairs we make in my home valley? But the rich spend their lives devising expensive ways of doing things a sensible man does for very little, and you could succeed here where I would fail. So I will work to your instruction for a month, two months perhaps; then we shall see."

"See what?"

"Whether you are worth supporting any longer," he replied blandly. "You need not concern yourself about my share; I will talk money with the Commandant. Such is my good fortune that he just cannot help himself being generous where I am concerned."

He left her without waiting for an answer, which was fortunate, since Eve could not think of one immediately. Joubaire was greedy, and his demands would increase if—when—she was successful; he also enjoyed his power over Guy and might destroy him for pure pleasure, or revenge if she angered him. Eve did not doubt that he could do it, when there seemed so little that Sergeant Joubaire did not know.

One day, he certainly would do it, unless she could somehow plan a way out of the trap he had baited.

Eve swore aloud, and experienced startled satisfaction at the sound. At Bois-Chauvert she had learned words she had never heard before, but this was the first time she had used one. She had no choice; no immediate choice, that is. She must sweeten Joubaire with visions of easy francs, wait and watch for an opportunity to claw him off their backs. When the time came, she didn't think conscience would bother her much.

She followed Joubaire out to the back courtyard almost immediately, on the principle that unpleasant medicine is best swallowed quickly. "I have come to accept your terms, on one condition."

"You are not in a good position to make conditions, madame."

"You need me. I could go now, at once, and tell the Commandant I find the work too hard."

"Then he would be forced to work long hours here himself, at night perhaps, after his duty finishes. Alone with me and my inconvenient memory. But tell me your condition, madame."

"That your memory is curbed. When my husband comes here, you speak to him only about our trade."

He spat out a sodden cigarette butt. "It isn't always possible. Perhaps I will try."

"You need to succeed, Sergeant."

"I will try," he repeated. "What do you want me to do first?"

Eve could see that Marguerite was astonished by the willing cooperation she obtained from Joubaire. He was a hard worker when he wished and also possessed enough initiative to interpret her orders without supervision; Eve soon came to see how easy it must have been for Guy to rely on him too much. By the end of that first day, between them they had moved nearly all the ground-floor stock elsewhere, and when Eve locked the outer door, late in the evening, her sense of excitement was stronger than ever. Which was ridiculous when she deliberately forced herself to remember Le Trésor's run-down seediness.

But there was no altering how she felt, because threat and uncertainty simply increased her anticipation. No matter if Joubaire was an unscrupulous bully, and the Rue Daunou unchic; everyone began somewhere, and this was her beginning.

Eve tipped her face to freezing rain as she walked home; already the claustrophobic hazards of living with Guy seemed less oppressive. Last night she had walked these same streets strangled by horror at what he had done and sometimes was; now she was able to bundle shock and panic on one side. A distant corner of her mind protested and was silenced. She had decided to stay with Guy because of his need and not hers; Le Trésor was her just reward.

She was tired, and her new mood banished disgust; indeed she wasn't conscious of thinking anything at all when Guy came in a surprisingly long time after she was in bed. He did not ask about her day; she felt provoked but not too displeased. If he ceased to concern himself with it, then Le Trésor would be all the more hers, very soon, when it ceased to be a junk shop.

CHAPTER 14

After Guy left Le Trésor, he wandered for a long time through traffic-filled streets. Noise battered at him until his body shrank inside his clothes; he found it difficult to breathe. His worst memory from the war was of lying helpless in a shell hole while mud slid to cover him, collapsing walls of it silhouetted against distant sky as his lungs filled and he could not even scream. . . . He spewed into a Paris gutter and people stepped around him, disapproving voices clacking. Paris was tired of veterans who thought service in the trenches excused anything, and a commandant drunk enough to vomit in the Avenue Kléber was altogether too much.

As soon as the spasm passed, he walked away, boot heels rapping like C Company's old *mitrailleuse* you could recognize from all the rest. He needed to find somewhere dark to hide, and instead the sun came out and struck gelignite bursts of light from his eyes. His mind swung uncertainly from where he was to where his terrors lay in wait, vibrating sound, flickering a ripple of distortion through his senses. Joubaire had said something about an attack and how they must advance before the barrage lifted, which meant he must lead his men into their own shells as well as Boche bullets. Everything else somehow he could bear; shells . . . shells and mud where he would drown alone, these were beyond the place where he could go. He did not know it but he was running, fur-coated women staring, horns honking; his heart hammered in ears and throat and empty belly; panic possessed and all but choked him.

A vision of Eve swam sickly behind his eyes, wanting— no, hiding something from him. Wanting, too, perhaps. Eve, in trenches where Bertrand said they must attack into shelling. He screamed at her to go back to Paris, leave him at once and go. Of course she must leave him, leave him, leave him, it was the only way. He fought to make her hear, his mouth gaping, hands on her throat to force her into listening. And leaped straight back into sense with the horror of feeling his hands against her throat.

He was kneeling and icy cold among some bushes; soon he realized he was hiding among the fantastic hutches of the Passy cemetery.

Jésus Christ, ayez pitié de moi.

The patter of childhood contrition in Alsace churches surfaced through the maelstrom in his mind, and he stood carefully, wiping his face with shaking hands. *Jésus Christ, ayez . . . Jésus.* At least no one had seen. Bertrand knew but had not watched; and this time Guy also understood at once that his hands on Eve were a foulness he only dreamed. He stared around him at life-size angels, marble bowers and brown frosted flowers: this was where he belonged.

Winter sun still shone, but he was shudderingly cold in a thin and searching wind, thinking clearly but sluggishly as he began to walk again. He would be all right, very soon.

One street he walked through was unexpectedly full of people, staring and muttering among themselves. There were a great many police and a flow of cars bringing black-suited men to a guarded doorstep. Guy paused and stared at it all abstractedly; he was in the Rue Franklin, so this must be Clemenceau's house; the atmosphere of waiting suggested that the old man was still alive, bullets in his chest or not.

Statesmen and officials were being received; they signed a condolence book and left again, looking annoyed but unconcerned. Clemenceau had made a great many enemies, and possibly there was also the unspoken hope that someone of lesser stature might be easier to deal with: all the same, one couldn't approve of assassins on the principal boulevards of Paris.

Guy joined the official flow, his decorations and prewar style of uniform marking him as someone gendarmes did not stop. The hallway inside was somber and full of hushed voices; Guy signed the book and came out into the street again beside a man he recognized as one of Clemenceau's aides who specialized in German affairs.

Guy introduced himself. "How is M. Clemenceau?"

The other grinned. "Cursing and coughing in a chair."

"You mean he will recover?" demanded Guy incredulously.

"I think so; the Tiger doesn't kill easily. He has already decided that decisions will be easier to manage now the main business of the Conference must be conducted in his bedchamber, which means by the Big Four alone. You're on Marshal Foch's staff, you say?"

"Only for the past ten days." Guy explained how he came from Alsace, and could recognize many of the woods and villages of the border area which were merely pawed-over plans to the delegates.

"Hm. I see." The other man was slight and dark, with a nervous manner which possibly came from serving so notoriously difficult a master as Clemenceau. "I remember seeing you now. Patrice Fabian, of the Prime Minister's private secretariat."

Guy laughed. "I know. Members of M. Clemenceau's private circus are important enough for people like me to discover their names." In fact, he had taken the trouble to distinguish French Foreign Office staff from Clemenceau's "enfants," as he called them, in case he might eventually need to confide in one of them.

Fabian gave him a considering stare. "In that case perhaps we should enjoy a cognac together."

Guy thought carefully before replying. He had no desire to become involved in the factional intrigues of politicians, but had been startled and dismayed by the predatory scope of French military ambitions to dismember Germany, which he had discovered once he took up his new appointment. "I think perhaps we should," he said deliberately, at last.

By tacit consent they chose a small, unfashionable bar, both realizing that this was a meeting they might not want to advertise: stained tables, sawdust underfoot, old men dozing over half-filled glasses which must last the afternoon. "It's the right kind of place to come after wrangling all week in the Quai d'Orsay," observed Fabian. "One understands how less of the world has changed than one thought."

"More than one could possibly imagine has changed, after four such years of war." Guy snatched at his own words as even the name of war shifted noisily in his mind; he must not, could not be upset again now. Alsace, the Rhineland, how Frenchmen and Germans gut-reacted to each other: this was familiar territory contained in the undamaged uplands of his memory. There he might still find something valuable to offer, an uncluttered clarity of thought where others floundered in emotion. He turned to Fabian. "You asked me here for a purpose, I believe."

Fabian raised his eyebrows. "Cognac is as good a purpose as any."

"Very well. If you prefer to probe and hesitate as a politician should, I will say it. You were interested when you heard I was on Marshal Foch's staff, and hoped I might become a useful source of information."

"On the contrary. I was interested when I discovered that one of Foch's officers had waited in line to offer his condolences to M. Clemenceau. Most would drink to his death."

"Believing he is selling France's interests?"

Fabian sniffed at his cognac speculatively. "One never knows what kind of brew one will find in a bar like this. Try it, *mon commandant,* and give me your opinion."

Guy pushed his glass aside. "I prefer a *café filtre.*"

Fabian sipped delicately. "Not bad. Not bad at all. Now, do you know, my father always told me not to trust a man who refused good cognac."

"How fortunate to have a father whose words fit every situation."

Fabian smiled unexpectedly. "I do not believe everything he told me. So let me see if I understand you correctly. You are an officer who feels that his loyalty is given to the Republic, and not necessarily to whatever orders your superiors may decide to give."

Guy considered; it seemed important to get it right, since he could cope with issues but not easily with more strain. "The war is over, so my loyalty is to peace. So is Foch's. We disagree over how it can be achieved: he a marshal of France whom I greatly respect, and I a farmer in uniform. I believe he is wrong and I am right, which certainly is arrogance and may also be criminal foolishness."

"So if you respect Marshal Foch so much, why should you reject his judgment?"

"Until four years ago I was a German citizen; I may still be one until the treaty is signed, for all I know. Foch is a Frenchman who looks at affairs from Paris; he knows we nearly lost the war and are so much weakened by it that certainly we would lose another if it came. So there must never be another. He need not even argue his case; it is self-evident and I have never heard a single military man disagree. So the Army intends to prevent another war, which they believe means advancing our frontier to the Rhine, ruining German industry, breaking the remainder of Germany into puppet states. Now, me, I am French by blood but German by training: I know that France lacks the strength to keep Germany down by force when none of her allies will cooperate in such a task. I also know that if we take the Rhineland and pile revenge on Germany, then one day another war is certain. I have served in the Wehrmacht, and understand how easily patriotic outrage could rebuild it out of ruin."

"Yet don't you think war may also come if we leave a defeated enemy tied down by little more than paper?"

Guy scuffed sawdust absently with his boot. "Yes. Yes, I am afraid so."

Fabian looked startled, as if that was not the answer he expected. *"Mon Dieu,* you are not a cheerful drinking companion."

"I don't drink," replied Guy dryly. Perhaps in the future he might drink cognac in good fellowship again, if the craving for oblivion ever passed.

"And I am wasting my time if you believe we haven't won a victory, after all."

"I believed it three months ago, when the Boches marched out of France. Ten days in attendance on the Conference has changed my point of view. But yes, monseiur, of course there is still a little time for hope. Yet if we are to hope at all we must not try, and fail, to rule ten million Germans in the Rhineland while leaving the rest in anarchy. Which is what Foch plans to do," he added. "He and our Army of occupation in the German Rhineland. If the Peace Conference refuses to give us a Rhine frontier—and they will—then Foch plans to start an armed insurrection there, and set up a French-controlled puppet government under the pretext of restoring order. Foch believes that a French-controlled state on the Rhine is the only way to give France security, and I am telling you all this because I believe that, on the contrary, it guarantees disaster. Our allies would never trust us again, and the Germans never be satisfied until they had thrown us out. Which means war again, a war that France would lose. So that is the reason I am here and willing to turn informer on Marshal Foch, a great Frenchman who deserves the respect of his countrymen."

"*Eh bien*," said Fabian meditatively, openly studying his companion. Soldiers who betrayed their superiors were always dangerous agents to handle, and amateurs who claimed to know better than the experts were lethal to a politician; this man was both. He also looked even more short-fused than most veterans of the trenches.

He didn't drink, either. Ah, Papa, thought Fabian, you were right; a Frenchman who refuses good cognac is a fool, and this one half a Boche as well. On the other hand, the French Government urgently needed to discover precisely how its Army proposed to achieve its ambitions in Germany, when the settlement which French negotiators must sign was certain to be very different. Clemenceau agreed with the Army's analysis of France's future weakness and was quite as determined as Foch to make her unassailable; he also believed he would fail if the Army destroyed American sympathy by attempting to seize the German Rhineland by force.

"*Eh bien*," said Fabian again, but definitely this time. Any information was better than none. "You are in a position to hear important developments?"

"No, but I hear them just the same. Foch trusts his staff and they trust each other." Guy could not keep bitterness from his voice. A grubby bar seemed the proper setting for what they both knew he was offering to do.

"We have not found that they are loose-mouthed with outsiders."

Guy shrugged. "No."

"But you are willing to keep us informed of what you hear?"

"Yes."

Fabian felt exasperated; he wasn't used to simple answers to complex questions, and loyalty was the most complex question of all. "You understand—"

"For God's sake, of course I understand. More than you do. It wouldn't matter that I was only squealing to our own government; if I were discovered, then the Army would court-martial me on whatever charges they thought would stick. And most of France is closer to Foch's thinking than to Clemenceau's at the moment, for all that the Americans consider him extreme."

Fabian dismissed America with a flick of his fingers. "Americans are children blundering over idealistic words dreamed up by sentimental journalists."

Guy had been disliking the grimy dealings thrust on him, but felt relaxed and certain in his mind. Now tension returned, because Rick Dwyer was the journalist most associated with the clamor growing in America in favor of more generous treatment for Germany. Dwyer, his enemy, who would take Eve from him if he could. To whom, perhaps, he should encourage her to go. "We need them, as well as their ideals," he said, voice jumping out of key. "I should tell you that my wife is American; until a few days ago she worked for the United States delegation."

Fabian clicked his tongue in dismay. "Really, Commandant Saulx—"

"Yes, I know. God help France when its agents must be Boche-tainted and married to Americans. Don't be a fool; you've nothing to lose." Prim, fussy little man with a clockwork brain, born bureaucrat. Give me Foch, every time.

Without waiting for Fabian to stop gobbling, he began to outline exactly the stage which army thinking had reached. The Allies already had a token occupation force stationed in western Germany, the French military headquarters established in Mainz. From there, the French High Command had already begun secretly releasing weapons to almost any German grouping with a grievance, with the sole proviso that they would shout for an independent Rhineland; at the same time, malcontents were encouraged to infiltrate more-reputable political organizations already demanding autonomy. "They will be ready in about six weeks," he added. "Lawlessness is growing anyway, and the Germans are in a mood to attack anything they see. Rioting and murder have become a pastime."

"Ready," repeated Fabian. "For what, exactly?"

"An armed coup under French tutelage. The German groups will be allowed to take whatever they fancy, providing France is asked to act as protecting power. So we gain the German Rhineland and armed scum are loosed over the countryside."

"That would not be France's fault. Germany has a surplus of armed scum at the moment."

"Yes, indeed. Which is another reason for not bailing any more out of the sewers."

Fabian smiled, very easily able to view armed gangs in Germany with equanimity. French policy was another matter. "So our commander in Mainz is part of the conspiracy?"

"General Mangin? Certainly. It is not a conspiracy, you must understand. It is a strategy which happens to require secrecy for its proper execution, like an offensive of the war. Our Army is still fighting and you are not, that's all."

"God damn all soldiers," said Fabian gloomily.

Guy stood. "Wishes, like policies, change with the season. Between now and Verdun, for instance. I'm sure you will find a way to contact me whenever I may be of further use." He pushed his way past crowded tables to the steep stairway which led up to the street.

Outside, the air was raw, sun vanished, fog settling over the roofs of Paris; two poilus saluted smartly, staring openly at Guy's medals and *brisques*, a hollow man whose façade deserved admiration. A man in whose presence generals were indiscreet, because he was part of a world they thought they understood.

A man who saw oblique meanings set at exploded angles, since even the thought of Rick Dwyer was enough to suck him away from cool consideration of high politics and back to the place where he must fight himself again.

CHAPTER 15

Eve decided that she must refuse to be rushed. In Paris, above all, originality was essential to success. She had some notion of what needed to be done if Le Trésor was ever to become a place the *beau monde* visited, but too little experience to put her ideas together in a hurry.

She spent most of the week following that first day studying the window displays of the great fashion houses. There were M. Poiret in the Rue de la Paix, Worth and a dozen others in the Faubourg St. Honoré, iconoclastic Gabrielle Chanel in the Rue Cambon.

Eve was enchanted by Chanel. She pretended to be a customer and went inside; the sparse, soft lines of Chanel's designs made every other style seem out of date, her restrained colors and new jersey cloth filling Eve with simple feminine longing to buy, and buy, and buy. She walked back to the Rue de la Paix afterward and mingled with the *midinettes* pouring out of Poiret's establishment: everything there was infinitely grander, the location more fashionable, rich colors imparting a sense of almost oriental luxury. Chanel and Poiret were utterly distinctive, and both enticed by sheer originality.

Eve might prefer Chanel, but that did not alter the fact that Poiret, too, had clawed his way out of nowhere into a position of great power and wealth, while Chanel had been an Auvergnat peasant who began her career as a prostitute.

Eve smiled to herself: well, she had been a Maine farm girl, and in New Moose she would have been damned from the moment she slept unwed with Guy.

She gave only cursory attention to *bijouteries* and antique shops: she possessed sufficient instinctive taste to realize that Guy had obtained a few splendid pieces, and a great deal more which was of good enough quality to attract buyers. But if she simply put them in the window and waited for offers, other dealers would snap them up and Le Trésor would be no better known than before. The well-known *antiquaires* might have fashionable addresses, but none showed a fraction of the flair which was commonplace among couturiers, so Eve continued to haunt the world of fashion, learning about presentation. She could hire advice on prices when she wanted it.

By the end of the week, Joubaire and Marguerite had cleared the ground floor at Le Trésor, the walls were painted, a fine carpet laid on the floor. Eve returned from her latest expedition and stood staring at Le Trésor's double frontage in dissatisfaction. Thirty yards away was the corner of the Rue de la Paix; once let gossip begin, and Le Tout-Paris would not find this too far to come to look at novelty. Until it did, the Rue Daunou was no more than a shortcut people used on their way to work.

Eve had considered and discarded a dozen ideas, tentatively tried new decor as stark as Chanel's designs; she had not liked it and instead attempted a setting of richly draped cloth, a single good piece on display.

Clerks stopped and admired it, a few *midinettes* and women on their way to market, but none of them could afford a single piece she stocked, and Le Tout-Paris did not come.

It was infuriating.

Eve sighed and crossed the street, then turned when she heard someone call her name.

"Eve! You haven't called at the Astoria for ages, so I thought we'd take our afternoon walk this way. Father has told me to be sure Mother gets out each day." Sarah Wyville's tone was ungracious, as if she resented being ordered to walk with her mother, but she looked around her curiously. "You said this place was outlandish, and I see you were quite right. Does every house in this street cook cabbage all day?"

"Only at mealtimes," said Eve, nettled. "Most Paris streets smell of cooking."

"Not the good ones."

"Only because they are wide enough to fill up with dung and exhaust fumes instead. How do you do, Lady Wyville. Would you like to come in and look around?"

"Yes, rather," said Sarah. "I've always thought keeping a shop would be fun."

Lady Wyville murmured something ineffectual and succumbed to her daughter's stronger will, as usual. She had once looked softly pretty, but that was before her only son was killed. More than three months had passed since then, and she had not even begun to recover from the blow; the fact that it happened on the last day of the war, when she believed Charlie safe, only made matters worse. She was dowdily and carelessly dressed; wisps of hair escaped from under her prewar hat, and she was hung with a great many chains and brooches, as if once she began fastening catches she forgot to stop.

Eve pitied her but felt uncomfortable in her presence; nor was she an enlivening companion for a daughter like Sarah, when the amusements of Paris flowed past on every side.

"Why, it's nearly empty!" exclaimed Sarah as soon as she went ahead of Eve through the door.

"It doesn't smell of cabbage, though," retorted Eve. "I've bought bowls and bowls of potpourri."

"Yes, but— Eve, it looks like a barn, and is nearly as cold! Where we live, in Norfolk, we're used to freezing-cold barns, but I certainly wouldn't want to shop in one. Stoneham has ninety-eight rooms and the wind comes straight off the Arctic."

"It is cold," admitted Eve. "There's a fire in the back, but the chimney here was right by the window and the stove looked quite dreadful. I've a feeling that customers won't linger over their purchases until the spring." Two months at most, Joubaire had given her; with an effort, she thrust worry back into its cage.

"I think it looks very effective with just one or two pieces to admire," said Lady Wyville. "The bureau over there is very similar to the one Charlie had in his room."

"Oh, Mother!" said Sarah impatiently. "It isn't in the least like, and even if it were, you'd be better not thinking about it."

"I can't help thinking about it." Tears slipped down worn furrows in her cheeks.

Eve brought over a chair. "If you would like to sit down for a few minutes I'll go and fix coffee."

She looked around for a table; Sarah was quite right: there ought to be some kind of fire. As she had discovered, cold made everything more unbearable. And fully fledged, the plan of what she would do came into her mind, just like that. As if ideas, longings, and half-grasped needs had all jostled together long enough, and synthesis took place.

As she bent to pick up a side table, images raced past and she saw exactly what she could do to make Le Trésor talked about.

It ought to work. She would damned well see it did work.

"What is it, Eve?" demanded Sarah. "Have you got lumbago or something? We had a gardener once who used to get stuck in a quite dreadful way; only, after a while he kept a pine knot in his hip pocket and swore he never had another twinge."

Eve laughed, and wanted to hug the silly child. She wanted to dance around Le Trésor and drink champagne out of a bucket. "No, I've just solved a problem that's been bothering me."

"Tell!" demanded Sarah.

So Eve explained about her desire to make Le Trésor chic, when she did not herself possess an *entrée* to the fashionable world of Paris.

"You said once that your husband's family owned a house on the Champs-Élysées." Sarah possessed a devastatingly accurate memory.

"We can't ask them to help," said Eve shortly. She liked Gabrielle and Pierre but had no intention of ever going near the Hôtel Daunay again. "It doesn't matter, because I've just decided what we need. A real, live stage set. This double window is exactly right. I'll restore the fireplace but with an open hearth, and when you look in from the street it will seem as if you're in a salon of Louis XIV or Napoleon, or whatever we decide for the goods we have. If it's Napoleon, then I'll have a full-dress hussar sprawled by the fire—"

"And the customers become part of the set and all the furniture's for sale!" Sarah went into a peal of laughter. "I'll buy the hussar!"

"You're welcome, since I expect I'll have to dress up Joubaire," Eve said acidly. "He won't enjoy being a powdered footman stoking the fire, either."

"When you've sold everything from Louis XIV, then you can have a different set and I'll dress up as Mme. de Pompadour."

"So long as you don't mind goose pimples in *décolleté*. All the same—"

"Eve, you're looking lumbagoish again. What have you thought of this time?"

"I was thinking we could also be up to date. Have the scene in Clemenceau's bedroom when the Council of Four meet there, with their papers all over the counterpane and the old man wheezing in a chair. Someone in Paris must make wax masks."

Sarah clapped her hands. "I'll ask Father what the room looks like, and the Salle d'Horloge, too, at the Quai d'Orsay."

"I am sure your father would never do anything *commercial*, Sarah dear. The Foreign Office would be dreadfully shocked." Lady Wyville spoke with unusual firmness.

"Mr. Balfour would never find energy to be shocked at anything," replied Sarah airily, "and the rest are too stuffy to bother about. Of course I wouldn't expect Father to do anything unscrupulous precisely, but there isn't the least reason why I shouldn't ask him what a room looks like."

"Of course you mustn't do anything improper," said Eve hastily, thinking that in fact Sarah would be a useful ally. "You could tell me how Stoneham is furnished; then we'll have an English week."

"I'll borrow one of Father's tweed suits and steal a club fender from the Embassy," promised Sarah. "But I don't expect you have a single piece here that my ancestors would have allowed into Stoneham. This French stuff is all marble and brass rails and horrid spindly legs picked out in gilt. They liked oak the hounds could chew."

"Our dogs never chew the furniture," expostulated Lady Wyville, looking bewildered.

"You know what I mean. Like Father suffering through course after course of French sauces and longing for mutton he can get his teeth into."

"I shall have to ask Lady Wyville to spare you to advise me on diplomacy and English furniture." Eve was impatient for them to go now, not wanting to wait another instant before starting on the pile of things she must do.

"I'm good at advice," said Sarah complacently. "I don't think you should accept what I say about diplomacy, though. We are giving a ball at the Astoria the day after tomorrow; why don't you and your husband come? I'm terribly curious to meet him."

"Because we aren't invited, nor are we diplomats," Eve said, exasperated.

"I'll have an invitation sent round. It'll be business, Eve! You can spend your time dropping hints about strange doings in the Rue Daunou. Between us, we could have everyone wondering whether you're starting a drug ring or just a gambling hell here! Do let us, Eve. It would be a splendid joke."

Anything Sarah said would be good publicity, Eve realized, stifling instinctive refusal. The diplomats would soon leave Paris, but a ball at the Astoria would also be attended by influential Frenchmen. Thank God none of the Daunay family was remotely connected with the Peace Conference.

So she accepted, secretly wondering whether she would ever persuade Guy to go and what she could wear if she did. Sarah was as good as her word, and a British dispatch rider came with their invitation just before Eve closed up for the night; she guessed that Sir Maurice's private secretary was well used to capitulating over unimportant matters where Miss Wyville was concerned.

Guy listened without interrupting when she poured out a jumble about fireplaces and footmen, stage sets and period furniture.

"You will need more money," he said when she was done.

"I know. We shall have to sell a few more pieces through the dealers, but we can't help it. This will succeed; it must. I'm sure of it, aren't you?"

"It depends. Such an idea needs a great deal of professionalism if it is not to become some kind of third-rate charade. Paris is very cruel toward anything or anyone it decides to ridicule; and taste here has long been sated by only the very best. I would not like you to be hurt."

"Chanel succeeded."

"She had an extremely rich protector during several vital years." His tone was dry. "It needs more than courage and talent to succeed."

"You aren't going to refuse to let me sell what I must, just once more through a dealer, are you?" She couldn't believe it; he couldn't deny her now. It was bitter to realize that although it was almost entirely her work at Le Trésor nowadays, he still possessed the power to stop her with a word.

"I was in the Rue Daunou for a while this morning," he said after a pause. "You were out, but Bertrand told me you had helped him to carry a great deal of furniture upstairs."

"Why not? He has been more civil, precisely because I work with him. I think he appreciates it."

His mouth tightened. "I wouldn't bank on it if I were you; Bertrand always lives through a honeymoon period with his victims. It merely makes what follows more unpleasant. But that wasn't what I meant. You ought not to be carrying furniture in your condition."

"My condition?" she said blankly.

"You are expecting a child in six months. Or had you forgotten, among the excitements of Le Trésor?"

Eve flushed. "I wasn't raised in a Paris salon. I'm used to hard work."

He frowned at the floor between his feet, hands clasped, elbows on his knees. Candlelight brought false color but exaggerated the lines of his face; deep-gouged sockets hiding eyes which recently had become bloodshot with continuing lack of sleep; the look of them in daylight often gave Eve a quiver of unease. "I am afraid I shall have to forbid you to go to Le Trésor unless you promise to take proper care of yourself. Rest sometimes, and work shorter hours."

"Perhaps I could, if you would come more often," she retorted.

"I can't. I have been kept very busy these past few days."

He would not look at her, and for the first time Eve felt contempt instead of pity. He detested being with Joubaire, and now that she was at Le Trésor, used her to hide behind. "So if you can't come, I must stay. Twelve hours a day if necessary, unless you manage to rearrange your duties." Some demon made her add: "I could probably arrange for Joubaire to be elsewhere if you warned me you were coming."

She watched his knuckles whiten. "I am not afraid of Joubaire."

"I didn't say—"

"It was what you thought. I try to face some issues honestly. I am very busy at the moment, but if I can last, I'll cure myself in time."

Eve knelt impulsively in front of him and covered his hands with hers. "I'm sorry. That was a horrible thing for me to say. Are you sure— I've meant to ask, but have you ever seen a doctor? Surely if you did, at least they'd see you were relieved from duty?"

"They know so little. A few more wars like this one and they'll have books and words which deal with the wreckage tidily, except that the human race will be extinct by then."

"But couldn't they help, even a little?"

He drew his hands from under hers and thrust them in his pockets. "No. They click their tongues and force drugs down your gullet. Study you like a rat under dissection. I must fight this my way; I need more time, that's all. It's just that Joubaire has a knack of defeating me very easily, but . . . of course that's part of it. I'll come with you to Le Trésor tomorrow if you don't mind being early. I must be at a meeting by nine." He was deeply involved with Fabian now, and also expected soon to be sent by Foch to Germany.

"So you will let me go ahead with my idea, and raise the money it'll need?"

He went over to the window, forehead against cold glass. "It's snowing."

Frustration burned like bile in Eve's throat. "For heaven's sake, Guy! Can I, or can't I?"

"I don't remember what you wanted to do," he said desperately. "Don't you see, you're going to have to tell me everything again. Stay there, I don't want you near me."

So she told him, including, after a brief tussel with her conscience, the promise he had wanted her to make.

"Thank you." His voice shook, and then steadied. "Comfort yourself that I should have made the same condition again, whether you reminded me of it or not. Tell me, Eve. Do you want this child?"

She was taken aback. "Naturally."

"I've wondered. Without it you would be free, still working at the Crillon among Americans. It wouldn't be surprising if you felt resentful. When you told me, I felt— I knew this marriage would be a disaster. But the child means a good deal to me; strange, isn't it? I've never lived in a family and hated most of my relations, but I suppose . . . most men . . . like to leave something to mark their lives, and there won't be much else to mark mine." He hesitated and then added awkwardly, "I don't think you need fear a tainted heritage; I— I was. . . . It was the war which made me what I am, and let us pray that our child will live its life in peace."

Eve flinched as if he had struck her, then sat paralyzed by shock. Horror and shame engulfed her, for over this past week at Le Trésor she had been waiting for the right opportunity to tell him she had lied. She was not pregnant and several times had needed to plead exhaustion to keep him away from her. She had become determined to marry Guy for reasons often scuffled through since; some she still considered justified, others less so as she understood herself better. In the end, sheer obstinacy had made her force him into it, using pregnancy as her weapon, and during those first weeks of near contentment her deception seemed triumphantly justified. A fraction of war's sufferings was eased because she'd had the courage to risk herself when he desperately needed help.

Eve had been certain that Guy's driving passions would soon make her word good; when they did not, she experienced faint relief, as if she expected his child to have shell shock too. Until now, it had never occurred to her that she ought to feel ashamed: Guy loved her and she had lied for his sake and to her own great cost.

In the short time since she came to Paris, Eve seemed to have lived through a wilderness of emotion. She had lost a great many illusions, and simple reactions like pity were being tempered into a more generous understanding: she was also tougher and more honest with herself. After that first, dreadful night, Guy had sometimes given her a great deal of pleasure, and she realized now that she had also married him because she no longer wanted to live alone in Paris.

His halting confession tore away another layer of self-deception: what she had done was bunglingly cruel, contemptibly naïve.

Unforgivable.

"I meant what I said once before. After it is born, if you wish . . . if you are able to take it to America I won't stop you." Guy was still over by the window, his back turned to the room.

Eve moistened her lips. "Guy—"

He shook his head, and bumped it painfully on glass, as if he scarcely knew where he was. "Of course we'll raise the money you need for Le Trésor, but you will take care, won't you? For your sake as well as mine; but I didn't want you to think me indifferent, when it's the reverse, in fact."

In a daze, she stood and went over to him. "Of course I'll take care, but—"

He turned. "Promise?"

"I promise," she said helplessly.

His lips quirked into a shadow of a smile. "I'll hold you to it, and for my part shall try to find somewhere better than this for us to live."

She reached out and touched him, felt braced muscles and the stark outlines of his body. She kissed him fiercely then, curving herself into the line of thigh and belly, pulling his head down to hers, demanding as she had never demanded from him before.

He seemed oddly hesitant, although whatever had failed him in the past, his physical demands seemed only to intensify. He responded eventually, almost with surprise, as if ardor from her took him off balance; then Eve felt the almost electrical crackle of desire which could convulse and thrust him beyond control. Before, she had wanted or not wanted this, responded or just suffered him; tonight she teased and kindled and drove him, because now she was utterly determined to have his child.

She also softened to him, and they laughed together as they had not since the day Eulalie came. Eve slept a little afterward, but woke when he would have left her as he always did, drowsily twining herself to keep and rouse him once again.

"Eve," he said, and laughed. "The Garden of Eden in the Rue Férou."

"Why not. Why not indeed, my love?" The endearments of drawn-out passion were something else which came easily that night, and fierce urgency each time she thought of the child she simply had to have to make confession bearable. Thought also of him, sensuously delighted and oddly contented by him, alone together on a board-hard bed. The shackles of guilt and dread and inadequacy snapped and forgotten, just this once.

He slept in her arms eventually instead of on the floor, muttering and thrashing sometimes but too exhausted to wake. Eve lay and could not sleep again, her mind racing and calculating: surely she must have conceived tonight. Surely this time when they'd both been happy would bring a child, when other, longer nights she'd hated, had failed to do so.

Illusion, indeed. Eve grimaced to herself in darkness; the God of New Moose punished sin and did not consider sex enjoyable. When Guy woke she must encourage him to want her again; and each night until her month ended. She would have to tell him then.

He stirred as Paris wakened into noisy activity and then lay quietly, though nightmares usually racked him into instant, sweating wakefulness. "Miracle worker," he said smiling.

"So now we know how to help you sleep all night." Eve felt miserably tired; it needed a real effort of will to move against him, to hold her face to his and set out again on the repetitious path of stimulating passion. There's nothing quite so boring, she thought crossly; guilt had returned and changed her mood of the night completely.

"We know how, and perhaps eventually you will always feel as you did by chance last night." He kissed her tenderly. "Sleep now, my love. You're tired."

Dismay struck at her again. It was scarcely surprising if he misinterpreted her reasons for responding so passionately to him; he had accepted that she did not love him; now he was allowing himself to hope.

She felt his instinctive reaction to her touch; then he caught her hands and thrust them into a trap of bone, physically forcing relaxation. "No, Eve. You're taking care, remember? Sleep now, and feel me nagging you whenever you're tempted to forget your promise."

She was too tired to argue, and probably it didn't matter anyway. The streets of Paris were full of children, conception commonplace, especially for women who possessed demanding husbands.

Eve remembered Sarah's invitation as Guy walked with her to Le Trésor. "Do you like dancing, Guy?"

"I haven't had much practice. In Alsace we didn't go where German officers might be present, and on leave during the war my leg was too sore to enjoy more than a turn around the floor."

"How is it now?"

"Do we have an invitation somewhere? As you know, it is sound for normal use."

Eve brought the invitation out of her bag. "Are you allowed to accept British hospitality? Unless the atmosphere at the Conference has improved since I left, you can't find a Yankee wife an advantage, and your bosses might get suspicious if you seemed friendly with the British, too."

"I shouldn't care if they did, when the British fought four years as our allies. You'd enjoy going?" The atmosphere at the Conference had not improved, and his own double-dealing made it no easier to endure.

"It would be good for Le Trésor. I don't know any of the people I ought to know, and—"

"That wasn't what I asked you. Would you *enjoy* going?"

Eve realized that she would very much like to go. Apart from the Opéra ball, she had been to a few enlisted men's dances at Bois-Chauvert and one illicit hoedown in New Moose. She was twenty-one, and recently had forgotten what it meant to be young. She nodded.

Guy kissed her fingers. "Then I shall look forward to escorting you." He glanced at the pasteboard. "Two days away. You'd better tell Chanel she must hurry."

"Chanel?" said Eve, bewildered.

"We can't have a Parisienne outshone by the English. Sell something extra and we'll worry about it another time. It'll be worth every sou."

Eve felt she made a wretched muddle of thanking him, embarrassment and shame warring with delight at the thought of wearing one of Elle Chanel's spanking-new creations.

CHAPTER 16

The ball at the Astoria was far more decorous than the one at the Opéra had been. Respectable embassies do not expect their diplomats to indulge in unseemly frolics, and the British were nothing if not respectable. Their Prime Minister, Lloyd George, who led their delegation, might be widely regarded as having the morals of a tomcat, but that made no difference to manners or etiquette, or indeed to Lloyd George himself. He put in an appearance, benignly at ease, and chatted without the least pomposity and entire propriety with anyone who caught his eye.

"He's a brilliant man," observed Guy. "He has an almost occult sense of what others will say before they've thought it for themselves, and a crook's insight into which concession will make an opponent bend easiest. If you could hire him to dress your window at Le Trésor you'd have the sensation of the season, since he also possesses the theatrical imagination of a Diaghilev. When the Conference was discussing the future of the Turkish Empire, he introduced a troupe of Arab chiefs complete with oriental headdress and British Army uniform to help make his point. Discussions are never dull when he is around."

"I've seen two of the three now, Wilson and Lloyd George." Eve gazed about the splendid ballroom with fascination. "I shall have to add Clemenceau to my score, and the Germans, too, eventually. Even though I'm not inside the Conference any more, it still sometimes seems extraordinary for me to be here when these few old men are fixing the future of the world."

Guy slid his arm around her waist. "Will you dance meanwhile, madame? This sounds about my speed; I'm not so good at *le turkey-trotting*."

The foot-tapping, exultant beat of ragtime swept the room into a kaleidoscope of stiff shirtfronts and shafted color: there was also the relief of very few uniforms, since the armistice gave the British sufficient excuse to return to their habit of wearing civilian clothes whenever possible, to the undisguised astonishment of their Continental counterparts. The evening had begun with prewar waltzes and polkas, but nostalgia shriveled as the pace grew hotter, the dancers turning capricious beat into a hilarious shuttle of movement, until one by one the couples admitted defeat before the triumphant blare of saxophones.

Eve threw back her head, laughing. "You said you weren't a good dancer."

"I'm not, but I can dance with you." He slanted her through the remaining couples until they reached the edge of the room. "I know when I'm beaten, though."

Eve had been fortunate in finding one of Chanel's dresses which had been designed for a client whose husband had returned it with the comment that he preferred his women feminine. Certainly its lines were uncompromising, waist and bust almost nonexistent, nor was ivory satin with a tracery of black embroidery really Eve's color, but no one in the Astoria ballroom would have agreed that on her it was unfeminine. Her appearance both shocked and delighted Eve when she first saw herself in the Astoria mirrors. Guy's shaving mirror had offered only unsatisfactory glimpses, and they had both felt nervous of arriving at the Astoria when Eve was forced to wear her Red Cross cape over such splendor.

Once she was rid of the cape, though, her morale swooped upward when Sarah exclaimed in frank jealousy at her appearance, and older women exchanged speaking glances over the daring V of her neckline, when they were still swathed to the ears in net.

"Everything is so loose and unfussed!" said Sarah, fingering soft folds. "I shall be at Chanel's in the morning, you may be sure. I've never heard of her before and was quite thinking Paris fashion not half it was puffed up to be. Especially when Father sent back cloth thigh boots and a stick I fancied for walking in the Bois."

"Perhaps he was right," said Eve, thinking of Eulalie.

"Oh, yes, but that doesn't make any difference! Especially when skirts are shorter every day."

"In New York they were still on the ground when I left. The established couturiers say it's only a fad left over from the war, but I think women enjoy walking in comfort too much to change now."

Sarah wrinkled her nose. "No more sodden skirts round your ankles each time it rains."

"And just think of the splendid sights added to the Paris streets," Guy said straight-faced. Sarah's naturalness helped him to relax, although Eve sensed how he needed to brace himself against the din in the ballroom.

"Why don't we go and find some refreshment?" Eve said now, as the band launched itself into the bunny hug. Lorgnettes snapped shut and there was a general exodus of the older guests.

Guy grinned. "As members of the older generation? You just give them a few more months to forget their gallant boys in the trenches, and the whole pack of over-forties will disown the postwar world we and our like will build."

"No going back?"

"No going back," he agreed. "Everything's changed too much, including *le bunny-huggant* in place of the waltz. I also think I can support a few more minutes in here so long as I have your company."

Indeed, concentrating on unfamiliar steps and consciously proud to claim Eve as his wife, Guy seemed completely the person Eve had only occasionally found in him before. As she was another person too, her hair pinned high and ivory satin sheathing her body, when her last dress made for company was home-tucked gingham from the store.

"I must have my hair shingled," she said aloud.

"*Pardon, chérie?*"

"I said how marvelous this all was. Guy, have you met Lloyd George?"

"Only as one of many in an anteroom. Why?"

"He keeps looking at you; then, a moment ago, he turned to ask Sir Maurice something and they both looked across. As if he asked to be told about you."

She saw the muscles of Guy's face contract, as though reality switched into waiting circuits, and immediately regretted words uttered with only casual interest. "Guy, let's rest awhile."

He shook his head, frowning, but the dance was becoming more frantic, and once concentration slipped his leg began to give trouble. Enjoyment was subtly soured as he refused to admit defeat and Eve became annoyed and then embarrassed by his stubbornness. "Guy, this isn't a competition, and I'd like some lemonade."

"As you wish." He led her off the floor.

Eve glanced across to where Lloyd George was talking to some dignitaries; his regard was casual, but his eyes had followed them.

"Eve, it's good to see you out on the town, and in a dress which makes everyone else look homely." Rick Dwyer was standing by the door.

Eve laughed. "It's good to see you, too. Have you met my husband? Guy, this is Rick Dwyer, Paris correspondent of the Washington *Times*."

"Only by repute," drawled Rick. He did not offer to shake hands. "I sure had me some surprises when I did an investigation on war profiteers of the Champs-Élysées, and your family was among the candidates."

"I expect you would," replied Guy evenly. "As no doubt I should too, if I decided to investigate the new rich of Washington."

"Oh, sure. Then you'd give the same advice to a girl living a long way from home as I gave Eve. Don't touch 'em, or they'll drop you in the dirt too."

"Eve asked you for advice?"

"Rick comes from New Moose, the same as I do, but I didn't ask his advice," interrupted Eve. "You remember, we left a note for him at the Crillon when I first came to Paris." She had been so unself-consciously delighted to see Rick again, she had forgotten that he had made it his business to discover the damaging gossip about Anselme Saulx's death.

"I just gave it, and then put in hand some investigations of my own." Rick watched Guy derisively. "If I'd been around when she married you, I'd have forbidden the banns, or whatever it is they do in France."

Guy tensed, ease of a few minutes before banished. "What precisely did you investigate?"

"Worries you, doesn't it? You don't deserve your luck, but by the time everything was checked out, Eve had married you. But watch your step; she's less alone in Paris than you thought."

Guy turned on his heel and walked away, leaving Eve with Rick. He smiled, eyes caressing. "Dance with me?"

She nodded, throat shut on words. Anything to be away from the ripple of attention which antagonism had stirred around them, but she had not expected to be held so intimately, nor that she would be forced to listen to the kind of endearments better left unsaid. "Rick, stop it! Either let me go or shut up."

He slid his hand down the length of her back. "It must be a relief to talk straight American for a change."

She laughed reluctantly. "Sometimes. I meant what I said, though. For heaven's sake, whatever possessed you to speak like that to Guy?"

"Why the hell shouldn't I?"

"Why the hell should you, when you've hardly met?" She knew why, and was also afraid of what more Rick might have discovered. Each time she and Guy achieved a few hours of peace, the first touch shattered it again. Both carried too great a burden of guilt, suspicion and fear for it ever to be forgotten for long.

"Because I wanted to. I'd watched the bastard flaunting you as his possession and enjoying every minute of it; then I thought of the file on him and his fine family locked in my safe and wanted to punch his face."

"We were happy until you came."

"Yeah? You sure didn't look happy when you came off the floor. You could be enjoying yourself now, though."

"I could, but I'm not."

"You're lying, sweetheart." She felt his lips touch her hair. He was taller and broader than Guy and she could feel the self-confident length of his body against hers. Insensibly, antagonism lessened; she was so very tired of strain and complication.

Eve sighed. "Just sometimes I wish I were back in Bois-Chauvert, where the greatest worry was a comforts fund which wouldn't balance."

"Well, you aren't, so enjoy what you've got. Which, at the moment, is me."

Rick was an easy companion, untiring on the dance floor, attentive, and cynically armored against the world's foibles, so Eve was able to say whatever came into her head. She did not notice how great a relief this was, but postponed from minute to minute the urgent need to go in search of Guy.

Then she saw him, talking to Sir Maurice Wyville.

Rick followed her gaze. "Does that surprise you?"

"Yes," confessed Eve. "Guy met Sarah earlier, but told me before we came that he had only encountered Sir Maurice in passing."

Rick reflected that Saulx was probably a liar as well as all the rest; all the same, it was odd. Worth investigating, in fact. If Eve had not denied it, he would have assumed Saulx was acquainted with the Wyvilles through Eve's friendship with Sarah, as others in the room no doubt would think, if they thought at all. If he wasn't, then Wyville was after something; the British were crafty bastards, and Rick was already interested in French plottings at the Peace Conference. Tomorrow he would add Commandant Saulx to his list of men worth watching there, and with the extra, intimate satisfaction of a marksman who hates the quarry he is paid to kill. "Have you mentioned to your husband that his old German buddy might be coming to Paris?"

"No. I meant what I said; I won't have you bothering him."

"Okay," Rick said peaccably. "It's a stupid thing to talk about with you in your Chanel gown, anyway." He kissed her fingers, and across the ballroom Eve saw Guy turn and look at them, before pushing his way out through the crowd.

"That's what I call real tactful," said Rick. "Let's go too, Eve."

Her heart bumped, and suddenly she could not lift her eyes above the studs in his shirt. "He'll be waiting for me outside."

"Want to bet? We'll dance again, though, before we fix the stakes."

They danced in silence; then a British boy claimed the next dance and Eve went with him thankfully, wanting time, answering him so much at random that his opinion of American women suffered a severe setback.

"This one is mine." Rick was there again, taking her hands as if all questions between them were settled. He brought his mouth close to her ear. "Don't you want to know the stake in our bet?"

Eve shook her head, pulse beating in her throat.

"I'll tell you anyway. If your precious husband has gone, I take his place as escort. If he hasn't, the choice is yours."

When they left the ballroom, there was no sign of Guy.

"That would seem to settle it, honey." Subtly, Rick's voice had altered; his assertive mouth softened.

"I'll get my cloak." Her lips felt stiff, Rick's rangy, carelessly dressed body belonging to a stranger.

The suite of bedrooms where maids guarded the ladies' wraps was arctically cold, but Eve welcomed it. She would have liked to walk for miles in the rain and numb sensations which Rick's frank sensuality had kindled while they danced.

Instead, she sat on one of the beds piled with sable and mink, and tried to force thought past the fact that Guy had simply gone off and left her. Why shouldn't she go too, with Rick, when this was Paris, after all? Why not, when she was twenty-one and chained to a man whom no mere impulse would have made her marry if Eulalie had only come with her accusations a short time earlier. A man who deserved unfaithfulness, when he ran at the first, almost casual threat Rick offered.

The snake of a deeper need slid into her mind. She had so little time, and if she could not get a child by Guy, then Rick's uncomplicated lusts ought to give her what she wanted. She thought feverishly and incoherently about dates: Guy was clear about some things and could not be fooled over two months' discrepancy. She would have to admit she lied to him, but say. . . . She knew then that she could not do it. Whatever imperatives trapped her, she could not add this treachery to the rest.

And with decision taken, she was instantly unable to imagine the cravings which had drawn her to Rick.

Eve stood and hooked her cloak at the throat, staring at herself in the mirror. She still looked, and was, a country girl among the exquisites, she decided. Chanel and ivory satin were all very well, but beneath it remained the uncompromising absolutes of her raising. Fresh, freckled skin and well-brushed hair; determination implicit in straight lines of mouth and jaw. She shrugged and turned away: she'd been a fool to think herself Parisian when all she did was live here.

But when she saw Rick waiting for her at the bottom of the staircase, she realized that though she was able to refuse him tonight, tomorrow or next week might be more difficult. And what could she hope for with Guy, when very soon she must confess to fraud, with nothing to offer in place of the child he wanted? Not love; scarcely even respect when she had so contemptuously tricked him. With her new, almost humble honesty, she decided she had given him very little beyond pity and some callow cravings, of all emotions the most likely to provoke gut-wrenching fury.

She was crazy to refuse Rick, but couldn't help it now. She smiled at him as she came downstairs, nerved for the battle he reckoned already won.

"Honey, you put the most chic of Parisians in the shade," he said with satisfaction. "I'll never let the French pretend their women have an edge on the world again. Give me a New England farm girl every time."

It was too close to what she had been thinking for her to enjoy the compliment. "Chanel helps."

"I can't see Chanel under a Red Cross cape," he pointed out. "Let's go, and take her off. Then we'll find out whether she helps at all. My guess is no."

Mercifully, his confidence stiffened her. "The Red Cross cape stays where it is."

"It's cold outside," he agreed. "C'mon, honey, my apartment's got heating with real hot water in the pipes. Have you been warm, I mean really warm since you arrived in France?"

Eve shivered involuntarily. "No."

He took her arm. "You'll remember tonight, then. In more ways than one. But it's too goddam difficult just to talk about these things. I want to kiss you, and the Astoria isn't the place to do it."

Eve swallowed; the trouble was her absurd lack of experience. A strict upbringing and then marriage to Guy Saulx at twenty-one had not prepared her for dealing with an approach like a subway train. "I'm not coming with you, Rick."

"For God's sake—"

"No, listen. I don't want to, and that's final. What other reason could there be for coming?"

He stared at her for an incredulous moment, then gave a snort of laughter. "I can't think of another just at the moment."

"Rick, I'm sorry. I'm so sorry. I couldn't think how to say it."

"You said it," he commented dryly. "D'you mind telling me why, when you went upstairs with your green eyes glittering, and came down armored like a preacher's wife? Did the gallant commandant leap out from behind the drapes?"

"I can't explain; everything's too complicated. Perhaps that's the trouble. I can't stand any more complication."

"You could call it a reason, though not a good one. I'm beginning to feel we wouldn't be complicated, but good and simple once we got started."

Which was a thought Eve did not want to pursue, when it might be close to the truth.

Rick shrugged. "Okay, I'll go call a taxi. But remember, I expect to be in Paris for a few weeks yet."

"No! I mean . . . I can't go home with you. Guy might not believe—"

His face hardened. "Just how much longer before you add that bastard's score up right? He ran out on you; how else do you expect to get home—walk in your Chanel gown through the streets of St.-Sulpice?"

"Leave it, Rick, please. I'll find Sarah and ask her to arrange an escort for me."

"So what makes that so different when Saulx could just as easily accuse you of hot-handing in a *fiacre* with a British attaché?"

"He wouldn't," she said shortly.

They stared at each other in quick-flaring rage, oblivious of the shifting throng about them.

"I have been waiting for you, *chérie*." Guy folded her hand under his arm and held it there. "Thank you for escorting my wife, monsieur. Your exposés of Paris life must leave little time for enjoyment."

Rick was taken completely by surprise, fists balled at his side and mouth an angry line, voice thick when he managed eventually to reply. "I've a few ends still to tie up; then I guess those same exposés will give me a kick worth waiting for." He felt like a fight after such an unexpected overturn of his hopes; a real teeth-in-the-throat ruckus, but recognized that this was not the place for it. "Good night, Eve. I'll see you around."

His fury showed as he shoved away through the throng, and Guy shook his head in mock regret. "The trouble with reporters is that one always does see them around. You have your cloak, I see; but would you like to go home or first enjoy another dance?"

"I thought you'd gone," said Eve in a small voice.

"I know. I haven't enjoyed waiting for you to decide what you wanted, but it seemed to me that I could skewer Dwyer in the Bois at dawn tomorrow and still be the loser. It was just that I couldn't . . . there was so much noise in the ballroom, and some kinds of mistake I couldn't bear to make. Dwyer's your kind. No, I didn't mean that when you're. . . . I needed to think, you see, and couldn't do it there. Then—"

"Then you were sidetracked by Sir Maurice?"

"That was later," he said vaguely, mind too busy scampering after how nearly he'd lost her to notice any query in her voice. "Home, I think, don't you?"

Eve nodded; she wanted very much to tell Guy while each understood a little of the other, that she did not carry his child.

Instead, they journeyed home together in stuffy darkness, each uncertain of the other's thoughts. And when Guy would have left her to sleep off exhaustion, Eve flogged herself to rouse him, and came close to hatred when she succeeded.

She felt jaded when she arrived at Le Trésor next morning, but there was so much to do she soon revived. She knew exactly the effect she wanted; a list of requirements drawn up in her mind, a date marked when everything must be ready. Her personal deadline before Joubaire's limit ran out, though success at Le Trésor would soon bring another crisis, unless she submitted to blackmail and became Joubaire's tool for the rest of her life. The filaments of menace and frustration were everywhere: entangling, tripping, catching at words and hopes.

But all she could do was try to grasp something from the future, and wait for whatever else would happen. "Where is the canvas and timber I ordered?" she called to Marguerite.

"Paul is working on it, madame, as you ordered." She hitched her shawl about her shoulders in rebuke.

"I'll go and see what he's doing." Eve abandoned accounts thankfully. They, too, pointed to disaster, very soon.

Paul was willing, but dull-witted. He followed designs skillfully, but if she drew a single line wrong, he never noticed until everything was snarled up. Over the next few days Eve prowled restlessly between Paul's workshop and the ground-floor showroom, hurried from theatrical wigmakers to costumiers, then back again by way of an ironfounder who was designing a grate he hoped would burn logs in their shop window without also burning down the Rue Daunou.

"I expect the police will ban it when they see a hearth just behind glass, madame," he said cheerfully. "You send them to me and I will explain how safe flames are when confined in one of Raoul Dupuy's grates."

"It would be good publicity if they did try to ban it," observed Guy when Eve asked him about this fresh worry. "You could fight them in the courts and everyone would take sides; there is nothing Parisians enjoy so much as a good legal squabble."

"So long as they're not paying the lawyers," said Eve pessimistically.

Sometimes her ideas seemed crazy; the Louis XIV scene was not yet finished and already she was trying to think about a Napoleonic library, with a Louis Treize setting to follow.

"My dear, it won't matter who pays the lawyers. This should succeed, and if it doesn't then everyone will wait for their money." Since the evening at the Astoria, Guy had seemed both less dependent on her and more reticent in behavior, occasionally locked in uncanny silence a whole evening at a time, but certainly easier to live with. He remained ridden by nightmares but his memory had steadied, his confidence revived; Eve was uncertain whether the improvement was due to interest in his work at the Peace Conference, or more simply to satisfaction because he had frustrated Rick Dwyer's attempt to steal his property. Either way, she was beginning to feel like a street-corner whore in her continuing design to have him in her bed at every opportunity, when Guy himself was now capable of restraint.

"I could use some help," she said resentfully now. He still came very seldom to Le Trésor.

"I know, I am ashamed to do so little, but at least you extract more work from Joubaire than I should do."

"Because he hopes I'll make his fortune! He'll suck the blood out of us for the rest of our lives."

Guy stared at his linked hands. "What do you want me to do, kill him?"

Eve jumped. "Guy, for land's sakes!"

"What else do you suggest?"

"What does one usually do with unsatisfactory employees? Fire him."

"*Exactement.* Why, therefore, do you imagine I have not done so?"

"Because you don't dare!" she burst out, then stopped, appalled. This was ground she simply must not tread, no matter what lead he gave her, no matter that for the first time he himself might want to probe the dark places of his mind.

"I don't dare because he could ruin me," he agreed calmly. "Stir up enough trouble to have the contents of Le Trésor impounded while its ownership is investigated, a score of ex-owners dredged out of the countryside to dispute such deeds as I possess. I ought to win in the end, but any delay now would ruin us."

"So we have Joubaire around our necks for life," said Eve silkily. He had said nothing of matters at the Hôtel Daunay: nor had she yet been able to decide quite how much of his mind remained entirely blank. Perhaps none, she sometimes thought; which, when she remembered his father's death, made everything seem worse, and just occasionally, better.

He shrugged and would not answer, fingers twitching as if his words about killing Joubaire had triggered a yearning he had not named before. Eve stared at him, mind fluttering, suddenly afraid. Evil festered, once put into words. I must get rid of Joubaire, she thought in panic; somehow I must force him to go before it is too late. She had often thought this before and so far discovered no way of ever being rid of him.

The formal reopening of Le Trésor was fixed for the middle of March, by coincidence the day President Wilson returned to Paris after a quick trip to the United States. It did not matter; he slipped back into the city with only jeering comments in the newspapers to mark his coming. The mood was far removed from his hysterical reception the previous December, the American delegation now regarded with sharp suspicion by the French. Since he lacked political support in Washington, he could no longer lecture Clemenceau and Lloyd George on the brotherhood of man: instead he had become a beggar needing concessions to pacify opponents sharpening their knives on Capitol Hill.

Eve had sent out invitations for Le Tout-Paris to attend the opening night at Le Trésor, laid in champagne and prevailed on Joubaire to wire up floodlights and wear the court livery of Louis XIV. Tomorrow her window setting would be unveiled and she would learn whether or not she had been a fool.

In fact, it was nothing like so simple as she had thought. She visualized instant success or failure, not the slow drift of curiosity. People came to drink her champagne and occasionally came again, witticisms at her expense made the rounds of gossip, which in Paris was a kind of publicity, even if not the best. Most of the Louis XIV pieces sold in the first week, their quality too good for such a display to remain unsold, but most of her purchasers were dealers still. Eve could have screamed with vexation.

A dozen women came one afternoon, sat sipping champagne and drawling incomprehensible Tout-Paris jokes before wandering around the shop for an hour. They bought nothing, and Eve missed a bonbonnière after they had gone.

"They're wasters," said Joubaire, and spat one of his sodden butts on the floor. "You know the Americans at the Crillon; why not invite them to come? Americans go anywhere for free champagne, and for them the quality need not be so good."

"Most wouldn't know Gobelin from Savonnerie," said Eve shortly. She pored over books and was learning fast, since nowadays Guy seldom returned before the middle of the night. He was tired and on edge as well, strung up by strain as he had not been even a week before. He no longer discussed his work with her, but said he might have to go on a mission to Germany soon. "We have to build up a French clientèle before our best goods go; then we can use our profits to restock and expand in the knowledge that we have customers who will come again. I want to start a workshop and hire restorers, not become a depot for other dealers."

"You're throwing good money in the gutter with your childish settings and costumes." Joubaire tipped his wig over his nose and rasped at his scalp. He had grumbled at fancy dress before, but accepted that one must suffer for success.

"Don't do that!" Eve felt her nerves jump. "You're on view all the time out here."

"Tight clothes and a wig were as uncomfortable then as now. I expect they scratched too, madame."

Annoyingly, he was certainly right. Eve went out into the windy street, shutting the door behind her with a snap, and stood biting her lips and staring at Le Trésor. It looked good; it really did catch the eye. Standing on the pavement, you seemed to be peering into a library, in place of the salon she had arranged before. A log fire flamed on the hearth, flickering light over the tooled bindings of precious books shelved on either side. A curved daybed which must have come from some Louis XV alcove softened scholarly severity, as did a méridienne settee in polished lemonwood. Ivory dominoes, a reticule and fan were scattered about, as if a spoiled beauty was about to return. A toy theater lay on the floor with crimson silk curtains drawn back to reveal scenery painted in gouache; a child sprawled on the rug in front of it, his hands on the strings of eighteenth-century marionettes: miniatures made of pasteboard and set in motion by a thread. The child was a dummy, but with his face hidden looked lifelike in the dusk, and as Eve watched, Joubaire came in to replenish the fire and light candles, stately in his livery. It was exactly as she planned, a peepshow into the past, the tremendous chimney worth a stare in itself. Only a book left open on a table revealed that this was a shop with wares to sell; inscribed on its pages was a formal invitation for those interested to come within and browse for as long as they desired as guests of Mme. Saulx.

While Eve stood there watching, plenty of people stopped, gesticulating and exclaiming with pleasure, but none showed any disposition to enter, and for the first time she wondered whether customers might be intimidated by such an elaborate display. But Le Tout-Paris was incapable of being intimidated, and she had gambled everything on catching the fancy of the clientèle she wanted.

An elderly, gray-haired woman followed her back into the shop, her eyes probing the shadows so Eve wanted to sweep her smaller wares out of reach, in case she lost another bonbonnière. "You have a mixture of styles in your design for the Régence period, madame," she said immediately.

"I think libraries usually are a mixture, don't you, madame? One furnishes a salon for effect, and desires everything of the latest fashion there. A library is for personal pleasure, and a husband easily angered if the Renaissance lectern he happens to like is replaced by an ormolu bookstand, which from that moment on he will regard with ineradicable loathing." Eve was prepared to defend every knot in the Chinese carpet from criticism.

The woman gave a cackle, possibly signifying approval. She was dressed all in black, gray hair elaborately coiffed, nose predatory and high-boned. Ruthless eyes which looked people straight in the face; you saw eyes like that behind every cash till in St.-Sulpice. She stood in the center of the shop, not moving but estimating everything.

"Will you pay me a visit to advise on which of your pieces would best suit my apartment?" She spoke with the grating intonation of the *beau monde*.

"Certainly, madame," replied Eve at once, although she had never done such a thing in her life. "When would be convenient?"

"Tomorrow at eleven precisely. I do not expect to be kept waiting."

Eve found that easy to believe. "Where should I come?"

She named an address on the Ile St.-Louis; where Guy once said he would like us to live, Eve thought with a pang. She asked him that evening whether he had ever heard of Mme. de Saint Luc de la Forestière, for the old witch had exuded the confidence of one whose name is known.

"Nathalie de Saint Luc? *Mon Dieu*, is she still alive? I don't know her, but she's a legend. Been around sixty years or more, she must be over eighty."

"She certainly didn't look eighty," observed Eve.

"She must be. People used to say stagecoaches were still on the road when she was young. She married three fortunes, the last of which very properly also possessed a Bourbon title; she's had a hell of a good run."

"She doesn't appear in the least like any of that," said Eve doubtfully. "A really *grande dame*, who'd make the sniffiest butler shake in his shoes."

He laughed. "She'd do that, all right. Enjoy her, but watch your step. She's one of the last of an extinct breed, which probably is as well. She also carries a great deal of weight with the prewar set. If she approves of you, you're where you want—and deserve—to be."

Eve felt her heart give a little skip of excitement. "Really, Guy? Just that one old woman?"

"Didn't she look to you as if she'd spent a lifetime getting exactly what she wanted, in judging the worth to herself of everything she saw? She's done and seen everything, and consequently suffers from almost permanent ennui; only novelty, but novelty in the most exact taste, has the power still to intrigue her, and with Le Trésor you did just that. Which is a triumph Le Tout-Paris will rate at its true worth, and come to admire." He had been working on some papers, but came over to hold her, oddly passionless, as he had been recently.

"But I could easily fail tomorrow! I've learned a little about antiques, but a woman like that could trip me at every step. I'd never spot a competent fake, and still get confused between Louis XV and XVI! It's a test, don't you see? She might even guess I'm a fake too, with looted goods to sell—why, some of those things could have come from the châteaux of her friends!"

He stood very still, hands on her shoulders. "Everything we have was bought, not looted; and if not bought fairly, at least I risked a good deal for it and dealt with people only too anxious to strike a bargain for their lives. Tell her so if she challenges you; she'll respect effrontery if all else fails."

She twisted in his clasp. "Guy . . . this once, couldn't you come too?"

"No, *chérie*. With Nathalie de Saint Luc, I think that this is something you must do for yourself. She means to approve you, or not, as she chooses. Should things go wrong I'll do whatever I can to help, but if you truly want to win, then this time you must win alone."

"What do you mean, 'this time'? It's been me alone from the first day I entered Le Trésor. How about you? You wanted Le Trésor badly enough once—" She broke off: once, perhaps he had wanted it badly enough to kill. Always it came back to this; whatever else he did could be forgiven; this only became more terrible with time. She had very nearly fought her way to lack of blame so long as blame was lost in pity; revulsion came easier now that only his drawn face remained to remind of torment. This distant stranger was not the man she married, any more than he had then remotely resembled the man she imagined he might be.

"I wanted Le Trésor once?" he prompted, hold reassuringly loose on her shoulders. Just sometimes, fear leaped out of nowhere when he held her.

Eve tried to read something into eyes sunk beyond expression; he still slept only in snatches. "You wanted it badly enough to contemplate marrying Eulalie, remember?"

His hands tightened abruptly. "I remember."

"And now you scarcely come near it from one week to the next."

"I had the infinite good fortune to marry you instead of Eulalie. You will succeed where I would have failed."

"You don't mind?"

"No."

"Why not? I don't think most men would have said it so plainly, without excuse."

"I am not most men, *chérie*, as you should know." Furniture was another world from intrigue along the Rhine, and he was too weary for mastering two different worlds.

I live with him but he is fleshless, Eve thought, almost with superstition. You touch, and probe, and try to find, and there's nothing behind skin and bone. She tried to twist away. "Let me go, Guy."

He dropped his hands at once and locked them behind his back. "I asked you once— I don't remember quite how long ago, but I valued your answer then. Are you afraid of me?"

Yes, no, don't answer; impossible alternatives flashed across the surface of her mind. In the end her silence answered, and she saw his muscles loosen, his lips tremble as if tears were close. "You are. You were not then, but now you are."

"No!" Eve cried out then. "Guy, no. It's just—"

He shook his head and stared at the floor, as if he would never look at her directly again.

She snatched at his hands and held them against her throat. "I'm not afraid, Guy."

He did not move, his fingers slack in hers. "Don't. I don't want to think about how often you must have imagined my hands like that."

Eve stared at him, appalled, and knew beyond doubt that it was too late for anything except the truth between them. She must discover the facts of Anselme Saulx's death, even though Guy's mind was still too fragile for safe probing into the fearful past, and he had a right to be treated honestly, too. She might not be safe once she confessed to squalid trickery over a child he very much desired, yet even risk no longer mattered, when set beside the overwhelming compulsion which possessed her.

Yet there was no easy way to explain, nor to begin explaining, and that was unimportant too; she started now on an end to easy ways.

"Guy. . . ." The odd note in her voice forced a blade into his consciousness, and he looked up. "Guy, I wasn't expecting your child when we married. Even now I'm not, although God knows I've wanted to enough."

PART II

Listen to
the Mockingbird

Out of the mockingbird's throat, the musical shuttle.
Walt Whitman

CHAPTER 1

Hugo von Kobis tried not to be delighted by Paris, and failed. He had come to undertake the most difficult diplomatic mission of his life, and consciously reminded himself of the ruin he had left behind in Germany—the emaciated children and anarchic rabble in the streets—but nothing could obscure his enjoyment. Hugo detested barbarism and had found the sheer crudity of existence in the trenches infinitely worse than either fear or pain. He could not help lingering over the watercolor softness of Paris, the way contentment stole up on him as he trod its boulevards after long absence, the sense of belonging brought by a place and people no longer in fear for their lives.

He could have walked directly from the Gare de Lyon to meet Rick Dwyer at the Crillon; instead, he wandered without knowing where he went, March sunshine on his face. Children went hungry on the streets of Paris as well as in Berlin, while underpaid, casually employed workmen seethed with discontent; Hugo saw only the first spring of peace and gray buildings luminous in the sun.

A chill wind eventually roused him from reverie, his undernourished system acutely vulnerable to cold. He was in the Marais, a strange place to find himself but not too far to walk to the Crillon: the embattled government of the newborn German Republic had no money to spare for unnecessary taxis.

He had not expected to find U.S. marines guarding the Crillon: Americans swore they were not militaristic but were surprisingly lavish with the more intrusive signs of power. He had seen U.S. military police patrolling the streets of Paris and heard bitter French comment on this takeover of their city: it was of course untrue, but Hugo thought it as well that few Americans spoke French.

He felt uneasy, though. He had come expecting to find America controlling the processes of peacemaking, but was sufficiently sensitive to atmosphere and enough of a diplomat to suspect already that matters were less simple than his masters thought.

"I'm representing the Züricher *Zeitung*," he said to the marine on duty in the Crillon foyer. "Is Mr. Dwyer of the Washington *Times* in the building? He's expecting me."

"No French press admitted except to the daily briefing," snapped the marine. "I've told you guys the same four hours a day, seven days a week. We're not helping you dip your pens in shit any longer."

"The Züricher *Zeitung* is Swiss. Neutral. Not French. We pride ourselves on reporting fact, not . . . er . . . shit." Hugo took a press card from his wallet.

"Yeah? We're used to all kinds of fact on the front desk here, mister. Including Frogs calling themselves the Zurker— Zurker . . . your Swiss outfit."

Hugo set himself to soothe the marine, enjoying the exercise of diplomatic skills. It's peace, he thought absurdly. No more barked orders so long as I live.

"Paris," he said to Rick when he finally discovered him in the bar. "It heals in a day the wounds surgical stitching can't touch."

"Another year and you could be First Secretary in your embassy here." Rick poured prodigal American quantities of Bourbon into two glasses. "You deserve it for getting yourself past the marines on your own. Those guys are shit-mad from all the French who come out of the street just to swear at them."

"Why?" asked Hugo curiously. "*Prosit!* I shall be drunk on so much after years of ersatz beer." The noise in the Crillon bar prevented any risk of eavesdroppers.

"Enjoy your luck, then," recommended Rick. "You'll get a hell of a thirst hanging around a pack of wrangling statesmen. The French think we're spoiled brats who should leave affairs of state to adults, French adults of course. They also want us to look the other way while they tear the guts out of Germany."

"They always knew you wouldn't do that," objected Hugo.

Rick pushed crumbs around the bar top, frowning. "They've added things up now, though. When Wilson came over in December, Paris was so damned delirious with joy, no one could think of anything except how they'd won, when a few months before they'd been so nearly beat that most of Tout-Paris high-tailed it to Bordeaux and Deauville. They've sobered up now, except for still dancing like crazy, and those with cash spending as if they'd printed the stuff. They probably have, since there's so many strange notes about and prices are through the roof. But you know the French." Hugo nodded. "They're a crafty bunch. It's not natural for them to dance in the streets and think only of the present. The mood's passing. It never came for Clemenceau and his like: they know they lost this war. It took half the world to throw Germany out of France, and next time half the world just might not be around. Germany's a mess right now—"

"Germany lost too," said Hugo. "Rick, you saw Berlin. *Grosser Gott*, you know Germany lost too."

"Lost what?" demanded Rick bluntly. "Public order? Germans won't enjoy anarchy long; you'll get that back fast enough. What Foch and Clemenceau see is Germany unravaged when a third of France is smashed to splinters; a Germany breeding sixty-five million Boches against forty million French. They mean to take what they can get and destroy what they can reach. They hate America because they're afraid we're strong enough to stop them, and despise us too, because we refuse to accept the realities of power."

"And you, Rick? What do you think in this year of America's strength?"

"I'm risking my job to have you here, sticking my neck out to introduce my good old Switzer buddy, Hugo Kobis, into Quai d'Orsay briefings. I think power talks, and if Germany is force-fed on resentment like a pâté-de-foie-gras goose, I'll live to regret that I didn't do what I could to stop it. But they say every American has two hometowns, his own and Paris. I like Paris better than Berlin, Hugo."

"So do I," said Hugo, smiling. "It's warmer, for one thing. There's thirty centimeters of snow in Berlin at the moment, and no coal at all."

"Oh, Christ!" said Rick rudely. "If I hadn't been listening to them for the past three months, I could find it in my heart to pity those selfish old bastards horse-trading scraps of Europe in the Quai d'Orsay. Have another drink."

Since President Wilson had declared that open diplomacy was the key to fair dealing between nations, and his allies having perforce acquiesced in this untried notion, the Peace Conference had opened in a blaze of publicity. Hundreds of reporters were assigned to analyze its deliberations, only to find that as disagreement multiplied and enraged populations outdid each other in demands for revenge, secrecy clamped down tight. Since the French ran the administrative arrangements and had been adept in such matters as inspired leaks and confusing rumor since before Columbus crossed the Atlantic, reporting the Conference became a steadily less rewarding experience. Besides, some concessions were inevitable, and no statesman wanted to be observed in the act of moderating his demands. Councils of diminishing size were set up with the express purpose of ensuring secrecy, and the rest of the Conference became largely a charade. The affairs of Europe were distilled into acerbic wrangles between Clemenceau, whom nothing could surprise; Lloyd George, who delighted in detonating firecrackers of surprise; Orlando of Italy, who understood six words of English but was resolved to make his ignorance work for Italy's benefit; and President Wilson, who was still capable of feeling astonishment that Europe could be so awful, but otherwise was too ground down by circumstance and the consequences of gratuitously offending nearly everyone of importance in Washington, to concentrate on detail.

Since the details of peacemaking included massive dealings with populations and lands whose precise location and composition were often unknown to the negotiators, considerable confusion prevailed over just what had been agreed and what remained to be done. British, French and Belgian opinion was inflamed by uncertainty, and the world's press was reduced to writing articles short on fact and extremely long on personal malice. The most respected reporters had drifted away from so unpromising a field, and no one found it remarkable that the Züricher *Zeitung* should accredit an unknown stringer to the disheartening task of extracting sparse handouts from the French.

"I've nearly left Paris myself a dozen times," confessed Rick to Hugo as they loitered in a café outside the Quai d'Orsay the following day. "But in spite of it all, this is where our next fifty years is being made. I've stuck around for so long, I guess I'll wait for the end now."

"How far away do you estimate the end is?"

"Christ knows. A formal covenant for a League of Nations has been agreed at last, which means that everyone thinks they've wrung as many concessions out of Wilson as it's prudent to get. Another month to tie the ends up, I guess."

"I have to find out exactly what it is they then expect us to sign. We need to lodge objections before the treaty's published, not after."

Rick nodded gloomily and beckoned to a waiter. A pile of saucers beside him showed the length of time he and Hugo had been drinking.

"No one in Berlin has any idea what to expect," added Hugo; beside him was a single saucer, which indicated both professional care to keep his head clear and finicking regard for Germany's finances. "We've set up a special unit at the Wilhelmstrasse to study the possible proposals the Allies might make, so we can offer an immediate, reasoned reply, but—"

"But reasoned replies may be too late?"

"We must know what's being decided. It's no good just having our representatives summoned to sign something we've never seen."

"You'll see it, all right."

"A week, two weeks perhaps before signature? Rick, things are so confused in Germany that hardly anyone is thinking about a treaty at all. They're thinking of Reds and Freikorps and murder in the courtyard. A treaty is like a dream. Not here and now, but something we'll talk about eventually. We can't hide like that in the Foreign Ministry, but believe me, in all Germany there's scarcely anyone else who gives it a moment's thought. And even in the Wilhelmstrasse, there's blood on the steps most days. It doesn't make for clear thinking."

"But Christ, Hugo! Everyone knows the Conference is meeting. Those old bastards have been here nine-ten weeks now."

"How could most Germans know? Newspapers are the trophies of revolution, their offices stormed several times a week in some cities. We do not feel Germany was more to blame for the war than anyone else, so the few who do wonder about the shape of peace mostly trust Wilson to force his allies into moderation. I'm beginning to wonder about so much trust in Wilson."

"I thought you'd come to subsidize publicity about allowing Germany to import food," said Rick uneasily. "To take the temperature here and report on how your case could best be put."

"In general terms, yes. But food is beginning to arrive; we now have better uses for such money as I can spend. I must see a draft of the treaty, and will pay to get it. Then we might be able to make the kind of objections statesmen respect before the world knows what the Allies intend."

Rick pushed back his chair angrily. "You bastard! That wasn't what you said before."

"Think about it carefully, and you will find my orders have not changed. The aim is still the one you agreed with, to do what we could to help obtain a peace which Germany could accept without lasting resentment."

Rick threw a handful of notes on the table and pushed his way outside without replying. The mild weather of the day before had vanished and a cold drizzle was falling, as if spring had been beaten too.

Hugo fell into step beside him. "You are angry with me, but unpleasant details are my affair; you only do what you agreed to do. Introduce me to colleagues and the ways of the press, report what you would have reported anyway, and ease my way into knowledge which would take too long to acquire for myself. You need do nothing of which your State Department disapproves."

"If you think that, you don't know the State Department!" snapped Rick.

Hugo laughed. "All foreign offices are the same; they want everyone else to keep their noses out. But tell me truly, Rick, do you not think it absurd that Germany's future should be settled without a single German here to listen to what is said? They could have told us we weren't allowed to negotiate, but still allowed an observer, surely? Every enemy we've ever had has been allowed his say; their evidence is accepted, their maps pass unchallenged. How would you like Mexico to decide for herself which parts of the United States belonged to her?"

"You goddam diplomats! You're all the same; when this is done, I'll never cover another peace conference as long as I live."

"I hope you won't have to."

"You're leveling with me this time? There's not some other crooked play you're holding behind your back?"

"I'm leveling with you. But if I weren't, I'd say the same, don't you think?"

Rick swore again, striding loosely, hands in pockets. Newsboys darted through clotted traffic, carrying placards which told of a Red takeover in Hungary, while the brutal jostling of passersby was made worse by his own uncompromising pace. "Okay," he said at last, "I'll help but reserve the right to quit if I don't like your play. And God help you if you're holding out on me this time."

Hugo looked up at the Eiffel Tower, freshly strung with lights. "Thank you. When this is finished, I hope you won't regret your choice. I hope I shan't either."

That night, Rick began taking Hugo around the places where information might be discovered. Not sinister bars, because Hugo sought the kind of secrets which existed largely in the minds of conference bureaucrats, and could only be fitted together piecemeal from chatter in restaurants and *tripots*, the illegal gaming dens of the Champs-Élysées, or perhaps from the gossip of *cocottes* who slept with men of position. Really exclusive gatherings were beyond Rick's grasp, but his rakish good looks found favor in many salons and he had long traded on the fact: bored women enjoyed his uninhibited virility, and would have been disappointed if he had allowed them to discover sensitivity in an American. Hugo, too, was an instant success, except for exciting mild surprise that so agreeably polished a man could be Swiss, whom every Parisian knew to be *ennuyeux comme la pluie*.

"The major occupation of this city is pouring cognac and gossip into newsmen," said Hugo after a week of this. "Why can't I discover what I need? It isn't as if anyone were in the least discreet."

He and Rick—two proper Parisians—were capping a liver-churning round of parties by eating onion soup in Les Halles at four in the morning.

"Imagine being in the office by eight tomorrow— today," moaned Rick. "The few people who really matter *are* discreet, dammit. I haven't filed a thing for days."

"If any editor published copy written with a hangover like yours, he'd deserve to be fired," observed Hugo unsympathetically. "I think I'm wasting my time. When every underling enjoys discussing secrets with the first listener he encounters, there's no means of judging what you hear."

"I hope to God you're right. Another week of all those silly women would turn me into a dipsomaniac."

"The best salons are very entertaining; I remember, before the war— well, it's lucky I wasn't in Paris long enough to become known. As it is, a couple of people said they were sure they'd seen me somewhere before."

"That settles it, then. Back to the Quai d'Orsay press briefing tomorrow."

"I suppose so. But I shan't get what I want there, either, when the French simply regard them as a means of deception."

Rick held his head; he had come to recognize some of the signs with Hugo, and needed to think carefully about his own ideas too. Guy Saulx, for instance. "What are you going to spring on me now, for Chrissake?"

"I think I have been trying to discover something which does not exist," said Hugo slowly. "I suppose I am German enough to expect a Peace Conference to have an exact schedule of negotiations, drawn up and enforced by a central secretariat, a set of proposals to debate, vary, or accept. I believe I'm wrong. I don't think Wilson himself could show me a document and say, look, we've reached article two hundred, there's just these points left to discuss."

"Wilson's had a stroke," said Rick abruptly. "I haven't told you before, and officially it's flu. It'll stay flu too but sounds like a stroke to me."

"Another casualty of the war; I'm sorry, Rick." Hugo did not say that he had heard the same story earlier in a darkened bedroom; nor did he think it mattered, when he had already decided that Wilson was a spent force. French and British squabbles over Germany's carcass were now more important to his purpose than Wilson's scruples.

Rick rasped at the stubble on his face; the onion soup was disagreeing with him and he felt like hell. "There's one bitch of a little story I've been following these past few days, which I don't mind sharing. My editor's a cautious bastard who'd spike something like this until I have all the evidence, and by then I guess it won't seem too interesting. Whichever way it breaks, there should be something in it for you, though."

Hugo looked courteous and receptive, although in his experience the confidences of newsmen were nearly always worthless. You could never tell, all the same. "I should be interested to hear anything you think might be of use."

"I bet. You told me once that you knew Guy Saulx, remember?"

"Yes, of course. Before the war, my father commanded the military district of Alsace. Guy and I ought not to have met, you understand, but we did, and perhaps our friendship prospered partly because it had to be secret."

"You said in Berlin that he might help."

"I meant that our affection would probably have survived the war, not that I thought he would be in a position to help over clauses in a treaty."

"Well, you could just be wrong. I've been watching Saulx, and he seems to be mixed into several helpings of the same pie, and the pie is Germany's western borders and how they're to be settled in the treaty."

"You've been watching Saulx," repeated Hugo. "Why?"

Rick hesitated and then explained how Guy was on Foch's staff, yet he had followed him to private meetings with Clemenceau's aides.

Hugo frowned. "You have not answered my question. Why watch Guy in the first place? It is clear to me that if you had not been watching him, you would never have known of any connection with Clemenceau. Nor do I see why a French officer should not report to his own government. Guy knows Alsace and was stationed in the Rhineland when he served in the Wehrmacht. He also has a clear and accurate mind; it is quite likely that he is useful to both government and Army."

Rick stared at him. "We're talking about the same man? Guy Saulx, a clear and accurate mind?"

"Yes," said Hugo curtly. "Why were you following him?"

Rick knew he needed to be careful but at that moment was incapable of subtlety. The clangor of Les Halles was fearsome in the early morning, the smell of cabbage, onions and horse dung overpowering. He also wanted Guy Saulx fixed, and Hugo was the man to do it for him: Rick's instinct pointed to it as soon as he learned the two were acquainted. And luckily, fixing Saulx would also help redress one balance set against Germany. "I was following him because I know his wife," he said baldly.

Hugo blinked, even his suave self-control not proof against total surprise. "I remember now. You told me he had married a girl from your hometown."

Rick thought of the marine at the Crillon. "She's a real nice girl. I could kill the bastard for marrying her."

Hugo stared at him, thinking fast. A real nice girl; to him that did not sound as if Dwyer slept with her, but he was aware that his judgment was less sound with Americans than Europeans. There could be no doubt, though, that Dwyer cherished personal animus against Guy, even if he did promise political information Hugo could not afford to ignore. "I have not seen Guy since I came here, but I did hear that he had had a bad war," he said noncommittally at last.

"He's crazy as a coot. Yet apparently he was present at a recent meeting, at the Deuxième Bureau, over which Clemenceau himself presided. The subject was how to catch French generals in the act, now that they're smuggling arms to German subversives in the Rhineland."

"You told me Guy was on Foch's staff!"

"He is, and it's Foch and his buddies who want to give guns to any German mobster they see, in exchange for some kind of coup where a pack of roughs will declare an independent Rhineland and ask dear, friendly old France to step in and take over sovereignty."

"A *cocotte* told you this?"

"Part of it. It's a goddam silly country in some ways, isn't it?"

"She was lying. She must have been. Even French *cocottes* don't know everyone at Intelligence Bureau meetings."

"It's surprising how Frenchmen blab secrets into a pillow, all the same. I believed her. She was enraged that her *amant de coeur* was also at the meeting instead of in her bed, and only mentioned Saulx in passing. If I hadn't also seen him meet Patrice Fabian two nights ago, I might have thought he'd strayed into the wrong room by mistake. He's screwy enough for anything."

"If he had, I should think Clemenceau perfectly capable of having him thrown out again." Hugo instinctively resented Rick's contempt for a man who had been his friend.

"That's what I decided in the end," agreed Rick. "Think, Hugo. Saulx knows Foch's plans for the Rhineland coup, right? He possibly also knows the details of orders drafted for Mangin, their commander in Mainz. The French must have so many millions of surplus guns that any general worth his salt could smuggle a few thousand without being noticed. But that isn't all. The French are really afraid. Another few years, they say, and the Boches will attack us again. The only way to stop them is to take everything as far as the Rhine and ruin the rest; now they find we won't give it to them under the treaty, so—"

"And you won't?"

Rick shook his head decisively. "No. Supervision over some military installations, perhaps, but Wilson would never agree to handing over purely German areas to the French. We'd be back fighting in the Argonne within a generation."

"So Foch plans his puppet state, which will appeal for French help so as to make it look cozily democratic. Surely everyone must see through such a maneuver?"

Rick stood and went over to the bar; only a precisely measured dose of spirits might clear his head for a while. "I don't know how he plans to do it, exactly; there must be a hell of a lot of tricky political dealing going on in Mainz, not just guns. But yes, I guess that's what he intends. Now, Clemenceau's in a different league altogether, and more crooked than my granny's knitting. He knows exactly what he can get away with, which a pack of generals probably don't. He can't steal the Rhineland without anyone noticing, for instance, so he's out to keep Foch from trying."

"And you think Guy is giving his Prime Minister information against his commanding general?" Hugo was not military enough to be incredulous, but sufficiently bureaucratic to be shocked.

"Yeah, sure. Unless Clemenceau's simply hired Saulx to kill Foch and be done with it," added Rick, unaware of spite. "I told you, the bastard's half cocked. He doesn't remember what he's done."

Hugo's eyes narrowed. He was completely sober, having drunk coffee all evening. "Even to a killing, do you mean?"

Rick nodded. "I was anxious about Eve and investigated some dirty gossip I heard about the Saulx family. I'll show you the file. Among other things, there doesn't seem much doubt that Guy killed his father for what he could get out of it; some quarrel about inheritance, and the rest of his family seem to think you can't blame a veteran if he forgets occasionally that the war is over. I don't happen to agree, that's all."

He was afraid for Eve, worried about her as he had never worried about any woman before, and was quite simply pleased by the chance which brought Hugo to Paris. New treason would be a far easier charge to prove against Saulx than a stale murder which Le Tout-Paris wanted shoveled under the carpet; and helping to avoid another war was a fair purpose, after all.

Hugo's mind was moving in a completely different direction. He was remembering Guy as he had been before the war; loss and disbelief jumbled together in his thoughts. "You keep saying he is crazy. Now you have suggested he is violent and a bad husband. I think this is something I must try to judge for myself."

"You don't believe me?"

"I have seen too many men broken in the trenches not to understand what war can do. It could and probably did break Guy, but the friend I had would not—" He groped over his own meaning. "I find it hard to believe he would have fragmented in the way you describe. Nor do I think Clemenceau allows madmen into his meetings even if he does

hope to employ them as assassins. If one must use such people, underlings are briefed to deal with them."

"As a diplomat from the Wilhelmstrasse should know?"

Hugo grabbed at his temper. "As anyone with a gram of sense would
know."

"Okay, okay. I don't know what the hell we're arguing about, when I
agree he's still got enough sense to be of use to both sides in the
catfight over the Rhineland. I just thought you'd be interested to hear
how France is playing skittles with bits of your Reich behind everyone's
back."

"Oh, yes, I am interested. Thank you. As you will thank me if Guy
should face a firing squad at the end of it all." A pulse of anger was
beating under Hugo's jaw, his training for once forgotten.

"Sure, why not? You won't make me feel guilty by staring down your
aristocratic nose like I was crap on the sidewalk, either. Eve is married
to Saulx, and my file says he's a killer. She's twenty-one and alone, and
looked about eighteen when she began living with him, four months
ago; you wouldn't make any mistake now about thinking she was
younger than her age."

"I understand. I should like to accompany you to your office and
read that file." Hugo felt weary suddenly, and not from the night he
had just spent. He did not want to discover just how harshly war and
circumstance had dealt with Guy Saulx, when Dwyer meant him to use
what he learned simply to remove an inconvenient husband. No nonsense about peace and war, but old-fashioned jealous hate lay at the
root of this. Yet Hugo had no choice if anything he discovered might
help Germany in her time of peril, and later today he intended anyway
to call at the Rue Daunou. After nearly a week of frequenting the
haunts of Le Tout-Paris, he had heard a great deal of chatter about Eve
Saulx, who ran a newly fashionable establishment there, sometimes
helped by Sarah Wyville, the daughter of Sir Maurice Wyville, a man
whom Hugo had identified as one of the few who might command the
kind of information on the treaty he was looking for. The British had
their faults, but their secretariat possessed such an array of administrative talent that the other delegations had given up trying to compete
with them. Instead they relied on British digests of information, as well
as their instant ability to produce a judicious resolution to smooth over
difficulty: which meant that if a draft treaty did not exist, then the British certainly possessed the skeleton on which one could be fleshed,
quite quickly, on demand. A man in Wyville's position would have the
salient points clearly marshaled in his mind, when even Lloyd George,
who regarded most facts as flexible and was still locked in combat with

his allies, easily might not. The Rhineland was important, but the treaty remained Hugo's most vital purpose.

Neither Rick nor Hugo spoke as they walked through waking Paris streets; the air smelled fresh and the first buds of spring were jagged against paling sky. Unlucky prostitutes trailed sullenly home, and a series of black behinds were visible through windows as work-worn women scrubbed floors for another day.

Rick fitted a key large enough to open a dungeon into the outer door of his office building. As usual, the elevator wasn't working, and he went up the stairs fast, nearly sober again, wanting only to be free of necessary unpleasantness.

He swung open his safe and searched hastily for the file he needed; there was really nothing else there which Hugo wasn't welcome to read if he could be bothered. His editor would bust a gut—express blasphemous disapproval—if he knew that a German diplomat had the run of the *Times*'s Paris files. Well, what the hell! There was just time to go home and shave if he hurried.

"The girl doesn't come in for another couple of hours; I'd like you out of here by then. You be okay if I leave you for a while? Lock everything into the safe before you go if I'm not back."

"Yes, thank you." Hugo glanced at the Saulx file with distaste. He wasn't surprised that Dwyer preferred not to sit watching his own betrayals. "I think this is something I might like to read alone."

Rick had chosen his apartment partly because it was close to his office. When the concierge let him in, he found Eve waiting for him there.

CHAPTER 2

Eve had so much dreaded confessing to Guy how she had lied to him, that until the words were spoken she had not realized how much greater still would be the relief of honesty again. Thus was her part done, and if anything of their relationship survived, then next must come the first steps toward the infinitely more complex task of bringing Guy face to face with Eulalie's accusations, and that was something Eve still had no idea how to tackle.

For a fraction of time after she had spoken, Eve quite simply forgot apprehension in relief, but that moment passed and dread returned, even though his fingers remained slack against her throat. His face was blank, swept clear by shock.

"I'm sorry," she said helplessly.

He shook his head. "No. You're glad."

And of course, beneath shame and compassion, she was. A child tied her to him, and to France, forever.

He pulled his hands away and went to stand by the window. He seemed astonishingly calm when she had expected— she did not know quite what she had expected. "I think you'd better go. I'd go myself, but the Rue Férou isn't safe for a woman living alone. Do you still know anyone living at the Crillon well enough to beg a room until I can let you have sufficient money for something better?"

Eve shriveled at his tone; she had thought of truth regained, but once pretense was gone there was frighteningly little left between them. "We're still married, Guy."

"Yes. Divorce on such grounds as we can offer won't be easy, but I expect we shall manage it in the end. We didn't have a religious wedding."

"I wish we had."

He was caught off guard, and turned. "Why?"

"Perhaps because it might make you feel some slight obligation toward me."

"If we are to talk of obligation, you, too, might have felt embarrassed, don't you think, on your knees beside me and confessing sin at nuptial mass?"

"Yes," she said, and felt her cheeks wet. "Can't you see, Guy? I'm so dreadfully ashamed I could grovel, but it wouldn't help. I thought what I did was for the best. I never dreamed you'd care so much, or . . . that having your child would prove so difficult."

"I expect it's my fault, like all the rest, since recently you've used me like a stud bull. I was simple enough to be surprised that you rejected tenderness when I was able to offer it, but you preferred me frenzied, after all."

His voice was rising, hands twisting, and Eve watched him with alarm, trying not to think how much alone she was. The time of their peace was now completely in the past; he had been better and now was worse again.

She moistened her lips. "Guy . . ."

He turned his back on her and savagely forced the window open. A pane shattered and glass fell on his hand, cutting it slightly. Bitter night air poured into the room, blowing curtains and rolling a cafetière on the floor. The hiss of wind was the only sound as he stood and stared at blood on his fingers. "Eve, I beg of you. Go. Now."

Words whispered, sensed rather than heard.

He was trembling so violently Eve could see the muscles of shoulder and back under the fine blue cloth of his tunic. Her nerves screamed at her to take the chance he offered and run for her life without waiting for anything at all, even while something deeper and tougher made her stay, to forget danger and remember that this was her fault. The blood he looked at was his own.

He was even more alone than she, alone with mirrored pain.

Eve moved at last and went over to stand close. "I don't want to go. Or cause a difficult and expensive divorce; I mean to hold you to our marriage."

She could see a pulse beating over his eye as he kept his face averted. "There's no way you can hold me to it. With the lie of a child you tried, and now you have failed."

The half-furnished room was refrigerated by the wind. "Why not accept what I want to offer? What I have already given you, in fact?" As soon as the words were out, Eve realized they were a disastrous mistake.

"No! If you had ever loved me . . . perhaps it might be different. I want you to go. I can't endure this any longer."

"Endure what, me?"

She knew every shade in his voice and change of breathing, had not realized how much she knew until she heard the harsh roughness of his worst times come again. "No."

"Then, what? I need telling before I'll go." She wanted to go so much that in imagination she was already down the stairs. Yet she had determined on confession, believing it might help, understanding that if it did not, then there was nothing more she could do for him. Every instinct she possessed now screamed of danger, but she refused to go until she was certain he had grasped that if she did, then it was the end. Danger, even courage, had very little to do with something she must finish, if ever it was to be truly finished.

He turned suddenly, violently, face sweating even in the cold. His hands had been thrust defensively under his armpits; now he seized her and she saw blood bright on his fingers. Too late, too late, she understood how the end had come, but she could no longer go.

He said something once and she heard him sob; his blood streaked her breasts as he tore at her clothes, it tasted salt on her lips when she cried out. Crude brutality was no easier to endure than on that first night, except she had learned a little since. He rolled free of her immediately desperation ebbed and lay with his face hidden, showing no sign that he remembered she was there.

Eve stood almost at once, washed in icy water before dressing, and then flung her few belongings into a valise. When she was ready, she stood and looked at the room which for a while had come close to seeming home, and then she left.

Outside, the night wind seemed suited to her mood, the quayside trees laden with water droplets, pavé streets deserted. She stared across to where the Cathedral of Notre-Dame looked like a battleship steaming downriver, darker ivy forming a shadow bow wave; today she had an appointment over there to call on the Comtesse de Saint Luc.

Well, why not?

She had to earn her living, and Le Trésor was more her creation than Guy's, since his interest waned to nothing as soon as she was there.

Her pace quickened and she went directly to the Rue Daunou, relieved by a decision taken. Until she discovered somewhere suitable to live and saved the francs to pay for it, she could camp at Le Trésor. There were empty rooms under the eaves which could scarcely be much colder than the Rue Férou. Leave sentiment behind, and be hard-headed, like a Frenchwoman behind her till.

She prepared herself carefully for a meeting which Guy had said

could make the fortune of Le Trésor. She paused, staring out from a
tiny eaves window, hairbrush in hand; could it really only be a few
hours ago that he had laughed and told her of Nathalie de Saint Luc?

She shrugged, and resumed brushing doggedly; no good thinking of it
now. No good thinking of it ever. Except . . . except she was still
bound, and would continue to be bound to him so long as she occupied
his premises and carried on his business. They could not simply part; in
fact, would have to meet again quite soon to decide on the practicalities
of living.

Eve walked briskly to the Ile St.-Louis, outpacing thought and savor-
ing instead the mixed smells of old Paris: wet stone, tar, spiced cooking, vegetables and houseplants sold in stalls; each district was distinct
to the nose of a connoisseur, and inexperienced though she was, Eve
caught the whiff of prosperity on the Ile St.-Louis.

Wrought-iron balconies decorated the house she sought, and stairs of
ochered stone led up to the first floor. There she found a velvet bellpull
ending in a fox's foot, and when she summoned courage to tug it, a
starched *bonne* opened double doors and showed her into a large drawing room.

Windows framed a view of Paris which might have been centuries
old; a narrow street, shutters, soaring spire and an unctuous cat
crouched on the balcony, viewing intruders like a goddess. The chandelier was draped in muslin; why bother to dust each droplet when important company was not expected? Heavy Second Empire furniture
cluttered the splendid room, the deposit of years silted into corners.

Eve fidgeted restlessly while she waited, then remembered how Guy
had agreed that this was some kind of test which she would best sur-
mount alone. Childishly, Eve wrinkled her nose at family portraits
watching her somberly from the wall: I bet Nathalie bargained for
them as she did for husbands, she thought uncharitably. She came from
the backwoods just like me, and see how well she has done.

Eve stood when the Comtesse came in at last, nor did a curtsy seem
out of place, just this once, to acknowledge success. For successful she
undoubtedly was, when from her bearing you would imagine a family
tree going back to Charlemagne. She wore black again, beautifully cut
and stitched with intricate designs; a five-fold string of pearls concealed
wrinkles at her neck, and she leaned lightly on a polished cane, the handle decorated with the head of a golden lynx.

"You come punctually on time, Mme. Saulx," she said.

Eve inclined her head. "Of course."

"*Bien.* Then, you shall tell me what you think of my salon."

"It is a very beautiful room, madame."

"Ah, I see you have an exact mind. My intention was to ask your opinion of the arrangement of furniture and effects within the room."

Eve laughed. "I think you must forgive me, madame. Like the statesmen at the Quai d'Orsay, I will do my best to refrain from comment on the internal affairs of others, since these are usually a great deal more convenient than appears to the outside observer."

"At least no one could mistake your meaning," said the Comtesse dryly.

"As no one could have mistaken yours, madame." Absurdly, Eve found she was enjoying herself. This was a duel of wills, and if she admired furniture which privately she disliked, then this woman could read her mind, and intended to do so, simply to disconcert.

"You have some kinds of judgment, then, even if not of furniture."

"I hope so, and of furniture as well, since I want to establish myself *comme antiquaire* in a city still foreign to me."

The old woman surveyed her mockingly. "There is always room for another woman of wit and looks to achieve her conquests in Paris."

Eve felt the blood come to her face; Nathalie de Saint Luc was intolerable. *"Merci du compliment, madame,* I am already married and look for my success in other fields."

"My dear Mme. Saulx, how praiseworthy! I also consider the married state quite excellent for its purposes. The quality of a painting is not decided by the manufacture of the frame, however, nor should one waste such gifts as one possesses." She looked at Eve pensively. "Which in your case include a femininity appreciated in Paris, as well as a character not entirely lacking in interest. And now, if you refuse to give me your opinion of the furnishing of this room, perhaps you would venture your estimate of that secretaire."

Eve turned away thankfully and went over to the secretaire. This, too, might be a test, of what she was not sure: a simple test of knowledge would be too ordinary to amuse the Comtesse de Saint Luc. "It is lovely, madame. We have one very similar at Le Trésor."

"My friend Henriette de Luxeuil informed me that you had. She says it belongs to her."

Eve touched golden arabesques. "Then, she is mistaken."

"She would disagree, Mme. Saulx."

Eve could feel her stomach clench with dismay; she had never expected this, in spite of her half-joking words to Guy the previous evening, but nothing was gained by admitting doubt. "If she valued her piece sufficiently to dream about a chance resemblance, perhaps she might be interested in purchasing ours to replace it."

"I don't think that was quite the proposition she had in mind." Hooded eyes watched Eve unblinkingly.

"A pair would be extremely valuable," Eve said earnestly. "If you would give me her address I should like to visit her to ask how we might track down the one she once possessed. If they really are alike I would be very interested in buying the mate to mine."

"I will inform her of your wish, madame." Thin lips curled into what might have been amusement. "You are perfectly correct, of course. Never admit error."

"Oh, I often admit it!" said Eve cheerfully. "My eye for period and decoration is far from attuned to French taste! In the United States such fancies as gilt and inlay are often crude and therefore regarded as somewhat vulgar, although our plainer designs are very good. After such a short time in Paris I can appreciate French style without yet finding it comfortable to live with."

"I feel confident that you will readily conceal such difficulties as you may encounter in so trifling a matter; which, as you are aware, was not precisely what I meant. Now, madame, I should like you to stay on for lunch, so we may arrange for me to visit your establishment. I have a whim to refurnish my salon with your very charming pieces, and when I have finished I will invite selected acquaintance to a soirée. Then we will see whether they also recognize items they consider to be theirs. Old age is a disaster but may occasionally be relieved by a really enjoyable scandal."

The lunch was delicious: *filets de sole au champagne* and young partridges *sur canapé*, served on Vieux Paris porcelain flanked by cut-glass goblets and table implements stamped with an impressive coat of arms. After a few mouthfuls Eve refused to think beyond her own enjoyment: she was ravenously hungry and had never encountered anyone remotely like the Comtesse de Saint Luc. An extinct breed and a good thing, too, Guy had said, but whatever her alarm over the future, Eve could not agree. The world might be a better place but certainly it would be duller, when the stringent intelligence of Nathalie de Saint Luc was dimmed and Paris no longer waited for the next devilment of her engineering.

How quickly had she realized that Le Trésor held not only a single secretaire but many items which her acquaintance might recognize? Eve could not decide; perhaps whispers were already circulating among the *beau monde* and it was only a matter of time before the police were on her doorstep. But somehow, she did not think so. Within hours of such a rumor beginning, Le Trésor would fill with curious scandalmongers even if not with customers, and so far nothing of the kind had happened. But whatever the position now, the Comtesse intended to stir up trouble in the future: Guy had said his purchases were legal, but Eve could no longer even guess how much reliance should be placed on his judgment.

"I will invite you to my soirée when redecoration is complete," the Comtesse said on parting. "There will be a great many people present who will want to meet you."

"I shall look forward to it," answered Eve. She most certainly would not, when every one of the guests would be invited in the hope they recognized something they would regard as loot.

"How agreeable for me also to be able to look forward to the future, even if only for a short while, when life had seemed devoid of interest. But you, Mme. Saulx? I find it surprising that you agreed to show me the pieces you and I have discussed today, or do you doubt my ability to discover precisely whom I should invite to view my new furnishings?"

"I would never doubt your ability to accomplish anything," said Eve. "You wouldn't believe me if I said I had nothing to fear, although I hope it is true, but my husband told me your interest could make Le Trésor; now you plan to come three days together to choose what you want, and then make sure everyone knows where you have been. For that, any risk would be worthwhile."

Nathalie de Saint Luc allowed herself a faint smile. "We shall see, madame."

I think I've done it, thought Eve exultantly as she walked back to the Rue Daunou. I've left her intrigued, but sure enough of her own instincts to be willing to pay whatever I ask for pieces she guesses may one day be recognized. She also wonders why I'm not worried. I wonder why I'm not worried, whether I wasn't crazy not to go down on my knees and beg that old witch to stay away from Le Trésor.

Eve laughed aloud, making several passersby turn and stare; one thing was certain, when the Comtesse opened her new salon to painstakingly chosen acquaintance, it would be the soirée of the season.

Eve was astonished by the speed of her success once Le Trésor became talked about. Word spread within hours that Nathalie found the new establishment in the Rue Daunou *bien amusant,* and Le Tout-Paris flocked to visit a place which caught so capricious a fancy.

Eve was overwhelmed by work, for she was determined that once the fashionable world accepted that Le Trésor was chic, they would truly find it so. Paris looked at novelty, but returned only to unmistakable quality.

Upstairs, Eve furnished a salon almost as if she were a couturier: it was carpeted in gray and provided with comfortable chairs in which clients could sit and sip champagne while settings of her choicest antiques were arranged expertly around them. She changed the downstairs window often—soaring sales forced change anyway, although the cost of such settings was disconcerting. Immediately customers entered the shop, they found banked flowers and warm hospitality, in the American rather than the French tradition, and quite different from the austere gray salon upstairs. The idea came when Eve saw an American rocking chair in a junk store, and immediately she traveled overnight to the U. S. Expeditionary Force Headquarters at Tours, determined to obtain anything American she could find.

She discovered some New England dressers gathering dust in an officers' club, and also a great deal of surplus food, which a friendly enlisted man offered to drop off in Paris next time he drove his truck there. She paid knockdown prices for everything, since U.S. forces were already alerted to leave Europe, but was surprised to find that her eyes kept misting in the train on her return. Until she encountered it again, she had not realized how much she missed transatlantic ease and casual generosity.

She ate alone before returning very late to the Rue Daunou through windswept streets full of carousing troops. She had never been so glad to reach Le Trésor, nor had it ever seemed so menacingly bleak; floor after floor of dust-sheeted shapes rustling in glacial drafts.

Eve slept in an Empire boat-sided bed, the rest of the attic almost bare. I must find myself a room, she thought. All I need is time, just a few hours squeezed somehow for myself.

Yet time was totally lacking. Customers came in a steady stream, and in this kind of trade each must be cosseted. She continually needed fresh ideas and felt herself becoming jaded; also, the question of stock would soon be urgent.

"Madame has sold so much that the store at Neuilly is nearly empty," said Joubaire with respect. "The Commandant must obtain military transport and take some of our profits to restock. So long as prices rise each day, there must be many families who wish to sell possessions."

Eve felt a quiver of distaste at such frank scavenging on distress. "Aren't there any auction rooms in Paris?"

"Of a certainty, madame. But touring the country with a *camion* is the way to profits at such a time; bumpkins don't know the value of what they have, and transport is still a difficulty for those less well placed than the Commandant. When will he come here next, so we may discuss what to do?"

"He won't come."

Joubaire's eyes narrowed. "I have been intending to ask madame what has happened to the Commandant."

Eve longed to tell him to mind his own business, but had pushed aside the problem of Joubaire too often during the ten days which had passed since she left Guy. "I don't know where he is. We have agreed to part for the moment."

"For the moment," repeated Joubaire. "I do not think such an arrangement will suit me at all."

"It wasn't meant to!" snapped Eve.

"You must return to him, madame. Le Trésor is his, and cannot be profitably run by you alone."

Eve felt anger burn all the way from her stomach to her throat, a completely physical sensation. "I could run Le Trésor even more profitably than at present without you."

"No, madame." His head was held slightly forward, his eyes opaque, like those of a lizard. "I have been patient, waiting for better times. I am not one of those who snatch at immediate profit and ignore the promise of the future, but I am becoming tired of patience. I see from your accounts that last week you sold goods worth over ten thousand francs and I am content for such profits to be used for restocking, when a child could see that these are exceptionally favorable times. I am not willing to see good francs squandered."

"Nor am I willing to see francs squandered," said Eve tightly.

"Then, make your peace with the Commandant, and instruct him what to buy. Otherwise those francs are mine; if I am to forfeit my living here, then, while it lasts, Le Trésor shall provide me with the reserve I need to build my future."

"It will do nothing of the sort. And after today, if you come here again, I will send for the police."

He shook his head, quite unruffled. "You have no authority, madame."

"Try me. I expect the Army would be very interested if I told them you were here instead of about your duties."

"It is arranged. I am on leave until the German delegation requires guarding at Versailles. I was not transferred to other duties like the Commandant. There are millions in the Army still, with nothing to do. I don't think anyone would be very interested in Sergeant Joubaire, even if you found the right officer to whom to complain."

Eve bit her lip; he had her there. She would miss Joubaire's efficiency, and certainly lacked time to unravel military bureaucracy. Nor did she know where to find the store at Neuilly, or how to get inside it if she did.

Joubaire struck a spitting sulphur match and lit a cigarette, incongruous against Napoleonic livery. "You could always lock me out in the street if you wanted."

"And stop trading?"

He shrugged. "It is your choice."

"No," said Eve slowly. "I certainly can't afford you outside, waiting to create a scene in the fashionable hour when Tout-Paris comes. If I can't dismiss you, then I shall have to charge you with theft. You took five hundred francs from my receipts last week, and this morning the two hundred which Mme. Rogier paid for porcelain."

"The *flics* would want proof, and also to know why you did not report the five hundred last week."

"I didn't report it because I wasn't sure," retorted Eve. "Today, Mme. Rogier will confirm her payment, and I have been in the showroom all morning. Only you went into my office, and the money is gone."

Joubaire took the notes out of his pocket and looked at them, grinning. "*Oui, madame. Et puis?* I will then tell the *flics* that you allowed me to take money each week for fear of what I would say if you did not."

"That's blackmail. If you admitted—"

"What have I to lose, if I am imprisoned for theft? It would make no difference to me, but a great deal to you, *n'est ce pas?* For what question do you think the *flics* would ask next, madame?"

"They would ask what it was I paid for rather than have revealed," said Eve deliberately. "Try it, Sergeant. Commandant Saulx told me he bought this stock legally and I believe him. I suggest you think further still: I have sold a great many expensive items recently to well-known people. They won't want any query about ownership, and are in a position to muzzle police inquiries. I have them on my side now."

Nathalie de Saint Luc had shown Eve this truth when she bought so heavily, clearly not expecting to lose by it. She planned to cause a scandal, but once she saw that Eve had confidence in whatever title existed to her stock, she had deliberately chosen pieces which would be recognizable.

Joubaire was still disturbingly unworried, though. "If matters were so simple, don't you think the Commandant might have tried to rid himself of me before?"

"We hadn't sold much when he was last here, and certainly not to people who could easily defend themselves from threat."

"And perhaps *Monsieur le commandant* was unable to think so clearly about these affairs as madame?" His tone was openly insolent again.

Eve shook her head, words stupidly congealed. It suddenly seemed intolerable that a bloodsucker like Joubaire should claim her connivance, however obliquely, in deriding Guy.

"He is not confused about one thing," added Joubaire. "They still guillotine people for murder. I have several fine tales to tell the *flics* if ever they tried to question me."

Eve stared at him, her pulse fluttering and blackness gathered behind her eyes. This was the other truth she'd intended to discover, if there had been anything left of her marriage to make such misery worthwhile. Yet only now, when everything had ended and Joubaire again dragged accusation from its hiding place to throw at her in malice and for his own profit, did she react with total disbelief.

It wasn't true and she knew it wasn't true, no matter what the evidence. Perhaps subconsciously she had always known it couldn't be true, but used this way to escape a man she did not love; as if wretchedness and fear demanded a focus she could accept without remorse. Only when Guy responded to her confession with desperate grief instead of fury did quite different emotions begin to unravel, and even then she had not noticed. Until now.

"*Ça c'est coupé l'herbe sous les pieds, n'est-ce pas?* That's winded you, hasn't it?" Joubaire remained competely confident. "You must have guessed, but were a fool to marry damaged goods even though you had an eye to property."

Eve clenched her hands. "I did not marry for property."

"No? Well, you enjoy it now you've got it. I've watched you thinking you own everything here, how you spit and scratch to defend it. Go and visit Mme. Benoit before you decide to call in the *flics*; she will tell you how the Commandant killed his father. Any court would chain him up and throw away the key on her evidence alone."

"I don't believe it." She did, though, since she had already heard what Gabrielle had to say. Whatever else had happened that night, Guy had been beside himself and was found by Gabrielle with an empty drug bottle in his hands.

Joubaire laughed. "The *flics* will believe it."

Eve went past him and shut the door deliberately. "I should like to hear from you what happened."

He looked surprised, as if he had not expected a pampered American to want to hear unpleasant detail, but told her willingly, enjoying watching her squirm. What he said tallied almost exactly with Gabrielle's account: he had been out of the Hôtel Daunay from the time of Guy's attack on Eulalie until he returned to sleep with a *bonne* he fancied.

"Everyone knows that Eulalie Daunay is a bitch for bitches," he added. "Why else would M. Daunay, who is a man of power and resource, be willing to hitch her to the Commandant, who is one of the walking dead? She enraged him, and I am not surprised, but from this came much else later, when he—"

"No." Eve heard thickness in her own voice. "You've told me once.
Daunay is to blame; he should never have considered such a way out. I
must think—"

"So I stay, madame?" interrupted Joubaire. "No *flics*, nor a lock on
your cashbox, and you will discuss with the Commandant how to use
your profit to restock?"

An unimaginable time ago, that was what they had quarreled over. "I
must think," Eve repeated dully. She had been sure these accusations
could not be true, but needed to grab at her own certainty again. The
trouble was, she had believed Gabrielle, and found herself believing
Joubaire, too, so far as his evidence went. "The drug," she said suddenly. "Those drops. What exactly do they do?"

Ever since she had lived with Guy he had spoken sometimes of them,
but more in fear than craving.

"A military doctor saw how it was with the Commandant before the
great offensive last summer, and gave him these drops to keep him on
his feet. They stun him when he is crazed but still can't sleep. I also
used to pour some down his throat when he needed oblivion before we
launched an attack, or gibbered after one. Whether he liked it or not,
the doctor said, so long as his regiment needs him, and we did need him
last year. So sometimes we held him down and poured; other times, I
hid the bottle to keep him from drinking it all; like I said, it's unwise to
marry damaged goods. Without those drops, your fine husband would
have been locked into a straitjacket long ago."

"Perhaps even that would have been more merciful," whispered Eve.
What dreadful specters Joubaire conjured up, of doomed battalions
thrust into war's furnace, no matter what the means. Foot in the chest,
nose held, drown in despair, in hate, alcohol or drugs; drain the last
drop of blood and sanity, nothing matters so long as the war is won.

Now it was won, and shattered, demolished men discovered how
peace was lost among the ruins.

CHAPTER 3

Eve felt quite exhausted when Joubaire left her alone at last. The duel between them seemed to have lasted forever, while somehow she out-faced insolence to hear yet again a repulsive sequence of events, this time recounted in such a way as to redouble grief.

She had learned a little more, though. She was now utterly deter-mined to discover exactly what had happened at the Hôtel Daunay on New Year's Eve, and sat trying to remember every word Joubaire had spoken, the inflections of his voice, the hesitations which meant some-thing left out. He was not a man who would ever say more than suited himself.

She looked up at the click of the door, thinking, No, I can't face him again so soon, but it was Sarah Wyville.

"Are you all right?" she asked doubtfully.

Eve nodded, and stood. "I'm glad to see you. Could you stay and keep an eye on Marguerite? I have to go out for a while."

"Oh, yes!" said Sarah enthusiastically. "Will you really trust me not to sell Louis Quatorze as Empire? Those old tabbies expect a bargain as soon as they hear my dreadful French."

"So long as you can count the number of francs they're offering, it's usually safe to double any figure they mention." Sarah always cheered Eve up, however exasperating she might be. She came quite often to Le Trésor as her interest in diplomatic parties waned and the weather remained too poor for outside diversions.

"There're always so many francs in everything, aren't there? I find I can't really think in such great quantities: when my couturier said my bust was eighty-something, I nearly died! Pounds and inches are so much more sensible."

"And dollars," said Eve, and laughed.

"I suppose so," conceded Sarah. "At least America uses inches, doesn't it? If the tabbies trip me over Louis Quatorze, I'll just tell them that the only French history I've been taught is how the British won. That'll keep them quiet."

"I should think it would," agreed Eve. "Don't lose all my clients, will you?"

"Oh, I'll say everything in such a sugary-acid voice they won't know whether I could possibly be as rude as I seem. Honestly, Eve, how often have you heard the French make even a compliment without a horrid, sarcastic dig?"

Eve felt tears sting her eyes. "My husband said he loved me; I wouldn't like to think he was being sarcastic."

"Well, I haven't received precisely that kind of compliment from a Frenchman yet," confessed Sarah. "Only two Englishmen and a Belgian so far, and I hope they weren't serious, because I didn't like them much. Really serious, you understand, because of course I shouldn't want them not to love me. I'm sure M. Saulx meant every word, though, Eve dear. I liked him and he wasn't a bit drawly-edged like so many Frenchmen; of course, he does speak English quite well, which helps."

"Like thinking in pounds and inches," said Eve gravely. Sarah was in fact quite shrewd, and Eve felt fewer qualms over leaving her in charge of Le Trésor than she would with unimaginative Marguerite.

Sarah enjoyed coming to Mme. Saulx's chic establishment; she had expected every day in Paris would be exciting but often found time heavy on her hands. Her father was always busy, and when he wasn't at that tedious Quai d'Orsay, had cases full of papers to wade through: such time as he spared he spent with his wife, who remained so wrapped in grief she usually refused to go out. Consequently Sarah was chaperoned by a succession of acquaintances, who usually regarded her with disapproval. Of course, she wasn't always chaperoned, since Sarah considered such constraints fustily Victorian, but junior diplomats were cautious about offending their chief and Sarah was fond enough of her father not to want to cause excessive anxiety. In London or at home in Norfolk it would be different: the sooner he learned to accept a style of life his daughter would enjoy, the better.

So Le Trésor was a pleasant diversion and Maurice Wyville sufficiently relieved that his daughter was kept out of mischief not to mind about her temporarily entering a life of commerce.

Eve returned to Le Trésor very late, and went into her cubbyhole of an office to fix herself coffee. She wasn't thinking about the lonely emptiness of the building or the crowding problems of a suddenly prosperous business; at that moment she was thinking only of Guy. She had been to the Rue Férou and the concierge had told her that she had not seen him in more than a week; when Eve went upstairs to their room, it had had the forlorn look of a place abandoned, the bed unmade and bread growing mold in the box. The window was still unmended too, the floor wet and the table smudged with soot.

Mechanically, Eve had tidied the room and swept up the glass, borrowed tacks and hammer and fitted a patch of cardboard over the broken pane; the room made her shiver, and not only with the cold. She had gone next to the cafés where they had sometimes eaten, but no one could remember seeing Commandant Saulx recently. It might simply be that he could not bear the places where they had been together, but she could not search Paris for him, especially when she did not know what she would say to him at the end of it. Nothing really had changed, except that she was anxious for him now.

Hesitantly, she had decided to go the Quai d'Orsay. She could not pass the guard, but the cafés round about were full of officers and clerks idling time away, some of whom might remember her. Guy wasn't there, either, but she did encounter an elderly staff captain who enjoyed gossip and offered to accompany her home when she left. Even so, she learned only that Guy had leave of absence after some disagreement with Foch. The captain knew nothing of the details and drew generously on imagination to persuade so elegant a *cocotte* to choose him in place of Saulx, who was not expected back. Commandants did not disagree with marshals of France and return to their posts next day.

"Rick," Eve said aloud, scalding her mouth on coffee. He possessed the means to trace missing persons, and suddenly she was also aware of how much she would enjoy seeing Rick Dwyer again. Tonight she felt horribly forlorn, left alone with Joubaire and the problems of Le Trésor.

At the back of the shop, a board creaked.

Eve tensed. In an old building, boards often creaked, but softly, timbers settling into ease; this was different. There was only one entry to her office and that in full view of the passage, so there was no means of slipping out unseen. She stood carefully, heart thumping, and moved behind an angle of cupboard; a glance would show where she was, but it was impossible simply to sit and wait for whoever came.

She had known it would be Joubaire, and it was: he must have slid back the courtyard bolts before he left, earlier. He paused in the doorway, then turned. "Ah, madame. We are not playing hide and seek."

Eve willed her voice into steadiness, for he was a man who would be brutal toward weakness. "Just what are we doing, then?"

He sat on the edge of her bureau, at ease, one leg swinging. "I am enjoying myself; and you?"

"I'm waiting for you to go."

He reached out and touched her arm. "I enjoyed our talk today, and did not cross Paris just to go again."

His touch and the bright glint of his eyes were alarming, the way he wet his lips as if his mind had been uncertain before and was now made up. Eve lifted her chin and gave him back stare for stare. As wife of Guy Saulx, I ought to have learned how to deal with men's passions, she thought.

His eyes slid away from hers and she felt a shadow of reassurance, but her fashionable calf-length skirt, which revealed the curves of leg and thigh, excited him afresh, when her expression might have made him pause. He snatched at her greedily, softness under his hands and perfume in his nostrils. Eve twisted away, farm-bred strength surprising him. He swore and came after her, while she used the space she had gained to face him again.

She was trembling in spite of her determination to offer no sign of weakness, and knew she could not get past him to the door. She also detested Joubaire and for weeks had nursed a bright glow of rage against him, which their clash of the afternoon had fanned into flame: she was in a mood to take risks to defeat him, and beneath her fear felt coldly pleased to be finished with pretense. "Leave here at once, Joubaire," she said quietly.

"Or you will whip on your fine husband to kill me, as he has killed before?" He stepped forward and held her again, laughing, red lips parted.

"Yes, he'd do it, don't you think?" She had not thought of it for herself, but saw at once that this was a threat worth having, when somehow she had to get Joubaire out of Le Trésor fast. She intended to fight him but on her own terms, which wouldn't be when he'd trapped her in a dark and empty building. "*Crime passionel*, I believe it's called in France, and usually left unpunished. It would be a tidy way for us to be rid of you for good."

She saw uncertainty in the sudden loosening of his muscles, the way anticipation changed to calculation. He had meant to taunt her but recognized truth as soon as his words were turned against him. It would indeed be a convenient way to be rid of him, with no loss except the one she faced, and after three months of being married to Saulx she might not worry overmuch about that.

Fury was like vomit on his tongue as he threw her violently away from him. Bertrand Joubaire was a sensual and ambitious man of limited imagination, who felt hotly and acted coldly; coming to Le Trésor tonight had been an unusual act of impulse, but sense quickly returned when he saw his interests threatened. He intended to have this ice-water bitch one day, but the prospect of being stalked by a deranged maniac afterward did not attract him. "I will be back," he said thickly.

The board creaked again as he left, and Eve ran down the passage to double-bolt the door as soon as she heard it slam. Everything had been so quick, a handful of minutes since she had heard the first creak of board, the whole happening like shadow on the ceiling. Yet it had happened, and told her something more: Joubaire had seemed the most likely murderer of Anselme Saulx, yet he was in no doubt at all that, for a strong enough motive, Guy was capable of killing.

She simply could not bear to spend another night alone at Le Trésor, even though it must be safe now Joubaire had gone again. Danger was there, stark and obvious even if not tonight, and alone she could not imagine rest.

Yet where could she go, in Paris after midnight?

The answer came as if it had long been waiting for her: Rick.

She realized afterward that she ought to have expected him to be out; he was not the kind of man who spent nights quietly at home. His concierge was resigned, though, and used to visitors at all hours for M. Dwyer. Females, more often than not, thought Eve wryly, as she sat through the night on a hard chair in the concierge's green-painted hutch, her courage ebbing with chill discomfort.

Tomorrow she must face Le Trésor again.

She slept in spite of everything, and was only shaken awake when Rick came in, having left Hugo studying files in his office.

"For Christ's sake, Eve," he said, staring. "What's happened? What's that bastard done to you?"

It took a moment to realize he spoke of Guy. "Nothing. I mean, it has nothing to do with him."

He took her arm. "Upstairs, and tell me later. Do you remember I promised you hot water and steam heat? You look as if you could do with both this morning."

It *was* morning too, Eve discovered when they left the dark stone entry and started climbing stairs. Her watch had stopped, but she judged it long past dawn. Rick's apartment was untidy, books and papers overflowing everywhere; he brushed aside explanation and instead ran hot water into a tub. "Later. I'll go get some croissants and boil coffee while you have a soak; you can tell me about it when you've shucked off your night in the concierge's den. There's fresh clothes on the shelf."

It was marvelous to lie in hot water with steam coiling past half-shut eyes. Eve drowsed until the water chilled, then reveled in thick towels from New York: in St.-Sulpice market she had found only gray linen worn by use.

There were certainly plenty of clothes on the shelf Rick had indicated: negligees and hand-stitched chemises carelessly tumbled with robes and sweaters bearing labels from shops in London, Paris, New York and Washington. Well, thought Eve, it's stupid to be squeamish when here I am, adding my share from the store in Main Street, New Moose.

"That looks good," said Rick as he seated her and poured coffee. "Isn't it pleasant to be able to wear lace without freezing for once?"

"Very," said Eve, and laughed. She wished she did not feel like a whore in someone else's robe.

"Want to tell me about it now?"

Oddly, the desire to confide had faded. It was all so complicated and she too tired for the effort of explanation. Still, she couldn't sit out the night on his doorstep without offering any explanation at all; anyway, she needed his help. It was difficult, though, when she had to decide on what to leave out while she spoke.

"So you've walked out on Saulx for good?" he said with satisfaction when she'd finished. "My God, do you mean to tell me that store of his is full of stolen goods, and the bastard left you alone to sell them around fashionable Paris?"

"Not exactly," said Eve wretchedly. She had been so intent on avoiding any mention of precisely why she had left Guy that she had not realized how the rest of her story would sound. In fact, Rick did not query that part at all; in his view, Eve ought never to have tried to stay with Saulx, once she understood more of the man she had married.

"Yeah, well, let's leave it at that, shall we? I must shower and go out; I'm late already. So how about you sleeping here today and telling me the rest tonight? I'll bring back steak from the Crillon and we'll eat here, so don't worry about a thing. You look tired enough to sleep for a week."

She was, and couldn't summon energy to protest. She ought to dress and go to face the usual array of problems, pack up a pair of jardinières bought two days ago and still not dispatched, decide what to do about stock, and tax, and hire another man to help Paul in the workshop. But her eyes kept closing and her body ached from hours on a hard chair; Rick's bed was wide and soft, covers fleecily warm. He knows how to live in Paris, she thought sleepily, and swooped down the slope exhaustion scoured for her. Tomorrow she would worry about Le Trésor again.

It was evening when she woke, to find Rick standing beside her with a tray in his hands. "Room service, ma'am."

Eve stretched luxuriously. "I haven't slept like that for months. Whatever time is it?"

"Cocktail time. Try the Dwyer double-dynamite mix while I fix the steak."

I must get up, thought Eve, but Rick returned as she threw back the cover and she lay back hastily, sipping her drink, as if caught out in deceit.

Rick served steak sandwiches on a plate, and sat on the edge of the bed. "Like the cocktail?"

"It makes me want to sneeze," confessed Eve. It was so dry it curled her tongue.

"No strong drink in the Ottoway homestead, I bet." He grimaced. "Nor at the Dwyers', either, but this prodigal son has gotten himself some different tastes."

"So I see." Eve touched the lace over her breasts.

He kissed her, fleetingly. "Enjoy your steak. I guess you could do with it. I don't suppose you've eaten many meals worth having since you left the Crillon."

Eve thought of the scantily stocked stalls in the markets around St.-Sulpice. "No, I haven't."

"There's more outside if you want it." He refused to let her talk until she had eaten every mouthful, drinking three cocktails while he waited and then producing a bottle of wine. "This is probably nearer your taste."

Eve had been hungry and now felt uncomfortably full; it was surprising how quickly you got out of the habit of eating such a solid meal. She also felt increasingly awkward about Rick sitting on her bed—his bed, she amended. His easy manner and the frank certainty of his design were disarming, the familiarity of American food, tobacco smells and intonations of voice subtly denying strangeness. She had been besieged by alien circumstance and overwhelmed by worry for so very long.

"Do you like Paris?" Rick asked unexpectedly, although the question tuned in with her thoughts.

"Yes. No. I could have." Honesty again seemed important. "It's just . . . well, Paris is another existence from New Moose, and so was everything else all at the same time."

Rick poured himself a tumbler of wine. "If you'd been happy here, you would have liked Paris."

"Rick, you mustn't keep heaping everything on Guy. Often we were happy. But for the war—"

"The goddam war, yeah, I know. Sometimes I think I'd like to quit Europe forever and set up as the *Times* correspondent in the Midwest."

"You'd be bored crazy inside a week."

"I guess so," he said ruefully. "Kansas City is a hell of a place for a reporter to earn his living in this year of nineteen-nineteen. How do you think you would feel the week after you got back to New Moose?"

Eve shrugged. "I'm not likely to find out."

He put down his glass and took her hands in his. "It's easier to go forward than back. I think you would enjoy Paris with me. Let's give it a try, shall we?"

"Rick—"

He put his fingers under her chin and kissed her. "Smile for me, Eve. You've a mouth made to smile as well as be kissed; I thought so when I first saw you. Now I've kissed it and know that part was right, not that I was ever in danger of being wrong. Now I'd like to prove myself right on the rest."

Eve laughed. "I bet you think that about every girl you meet for the first time."

He kissed her again. "I was right. That's the way you should look, with a smile in your eyes and a kiss on your lips." And he thought how strange it was that anyone as lovely as she should be so unconscious of her power. Strange, too, that resolute bones, tilted nose and curved mouth should subtly become loveliness when she possessed little conventional beauty. Then he thought only of how to overcome instinctive prudishness left over from New Moose, the recoil of a body to which that bastard Saulx had helped himself without troubling to arouse.

There was a roar of traffic outside the window, the wide bed and Rick's skills playing on her senses; Eve had not wanted this, still did not truly want it, being weary of men's bodies wanting hers, but had known when she came that this would happen. And after Guy, Rick was joyfully uncomplicated; he did not suffer nightmares or attack her in the night as if he loathed instead of loved her; she could sleep peacefully in his arms instead of lying as the anvil for another's torment. Rick roused her easily and regarded having her in his bed as the most natural thing in the world; he teased and laughed with her, and slept while they were still warm together.

It's all so easy, thought Eve, amazed. He had been half drunk, but that hadn't seemed to matter either. He woke while she watched him in the sunlight of early morning and came instantly awake, his mouth seeking her breast. It was easier still in the morning, when she was rested, and thoughts of adultery put behind her. Afterward they dressed and breakfasted together, whatever they did miraculously set apart from strain.

"I can't quite think why I don't feel guilty," said Eve suddenly. "When I came—"

"You're not telling me you came to my apartment in the middle of the night just to find a good old buddy from home?" he demanded.

She had come in fear and loneliness as to a bolt-hole, and probably would have gone to the Rue Férou, except she knew Guy wasn't there. "I don't know."

"Of course you know," he said impatiently. "That's one thing which makes my reporter's hackles rise. Witnesses who say they don't know, yet choose and do the thing they want. Which for you last night happened to be me. You'll never get a priest or minister to admit it, but joyful sin is nearly always better for you than the thicket of thorns."

"I told you, I don't feel guilty," Eve repeated.

"What do you feel?"

"Rested."

He drank his coffee, unexpectedly disconcerted. "You'll come again tonight?"

She nodded, thinking of Le Trésor and Joubaire's foot on creaking boards.

Tranquillity held her all through a difficult day. Joubaire was surly, Marguerite snuffling with a cold, Sarah obviously charmed by a new customer who spent an inconvenient length of time examining porcelain. He was personable, though; Eve wasn't surprised a girl like Sarah fell for such good looks and address. She sighed, hoping he would soon go. She could do without the complication of Sarah in love with some Parisian man-about-town, when she had met him in her store.

"He isn't Parisian," said Sarah when he went at last. "I don't think I like Frenchmen much, except for M. Saulx, of course," she added hastily.

Eve had avoided thinking about Guy all day, and her tone sharpened as she thought about him now. "Where does he come from, then?"

"He's Swiss, and collects porcelain as a hobby. He's in Paris to report the Conference, but I shouldn't think the Swiss care much, would you? He says he has to pass a great deal of time just waiting when everything that matters is shuttled secretly among the few men at the top, so uses it to improve his collection."

Eve's heart sank; the Wyvilles were unlikely to regard a Swiss newsman as respectable. "Is he coming back?"

"I wouldn't be surprised," said Sarah saucily. "He bought a Sèvres candlestick, or at least he paid a Sèvres price for it and scarcely even tried to bargain."

"Did he realize it might not be Sèvres?"

"Oh, yes! He seemed very knowledgeable, but said he never liked to take advantage on the first day of a new acquaintance. The second and third would be different, when I wouldn't be constrained by shyness and able to bargain franc for franc with him."

"He must have been deaf and blind to think you were shy," said Eve dryly.

"He didn't, of course. He probably always says things like that, and was rather surprised to find I wasn't shy, so this time it didn't fit at all. He's gone away to think about it, I expect."

"Well, with any luck you won't be here if he comes again." Whether she was or not, Eve resolved that if he did come again, she and not Sarah would serve this Swiss.

Sarah squeezed her hand warmly. "Don't worry about me, Eve. I've quite decided that next time he comes I shall be quite dreadfully tongue-tied and shy. It should be amusing to see what he tries then."

The Comtesse de Saint Luc came in soon after, and Eve forgot Sarah in the flurry her presence always caused. The soirée which would mark the refurnishing of Nathalie de Saint Luc's salon was set for two weeks hence and Eve invited to attend. It was another of the things she had been trying not to think about, for this could be a quite appalling show-down. I must think about it, and very quickly too, she reflected. Whether I like it or not, I simply have to find Guy and ask him to give me the receipts he said he had.

And as urgency drove at her, she felt her stomach lurch. She had not felt guilty breakfasting with Rick this morning; but how would she feel when she saw Guy again?

CHAPTER 4

"Eve, no. You'd have to think a great deal more carefully first about what you want."

"I have thought," she retorted. "Care hasn't got much to do with it."

"You wouldn't be in this goddam mess if you'd thought a few minutes before you married Saulx." Rick pushed his plate aside and poured more wine for them both.

"I don't know," Eve said, reflectively. "I was a fool in more ways than you know, but what I did seemed right at the time. Thinking longer probably wouldn't have made any difference."

"I suppose you were just a starry-eyed kid full of damfool notions and preacher's charity, but he— My God, he wasn't so crazy he didn't know it was criminal for him to marry you."

Eve winced. "I don't want to talk about it, but that part wasn't his fault. None of it was as simple as you seem to think, so let's leave it, shall we? Which brings us back to me asking you to find Guy for me."

"No," he repeated flatly. "I'm glad to see the back of the bastard."

"But I've explained to you why I must find him!"

"I didn't hear how your explanations included plans for divorce."

"I'd still need to find him if I had any plans."

"Have you?"

Eve stared at her wine. She had lived a week with Rick, letting the world slip, and felt enormously better for it; but the world was intrusive again, and as her usual vigor returned, she had become impatient to tackle the confusion engulfing her life. She disliked shuffling matters aside unresolved, but successive shocks had simply brought her to the end of her resources.

That was a week ago, and now she felt quite different, yet everything was more complicated than before; above all, she needed to find Guy within the week before Nathalie de Saint Luc's soirée, within the very short time before Joubaire again demanded more from her than petty pilferings. She had considered and rejected a dozen plans for defeating him, but he was still there and bolder every day. Also she was worried by Guy's disappearance, had thought everything was finished between them only to discover that that, too, was less simple than she expected.

She looked up. "I think Guy will have to say what he wants."

"For Christ's sake! You walked out because you couldn't stand him any longer. What makes you think anything has changed, except for the worse?"

"I'm his wife, Rick. You'll just have to accept that's how I feel. I don't feel able just to set him adrift, unless that's what he wants."

"You're as crazy as he is," said Rick with conviction. "He'll kill you one day when you're all sweet and anxious, bathing his bruised ego."

Eve flushed. "You've said that before, but he's never harmed me. Yes, I've been frightened, I'll admit it, but he's torn himself apart trying to recover decencies he once possessed, and keep torment chained out of my sight. He didn't always succeed, that's all."

"Then, he's certainly best left howling in a corner by himself. You won't change me, Eve. Anyway, I couldn't find him if he's foamed all over Foch's boots and been locked away in some French Army stockade, and I'm not going to try until you've gotten him out of your system." He came around and kissed her. "You stay here with me. Have you looked in the mirror recently? Rick Dwyer is good for your health."

"I know you are," Eve said candidly. "But I can't spend my life nursing my own health."

"Why not? Then, one day, when you've decided on that divorce—"

Eve laughed delightedly. "Rick! Is that a proposal? And you with an apartment full of lingerie and a bed like a room on its own?"

"You enjoy the bed, and we could always give the clothes to the concierge. I find I'm quite often leaving the Peace Conference to wrangle on its own so I can hurry back here to you. To me, we fit together fine, nor do we get in each other's way."

"We should. We ought to. That's really what I'm trying to say. Marriage means getting in each other's way, not necessarily unpleasantly, but it does close some roads if others are to be opened, or it should. I think you'd hate it, Rick dear."

"I sure don't hate this," he said, and kissed her again. "I've felt very married having breakfast a whole week with the same woman. I usually can't look at them in the morning."

Eve said nothing and allowed herself to be taken to bed; argument was getting them nowhere.

Sarah's Swiss newsman, M. Kobis, came into Le Trésor again next morning, their easy exchanges suggesting to Eve that he must have been there several times when she was out.

Since Eve was feeling in the mood for settling uncertainty, she went over as soon as Sarah had the contents of a cabinet spread out for his inspection. "*Bonjour*, M. Kobis."

He turned and bowed. "*Bonjour*, Mme. Saulx. If the Peace Conference does not settle its affairs soon, I shall be seriously embarrassed financially from all the porcelain I have bought."

"You will be much better educated, though," said Sarah mischievously. "Do you know, Eve, Hugo did not know a single one of the modern dances? He still thought the fox-trot rather daring! They must be dreadfully stuffy in Switzerland."

"We have to be very careful there," said Hugo seriously. "It's all those Alps, you see. Saxophones set off avalanches, so we prefer to be safe, but solemn."

Sarah gurgled with laughter. "How about yodels? They must bring down the avalanches like anything."

"Not like a bunny hug or black bottom," he said firmly. "Just little ones, which only bury you deep enough for the dogs to find. You know, the sort who carry brandy. All the best Swiss parties depend on being rescued at the right moment by a herd—flock—is that right? of those excellent dogs."

"A shoal. Because of all that brandy," explained Sarah kindly.

"Thank you, Mlle. Sarah. A shoal describes what I had in mind exactly."

Eve laughed too, but listened with increasing misgiving. She found Hugo Kobis attractive, and suspected that most women would, but he was several years older than herself, perhaps thirteen or fourteen years older than Sarah. It was not surprising a seventeen-year-old should be taken by his charm, but unlikely that a man who possessed such obvious gifts was more than fleetingly amused by her. One day, Sarah Wyville would be a personality to be reckoned with, but not yet.

"Sarah, would you go and find the porcelain catalogue for M. Kobis? I think that if he is anxious to add to his collection, we should at least inform him of the provenance of items he buys," she said.

Sarah laughed. "Dear Eve, I showed it to him yesterday. No, I don't think I want to go rooting in your office while you scold poor Hugo."

Eve bit her lip. "I have no intention of scolding M. Kobis."

"In that case you won't mind if I stay to listen while you tell him all about porcelain. I have become very knowledgeable, you know; he doesn't catch me out nearly so often as he did. Father was astonished by my industry when I stayed at home three nights in a row with fusty old books on Limoges and Sèvres."

Eve picked up a pair of bronze gilt dishes enameled with flowers. "What are these?"

"Vincennes porcelain," interposed Hugo, smiling. "Mlle. Sarah cannot learn everything in three evenings, when she must also find time to teach me the bunny hug."

"You have taken her out?" Eve abandoned subterfuge, since it was clear that Sarah intended to remain stuck like a burr.

"Twice to a *thé dansant* in the Champs-Élysées; do you, then, object?"

"It isn't for me to object, but since she is under age and met you in my store, I shall feel bound to inform her parents."

Something flickered in Hugo's eyes but was gone before Eve could decide she must have been mistaken when she thought it was satisfaction.

"You wouldn't be so mean!" said Sarah indignantly. "Eve, I promise you that Hugo behaved exactly like a gentleman the whole time."

Hugo grinned unexpectedly. "Sarah was most disappointed, I assure you, madame. Although of course only the English can actually be gentlemen."

Against her will, Eve laughed. "Wretched child. You haven't changed my mind, though."

"I am sure you are right, madame," agreed Hugo placidly. "I should be very happy to meet Sir Maurice Wyville."

A faint suspicion uncurled in Eve's mind. "As a reporter, M. Kobis?"

"That, too, of course, although I should be a fool if I expected the Züricher *Zeitung* to obtain much of interest from a man well used to keeping his mouth shut. No, I should simply like to set your anxieties at rest if I could." Hugo's eyes dropped to the porcelain between them. "And now, I think that today I should like to purchase some Meissen for a change."

Eve left them to it; there was nothing more she could do except send a note to the Wyvilles when the car came to pick up Sarah. She went out into the street instead, and stood, sketch pad in hand, staring at Le Trésor's window. It was more than time the design was changed, and on this occasion she wanted something exotic and completely different, since so many of her best French pieces had sold, while there was still a considerable stock of lacquer and oriental goods of all kinds. She frowned, reviewing in her mind which items would look best in the window while trying to visualize some unifying design.

She looked up, and discovered Hugo Kobis waiting beside her. "I'm sorry, I didn't know you were there. Were you able to find something which pleased you?"

"Indeed, yes. I wanted to tell you that I understand your anxiety for a girl under your protection, but you may set your mind at rest so far as I am concerned. Mlle. Wyville will take no harm from me."

Eve studied him and then nodded. "I believe you. But as you must know that you possess considerable charm of manner, I don't mind mentioning it. I'm surprised you don't understand women better, monsieur. You may behave as much like a gentleman as you choose and Sarah still take a great deal of harm at your hands, when you tire of filling a few idle hours with flirtation."

He flushed unexpectedly. "She is very young and simply enjoying herself, too."

Eve shrugged. "Yes, she's young, but you know I'm right. Otherwise you wouldn't have apologized. Send her some flowers and a pretty message; then don't come back."

He looked away, face set and somber. "I will do my best, you may be sure."

"It only needs a little resolution and address," Eve replied briskly.

He laughed. "How easy it is to arrange the lives of others, madame."

Eve felt her face tighten; that particular remark was too close to the truth for comfort. "You are an unusual reporter, M. Kobis."

"No, why? We are all unusual, surely. You, for instance; I was very interested when Mlle. Sarah told me you had no experience of antiques, yet had made a success of so difficult a business within a matter of weeks."

"You could certainly have discovered holes in my knowledge of fine porcelain," Eve acknowledged.

"I doubt it," he said dryly; like Sarah, he had spent many hours over fusty tomes. "M. Saulx is fortunate to have married so charming and accomplished a lady."

Eve could feel herself blushing; she wasn't used to the kind of compliments Europeans offered with complete solemnity.

Hugo watched her, smiling faintly. He wanted very much to discover where Guy Saulx had gone, but was both disquieted and delighted to find his wife so charming. Guy deserved a turn in his fortunes and surely could not have been so completely annihilated by war as Dwyer suggested, when he had recently married a woman of such warmth and intelligence; either that, or Dwyer was right, and she had no business to be married to him. "I always understood that American women are very capable," he added after a pause. "Certainly, you have proved this for me. You are planning a new . . . layout, do you say? . . . for your window?"

"It's something I really enjoy, so long as the idea comes," Eve replied ruefully, and found herself explaining about the need for an oriental setting. He was a good listener, and somehow she began telling him about her worries over stock, too, a couple of oblique questions she did not notice establishing that Guy was away and that she did not know when he would be back.

She's worried about him, Hugo thought, adding aloud: "I am forced to haunt the lobbies of the Peace Conference for the Züricher *Zeitung,* although it is wasted effort. If I should encounter Commandant Saulx I will suggest that he visit Switzerland when he is free; there is a great deal more to buy there than cuckoo clocks."

Eve's fingers twisted with her pencil. "If— if you should happen to see him, do you think . . . could you ask. . . ." Her voice trailed away. She could not beg a complete stranger to ask her husband if he would visit her. Nor was Guy at the Conference any longer.

"I will tell Commandant Saulx that however urgent are his duties, he should apply for a few hours' leave," said Hugo, as if he accepted that it was impossible for Guy to cross Paris without major formalities.

"I wish you would," said Eve gratefully. "You ought to be a diplomat instead of a reporter, M. Kobis."

He gave an involuntary chuckle. "Yes, perhaps. And now, madame, I might also be a window designer if you will permit me to make a suggestion. *Les ballets russes.* Diaghilev is all *surréalisme* and cubist settings now, but not many have accustomed themselves to this change, from what I understand. I remember the great thunderclap caused by Stravinsky and Diaghilev before the war, though, and so will your rich patrons. That could be your oriental background, yet sufficiently linked with the life of Tout-Paris to be acceptable."

"What a marvelous idea! I have just the silk brocades which would— M. Kobis, are you sure you're not looking for a job?"

He laughed and bowed formally. "*Au revoir,* madame. I shall look forward to seeing the results of our inspiration."

Only afterward did Eve remember that she had intended to make him promise not to see Sarah again.

Eve threw herself into the new setting for Le Trésor; perhaps Tout-Paris had begun to take her Louis Quatorze and Empire ideas for granted, and this would be triumphantly different, prove that nothing could be taken for granted in the shop in the Rue Daunou. Jewel-like "Firebird" colors would dazzle the eye, caskets of barbaric *objets d'art* spill carelessly open to display the carved ivories and gilded glass which Paris taste normally despised. A backdrop of the steppes, thought Eve feverishly, with the fire made up so it reflects on a burning village. I must try to find someone who will carve Petrouchka puppets. . . . I wonder whether I dare turn right away from antiques just this once, and stock a few wickedly expensive fur cloaks and capes?

Rick found her inattentive the next few nights, and she was often late getting back as she rushed around Paris trying to find the people she needed: she decided to risk stocking the furs when she discovered a Russian émigré furrier with exactly what she sought; of course they were fabulously expensive, but the *beau monde* of Paris did not lack money to spend, once something became fashionable. For everyone else, it was different. Decorative *tricolores* and flags of the Allies were beginning to be overshadowed by the red of working-class discontent, as spiraling prices brought real distress. Wages fell and unemployment grew as the vast complex of war industries in the Paris region faced the reality of peace. The Avenue de l'Opéra and the Champs-Élysées were often filled with shouting crowds, and Eve came to dread the need to go out when she wasted so much time forcing a way through belligerent mobs.

The statesmen, too, remained trapped in dissension, although well aware of mounting unrest. They were barracked by shouting groups, harried by delegations, besieged by hostile, often hysterical criticism. Elderly and already exhausted by years of strain, they no longer contemplated the wider vision, when only crude bargaining would ever allow them to finish the impossible task they had assumed. President Wilson became ill; Lloyd George was forced to scurry back to Westminster to cow a dangerously shrill opposition; Clemenceau became the victim of scurrilous cartoons, and deputies in the National Assembly openly referred to him as a traitor selling the interests of France.

In Bavaria, a soviet republic was proclaimed, but the agony of Germany was not news in Paris. The loser in any war must expect some difficult moments, though it seemed unjust that the victors should experience them too.

Hugo searched the newpapers in a frenzy of frustration, trying to discover what was happening in the Reich, whether indeed a Reich remained. Red Bavaria had declared itself an independent republic; the Freikorps had stormed Berlin and imposed a reign of terror; the French openly gloated that with their help the Rhineland would soon secede. He continued to meet Sarah Wyville and take her dancing, the nag of conscience over a girl's sensibilities unimportant at such a time; instead, her fresh and unspoiled vivacity became a relief from crisis.

As uncertainty increased, volatile Parisian emotions continued to boil over in a mad orgy of dance: Eve certainly struck the right mood with her exotic and faintly decadent swirl of color in the windows of Le Trésor. It didn't matter what the hour, there were orchestras, jazz bands, drums, half-gutted pianos and brass bands playing to frenzied dancers, and since Hugo would never be allowed to take Sarah out at night, they went in the afternoon to cafés and boats along the Seine, where dancing never stopped, to restaurants where it was now normal to danse-tango between courses, and to the morning *"dansomanie"* in the vestibule of the Casino de Paris.

Hugo was puzzled and impatient as time passed and still he wasn't summoned to the Hôtel Astoria to give an account of himself, but at least Sarah knew a great number of the younger attachés to the Allied delegations, and he was able to piece together a jigsaw puzzle of useful information. There was nothing particularly secret in the sprawling deliberations of the main Conference; only the vital horse-trading in Clemenceau's salon remained completely unknown. It was, rather, that discussions in dozens of committees were imperfectly collated and their decisions often contradictory or imprecise; it was only possible to estimate the final shape of any settlement by sifting gossip from a great many sources. The newspapers printed everything, the most exaggerated rumor and the most detailed confidential leak: usually it was impossible to distinguish between frivolous invention and possible fact. Hugo hoped fervently that a government still existed in Germany which would read his dispatches, for the framework of the eventual treaty which he was so painfully assembling bore little resemblance to expectations which he knew existed in the Wilhelmstrasse.

In Berlin, the experts believed that the Allies valued Germany as a bastion against Bolshevism and would not be tempted to weaken such a fragile state any further; anyway, President Wilson had repeatedly said that they had no quarrel with the German people, only the aggressions of its imperial government, now defunct.

Well, Hugo had news for the experts of the Wilhelmstrasse, if they were still capable of absorbing it. Wilson was sick and politically weak, the Allies not in the least grateful for Germany's stand against Bolshevism, while France and Belgium certainly regarded themselves as invaded and ruined by the German people, not just its government. They intended to hang the Kaiser if he could be reached, but personal revenge was insignificant beside their determination to castrate German power, which for the French at least meant extending ruin to the people whose power it was and breaking their state in pieces.

Hugo felt intensely depressed; there could surely be no worse situation than being a secret German in Paris at such a time. *Gueules cassées* begged on street corners, while undernourished children and the unemployed piled tinder-dry fury around the sunburst of luxury in the city's heart. Also, Hugo understood French fears only too well, when France was so profoundly ruined by the war; but not even understanding helped, because all of Europe was caught in the mills of tragedy, the juggernaut of fear and revenge laying waste what was left of peace.

Oddly, Hugo came to sense that uneasiness afflicted the British first. There was no sign of moderation in the British press or parliament, but the younger members of the British delegation had shared American idealism at the beginning of the Conference and were disillusioned by the way their hopes were allowed to crumble. Also, British leaders were not devoted to abstract principles, none less so than Lloyd George, a realist of realists.

As tension mounted in Paris, Hugo thought he wasn't mistaken. If there were to be second thoughts, they would start with the British.

Then news broke on April 18 that a German delegation had been summoned to receive the text of the treaty a week later, although to Hugo's knowledge no such treaty existed. Decisions, concessions, and compromises littered the delegations' offices, but no treaty was yet drawn up for negotiation.

It was very hard to dance and pretend lack of care, when the Wilhelmstrasse sent back a dignified response to the summons, apparently still expecting leisured dealings between equals when Hugo had repeatedly warned them that this was far from the Allied intention.

"You are in the clouds today," said Sarah, pinching his arm.

"They are at least more attractive than the reality of Europe." Hugo looked at the vivid, mischievous face at his shoulder, and smiled. "None of which is your affair. I am sorry to be such poor company."

"It would be odd if you always were good company. I know you think so, but I'm not at all one of those brainless creatures who expects everything to suit me all the time, and people to have nothing on their minds but the latest gossip."

"I never thought you were," said Hugo, touched.

"You did, but never mind that now. Would you like to come to England?"

"To England!"

"I live there, or had you forgotten? You see, Father accompanied Lloyd George back there last week and goes to Stoneham for the weekend before returning here on Monday. Now Mother has decided there is nowhere she wants to be so much as Stoneham, and I told her I knew exactly the person to escort us."

"You did?"

"Well, of course. Dear Hugo, I am sure there must be some scandal in England which you should investigate for your newspaper. I told Mother you had business in London and would not mind a bit going on the same train as us and managing tickets and porters and all the things she always drops or forgets. Don't you see, she has that wretched letter

Eve wrote about you? She certainly intends to show it to my father, but of course will disbelieve every word Eve wrote once you are attentive and agreeable. And if you manage well, and don't drop or lose anything, as of course you won't, then she can hardly help asking a Swiss with no friends in England down to Stoneham with us, can she? I shall remind her if she doesn't think of it for herself. *Then* you will be perfectly respectable and able to take me to the Canadian Delegation Ball next week!"

"If your mother has Madame Saulx's letter, why hasn't she forbidden you to come out with me?"

"Oh, she did," said Sarah blithely. "But I assured her that Eve was making a great fuss about nothing, and since my brother was killed, she lacks resolution to do so much as leave the hotel. That is why she wants to bolt back to Stoneham, I think." She frowned. "I am very much afraid she won't return to Paris, which would mean I'd have to stay with her."

"Will you mind?"

"Of course I shall. But you knew that, didn't you?"

"Mme. Saulx was perfectly right. I ought never to have continued seeing you in this way."

"I couldn't at first work out why you did," confessed Sarah. "When I know that often you think I'm scarcely out of the schoolroom, which, I assure you, I am not! I've had to do a great deal at Stoneham with everything upset by the war, and then Charlie in the Army."

"I've found you enchanting," said Hugo truthfully. "A burned-out world needs the untouched young from their schoolrooms."

He kissed her undemandingly, as he had a few times before when she seemed to expect it, but this time it was different. The flame of response was lit, shriveling the amused indulgence he had felt for her before. Sarah Wyville was no longer the enchanting child he thought her, but vividly loving in his arms.

She smiled wickedly when he tore himself from her. "It's quite your own fault, you know. I could have loved you to distraction from a distance and you have known very little about it, except that you thought I would be useful. I hope your editor thinks your articles are worth the trouble you have taken, because they've really landed you in rather a scrape, haven't they?"

Hugo was shaken by laughter. "Do you never care what you say?"

"Do you never care what you do to follow a good story?"

He kissed her again, but gently this time. "Yes, I care very much. How long have you known?"

"That you found my friends useful? Nearly from the beginning. It is often rather awkward, but I can usually tell what people are thinking even though they say or do something quite different. It's useful, too, of course," she added. "You aren't thinking of the Züricher *Zeitung* at the moment, for instance."

"No. Nor have I always thought of it with you."

"I know. So will you escort us to England? I told Mother you weren't in the least what Eve wrote in her letter, if only she would take this chance to become acquainted."

"But I am, my dear. As you have said, you knew I was, nearly from the beginning."

"That's horrid, Hugo."

He stared at her, but her eyes did not waver from his, and after a few moments it was he who looked away, out across the Seine from the moored barge where they had been dancing. "I apologize. I never felt with you as if I were simply a vulture seeking his carrion of inside information, although often I needed to offer excuses for myself."

"And you will come to England? You can be back on Monday."

He nodded, and was uncertain whether he went because it was unthinkable for a Wilhelmstrasse spy to refuse an invitation to Sir Maurice Wyville's home, or because his reward was Sarah's hug of delight.

CHAPTER 5

Eve dreaded the day of Nathalie de Saint Luc's soirée, and because of it time seemed to hurtle past with nothing settled. No chance of settling anything, nor time to go to the Hôtel Daunay again, as she must if she cared . . . if she still cared enough for Guy to want to solve the mystery of his father's death. The very next day in which there was an hour to spare she would go, but spare hours vanished as the hectic, spendthrift atmosphere of Paris spilled over the threshold of Le Trésor. The only relief was that Sergeant Joubaire had been called back to duty, now the German delegation was expected within days. Eve hoped this might mean that Guy, too, would reappear, but when Joubaire came into Le Trésor, he said that someone else had been appointed to command security for the Germans, and no inquiry produced any information on Commandant Saulx's whereabouts; Joubaire felt quite as much at a loss as Eve did over what to do next. Threatening her became pointless when she had banked profits in ignorance of French law which made it impossible for a married woman to withdraw money even from a joint account without her husband's consent. Because of this, Eve was already in severe difficulties, having started by banking everything to keep Joubaire's hands off it. Now she was forced to keep cash back, above all because the question of replacing stock had become urgent, which meant that the problem of limiting Joubaire's pilfering became acute. The relief when he was sent off to Versailles was enormous, temporary though it might be.

Before he went, he had begun quite openly intercepting her after a client had left, and since French customers often paid cash, Eve came to dread rather than delight in a sale. But the real problem remained the whole future of Le Trésor, which was bound up with the fat balance of francs no one could touch until Guy was found.

"How long do you suppose the Germans will be at Versailles?" she asked Rick. The longer the better, while Joubaire froze in cold rain outside their quarters.

He shrugged. "God knows. As long as it takes the Allies to concentrate their minds and print a treaty for them to read."

"Do you mean there isn't one?"

"Nor anything like it. The Italians and Japs have just walked out of discussions in a rage, and most of the smaller nations are plotting in cafés, while the diplomats scuttle around Paris like maggots in bad meat. It wouldn't look good after all the high-minded speeches if just the U.S., Britain and France fixed the future of Europe to suit themselves."

"For land's sakes! Why send for the Germans if nothing is ready?" Eve had paid only passing attention to peacemaking since she had so many other preoccupations, but even so, it seemed an improvident procedure.

"Because everything is in such a tangle there was a danger the Conference would fall apart with nothing settled. They're gambling that, faced by a deadline, everyone will settle for what they can get. Also, we want to get our Army out of France: the British have already demobilized a couple of million and we've had God knows how many desertions. Soon we won't be able to invade Germany if they refuse to sign."

"Of course, it could work the other way around," said Eve thoughtfully, remembering intransigent delegates from her time at the Quai d'Orsay.

"Say again?"

"Italy and the rest who want concessions could feel that a deadline offered them their chance. Force the rest into giving them what they want so the Conference doesn't sink."

"Sure. It depends who has the nerve to outlast the rest."

"Or enough statesmanship to yield a little, and so bring the peace we long for."

"You long for," amended Rick. "There are a helluva lot of aggressive guys with their heads together in corners at the moment."

"But no one could dream of another war like— For God's sake, Rick, that's what we fought for!"

"So I've heard it said. The U.S., Britain, France; we've won and want to keep it that way. There's others with different interests, and I don't only mean Germany."

Eve felt so dismayed by this conversation that she tried to follow events more closely, but nothing seemed to make much sense. Paris newspapers were full of spring fashions: breastless, hipless, scandalously short fashions which made women look like adolescent boys. Paris society was not yet completely resigned to following where Chanel led, but short hair, short skirts, *le pullover*, and soft jersey material had subtle attractions for women, offering freedom after the centuries of cluttered imprisonment.

The Paris press had long regarded factual politics as something reported in the spaces left between criticism, the latest scandal and whatever literary and artistic polemics titillated the taste of the day: while the Allies waited in disarray for the Germans to arrive, speculation centered on the forthcoming prospects for the Ballets Russes, on Proust and Cocteau, the excesses of Dadaism, cubism and surrealism. In the spring of 1919, Paris was not only the political storm center of the world, it was also the liveliest, the most wildly extravagant, the noisiest, the most amusing and depraved city of the postwar world. Taste and behavior became more wildly eccentric from day to day, theft almost commonplace. Eve sold almost her whole stock of oriental and lacquer goods, then Mistinguett came in one day and bought three sable capes without even asking the price: she had seen Eve's "Firebird" window and immediately decided to receive her dinner guests naked except for thrown-back sable and cossack boots. Some Renaissance rings were sold to a woman who wanted to wear them on her toes in bed, a sixteenth-century steel breastplate to a *demi-mondaine* who wore it in the Ritz bar. Men came in dressed as women, women arrived smoking cigarettes in holders a yard long.

Sex in a certain inner Paris set, where money, art and salon life mingled, was explicit and perverted enough to shock the hardworking bourgeoisie quite as much as at first it had shocked Eve. Secretly, she was still shocked, but hid it better than she had. However hard she tried to outlive it, Maine puritanism was ingrained in her, and she was a little comforted by Marguerite, who regarded postwar Paris as she would a leper seated in her kitchen. "It is an abomination, madame. The good God must wonder what *espèce de bête* now inhabits this world. He weeps, madame, and who can wonder?" She flipped a stubby finger at rain beating on the window.

"I have never lived in a city before and expected Europe to be different, but—"

"Paris was the most beautiful place on earth, madame." Marguerite spoke with the conviction of one who had never been anywhere else. "Naturally it is a city, what of it? Before that accursed war, ladies clothed their bodies and decent men did not behave like pimps in a gutter."

After that exchange, Eve's relations with Marguerite eased. Before, she had been grudgingly civil; now she brought every fresh scandal to share with her employer, her eyes glistening with pleasurable disgust.

One day, Rick told Eve about a family living at St.-Cloud who wanted to return to La Rochelle, where they had come from thirty years before. Their four sons had been killed in the war, and the father had given up his business to work for the Red Cross when the last of them died of wounds. They intended to sell the entire contents of their house to a single bidder, and Rick only told her the story because he thought there might be profit in it, when only junk dealers had shown interest in such a time-consuming business. So Eve squeezed a few hours to go out to St.-Cloud one evening, since she was becoming desperately worried about stock. If there was anything worth having, she'd work nights to clear the house if necessary.

"I don't want a single thing left." The elderly woman who received her looked as if she had wept her last tear long before. "We return to La Rochelle because we may best wait out the years there, but I cannot bear to take anything with us which will remind me of the past. Nothing. Not a photograph, not a table where my boys sat, nor any plate from which they ate. Do you find that strange?"

"I'm not sure," said Eve slowly. "Perhaps I might need something to remind me that happiness once existed."

"Whenever I see the young, I pray they will never know a time when the memory of happiness is the one remaining burden which cannot be borne. You are long married, madame?"

"Four months," she said reluctantly.

"And to a Frenchman, from the name, although you are American, *n'est-ce pas?*"

Eve nodded, wishing people would stop prodding the aching stump of her marriage.

"Our poor France can do with a transfusion of blood from across the Atlantic. May your sons live out their lives in peace." She touched Eve's stomach in frank French acknowledgment of physical functions which Eve found embarrassing at the best of times, and on this occasion cruelly hurtful. "And now, Mme. Saulx, you may look at the house. I sell the whole contents to one buyer, as there are rooms I do not wish to enter and haggling would be beyond endurance. You may come afterward to my salon and offer your price, if you wish."

"It was unbelievable," Eve told Rick that night. "I've had to take everything from kitchen to attic, they're going to leave for Rochelle in the clothes they wear and possessing nothing else. Not even a valise."

"Except a fat bank balance."

"Not from me. I offered as much as I could, but I've only the cash I've kept in hand. I told her my price was absurdly low for what was there, but I don't think she would have cared if I'd named a sum half or twice as large. Her only thought was that now she could go tomorrow."

Rick whistled. "Just like that?"

"That was the deal. I write to their lawyers when the house is empty, so they can sell it. No time limit, and nothing except her husband's signature making over the contents to me. He never spoke once."

"So now you've got to clear out some goddam great mansion at St.-Cloud, as well as all the rest? I was a fool to tell you, I guess."

Eve sighed. "It's all so terrible, Rick. Those poor people . . . can you imagine stripping yourself of everything and not even caring about the price?"

Rick looked at his apartment consideringly. "I hire and sell nearly everything each time I take a new assignment. It never bothers me."

Eve did not answer: a home where a whole family had grown up was different. She doodled restlessly on some paper, nerves strung tight from the breakneck pace she was forced to set herself, as well as from glimpsing the unendurable at St.-Cloud. And tomorrow was the day of the Comtesse de Saint Luc's soirée. She had thought that if she could only bluff her way through whatever the Comtesse planned for her—and what could she prove, or do to her, after all?—then afterward she could face Joubaire and then fire him, daring him to tell everything he knew, since by then the scandal would be open but discredited. Now that the soirée was tomorrow it seemed a crazy risk to take; she ought never to have agreed to go, should have done anything to make the Comtesse change her purposes.

I don't care any more, she thought wearily. Let the society harpies tear me to pieces so as to provide Nathalie de Saint Luc with entertainment: I'll remember St.-Cloud, and believe I'm lucky, compared to some.

She did not feel lucky the following evening, driving in a *fiacre* to the Ile St.-Louis. Rick had left to cover the arrival of the German delegation at Versailles, and she missed his buoyant presence while she dressed. Despite her success with Le Trésor, she was oppressed by a sense of failure, and not even the sleek gown she was wearing lifted depression. Absurdly, she had felt hurt that Rick did not stay when he knew how much she dreaded this evening. But of course he could not come with her to the Comtesse de Saint Luc's salon without an invitation, and Washington would expect a dispatch on the arrival of the Germans.

Eve made a face at her own reflection in dirty *fiacre* windows; whatever happened, she must not fall into the trap of self-pity. All the same, she could not help thinking that she had formed an unfortunate habit of trusting too much to unreliable men. Rick loved all women and not one woman in particular; he was cynical and drank too much and called her the wrong name in his sleep, since to him relationships weren't something you made much effort over, but certainly he was fun. Eve considered her own tight lips and narrowed eyes lined into glass: she might be more conventionally attractive than before, but this elegant reflection was becoming a stranger to herself.

Eve's mood hardened abruptly; since she wasn't a wet-eyed kid any longer, the sooner she stopped behaving like one, the better.

She loved Nathalie de Saint Luc's salon. Redecorated in pale green and white with plastered medallions picked out in gold, the whole suite was gloriously, effortlessly elegant now it was refurnished. The Comtesse had purchased from Le Trésor the four or five pieces Eve would most have liked to own herself, and then placed them to the best advantage. She had also bought a few small *objets d'art*, and because her taste was faultless it did not matter that their periods did not blend. A fourteenth-century ivory Virgin smiled down from a velvet-lined recess; there were four Louis Quatorze vases in green jade, a Fragonard over the fireplace and a pair of Coromandel screens, painted with tangled flowers, either side of the door.

The salon was uncomfortably full of people, and Eve felt awkward entering on her own. She at once became the cynosure of all eyes, heads turning, the babble of talk dying away the moment she went through the double doors, so she was certain the Comtesse had spent the time before she arrived telling everyone how Le Trésor was filled with furniture they would recognize. Not that she had expected anything different; Nathalie de Saint Luc had been explicit about her purpose.

"Ah, Mme. Saulx," the Comtesse greeted her. "M. de Rouay cannot believe I was so fortunate as to discover all these exquisite pieces in your shop."

"They certainly look exquisite here," replied Eve coolly; she knew how vital it was to cling to the determination she had felt in the *fiacre*. "I was fortunate to encounter someone who would give my wares so splendid a setting."

"You have the effrontery to call them your wares?" M. de Rouay was small and extremely angry, like a ruffled crow in ancient, molting clothes.

"Why, yes, monsieur. Did not Mme. de Saint Luc tell you? By proclaiming her interest in Le Trésor she has set my establishment on the road to fortune. Without her to vouch for me I would still be struggling against the power of the Paris dealers."

He looked as disconcerted as Eve had hoped. If Nathalie de Saint Luc vouched for Le Trésor and did not simply buy there, then her prestige was a factor which must be considered before embarking on any scheme to recover lost property.

"Michel was always timorous; I understand he ran away from his château in 1914 when the Germans were still fifty kilometers away," interposed the Comtesse suavely. "However, I am sure some others here will not count the cost of indiscretion so exactly. Allow me to introduce M. and Mme. Vercours, who commented earlier on the likeness my favorite bureau bears to one they own."

"Owned," interrupted a man with a corseted stomach. "It was stolen from us in most atrocious circumstances."

"And what were those atrocious circumstances? Do tell us, *mon cher* Henri," said the Comtesse cordially.

He ignored her, a social solecism in itself, bitter eyes fixed on Eve, as if he wanted her blood on the Aubusson carpet. "Stolen, Mme. Saulx," he repeated. "And now I discover it in your shop."

"No; if by chance it should have been yours, you find it in the salon of the Comtesse de Saint Luc." Eve's heart was thumping; this was a wolf pack, and lacking the proof of legal purchase which Guy might or might not have, she was the kid tied down for slaughter.

M. Vercours was not to be diverted. "You dealt with the Comtesse under false pretenses. See here, Nathalie. This grain and patterning of tortoiseshell, I'd know it anywhere."

"So would I," interrupted Eve. "Since I catalogued and sold the piece, with the reverse grain of the left-hand side noted as a defect."

"*Quelle horreur,*" he said ironically.

"One may argue about the ownership of a bureau, and from which atelier it came forever," observed one of the women. "A medieval ivory Virgin is quite different. This one you have in your niche, Nathalie, is listed as belonging to us by the Beaux Arts."

Several other voices joined in the clamor. It was clear to Eve that these people had been here some time; the Comtesse must have invited them well before the hour she had named to Eve, so they could browse among treasures she expected them to recognize, and stoke up anger which as guests they might have hidden, if taken unawares. The Comtesse was leaning lightly on her cane, elegantly groomed and gowned, lips slightly parted in malicious enjoyment.

She turned to Eve. "Well, madame? I think perhaps my guests have a case which you should answer, since I bought only a small selection of your goods and *hélas!* each one finds an aggrieved claimant to ownership at the very first soirée I hold. It is unfortunate, to say the least."

"Very unfortunate." Eve refused to give the old harridan the pleasure of appealing to her for support.

"How do you account for it?"

"*C'est clair comme le jour,*" growled one of the men. "The woman is nothing but a thief, but too simple to realize the danger of selling such goods openly. I propose to fetch an officer from the Quai des Orfèvres; it is not far and he may take her back with him to investigate our charges."

"Mme. Saulx?" repeated the Comtesse, unmoved.

"It isn't true, and Mme. de Saint Luc knows it isn't. M. Vercours, you said that your bureau was lost in atrocious circumstances; would you be good enough to inform the company what those were?" She had decided that this was her only chance. These people might not like, after victory, to recount how they had sold possessions at ludicrous prices in order to scuttle from the Boches.

The Comtesse smiled at him, lightly, almost childishly, so Eve suddenly wondered whether her object, after all, might not be to expose these self-important people for the humbugs they were, rather than to discredit her and Le Trésor. Both, surely, and for sheer devilment. "Well, Henri? I think you should offer some explanation before fetching a policeman from the Quai des Orfèvres."

His face mottled angrily. "Why should I? I can produce a dozen witnesses to swear that bureau was mine, servants who polished it for years and know each scratch and scrape."

"Henri, *chéri*, we are here and waiting, your servants *le bon Dieu* knows where. This bureau, then; it was at your house in Artois?"

His eyes flickered, and Eve guessed it had just dawned on him that he was as much a victim of the Comtesse de Saint Luc as she, but it made little difference when he had the support of those around him. They had been robbed and humiliated too; in this company he would be free of censure. "Yes, it was in Artois. Together with many other things which I have no doubt are in Madame Saulx's shop now. In August of 1914 I lost much that was precious to me, when the Boches were advancing. We were packing to leave, since we did not fancy an occupation; in our district, atrocities from 1870 are still remembered." There was a murmur of sympathy. "We had horses and carts, but not many. Then a man drove down our lane in his *camion* and offered us transport as far as Soissons. We were grateful and my children wept with relief, but then he named his price. Half the *camion* for our use, half for goods of ours which he selected. I accepted; what would you, madame? My wife was hysterical." He glanced at the woman by his side, who stared at the carpet. "When we reached Soissons I expected him to bargain with me, to offer money for the pieces he had taken, but no. He drove off with everything as we dismounted into the road. I tell you, madame, my wife sprawled on the pavé, he drove off so fast. Is it not so, Marie-Claire?"

She nodded but did not look up. It isn't true, Eve thought, or not the way he tells it; but such details enlisted sympathy and were impossible to disprove.

Murmuring gathered force as others in the room began to tell of similar experiences and also found ways of making their actions creditable. On one point they were all agreed: no one had signed anything or made a witnessed contract to sell the items which they now saw in the Comtesse de Saint Luc's salon. She's told them, Eve thought bleakly. She's hinted that I lack proof, and the Daunays could tell her about Guy's state of mind; they've probably heard he's disappeared. None of these people would dare to sue the Comtesse for what she'd bought, but would claim everything at Le Trésor, whether it was theirs or not. And make sure I went to prison while they did it.

At least she could make the Comtesse pay for her entertainment, force her into fighting for what she had bought. Eve did not approve of what Guy had done but, in that moment, wished he had stripped these people's châteaux bare. She was being pushed and jostled now, and recoiled sharply as pain flashed through her arm from a spitefully driven pin. "I would like you all to think about this for yourselves," she said, voice diamond-hard. "When one of you scampers off to the Quai des Orfèvres, will the rest begin to carry out from here the goods you say belong to you? Mme. de Saint Luc might call that robbery too."

A woman laughed, delighted by the thrill of it all. "We will wait for an arrangement; dear Nathalie was not to blame."

"I think you're wrong. If a purchaser buys stolen goods in innocence, then only conscience might suggest she offer some recompense to the robbed." Eve turned to the Comtesse. "Well, madame? How is your conscience on this night of your enjoyment?"

Candlelight sparked over the Comtesse's face; only the mocking eyes remained dark. "It is all the better now I have watched how rats squeal while they invent fine motives for their . . . er . . . rattery. I am sure there must be a better word, but that one suits my meaning very well. I doubt whether my conscience would ever oblige me to reward cowardice."

"I suppose you would have stayed to greet the Boches on your doorstep?" demanded M. de Rouay.

"I would. I did, and the Boches behaved correctly while I remained there. Later Saint Luc became a battle zone and the château was demolished, but that, I feel, was *force majeure*." Her eyes scraped contemptuously over the company. "You, Mme. Pollinaire, I believe, spent the war in Deauville, occasionally wearing a chic Red Cross gown designed by Chanel?"

There was a brief silence before a woman laughed and touched Eve's sleeve. "All that is part of a past which everyone wants to forget. Mme. Saulx enjoys Chanel also, on profits to which she has no right. Keep your few pieces, Nathalie; we'll search her shop and see what else she has stored there."

Eve exchanged a small smile with the Comtesse, as if in that room they alone were allies. "You can't do that. Why do you suppose you are here tonight? Because the Comtesse de Saint Luc thought she recognized some pieces in Le Trésor, and wanted to enjoy watching you face some facts about your behavior during the war. If I were guilty of any fraud, a judge would never believe she bought my goods in innocence, when chance could not have brought you all together here tonight."

The Comtesse pensively twisted her rings. "Losing would be a fresh experience at my age, so you may be sure I should fight to retain what I have bought."

"But you would lose," exclaimed M. Vercours. "It is a clear case, after all."

The jostling which had been stilled now began again, one of the men sending Eve staggering as he brushed past, saying something about the Quai des Orfèvres. Her sleeve tore; in a confined space, emotions ignited easily and were immediately fueled by the volatile hysterias of postwar Paris; even a small gathering could become a mob. Eve felt her calm crumble; nothing much could happen to her here, but beyond lay the horrors of officialdom and ignominy. Heat and spilled hate made her head spin; hate shakes the soul when it is met face to face, and alone.

She backed, groping for a wall, but felt herself held instead; hands tight on her arms as someone stood squarely behind her. "Rats, I think Mme. de Saint Luc called you, although I would include her in your number for the whipster's role she has played tonight. Address yourselves to me instead of to my wife, and I shall be delighted to recount exactly what happened in 1914."

It was Guy.

Eve twisted in his hold and stared disbelievingly at the familiar bones of his face; he looked exhausted but completely collected, so far as she could tell. She had felt dazed by heat and shock; now sight cleared, and she turned back to face the crowded salon, seeing doubt flicker from face to face. Guy was formally dressed in the prewar blues issued only to officers in attendance at the Peace Conference, his sleeves striped with gold and silver of *brisques* and commandant's bars, his appearance made even more impressive by the array of medals lavished on those who survived the years of war to wear them.

"I believe this must be Commandant Saulx," said the Comtesse musingly. "The ruffian who allowed women to fall off his *camion* while he stole their possessions."

"That isn't the man who came! He was—" M. de Rouay broke off uncertainly.

"It was I, but four years of war changes a great many things. M. de Rouay, is it not? I remember perfectly how you ordered your servants to load up whatever I chose, since you knew that once your château was deserted, the Germans would destroy or loot whatever remained. Then you deserted people who had served your family for generations, while you drove off to safety."

"What of it? I couldn't take them with me!"

"No. What of it, indeed?" Eve felt Guy move, although he still held her left-handed. He pulled some papers from his pocket and held them where everyone could see. "I don't remember all of you, but I expect most signatures are here somewhere. Whether these are legal I don't know any more than you, but I am satisfied that I would win if you dare offer the matter for adjudication. I also serve notice on each and all of you. You summon me. My wife, as you and especially the Comtesse de Saint Luc knows, was a child in America at the time of which we speak; her only crime is to have married me. If you harass or threaten her, then I shall be on your doorstep again, but not this time to purchase goods." His voice was harsh, bloodshot eyes and eroded face doubly disquieting when linked with the degree of distinction implied by his clothes. He turned to the Comtesse. "I believe my wife is sufficiently generous to accept your apology for what has happened here tonight."

She smiled, still enjoying every moment. "My credit has established your shop."

"I don't dispute it. Your apology, if you please, madame."

"And now a word from me can make it *démodé* overnight."

Eve could feel the tremble in his body, the mask of coolness most painfully maintained. "Speak it, if you wish. My wife and I prefer not to be beholden to those who crucify for pleasure."

"I have enjoyed various kinds of pleasure this evening; I regret it if Mme. Saulx felt herself in any way ill at ease in company unsuited to her tastes."

It was apology of a kind, though sufficiently barbed for a few guests to exchange covert smiles; skill in riposte was better appreciated in Paris than most other kinds of virtue.

And suddenly Eve could not bear the whole charade another instant, feared above all that Guy's control would crack. How very much these people would enjoy seeing him plunge into the cavern of stripped emotions here, gloat as his dominance was destroyed before their eyes. He ought never to have risked such a scene in public.

"Thank you, madame," she said clearly, and curtsied, since some gesture seemed called for, before pushing her way past hostile faces to the door. She no longer cared that such a hasty withdrawal might look like defeat after the advantage which Guy had won.

Wide, polished stairs and the grilled front door: Eve stood for a moment, then crossed the road and leaned on the parapet above the Seine. Wind rattled branches over her head, foam flecked the current racing past; a few lights spilled across the water; otherwise it was very dark.

Stone rough under her hands. Eve shuddered and looked up, when for an instant the wish to finish it all had been insidiously there. The wish to accept what Guy had given her tonight, and escape the misery of telling him how she lived with Rick Dwyer now.

Then stubbornness held her again, although for what purpose she no longer knew. She turned, skin gooseflesh-cold, since she wore only a thin evening gown.

Immediately behind her, Guy was thicker blackness against black, and breathed as if he had been running.

CHAPTER 6

Eve's teeth were chattering; her fingers pressed against her mouth could not stop them. Tears on her cheeks and blood as cold as the currents of the Seine. She was conscious of a *fiacre*'s rank smell and Guy holding her, his touch a gesture to her distress and lacking any sense of intimacy at all. His tunic was wet under her face, and a button rubbed at the corner of her mouth.

Eve looked up and saw his face in lamplight, a mask of light and shadow; then he felt her move, and shifted, all shadow now. "We're going to the Rue Férou. I hope you don't mind."

Eve shook her head, words stuck in her throat.

He hesitated as if about to say something else, but whatever it was, he changed his mind, and after a moment took his arm from about her too.

The concierge at the Rue Férou was almost welcoming when she saw who it was wanting admittance: they were by far her most interesting tenants, and she had found life very dull without them. Neither noticed her, the stairs treacherously black when the light went out as usual. Eve stumbled over her long skirt and would have fallen except that Guy held her again. The same impersonal grip, the same tremble betraying something quite different. And unpremeditated, unexpected, a flash of desire went through her body.

She heard him fumble with the lock, each move and rustle of cloth fresh to her senses; the scrape of metal and then stale air on her face as the door opened. He dropped her arm while Eve stood wondering at herself; when he lit a candle, she stood and stared at him across the cold and familiar room as if she saw a stranger.

He jerked a blanket off the bed. "Wrap yourself up while I light a fire. I thought of going to a café with a brazier since I didn't want— I knew you'd sooner not come here. But you'd left your wrap at the Saint Luc place and would freeze in café drafts." He knelt by cold embers in the grate.

"I don't mind coming here." Eve hugged the moldy-smelling blanket and glanced around the room; nothing had changed since she tidied up when she came looking for him. Until tonight, he had not returned to the Rue Férou.

"You're still crying."

"I know. Stupid, isn't it? I despise women who weep all over the place. Your tunic is wet too."

She saw his hands quiver; then they continued carefully paring kindling. When he struck a match, the flame danced unsteadily in his fingers.

Awkwardness stifled words, made each of them shape sentences before they were spoken and then decide against the risk of speaking. With a blanket wrapped over her expensive, crumpled dress, Eve felt absurdly vulnerable, ridiculously aware of each move he made and how he avoided looking at her. She had wanted to see him for so many mundane reasons, and never once considered the fact that she wanted so much to see him. She could still fear Guy Saulx the way he sometimes was, but no longer remained indifferent to him. She had known too little when she came to him before, too many shocks too quickly had exposed the inadequacy of what she offered him; too late, senses unfolded which he might capture if he could.

Too late, because Eve had been nerving herself to tell Rick that she thought herself pregnant with his child. She expected Rick would simply be annoyed that he had overlooked her probable ignorance; impossible to add this hurt to the rest, when with Guy she had failed to conceive no matter how hard she tried.

"Where have you been this past month? I've searched everywhere for you," she asked at last. Her voice sounded odd, and his eyes flicked to her face before he busied himself with straightening the remaining covers on the bed. Eve chuckled involuntarily. "I'm sure it is not all *comme il faut* for a commandant complete with medals and high polished boots to make beds."

He shrugged, and when he had finished, drifted over to the window, where she so often remembered him standing. "You mended the glass?"

"Yes. Guy, where have you been all this time? Someone told me you weren't with the Conference any longer, but not many French soldiers are dressed as smartly as you tonight."

"I've been in Germany. On my way back I was drafted to accompany the German delegation on their journey to Paris."

"In Germany! No wonder I couldn't find you. I remember you said you might have to go, but I never guessed—" She had never guessed he might have been sent on a mission to Germany when gossip said he had left the Conference because he was in disgrace with Marshal Foch.

He did not reply; talking to him now was like prizing inlay out of buhl. It was difficult to imagine how concisely he had denounced the Comtesse and her guests so short a time before.

"The German delegation. They were only expected in Paris tonight; Rick went to cover their arrival." Eve spoke half to herself.

He was utterly still, staring at darkness beyond the window, hands behind his back. Eve watched his tight-gripped fingers; in the light of a single candle the rest of him was indistinguishable from shadow on the wall. She took a deep breath. "Guy, how did you come to be in Mme. de Saint Luc's salon just when I needed you so much? I'd thought perhaps she'd invited you and then kept you out of sight, so her guests might be confounded once she'd enjoyed her fun. But if you were in Germany until a few hours ago, then she can't have been able to find you, any more than I could."

"You thought I would do that? Listen at a keyhole and wait until you had suffered sufficiently for that woman's pleasure?" He had turned, but it was too dark to see his face.

"Not if I'd had a chance to think about it, no. It was just— I was confused and stupid by the end and simply puzzled by how you came to be there. Thankful, too."

The candle guttered and went out; only thin flame from the grate remained, so his voice came disembodied from the dark. "I saw Dwyer at Vaucresson, where the Germans were taken off the train to be driven to Versailles. He told me where you were."

"You saw Rick," said Eve stupidly. She could not assimilate the shock of it.

He knew, he must know she lived with Rick now; Rick Dwyer did not regard women in his bed as a matter for discretion, and he detested Guy, wanted to force divorce on her no matter what his motive. Yet, knowing, Guy had come to her immediately he understood what she might face at Nathalie de Saint Luc's salon.

"It— it was lucky you had the signed contracts within reach." Eve sought refuge in inconsequence, then hated her own cowardice.

"They're at Le Trésor. I showed them army movement orders, but it didn't matter. They saw what they expected to see."

"Guy . . . we have a great deal to discuss."

She heard the creak of leather, saw the shift of shadow as he turned back to the window.

Then silence.

The silence of caught breath and stopped blood; Eve felt her own cheeks wet again and feared that he wept too. The space of cold room between them and no comfort anywhere.

"I must go," she said helplessly at last.

Absurdly, she had thought he wouldn't be able to bear her simply leaving, but realized as soon as she spoke that it was her presence he could not endure. He muttered something about finding a *fiacre* and went out of the room, forgetting to shut the door. Eve heard him stumble on the stairs in his haste to be gone.

She wept then with the abandon of the youth she had left behind, for them both and for the child she carried. In that moment she wished quite simply she were back in New Moose; only frugal simplicity seemed to offer the peace she craved. She could not imagine why she had ever left it, how she could have found it oppressively confining and dreamed of seeing Paris.

She straightened at last, and dropped the blanket on the floor. There was an old trench coat of Guy's hanging behind the door and she put it on, cloth harsh against bare skin. She piled fresh fuel on the fire, thinking of him returning here alone, then stood irresolutely, wondering whether they would ever be together at the Rue Férou again.

It was quite a long time before Guy returned, *fiacres* being difficult to find in the middle of the night. When he did, Eve followed him downstairs without a word.

He stopped in the dark entry by the concierge's hutch. "Will you forgive me if I don't come with you? I must go back on duty tonight."

"Tonight! Guy, for heaven's sake, you have to rest sometimes. Tomorrow will do; the Germans can't run away from Versailles." Rain was beating on the outer door, a single lamp swinging in the courtyard. Great God Almighty, would spring never come?

"I don't think I should rest tonight."

"Guy . . . why not take some drops?" This was a crazy time to probe for information she had meant to extract by subterfuge, but she realized that after tonight she was unlikely ever to have another chance.

He stiffened. "I haven't willingly taken anything since the war ended."

"Then, shouldn't you? Just sometimes, when you simply can't manage without proper sleep any longer?"

"No. What has Joubaire been saying?"

Eve was completely taken aback. "What about?"

He sighed. "I suppose it doesn't matter. Eve . . . I'll send you word.

I know we have to meet once more, to decide what we must do to cut ourselves apart. But not here, and not alone. Some café perhaps might do."

She held him then, no reckoning or calculation to it, not even passion. Just the need to feel him still there, when soon they must do the best they could apart. She felt him recoil; then he held her, too, cheek resting against her hair.

He was shaking so badly he almost needed her support. "What address shall I give the driver?"

Eve swallowed. "The Rue Menars, not far from the Bourse."

He followed her out and gave the address to the *cocher*, apparently no longer intending to let her go alone, though now it was too late, Eve understood why he had refused before. She would have felt easier if he had changed his mind again. What could make tolerable the fact of being delivered by her husband to Rick Dwyer's door?

As he climbed up behind her she felt his hand fumble with the ungainly folds of the coat she wore. "They're useless garments; I had some linoleum I used to wear strapped to my back. I wonder what's happened to it? I shall need something better than war profiteers' cloth if this rain continues."

Eve cradled his hand to her lips, tenderness as physical as pain. This time she knew precisely why his mind slipped. If only he, too, could have some peace. "Guy, my love, come home to bed. You needn't lie out in the rain tonight; the war is over."

"Whatever made you think so?" he demanded. "We took two days to cross the battlefield."

Eve knocked on leather and called to the *cocher* to drive back to the Rue Férou. "You crossed it by train, remember? The battlefield is still there but in war you marched to it, then lay in mud. The war is over, so you crossed by train."

"It took two days. Do you know, it took two days to cross? The French—" He broke off, bewildered.

Eve kissed him, overwhelmed by emotions she could not name. Except for relief that at this moment he no longer remembered about Rick Dwyer. "You are French, my love. You were with Germans on the train, but at least you won and they lost."

He said something, very fast, eyes rolling, in German she was certain.

She had thought that this time she understood the why and how, yet could not reach him at all. Leather was tight-buckled at his waist and across his shoulder, harsh edges of medals and braid overlapped each other like armor plating, high collar cutting at his throat when his head rolled to the motion of the *fiacre*; military clutter defeated even the touch of her hands.

"Alsace is French again, you're French," she said steadily. "Speak to me in French; I don't understand German."

He spoke French immediately, and apologized as if for some social gaffe. "We stopped so many times. They wanted to be sure the Boches saw the destruction they had caused. We waited for hours on sidings chosen because the towns they once served were nothing but piled rubble. The trenches . . ." he gulped, hands crackling bones together. "I tried not to look, but . . . the train stopped so often. The shelling was too heavy to go on. . . . I suppose it's dangerous for a train in shelling. Once, I was buried when the line was blown up and thought I drowned again. . . . I nearly did, you know. Twice they dug me out with lungs and belly full of mud."

"And this time?" asked Eve quietly, wondering whether Guy Saulx screaming with shell shock on their train was also part of the punishment meted out by the French to the German delegation.

"I don't know. That's strange, isn't it? I don't know. Drops, I suppose." He frowned. "No, Bertrand wasn't there; he loses patience, you see, and makes me take them. Or leaves them under my nose when I can't sleep. I've managed better since he's been away, although I can't sleep, of course. Where's he gone? I haven't seen. . . ." He turned and looked at her with dawning surprise. "Eve?"

She kissed him again. "You'll sleep tonight; I'll stay until you do."

"Oh, God," he said dully, and then with a single convulsive movement freed himself and leaped out of the *fiacre*. Fortunately, it was slowing for the turn back into the Rue Férou, but Eve cried out as he almost fell under the wheels, the driver heaving at the reins so the half-starved nag nearly fell too.

"*Sacré nom!* Are you mad, monsieur? An accident and my license will be revoked; then how shall I live?"

Guy crammed some notes into his hand. "Madame will give you the address." He looked at her fleetingly, head bare in pouring rain, then turned and disappeared into darkness.

The *cocher* scratched his chin. "*Merde, alors. Qu'est que vous avez fait, madame? Et où voulez-vous aller maintenant?*"

"To the Rue Menars," said Eve wretchedly. There was nothing more she could do here tonight.

"*A la Rue Menars! A la Rue Férou! Non, encore, la Rue Menars. Et puis? Encore la Rue Férou, évidemment. Merde! Dites-donc, madame. C'est vraiment la Menars cette fois?*"

Eve nodded. Back to Rick, and heaven knew what he would say too. Tomorrow she must find somewhere of her own to live.

She lay the remainder of the night in the warm comfort of Rick's huge bed, listening while rain turned to sleet against the window. Mercifully, he had not returned from Versailles, so she had this short time alone. By dawn it was snowing, wet April flakes splattering against glass; Eve stared at gray light on the ceiling, lying flat on her back with a hand to her belly. She had calculated days a dozen times during the night and there was no mistake; normally completely regular, she was two weeks overdue. A little while longer to be certain, but she hadn't really any doubts.

She heard Rick's key in the lock as she was dressing, and he kissed her hungrily, snow melting on his face. "Christ, it's cold. Honey, I just decided. I love you best in slip and panties."

Eve turned to find her dress, annoyed he took intimacy so much for granted. But it's his own bedroom, after all, she thought wryly. He came behind her and slid his hands around to her breasts. "I like modern fashion. A year ago even, and I'd have had whalebone and God knows how many hooks between me and finding my way in."

She stood rigid while his hands moved lingeringly downward. Yesterday she would have responded unself-consciously to him in the few minutes before she must leave for Le Trésor; not long ago, she had felt only tight disgust when Guy tried to reach her, and lost himself in the attempt. How little we understand, she thought. How did love kindle and attraction wither; why should comfort with Rick turn into wretchedness when the alternative lacked any prospect of contentment, her body now reject the man whose child she carried?

Her eyes met Rick's in the mirror. "You told Guy last night, didn't you?"

His hands stilled on her nakedness. "How the hell do you know about it?"

"He told me. No, that's not true. He came to Mme. de Saint Luc's and I guessed from what he didn't say that when you saw him at Versailles you'd made sure he knew."

"Vaucresson; the Germans were driven from there to Versailles. The French didn't want to risk a mob in Paris."

"Vaucresson, then," she said impatiently. "Did you enjoy telling him in front of everyone at a railroad station?"

"Now I come to think of it, yes, I did." He turned her to face him and kissed her again. Eve remained completely still, thinking of Guy at a steam-filled railroad station, somehow facing Germans and French ceremony while scarcely aware of what he did or whether he stifled under mud or nightmare, and there confronted by Rick's complacent taunts.

"Didn't it occur to you that you had joined the rest of the world in inhumanity?" she asked when Rick drew back, surprised by finding no response.

"For God's sake, what is this? The bastard had it coming, so why make a tragedy of it? He didn't treat you to a scene at the Comtesse's, did he? I'm sorry, honey. I never dreamed he'd bolt off to beat the tar out of you there."

"He came because he thought from what you said that I was in trouble and might need him. He was quite right, as it happens."

"Attaboy, Guy. Look, Eve, I'm tired after a night with Germans at Versailles. If we're going to quarrel, let's leave it until this evening, okay?" His hands slid to her thighs, then gently asking up to hip and pelvis. "You're a mite distracting to argue with like this."

"All right. Take your hands off me and I'll finish dressing."

"That wasn't my idea at all."

"You should have thought of that at Vaucresson. You can't enjoy revenge as well as the victim's wife, all in one night."

He glanced out at gray light and thickly falling snow. "It's day, God help us. Not last night at all. Look, Eve, I've said I'm sorry if what I did annoyed you. I was surprised to see him and went to say you'd been searching all over for him; the rest slipped out. I wanted to boast, I guess. Christ, any man would want to brag if you were waiting in his bed, and you'd walked out on him, after all."

"Yes, I'd walked out, I went back to him last night."

Eve hadn't intended to say anything of the sort, especially not this particular untruth, but was unable to resist the temptation to show Rick how much some kinds of taunt could hurt.

His hands tightened and anger lit in his eyes. "You did what?"

She could not move, paralyzed by such a grip on the soft places of her body. "Rick, let me go."

"Sure. Later. As it happens, just at this moment I've other plans for you. Which you've enjoyed these past few weeks, or had you forgotten?"

"I've enjoyed them. I won't enjoy this, do you think?"

"You'll enjoy it," he promised. "And Eve . . . we've had a good time together. I don't intend you to forget it just because a sonuvabitch pitched you a good line."

And in spite of anger and feeling no desire at all, in the end she wasn't able to avoid the flare of purely physical pleasure. Rick was too skillful not to achieve it for her, once he offered all the experience he possessed; he was insistent, utterly determined, and savored also the full range of his own arts now these were needed not just to rouse a woman he desired, but to force her into thinking only of him. The realization that Saulx had reclaimed so dangerous a loyalty only hours before incensed him, anger and fear for her hardening passion into a weapon.

Eve cried out once, face taut, and then her self-imposed immunity broke as the tensile rope of him and her whipped tight.

Rick had succeeded in what he had set out to do.

CHAPTER 7

On the day after he arrived at Stoneham, Hugo went out shooting rabbits with Sir Maurice Wyville. It was Saturday, and on the Monday they both had to leave for Paris again. Cold East Anglian sky arched over a flat land, the earth smelled of drying furrows, and birds sang in copse and thicket. Occasionally geese wheeled upward from a mere, but most of their journey to Stoneham had been through intensely cultivated fields. As they'd come closer to her home, Sarah had eagerly pointed out landmarks Hugo could not distinguish in such undifferentiated land.

"The soil isn't rich around here, so this is one place the war has helped, when we had to grow everything we could. People were poor before, but it's good to look at now, isn't it? Oh, look, Hugo! Old Daventry has tried a crop of clover at last! He promised me he would, but I never believed him, he's such a stick-in-the-mud. Did you tell Barclay to give him a dreadful scold, Father?"

"I believe I did. Such flatness must look odd to you after Switzerland, Mr. Kobis, or have you visited this part of the world before?"

"London, but not Norfolk, Sir Maurice. I like flatness, though; one becomes tired of being dwarfed by mountains." This was an understatement, because here he felt at home, found his affection for Sarah growing into something more in a setting where she was so exactly and simply part of everything they saw. The Kobis estates in West Prussia had the same wide views and feel of great distances; whenever he went there he felt this same sense of conscious exhilaration. One day he would like very much to take Sarah there.

Norfolk, like West Prussia, was a land for the hardy, and here Sarah's cheeks glowed, her dark ringlets whipped into a tousle by a wind which worried her not at all; she climbed through hedges and walked for miles by Hugo's side over clodded fields.

"Don't you ever need a rest?" he demanded, when after a morning spent in viewing all the most precious places of her childhood, she proposed to accompany him and her father shooting in the afternoon.

She shook her head vigorously. "Oh, no! At least . . . sometimes in Paris or London, but that's because I'm bored. Never at Stoneham."

"Most people would be surprised to hear you're less bored in the wilds than anywhere else."

"But those are the people who make me feel tired in cities," she pointed out. "Besides, I'm not *often* tired or bored there, either. I must say, though, Stoneham will never be quite the same now Charlie isn't here; I was very glad when we went to Paris. I keep expecting him to call me, and still save up things to tell him. It's a *haunted* kind of feeling, if you understand what I mean."

Hugo tucked her arm under his. "Yes, I understand it. But that is the debt you must pay for your childhood happiness, and worth it every time. The fables are quite wrong, you know. We aren't haunted by unhappy ghosts but by the memory of those we loved, and who loved us. The rest we forget."

"That helps, Hugo. I hated to feel Stoneham was spoiled for us all, when that's the last thing Charlie would have wanted. It's strange you do understand, though, when Switzerland is peaceful: I thought you needed to feel such things and not just read about them."

"People die in Switzerland."

"Well, of course I know that," she said with dignity. "It isn't the same, though."

He was silent; certainly it wasn't the same. His three brothers and five out of eight Von Kobis cousins had been killed in the war; like many frontline soldiers, he felt little bitterness against their killers but was oppressed by loss and waste, the sense that such butchery had poisoned what remained.

After Sarah had spent a couple of hours in the undergrowth flushing out rabbits, Sir Maurice sent her home.

Sarah made a face. "I can see your diplomat's look being dusted off. Don't terrorize poor Hugo, will you?"

"Be off with you, baggage," commanded her father. "It's just that we don't want you counting our misses as it gets dark."

"Dear Father, you must think I'm a fool, but I don't mind. I know you like Hugo, but of course you can't start approving of him until you've explained just how badly he behaved in Paris. Really, I'm sure I would be able to arrange your old peace treaty in a quarter the time it's taken so far, because everyone wouldn't waste so much effort explaining just what they meant in all those gloomy clauses."

"Feminine intuition," said Hugo. "Perhaps your British Foreign Office should retain Sarah's talents, Sir Maurice. A thought-reader must be an asset in negotiations."

"I don't read them, exactly; I just know," explained Sarah. "And since I now feel quite out of charity with you, I shall certainly abandon you to a good scold. Don't be late for tea, Cook's making muffins." She waved a hand and raced off, pursued by both the dogs, which were meant to be retrieving rabbits.

"Dogs don't have any difficulty in making the right choice," observed Hugo, eyes following her. A rabbit broke out of a hedge to their right.

"Yours," said Sir Maurice.

Hugo sighted and then lifted his shotgun fractionally before he fired. The rabbit jinked in terror and disappeared. "Sorry, I haven't much experience of shooting." He was in fact an excellent shot, but sated with killing; on this brisk and lovely day when Sarah had been by his side he wanted to let things live, and had missed every rabbit so far.

"You handle a gun well enough," replied Sir Maurice noncommittally. He looked around him. "It was a mistake to come to Stoneham when it makes a return to Paris seem so very undesirable."

"The negotiations are not yet completed?" asked Hugo tentatively.

"I was thinking more of how this setting reinforced a sense of one's own fallibility. I expect always to look back on these months in Paris with horror, as a time when men were dwarfed by circumstance. Blazing lights, hard chairs, the windows shut and heating stoked so hot you can't think. But you must think and make mistakes, know one is making irremediable mistakes when it has become impossible to extract from hatred and double dealing any real impression of what will yield a lasting peace."

Offered such an unexpected opportunity, Hugo hesitated, torn between compunction and the need for information which might be vital to the German delegation. "You are worried, sir?" he asked at last.

"Of course. Any thinking man must be."

"Is there nothing to be done when you—the delegations—know mistakes are being made? So long as they are recognized for what they are, mistakes can't be irretrievable."

"There comes a point beyond which a course of action cannot be reversed. Yours, for instance. You regret what you have done, but haven't turned aside from it."

Hugo stiffened. "I regret some things, I could not now ever regret meeting Sarah."

"You think not? I'm afraid I disagree. As Sarah said, I like you, Herr

Von Kobis; if I didn't I should accept that you enjoyed arousing a girl's affections and then leaving her when your purposes were complete. As matters are, I think you may suffer as well as she, but that isn't my concern. Sarah is, however."

Guns cradled underarm, they walked like two friends, boots clinking on Norfolk flints. "How did you know?"

"That you were no Zurich journalist? I used my eyes; a man in my position needs to develop an instinct for the breed. Then I looked up the name in the Almanach de Gotha; you were unwise to use your own."

"It helped make imposture more bearable," said Hugo frankly. "I'm not— I was a diplomat before the war."

"I didn't expect to discover that you had introduced Mata Hari into my dressing room. Why did you choose Sarah to help in your plans?"

"Why anyone? I combed Paris for whatever information I could find, but it wasn't easy. I— I suppose I continued to see Sarah because I wanted to. No, that's not quite true. At least, it is but not all of it. I became sufficiently fond of her to know that continuing to see her was precisely what I ought not to do, but the job I had undertaken prevented easy retreat when she was acquainted with so many people who were useful to me. Then it was too late; I have become very much attached to her, sir."

"The irretrievable mistake," Sir Maurice said dryly.

"Yes," said Hugo after a pause. "Though in the end I hope that I and not Sarah will be the loser. I have come to love her, but I think she is too young for fixing her affections."

"It's clear you don't know my daughter as well as you suppose."

"I have come to know her better than I know myself at the moment. Are you going to hand me over for trial as a spy?"

"My dear boy, how very melodramatic! Why should I? Or are you proposing to extract information from me under the muzzle of a shotgun?"

Hugo laughed, then broke the breech of his gun and slipped cartridges into his pocket. "I hadn't thought of it, no. But I am a German officer out of uniform in your country. The peace treaty isn't signed yet."

"So I understand," said Wyville ironically.

Hugo flushed. "I'm sorry, sir."

"Yes, I think you should be. I am old-fashioned, I suppose, when in our fine twentieth century there are already so many greater wickednesses than betraying a girl's affections, and of course you have your duty to plead."

Yes, I have my duty to plead, reflected Hugo. I haven't accomplished much and probably the Wilhelmstrasse hasn't taken notice of anything I said, but one day when I remember how I would have liked —loved—Sarah as my wife, I shall be able to recall how faithfully I did my duty. Orders are fine things to follow, after all. "I don't think I shall speak so easily of duty in the future, sir," he said aloud.

"Neither war nor peace is simple, once we are face to face with those we call our enemies. I certainly should not find my son's death easier to bear because you faced a firing squad. But Charles would have inherited Stoneham and now it will be Sarah's; I could accept you as a son-in-law if Sarah still loved you in a couple of years, as I think she would; but my wife . . . has had enough to bear. A Prussian in Charles's place at Stoneham would seem intolerable to her, and a country mourning a million dead will generate sufficient hatred to split more than marriages apart. You and Sarah are both tough, it's possible that even so you could find happiness together, but I doubt it."

Hugo frowned. "Why not? In two years— I understand why you think Sarah is too young now and I'm— You don't know much of me, you've been incredibly generous as it is. Naturally, I'd expect her to need time, and in two years the world will have settled down."

"Would you live in England if you married?"

"We should come of course whenever my duties permitted. . . ." His voice tripped on the word duties. "That is, whenever we could, we would come. But of course we would have to live where I was posted; in effect I am accepted back into the diplomatic service now."

"You would remain a German subject?"

"Of course," said Hugo, astonished.

"In that case, there is no possibility I would agree to your marrying Sarah. She might or might not defy my judgment when she is of age, which is nearly four years' time."

"I expected you to have me thrown out as an intrusive reporter, shot if you discovered my deception," said Hugo slowly. "I confess I am somewhat at a loss now, sir."

"Because I am immune to popular hysteria over Huns, yet would forbid my daughter to marry a German? And have no doubt on that score, I am well able to enforce my decision and break you if you attempt to circumvent it. Would you allow a daughter you loved to marry a Russian at this moment?"

Hugo thought of the bloodthirsty, half-understood chaos sweeping the Russian Empire. "Of course not, but I assure you Germany won't go the same way. It's not good there now, but the Reich is too rich for revolution to be attractive long. It's sprung from defeat, and once peace is signed—"

"What do you suppose will then spring out of peace? Not love of the

British, but resentment, hatred and revenge, surely. You would be ruined, married to an English wife, and she ostracized." He looked down at his hands, slack on the polished wood of his shotgun. "It isn't over, Hugo. It's only just begun; that's why I so much detest returning to Paris. We have sown the wind, the whirlwind is still to come."

"Is there nothing to be done?" Hugo felt the older man's despair like a contagion.

"What would you say?"

Paris. Hugo thought of blaring saxophones and rage in the streets; the fear of Germany which showed as hatred you could touch, which would write fear and hatred into the peace. Blood and destruction spawned half-crazed men and women unhinged by grief; statesmen so physically and morally exhausted that they had given up attempting to shape opinion and followed it instead. The wild stampede for pleasure sprang from the war itself and was tainted by the same depravities; in defeated Germany as well as in victorious France Hugo had touched a secret known to those who seek to lead doomed peoples to destruction: that the rabid, mad-dog strain is not easily outlived by those who have tasted blood.

He looked up. "In a place like this it is possible to imagine that the fever will burn out. Paris, City of Light. I must believe it will be that way again. Germany, too; we're a tough people and not easily defeated."

Sir Maurice gave a crack of laughter. "I'll give you that. It took half the world to defeat you. Soon, you won't even believe you were defeated. The latest word east of the Rhine is *Dolchstoss*, so I am told."

"*Dolchstoss*—the stab in the back," repeated Hugo. "They talk of our Army stabbed in the back?"

"By civilians, Communists and Jewish profiteers. And armies which believe they haven't been defeated hanker to demonstrate the fact."

The windows of Stoneham glowed gold in the dusk, frost crackled underfoot; a solitary star glittered in wide-spreading evening sky.

"I hope you're wrong, but of course I'll go tomorrow," said Hugo. "I think I must tell Sarah exactly why. She has a right to know, and it would seem to me better for her to understand that I go because I love her, rather than believe it is because I don't."

Maurice Wyville nodded without speaking. His daughter and Stoneham, both would have been in good hands if this man had married Sarah. Another fraction added to the staggering toll of destruction left by war.

Hugo dreaded the evening, first dinner in a paneled dining room, then confronting Sarah with what he had to say. He had wanted to argue, protest, deny, but once argument was thrust on him, he wasn't able entirely to disagree with Wyville's judgment. Hugo was trained to report situations and assess possibilities accurately; he was not aggressive, yet had experienced humiliation every day he lived in Paris. He knew Germany had been defeated, but also that only a vast alliance had dragged his country down. He had watched arrogant French and British prating of victory and wanted to shout that, alone, neither could have stood against the German Army. America, too; it had taken them three years to argue themselves into the war and another ten months to put one solitary division in the front line. Hugo loathed war but would have liked to rub insolent French, British and American noses in the fact of his country's strength, as they were employed in rubbing Germany's in defeat. And if he felt so, then others would certainly cherish even more bitter hatreds.

So protest died while loss remained. He did not love Sarah deeply yet, while adolescent admiration must still be tangled with anything she felt for him; probably he could cut them both loose before it mattered much. Yet in his heart he knew it wasn't so; the roots of love had struck, and given time, would have bound them tightly into happiness.

After dinner, Wyville suggested that Sarah find their visitor a book in Stoneham's library, and so arranged Hugo's opportunity.

"Light candles, will you, Hugo? I hate those smelly lamps," said Sarah, pushing open the library door. "Before the war, Father was thinking of installing electricity and I must say it would be convenient, but not so cozy as candles on a winter night."

A splendid chandelier was ready lowered for lighting, and sparked reflections over tooled leather as Hugo hauled it up again. "The pulley is a good idea."

"Better than dripping tapers ten feet long," agreed Sarah. "What's the matter, Hugo? You were in the mopes all through dinner. I know Father can be very disagreeable when he wishes, but you ought not to take him too seriously."

"Don't you?"

She reflected. "Well, I suppose I take him seriously, but I don't really mind him telling me things, if you see what I mean. I rip up at him, and then we're the best of friends again. I thought you'd get on well, and not let yourself be put out of countenance."

"Disappointed in me, Sarah?"

"Well, I must say I think it rather poor-spirited," she said candidly.

Hugo laughed. "Who is the lady over the fireplace? You have a great look of her when you sit in judgment over me."

"It is quite dreadful, isn't it? It was painted the year Mother came out, and she told me the artist was a horrid little man and she spent hours sitting in a freezing studio, simply hating him. But in spite of it she was accounted a great beauty and not at all disagreeable, which is what you meant to say I was being."

Hugo stared at the portrait. He recognized Lady Wyville now, but would not have done so without Sarah to tell him who it was. She had been a beauty, in a delicate, peach-and-roses way; in the picture she was considering the human race with contempt, and her mouth had a petulant droop, which did at least add character to insipid regularity of features. "Lady Wyville has changed a great deal," he said at last.

"It isn't her fault, although I need to tell myself so very often. Charlie and I used to love her very much. . . . I still love her now but find it more difficult," she added. "She adored Charlie and literally took to her bed the day he joined the Army. She seemed like a ghost, you know, one of those spirit thingummies, not the fat sort wrapped in sheets, until the day war ended. Then, I couldn't believe it. I mean, I'd been ridiculously busy with affairs here when Father was nearly always in London and I hadn't much time to sit and make soothing noises, especially when I got angry if I tried. The day the armistice came, she joined the village singing round the bonfire and then went up to London to join Father, when he'd been alone there most of the war. I thought— I'm afraid I thought that's what she could have done before, if she'd made an effort."

"When you're strong it's natural to find supporting the— the less strong rather tiresome."

"The weak; yes, that's what I thought her. I still do, I can't help it, although I know it's horrid. Two days later the telegram came which said Charlie had been killed. He was shot five minutes before the armistice, which made things even beastlier."

Hugo couldn't take his eyes from the portrait. "I wouldn't like you to change as your mother has done."

"Me?" said Sarah in astonishment. "Why, of course I won't! Whatever made you think I might?"

"Things . . . happen. If your mother had been born at a different time she would not have been destroyed by tragedy."

"Well, I don't know. It's nearly always something, isn't it? I should think anyone is lucky to get through life without a few tragedies to trip over. Fifty years ago, Charlie might have caught the cholera. I get angry or weep, I don't lie in bed with the curtains drawn when things go wrong, and I shouldn't think that would change, would you?"

"I hope not. No, I don't think so."

She shook out her skirt. "That's settled, then. Now you can tell me what's bothering you."

"Do you never allow yourself to be diverted from an awkward question, either?"

Her eyes danced. "Poor Hugo. No, never."

He went over to her then, and held her hands in his. "I'm going away tomorrow, back to Paris. I shan't see you again."

Her smile faded. "That's silly. Has Father been reading you some lecture about the honor of a gentleman? I might as well tell you now that I don't pay much regard to antique notions."

"Yes, you do." He kissed her fingers. "But no, Sir Maurice lectured me on the international situation. Honor he left to me."

"The international situation! Hugo, really! I'm sure it is important, but— but not precisely at this moment." She snatched her fingers from his.

Her vivid little face scowled at him; lips curled, brows tight above defiant eyes. Sarah Wyville did everything completely, including expressing displeasure.

At that moment, Hugo loved her completely. "I'm not Swiss, you see. I'm German. You knew I took care to meet you because I thought I could gain information, but I wanted to send it to Berlin, not Zurich. That isn't important, though. I think I could make you understand that what I had to do then makes no difference to us now, but it changes things in a different way. I'm afraid I'm to blame, because I didn't want to think about it clearly before." He kissed her gently on the lips. "I'd come to love you, you see. Imagine you one day as my wife. I think perhaps it was the same with you?"

"Husband," said Sarah, and kissed him eagerly in return. "I don't know that I considered you as a wife, exactly."

Laughter locked into misery and he held her hands to his face. "I can't ask you, my love. Ever. Simply believe me when I say this is because I love you so very much, and then one day you'll understand why it was. I think you won't understand or forgive me now."

"I shan't if you just tamely go. Bed and drawn curtains, or scuttling off because of what people say, it's all the same, Hugo."

"It isn't, but I said you wouldn't understand at the moment. One day, if our countries are ever at war again, perhaps you may."

"At war! Why, that's ridiculous, Hugo! Of course there couldn't be another war or we'd all be dead. Do you mean that's how Father frightened you off?"

"He thinks peace won't last. He believes you would be made wretched if you lived in Germany." Hugo's eyes strayed to the portrait again: Sarah was like her mother in feature and coloring, and nothing else at all.

"And you? What do you think?"

He licked his lips, thought whirling, words hopelessly jumbled. "*Ja,*

Liebchen. . . . I think, too, perhaps it could happen. The risk is too great; I love you too much."

"What is life except risk?" demanded Sarah scornfully.

He turned her away from him, forcing her to face the portrait. "Your mother looked at the world with the same scorn you feel for me now. The world destroyed her just the same, and I don't intend to help it destroy you, too."

She quivered under his hands and broke away to face him. "You're just being absurd, Hugo. I don't go round Paris remembering all those fusty old wars we fought against the French since the time of Joan of Arc. Before then, too, I daresay, only no one bothered to teach me. Five months after such a great war ended, of course everyone thinks how the Germans are our enemies, but time passes. I don't suppose we should find everything agreeable just to start with, but as I said before, everyone has something to trip over."

"To trip over, yes. Not piled deliberately by my hands into a design well calculated to crush you."

"So it is to be drawn curtains and your head under the bedclothes," said Sarah tightly.

"If that is how you see it, yes."

"I do."

Hugo clicked his heels and bowed, very formally. "*Mit Ihrer gütigen Erlaubnis* . . . with your permission, I will withdraw. Think of me kindly sometimes, how it might have been with us. But it is over, Sarah. Believe it and go forward into your life, or you will be behind those curtains too. In such a matter obstinacy is not a virtue."

CHAPTER 8

It took Hugo an unexpectedly long time to return to Paris. His journey to England escorting Lady Wyville had been so smoothly prepared he was disconcerted to find that alone, and carrying somewhat suspect papers, it took him three frustrating days to argue his way across the Channel and then hitch to Paris, after having decided at Boulogne that policed and overcrowded trains were too dangerous to attempt.

But once arrived in Paris, he found himself at a loss. The German delegation had arrived at Versailles, the innumerable committees of the Peace Conference scurried in every direction, the mood in the boulevards surly rather than triumphant; whisper and rumor abounded. Hard information was another matter; everyone Hugo approached was either concerned with minor matters or contradicted whatever he had learned from his last informant. He went out to Versailles with the idea of contacting the German delegation but discovered that, diplomatic guarantees or no, its members were immured behind barbed wire. The street outside their hotel was guarded, and a small crowd at the corner jeered any car which might conceivably be carrying Germans.

He returned to Paris, profoundly depressed. It wasn't as if he had fresh news which made an attempt at illicit entry necessary; only instinct nagged at him, suggesting that in spite of everything, the German delegation might have come prepared for entirely the wrong kind of negotiation. As if to emphasize foreboding, the weather continued cold and stormy; wet snow weighed down trees struggling into leaf and drove in scudding flurries across exposed street corners. People had believed the winter to be over and burned their last supplies of fuel; consequently heating was almost totally lacking. Wet logs smoldered in damp chimneys, and the most fashionable salons were full of smoke.

The next day was the first of May and the workers came out on the streets. The area around the Place de la Concorde, the Opéra and the *Grands Boulevards* was crammed with angry, underfed people waving fists and red flags, shouting about how victory had been betrayed. They should taste defeat before complaining about victory, thought Hugo sourly. He was kicked and jostled, not for any reason but because he happened to be there, passions rising as mounted police and troops appeared. The workers weren't armed or organized for revolution; otherwise Hugo could have believed himself back in Berlin. He stared at angry, unforgiving faces and reckoned these people were as divided as his own.

On impulse, he turned down the Rue Daunou. Sarah would not be at Le Trésor, almost certainly had not returned to Paris, but it must be unpleasant for Eve Saulx to be responsible for a luxury shop when such a mob was out on the streets. She was unlucky in the situation of Le Trésor: on the far side of the Rue de la Paix a sabbatarian calm began, which extended over most of the rest of Paris. No public transport ran, cafés and theaters were closed; today you either demonstrated or stayed at home, and the dividing line was exact.

The Rue Daunou west of the Rue de la Paix was full of arguing and gesticulating people; women dragged children from underfoot; bold-faced girls screeched insults as they linked arms four or five abreast and shouldered everyone else aside. They had had a good war and intended to enjoy a good riot; for them this was not serious at all. For nearly everyone else it was savagely serious: essentially Paris was not frivolous but a hardworking, hard-eating, impatient city, and a large proportion of those milling about the Rue Daunou had little or no work, ate inadequate food and had long since exhausted their patience. Hugo several times had to show his press card, and change menace into backslapping good humor by swearing that he would report the hardships of Paris workers to the friendly Swiss proletariat.

Le Trésor was shut, and some planks had been hastily nailed over its windows. Hugo hesitated, not wanting to waste time when Paris discontents were not his business, yet certain Eve Saulx would be inside her shop, quite possibly alone. She was not the type to abandon her belongings to the risk of casual plunder; Hugo reckoned Guy a lucky devil to have married such a courageous, attractive wife, and an ungrateful one as well when Sarah said he never came to Le Trésor.

If only there were a café open, he would watch the mood of the crowd for a while from inside. He eyed blank frontages speculatively, but the Paris bourgeoisie had long practice in surviving riots, and everything was locked tight. It was raining steadily, icily; deprived of warmth and sustenance, the crowds would soon return to their slums and life would resume as normal.

Quite close behind him came the sound of shots, a volley first, then spaced, irregular fusillades. Hugo jumped, nerves instantly strung tight, and ran without shame for the nearest cover, a foul-smelling archway leading into a back court. A year in the trenches was quite long enough to outlive any feeling that shooting was something you waited to investigate. He was joined by a scramble of others, most of whom looked as if they had been soldiers, and the Rue Daunou itself filled even tighter with people. The shots had come from somewhere near the Opéra, and those who could, sensibly retired down the nearest side street. More shots came, single harsh reports followed this time by screaming; in the Rue Daunou there were shouts of anger and people began levering up pavé to use as missiles.

Hugo made up his mind and left his cover. Across the street lay the entry to another maze of back courts, and if he could find it, he could enter Le Trésor by the freight entrance without drawing attention from the undesirable.

In fact, he had no difficulty, since there was a nameplate nailed to brightly painted gates. He grinned to himself; trust an American to scrub and paint a back entrance.

Everything here was quiet, so he hauled himself over the gates to land with a clatter among discarded pipes. The inner door was locked, and bolted, too; the whole place looked deserted. Hugo thumped on woodwork but did not dare call too loudly; there were screams from the Rue Daunou now, and feet clattering on cobbles.

He wondered why he was so certain Eve was there, afraid but not running away; he only knew her slightly, after all. He knocked again, then bent and put his mouth to the keyhole. "Mme. Saulx? Eve? It is Hugo von Kobis; let me in."

No sound. He stood with his palms against woodwork, thinking. He ought to be in Versailles, at the Quai d'Orsay, in the hotels frequented by diplomats and press corps. He owed Eve Saulx nothing. Except, she was the wife of a man who had once been his friend, and he had taken some advantage of her to meet Sarah; he did not want to plead duty again and leave another woman to cope as best she could alone. Damn Guy; he was the one who should be here.

He was being watched; Hugo spun around, sidestepping the instant his senses sharpened, so weight landed on his shoulder instead of his head. The pain of it blurred his sight and made him cry out, and when he fell he hardly felt the cobbles under his face. He rolled, throwing up his left arm to protect his face; he could not use the right at all. He felt a hand grope for his throat, and jerked his head down in panic. Fingernails raked his face and blood ran into his mouth; convulsively, he jackknifed his body and butted his head into the half-seen shape above. The force of his own blow was stunning, and his assailant staggered back, hands to his face. Somehow Hugo came to his knees; he must get up, attack while he'd gained some shadow of advantage.

Then weight hit his legs and he was down again, flattened in dirt with knees in his back. His thoughts whirled; he must turn, throw the bastard off before a knife was stuck between his shoulders. He gritted his teeth and gathered his remaining strength into a single effort: it didn't amount to much, but the weight on his back lost balance momentarily, swore and grabbed at him again. He caught Hugo's bad arm and he heard his own voice scream before blackness exploded behind his eyes.

When Hugo regained consciousness, it was dark. He lay for some time feeling himself shiver. His clothes were sodden, and when he tried to raise himself vomit gathered on his tongue. He lay again, trying very hard to think.

Footsteps were coming, heels clicking on stone, and light dazzled his eyes. "How awful do you feel?" asked Eve Saulx.

He licked his lips, feeling crusted blood. "I've felt better."

"I bet you have." She knelt beside him, cloth in her hand. "Do you think you could stand if I helped?"

"I'll try."

"I couldn't move you any farther. I pulled you inside and I suppose a stone passage is better than cobbles, but you're too heavy for me alone."

"You pulled me inside?"

She wiped his face carefully. "I heard someone at the back door and was really scared until you called. Then I couldn't make out what was happening, and it seemed to take forever to pull the bolts."

Hugo thought about it muzzily. "I remember I was dead."

Eve laughed. "I think you would have been; he had a knife and you'd hurt him enough so he wasn't only thinking of your billfold. Luckily I'd put a Louis XIII andiron by the door in case I needed it. I hit him and he ran off."

"You hit him and he ran off," repeated Hugo.

"Yes, I'm afraid I didn't aim too well. I meant to catch his knife but had to hit twice before he dropped it."

"*Mein Gott,*" said Hugo blankly.

Eve stood and brushed off her skirt. "It was very good of you to come, but Sarah isn't here, you know."

"I thought perhaps I owed you something too. I only hope I haven't brought a gang of scavengers set on vengeance into your yard."

Eve smiled. "I would like to believe that it isn't our fault if good intentions bring unexpected retribution. Thank you for coming, Herr von Kobis."

"Hugo."

"Hugo," she said, and touched his swollen lip. "You were once a friend of Guy's, weren't you?"

"How did you know?"

"You called yourself Von Kobis through the keyhole," she pointed out, "and you didn't correct me when I repeated it, just now. Anyway, I'd been wondering ever since you went to England with Sarah. Rick told me a long time ago that a German Guy once knew might come, wanting to blackmail him into helping with some mission. When you came I didn't at first realize who you must be, when you weren't at all what I'd imagined. Then, two nights ago, I was trying to think about . . . to sort out some of the things which have happened to me these past months, and I remembered Rick had named Guy's friend as Hugo, although he'd given no other name. I was angry with you then. I'm still angry now."

Hugo moved his head on the hard floor. "Don't worry. I've paid my bill."

"Sarah?"

They both heard the sound at the same moment, a stealthy grating as if someone was trying to fumble with the outside door. Eve swung around, light from the candle she carried falling on the massive key protruding from the lock. It quivered while they watched.

"Help me up," whispered Hugo. He felt dazed and his arm hurt fiercely, but somehow he managed to stand. "Blow out the candle."

They both listened tensely in the dark. Shouts and chanting echoed from the front of the shop; here all was still until the lock rattled sharply again. Sweat was drying on Hugo's face, and his body felt brittle: he was in no condition for another fight. Eve's hand fastened tightly on his. "He's trying to fit a key," she breathed. "It's Joubaire. It must be."

Hugo's head reeled. "Why doesn't he say if he's come to help?"

"Because he hasn't come to help. It's all right; he can't get in while I'm here; the bolts are shot and the key inside."

They listened again, scarcely breathing, Eve with her ear close to the keyhole. She heard a muttered curse, the scrape of hobnails, then silence. "He's gone."

Hugo tried to clear his head, and failed. "I don't understand."

"You're lucky enough not to know Bertrand Joubaire. I'm wondering whether he knows anything about the attack on you: it seemed odd to me that someone had broken into our yard and then decided to try for your billfold. Let me help you now; we've got some time while he decides what to do next."

Hugo made it through to Eve's office without help, and revived on black coffee, but the slightest movement of his shoulder was acutely painful. "I shall be very little use if anything happens," he said ruefully.

"You're a witness."

"A witness of what?"

"I'm not sure," said Eve slowly. "I keep thinking I see a pattern, but it disappears each time I look closer. So much has happened and I've been too busy with Le Trésor to sort it all out. I ought to have forced myself to go back to the Hôtel Daunay; that's where everything began, but I hated the thought of it too much. I will when this is over."

Hugo remembered the file on the inhabitants of the Hôtel Daunay he had read in Rick's office, including accusations against Guy which had seemed damning but which he still could not credit, and had not brought himself to use as Dwyer wanted. "Guy," he said carefully. "How is he these days?"

Eve stared at a cup of coffee held between her hands. "Sick. Desperate. He ought to be in a hospital, but he won't go to a doctor, so instead the Army sends him to Germany."

"To Germany!"

She looked at him derisively. "Not, I think, as a spy."

Hugo flushed. "In any normal peace negotiation, the defeated would be at the conference table, not picking up gossip in the streets."

"I can't worry about it," said Eve frankly. "I don't understand what's going on; all I want is for it to be over."

Hugo entirely agreed and drowsed for a little while after that. When he woke, Eve was at the window. "Is anything happening?"

She nodded. "There's been quite a bit more shooting and people running away. The street is fairly clear now."

Hugo stood carefully and went over, holding his arm with the other hand: he thought his shoulder must be dislocated. A few figures were hurrying past, furtive in the gloom. No lamps were lit, and electricity had been cut off all day. "In the Bois de Boulogne I expect the evening promenade has been quite as usual."

Eve laughed. "And the fishermen along the Seine will have sat all day in the rain and caught nothing, also as usual."

"Will you be all right if I leave now?"

"Yes, of course."

Hugo caught the hesitation in her voice, and his mind returned to that furtive scraping at the lock. But for that, he would have been able to go and find a doctor; soon he would have to go or risk passing out again. "Let me take you home first."

"No!" Eve heard her own voice rise; last night, she had slept here again instead of at Rick's, and come no nearer to resolving the confusion of what she must now do. Until she had made her decision, she would not go to Rick again. A pack of men ran helter-skelter past, their shouted defiance echoing off shuttered housefronts; another walked warily along the center of the street. Eve stared at him, and the sense of inevitability closed on her again. That and relief after two days of worry. "It's Guy."

Hugo muttered something about it being time he showed up, but Hugo didn't understand. No one understood; except perhaps she and Guy, a little.

Eve went through to the front of the shop and slid off the bar when she saw Guy through chinks in nailed planks. She opened the door and smiled at him. "You make a habit of coming when I'm in trouble."

He took off his *képi* and stood in shadow. "You shouldn't be here alone."

"You came from Versailles to tell me that?"

"I haven't been in Versailles. I've been— I only heard of trouble in this district when I came out from a meeting. It's quiet elsewhere in Paris."

"So then you came?"

He was silent.

Eve touched his arm. "Come in, now you are here. I mustn't leave the door unbarred."

"No. No, thank you. I . . . Eve, is Dwyer coming to fetch you? You mustn't walk the streets alone tonight."

"I can call a *fiacre*," she said gently. "Don't worry about me, Guy."

"There aren't any." Across a yard of darkness she heard him swallow, and gag on dryness. "He isn't coming?"

"Not so far as I know." Rick Dwyer understood the cracksman's skill he had used on her two nights ago; he would be annoyed, perhaps even amused when she stayed away from him, but not disturbed. He would not come, but wait confidently for her to return. And as matters were, his judgment probably was correct.

"I can't," Guy was saying. "Eve, don't you see, I can't? You can't ask that of me. The other night, I wouldn't— I didn't know what I was doing or I'd never have come even part of the way."

"Guy, for pity's sake, I haven't asked anything of you. I wouldn't ask you to take me to Rick. Ever."

"You haven't left me much choice."

Eve wanted to kiss him and knew he could not bear it, knew also that unless she did something fast his mind would take its own escape from distress. "Guy, I'm not alone." Then, as she sensed his recoil, she added hastily: "Hugo von Kobis is here. You must come in; he's been looking for you. I was angry with him when I thought he was some kind of spy making trouble, but he isn't like that, is he? He came today because he wanted to be sure I was all right."

"Hugo?" Guy echoed blankly.

"Guy, you must come in. We can't argue in the street!"

Another clutch of running figures swept down the street to add point to her words; he followed her in and slotted the bar into place, touching furniture with an oddly yearning gesture as he went through the darkened shop. For the first time, it occurred to Eve that Guy's troubles were rooted deeper than the war: brought up between two hostile nations and regarded by his father as little more than a convenient garrison for an empty house, he reacted with instinctive longing to the trivia of domesticity, yet lacked knowledge of how to create the certainties he craved. He had been taught by whores and Prussian schoolmasters, toughened by drill sergeants and thrown into war without anything to tie him to a saner past. He had loved and married her but not expected it to be other than a disaster; desired a child only as something snatched from a future he had lost.

"Hugo is actually here at Le Trésor?" His voice jolted her into the present. It was unemotional again; he seemed to cope efficiently with impersonal crisis.

In stark fact it was she, and the whole intolerable situation she represented, who now prized his control apart as easily as did war's bestialities. She was not helping him any more. "Yes, he's been here quite often these past few weeks, but I didn't know who he was until today."

"I've upset you," Guy said at once, although she had thought her words unrevealing enough.

She shook her head, which in the dark he could not see, and opened the door to the office, thankful for any distraction when it seemed that she and Guy could not last even minutes alone together.

Hugo was standing where she had left him, and his eyes flicked at once from her to Guy, widening in shock before training hid it.

"Yes, I've changed, haven't I?" said Guy ironically. "You never needed that diplomat's mask with me before. Dammit, I'm glad to see you, Hugo."

"Me, too. I'm sorry I can't embrace you in the best French manner, but my arm feels as if it would drop off if I let go of it."

Guy grinned. "What's Eve been doing to you? You'd better let me have a look at it."

"I haven't done anything to him," said Eve indignantly. "He was set on in the backyard while he called to me through the keyhole."

Guy frowned; clearly he thought it as odd as she did. After a careful investigation of Hugo's arm, he straightened. "I can probably put it back in joint for you."

Hugo nodded, looking rather green. "*Ja, bitte.*"

"It'll hurt like the devil but save you having to go to a hospital."

Hugo said something in German and Guy replied; Eve had forgotten he would be bilingual. "Guy, surely a doctor should do it," she said anxiously.

"Yes, of course, but I don't think he's too anxious to encounter officialdom at the moment. What are your papers like, Hugo?"

"Not good. The press card is genuine."

"The hospitals we could reach from here today are all military. I'd lend you my army identification but it wouldn't help."

Hugo grimaced. "No, my French is rusty and I have altered too. It's strange to think that in the Prussian Jaegers we were thought to look somewhat similar."

"And you got into trouble for talking to an Alsatian pig of a recruit. Eve, can you find something to pad his arm while I pull it flat? We shall need a knife, too, and cognac. There should be a bottle in the cellar unless Bertrand has drunk it all."

Eve had never seen Guy so easy, and her anxiety that Commandant Saulx and Hauptmann von Kobis might be compelled to regard each other as enemies suddenly seemed absurd. Here at least were enduring ties with the past, and under their influence Guy showed even more clearly how damaging was the lack of them elsewhere in his life.

When she returned, they were talking German, Hugo looking close to fainting. Guy turned as she came in, his eyes unconsciously softening as they rested on her. "Right, Hugo. Relax. Drink as much cognac as you can and don't try to help."

Hugo leaned back, eyes closed. "I couldn't."

Guy was brutally swift. The knife to cut coat and shirt free, rolled cloth to help keep the arm straight, both hands on Hugo's shoulder, a brief struggle, then a twist and a highly unpleasant click. Hugo gasped something unintelligible and retched.

Guy wiped sweat off his face. "Sorry. It's too swollen where the bastard hit you to grasp properly. It'll take a few days to settle, I'm afraid." He poured a coffee cup full of cognac and held it for Hugo to drink.

Hugo shook his head. "I can't afford to get drunk."

"You won't be going anywhere tonight. Don't be a fool; my cognac will be the best thing to happen to you in a long time."

Hugo chuckled feebly, and drank. "Don't disappear again. I want to talk to you."

Guy poured more spirit and left the cup in his hand. "I've just realized that perhaps I need to talk to you, too. The German delegation will be summoned to receive the treaty in a couple of days; I'll see you there. If your press card is genuine, you're entitled to be present."

"Before," said Hugo muzzily. "I need to see you before they receive the treaty."

"No. I'm sorry, Hugo. There are some things I can't do for you, and that's one of them."

"You know what's in it?"

"Drink your cognac and stop worrying for tonight. No one knows what's in it. Committees of Three, Four, Five and Ten, as well as God knows how many subcommittees, are throwing everything together at this moment, and even they've often mislaid that they've decided. But yes, I know too much to be able to discuss it with you now. Afterward, I will try to give what little help I can."

Hugo gripped Guy's sleeve with his good hand. "Afterward will be too late. Don't you see? Once it's in formal treaty shape—"

"It won't make any difference what people like us do, when Clemenceau himself is swept away by circumstance. I've said I'll help, but it isn't the kind of help you're expecting. After the treaty has been presented, you can come with me where I'll probably be sent, and together we may achieve something for both France and Germany."

Hugo wished he had not drunk so much cognac. "For God's sake, Guy, afterward is too late. You know I wouldn't ask you to harm France. It's just. . . ." He set his teeth as his head swam. "It's justice I want, the same as you. So there won't be another war."

Guy had not moved, standing with Hugo's fingers gripping his sleeve. "There is no justice after such a war. It died with all the rest; I'm surprised you had not realized. Only perhaps a faith still to be kept. I am a French officer in a position of confidence; I can't do what you ask. If you were in my place, you wouldn't do it either."

"Then, why not take me to the nearest police post, since you're such a fine officer of France?" said Hugo bitterly.

Guy detached Hugo's hand from his sleeve. "It isn't the same and you damned well know it isn't. Go to sleep and stop behaving like a Junker."

Hugo spoke German then, apparently repeating his arguments.

Guy glanced at Eve. "Speak French, *mon vieux*. Or English if you prefer; mine has improved with practice recently. Best of all, don't speak at all." He lit a cigarette and put it between Hugo's lips. "They taste like manure, but are better than any I found in the Rhineland last week."

"How was it there?" Hugo remained enough of a diplomat to accept so definite a change of subject, but was too muzzy to attempt questioning Guy on what he had been doing in Germany.

"Better than when you saw it last, I imagine. No disorder, since the cities are full of occupation troops."

"You call an occupation better?"

"At least where the Allies rule, the killing has stopped. In Munich, it's still bloody massacre. The Reds there are killing hostages in a panic, while the Freikorps gather to storm the city. They'll kill a great many more besides hostages when they take it."

Hugo closed his eyes, despair and cognac making him feel hideously sick, the effort of further persuasion beyond his grasp. He had bungled his approach to Guy and could not think how to try again. Munich. He had been there on his last leave before the end of the war, and danced at the Residenz. Even in war, Munich had been a lighthearted city. Now it, too, was engulfed in blood and hatred. He slept uneasily, stirring and grunting against the pain in his shoulder.

Guy took the cigarette from Hugo's mouth. "Do you think I was wrong to refuse him?"

"I understand so little of what is going on. No, I was only surprised you found it easy to decide. I told— I said I wouldn't have anything to do with trying to divide your loyalties further."

He stared at her. "Told whom?"

"Rick," said Eve wretchedly, and then, as he exclaimed aloud, "long ago. Just after we were married. It hadn't anything to do with what's happened since. He— he was furious when I married you, and met Hugo when he went to Germany last December."

The old building creaked about them while they stared at each other, the smells of beeswax and rich fabrics a reminder of the precious wares surrounding this tiny, cluttered cubicle.

"Tell me," he said at last. And turned to stand with his back to her, as he had done before when he feared himself. Eve had learned the signs by now, though not how to save him from what they meant, when peace for them both was as far away as ever.

"Guy—"

"Tell me," he repeated. "I want to hear it from you. Everything, since I'm not sure how much I don't know, nor how far I have confused myself. Vaucresson . . . even that I would have preferred to hear from you."

"It starts so long ago, perhaps on the night I met you," Eve said desperately.

"Then, let us start on the night you were unfortunate enough to meet me."

It was too soon; his mind survived by obliterating the unbearable, and before she forced him to face the many horrors of the night his father died she simply had to discover for herself exactly what had happened. Perhaps it would be enough for her alone to know. Whatever her reluctance, the pressures of Le Trésor, she ought long ago to have gone back to Gabrielle and admitted she needed help.

"I'm sorry," she whispered. "I'm sorry, Guy, but I can't."

"Why not?"

She hesitated, enormously tempted. The risk to him was clear; yet now that she could imagine love for him, almost any hazard might be worthwhile when they could gain so much. Just possibly, he might understand for how few of the usual reasons she had gone to Rick. Eve put her head in her hands: the child. Such risk was unacceptable when there was nothing to be gained. Rick Dwyer's child was fact, and could have very little to do with forgiveness or understanding. "There's no point in raking over what's past, when I never even see you long enough to fix how to keep Le Trésor alive."

He turned and leaned his back against the wall, arms folded. "I always heard American women were practical."

Eve flushed. "Someone needs to be."

"Evidently. Do you know, I didn't believe it before? But then, my only experience of American women was of your grace and mercy."

Eve shook her head, words caught in her throat.

"Courage, too," he added, voice flat. "Eve, I want you to remake your life. Don't blame yourself for the lie you told me. I couldn't think straight on the night you went, but I understand a little of why you did it and how much it cost you. If it's any consolation to you now, I don't think I should have survived those first weeks of peace alone."

"And now? What will you do alone?" Her lips framed the words and he understood them, although she did not speak.

He moved and came over and kissed her hand. "I don't know. Don't worry, *chérie*. Mostly I'm too damned tired to care very much."

Her fingers tightened on his, on hands she had once feared about her throat. "You still can't sleep?"

Sunken eyes met hers, and somewhere in their depths was the glimmer of a smile as both remembered how in her arms he had slept one whole night through. "I manage in snatches. Tell me instead of these practical matters we must arrange."

He listened, frowning, while she poured out the story of these last weeks at Le Trésor. Clearly, he was as taken aback by French banking practice as she, and the furniture and *objets d'art* he had obtained at the beginning of the war loomed so large in his mind that he had failed to grasp that success would mean restocking. Eve did not even mention Joubaire, although she longed to do so, and he did not ask. Some matters seemed completely clear to him, his judgment sound and swift. The rest inhabited recesses in his mind, some locked, some kept shut by desperate force of will, some requiring fresh effort each time he needed to sort them into sense.

"I came past a couple of times," he said when she had finished. "But the whole place looked so prosperous, I thought . . . I thought you were best left alone."

"Well, I didn't think so," said Eve tartly, remembering the many occasions she had been desperate for help.

He avoided her eyes. "I'm sorry."

"For land's sakes, Guy! I'd never seen so much as a Louis Treize chair before! How did you think I'd manage?"

"How you have managed. Successfully."

"If that isn't just the limit! I was worried you'd been ill, but instead you went off with the Army to Germany and simply guessed I'd manage somehow."

"We did not part in a way which made it possible for me to come without good reason."

Eve bit her lip. She was ranting at him like a shrew, yet he had come to her now, and also two nights ago at the Contesse de Saint Luc's, when she needed him. Very soon she would be alone again and panic was making her shrill. She smiled and lifted her head to look at him out of clear eyes. In some ways I am not alone, she thought.

He did not meet her gaze. "I'll make whatever arrangements are necessary with the bank, and let you know what I've done. Eve . . . one matter I have investigated. It is possible but not easy for us to be free of each other."

My adultery, she thought; and for the first time realized how horrified everyone at New Moose would be. She could never return there as a divorced woman with an illegitimate child. "How long will it take?" There wasn't an easy way to phrase such a question.

"Perhaps two years if you're lucky." Since she was a foreigner recently married to one of France's war veterans, almost any evidence she offered would be discounted.

"Two years!"

"That is ordinary civil divorce; at least I had enough sense to avoid a religious ceremony. My cousin Pierre must know a slick lawyer who would cut some corners for you, but even so it will be complicated. The grounds on which a woman can divorce her husband in France are narrowly defined, and I don't want. . . ." His voice trailed away.

He could not bear to expose her to the squalid humiliations which would result from the much easier alternative of him divorcing her.

Two years; his words seemed to blaze in front of Eve's eyes. She had not truly faced before that there wasn't the slightest chance of her child being born to the rightful father. "You mean that? It could be so long and in the end—"

He winced at her obvious shock. "In the end we might still be tied, yes."

"I never knew," she said numbly. "In New Moose no one ever spoke of divorce, but in Paris I thought it would be different."

He smiled painfully. "Paris is not such a wicked city, except for the few who preserve the forms and do not care what else they do."

The street outside was silent, swept clear by police and troops. Only the occasional jingle of military equipment or tramp of a patrol echoed between the shuttered houses. The crisis which had briefly brought them together was over and there was nothing more to do except perform the courtesies of farewell.

Guy roused himself. "Hugo is best left to sleep. I made him drink nearly a tumbler of cognac and he'll have the devil of a head in the morning, but he should be able to take a taxi to his hotel. You'll stay here tonight, won't you? I'm late and ought to have gone long ago." A French-inspired rising in the Rhineland was imminent, but Clemenceau would be swept from power if he attempted to dismiss Marshal Foch, *le maréchal de la victoire*. Tedious, treacherous undercover work now filled Guy Saulx's days.

Eve stood and without thinking lifted her face to be kissed; in spite of everything it felt so natural to have Guy there, impossible to think of him gone again. Tomorrow she would once more be overwhelmed by things to do, above all by the problem she could not dodge much longer. The problem of how to sort any kind of sense into her life again. Rick was a generous man; if she had been free, probably he would have married her for the child's sake and a little for her own. Like this, she would simply be a burden; in two years, someone to whom he sent money from Bangkok or Berlin.

"You'd better come to put back the bar when I've gone." Guy had not kissed her.

Eve remained dry-eyed while he was there, and only wept as she listened to his footsteps fade.

The shop was dark and trapped with sharp-edged furniture, porcelain and jade ready to fall if she stumbled. She waited until she felt steady again before picking her way back to the office, the candle there a spark which made the rest seem darker. She had no handkerchief and scrubbed her eyes fiercely on her sleeve, feeling sullen satisfaction at ruining Faubourg St. Honoré cloth. Let it be ruined, since ruin suited the night.

"Ah, Mme. Saulx. *Quelle chance, alors.* I have waited a long time for you to finish arranging matters with the Commandant," said Joubaire out of darkness.

CHAPTER 9

His bulk moved between her and the glow of candlelight, his hand brushing hers before fastening on her arm. He was so close Eve felt warmth from his skin.

The shock was immense. She made no attempt to struggle against his grip, and her heart shook against her ribs.

"I began to wonder whether I must watch the pair of you on the floor together," he added with a shade of disappointment. "You're very long-spoken for a couple who haven't bedded together for weeks."

"How did you get in?" demanded Eve, and was pleased to find that her voice was not too shamingly unsteady.

"There are shutters upstairs with rusty locks, if a man knows where to look." Eve heard cloth rustle, and a cold edge was laid across her throat. "Don't try to rouse your sotted friend from his sleep, although I think you'd try in vain. Who is he?"

"Herr Kobis. You must have seen him before you went out to Versailles. The Swiss journalist who collected porcelain and liked Mlle. Wyville so much. He came to see whether I was all right, and was attacked on the doorstep." Eve could not guess how long Joubaire had been listening, but if he had not learned that Hugo was German, then at all costs he must be kept in ignorance. She could not afford to offer Sergeant Joubaire any more hold over Guy and Le Trésor than he already had: Hugo here when Guy had just left in what could look like secrecy would certainly mean court-martial for Commandant Saulx, and at the very least, imprisonment for Hugo.

"*Sacré fouinard,*" said Joubaire morosely. "Why must journalists always be where they're not wanted? It's a pity Michel le Loup didn't hit him harder."

So Le Trésor was watched, and Hugo attacked because he was coming here.

The candle in the office guttered out, Joubaire's bulk no longer even black against blackness: absurdly, Eve's imagination immediately transformed him into a giant of height and strength.

A board creaked overhead, and Joubaire called softly. He shifted his hold, and the knife edge was withdrawn. "Come."

"Not unless you tell me why and where."

He jerked her roughly. "Do as you are told."

She had no choice and, herded in front of him, picked her way up the narrow stairway. A soft and powerful moonlight lay in corrugated shutter slits across the carpet of the first floor showroom, treasures close by on every side. The previous afternoon, Eve had staged a private viewing for half a dozen chosen clients, and some fine pieces from the St.-Cloud house were arranged against draped brocades, fragile ornaments too, and only finicking care would avoid them in the dark. Eve turned. "There's a pair of jardinières on your left and a Renaissance triptych somewhere close ahead."

"Be at ease, madame. I have more interest than you in the profits of Le Trésor."

"Then, tell your henchmen upstairs to stay where they are."

"*Certainement*. I have achieved what I came for, a private talk with you. Though perhaps you feared something else." He dropped her arm and groped instead for the nape of her neck.

Eve's skin chilled. "Remember what I said before."

"I think matters have become a little different. The Commandant has not committed passionate assault on M. Dwyer, I observe, merely spoken of divorce. So you see, madame. . . ."

Eve cringed from the realization of how much he must have overheard, his taunts more unendurable than lust, and she broke violently away from him the moment his overconfidence offered her a chance. Yet even in desperate urgency to escape she remembered frail furniture very close, and slipped light-footed behind brocade and away from the moon. Silence, rather than speed, must be her ally here.

There was an inlaid table somewhere to her right, displayed between Louis XVI paneled screens; beyond that, a dresser and a sixteenth-century clock in rock crystal. Eve was just trying to remember exactly how she had set drapes and furniture within a space about forty feet square, when a dreadful clashing twang told of Joubaire blundering into a harpsichord.

Eve slipped into a curtained crevice before calling out: "Take care. That harpsichord is inlaid with *vernis Martin* and gold; it must be worth eight thousand francs."

He swore, and came feeling his way toward her. By the time he reached where she had been, Eve was crouched behind a billiard table, her hands on the Vincennes porcelain that formed its surface instead of baize. She possessed this single, slim advantage: Joubaire knew Le Trésor but not the profusion piled into this display. A voice from above demanded to know what was happening in barely comprehensible argot, and Eve, too, thought she would very much like to understand a little more. She retreated again while Joubaire was distracted by cursing his henchman into silence. He struck a match but the wax flared and dazzled, showed close obstructions without revealing anything more. He had moved to the top of the stairs, knowing as well as she did that with men on the floor above, there wasn't any other way for her to escape.

"You said you wanted to talk." Eve spoke very softly, so her position would be more difficult to place. "You can do it very well from there."

He struck another match, and she could just make out how his head was poked forward, shoulders hunched, menace in every muscle. Shock, followed by alarm for Guy, had helped control terror until then; now she was quite simply determined not to show her fear. It helped a little.

She realized she ought to have moved again and had not; in this deadly game of hide and seek, safety depended on using extra seconds to move in silence. He nearly caught her that time, coming out of nowhere with a pouncing rush.

She moved just in time but then was trapped in an angle of wall and could not remember what lay beyond. A cabinet full of Sèvres . . . no, that was closer to the stairs. She felt tentatively and encountered emptiness but knew something was very close, brain scrabbling frantically to remember her design. Silence was intense now, instinct telling her that Joubaire was controlling his breathing, as she was, crouched to take her at the slightest sound.

"Come, let us talk reasonably, then," he said, his voice so unexpected that Eve jumped. "We are behaving like children."

She nearly answered; from the edge of panic she had very nearly responded instinctively to human contact.

He swore again when she stayed silent, and she placed his position at once. He wasn't as close to the stairs as before, since he was trying to hunt her as well as prevent escape. Thank God for avarice, which kept him from summoning his men from upstairs, fearing their clumsiness might splinter priceless treasures. Two patches of sliced moonlight lay across the middle of the floor; she could not cross to the stairs there. Elsewhere all was black and trapped with obstacles.

Joubaire's indecision heartened Eve. Her senses steadied and she decided that only bluff might give her the few safe seconds she needed.

There was a collection of antique mechanical toys displayed on the billiard table, some of them already wound; if she could set one off, then the diversion might clear Joubaire far enough from the stairs to let her slip past. Very carefully, she moved sideways; it was infinitely difficult to avoid making any sound at all. At last her fingers felt the outlines she sought: a gold miniature carriage fashioned for the Duc de Mayenne, a collection of dolls . . . a preacher in an ivory pulpit. That would do. There was a catch, and once it was released he waved his arms and clicked his jaws, so good Catholics could laugh at sermonizing Huguenots. Carefully, she disengaged the lever, keeping one finger on it while she nerved herself to move again. Fast. Very fast, this time.

Quite close, Joubaire decided he could wait no longer, and called the others to come and help, cursing them into care.

Eve released the lever and took two carefully calculated steps to her right. The preacher whirled and clicked in pantomine play, and Joubaire went past so close that if he had been less intent he must have sensed her there. Then the toy tinkled into unmistakable music-box discourse, and he realized the trick that had been played on him. Being a man of swift decision, he guessed the reason and turned to find the stairs again.

Eve had less time than she had hoped and could not afford to use up any of it in avoiding sound. She streaked down the stairs, then hesitated: she would never have time to lift the bar or unbolt doors.

She ran for the office and slammed the door, wedging a chair beneath the handle. There was a telephone there, and Hugo. If he could rouse, then his presence alone must make Joubaire pause in whatever he planned. She unhooked the telephone in a frenzy of haste; French exchanges were sluggardly at the best of times, and like the electricity, might easily be on strike tonight.

Nothing.

The door rattled, and she dropped the receiver and ran over to Hugo, shaking him so he moaned sharply. "Hugo! Hugo, please!" She looked around frantically, saw a jug of water she had brought, and threw the icy contents in his face.

He gasped and spluttered as the door splintered open.

Joubaire stalked in and picked up the telephone, listening intently before replacing it on the hook. "I will not complain of our *femmes de téléphone* again. *Eh bien*, Mme. Saulx. You have behaved with the most abominable stupidity."

Behind him stood two men of the true *apache* type: lithe bodies, bad skin and depraved eyes.

Hugo pushed wet hair out of his eyes and said something in German, more than half dazed still.

Joubaire laughed, and snapped his fingers at the other two. "Throw him out."

They exchanged sly smiles and nodded; both held knives.

"They'll kill him!" Instinctively Eve moved between them and Hugo.

Joubaire shrugged. "It is your fault, madame. If you'd left him on the doorstep he wouldn't have suffered more than a bad shoulder. Or if you'd behaved sensibly upstairs and left him to his sleep."

"He's a journalist! Swiss! If you kill him, the police will never give up until they've caught you."

"How should they catch us? He is here by chance, and the Seine takes rubbish a great way downstream."

"Unless you get rid of me, too, and I don't think you want to yet; then I can tell them exactly who they are looking for." She stared at the two *apaches*. "I have a good memory for faces."

"Shut up, woman," said Joubaire roughly as one of the men jabbered something in argot. "You are an accomplice and will do as you are told. Take him."

"No." Hugo cleared his throat and then repeated more strongly, "No. Stay back or I'll kill you."

He had been sitting half hidden behind Eve. Now he stood, gun in his good hand aimed at Joubaire's stomach. "I'm only a passable shot with my left hand so it will have to be the belly. I can't miss at this range."

Joubaire stared at him, his face working; then his eyes dropped to the weapon Hugo held. "*Boche. Merde, un Boche.*"

"He's Swiss—" Eve began.

Joubaire spat. "I know Boche weapons, and Swiss journalists don't carry guns in Paris." He jerked his head at the two *apaches*. "Get out, and if I don't join you, then put a knife in the bastard's ribs next time he goes into the street." He sat on the edge of Eve's desk and folded his arms insolently. "Well, M. le Boche, what next?"

You had to admire his nerve, and also the swiftness with which he robbed them of advantage. Eve stared at him in hatred, unable to make sense of anything that had happened.

"I think that's for you to say," replied Hugo mildly. He sat again, gun hand propped on his knee. "Mme. Saulx, stand behind me please. Well away from anything he may try."

"Mme. Saulx," sneered Joubaire. "You and she and the Commandant were mighty friendly earlier, from what I saw. You'd never make me or the *flics* believe you weren't all treacherous swine together. I am thinking how Michel le Loup was a patriot, after all, when he hit you by the door."

"Think of it, indeed," agreed Hugo ironically. "Madame, what do you want me to do with this looter on your premises?"

He must guess there was more to it than that, realize that once he drew a gun they would probably all be compromised, but disabled as he was and pitchforked from alcohol-thickened sleep into crisis, he had had no choice.

Eve bit her lip. What could they do to Joubaire without inviting disaster? "Let him go; he— he thinks he has an interest in Le Trésor. He's too greedy to run to the police with imaginings of Boches here, when the most likely result is to cut off his profit as well as mine."

"He's blackmailing you?"

She nodded. "Guy. Me because of him."

Hugo again remembered the file he had seen on Guy and supposed he understood. He felt horribly sick, needed to sit to keep his gun hand steady; incisive thought was impossible. "If I let him go, he'll be back on your doorstep tomorrow."

"And either way you'll need to watch your back," said Joubaire with enjoyment. "My boys will relish a hunt when you're one corpse the *flics* will enjoy finding in the gutter."

Hugo stared at this man he had never seen before who wanted his blood in the gutter, struggling to clear his mind and wishing to God that Guy were there to clear up his own mess. Guy, who had changed so terribly, yet in some ways had not changed at all. "Eve, go and unbolt the door," he said at last. "Then leave us alone."

"No. None of this is your quarrel."

"I doubt whether it's yours," he said dryly. "Do as you're told, there's a good girl. I'll be gone from Paris before a pack of sewer rats catch up with me."

For the first time, Joubaire looked alarmed. "I have a proposition to make; that's why I came tonight."

Hugo shook his head. "I've met your type before. It is impossible to negotiate with someone to whom a deal is only words, to be changed when it suits him, for any reason or for none."

Joubaire jerked off the desk. "Murdering Boche! Ask Mme. Saulx. She knows she can't afford the *flics* in here."

"Stand back," said Hugo softly. "If Madame had left the room, you would be coughing up your life at this moment. I won't have time to warn you again."

Eve had not moved. "Hugo, wait. Let him tell us why he broke in tonight, when he could have called to see me any time."

Hugo glanced at her disheveled clothes. "It seems obvious to me."

"Not quite, though that, too, I suppose." Eve realized she wasn't making much sense.

Joubaire smiled; he possessed a kind of virile jauntiness when he smiled, which was quite often. "That, too, as you say, madame. But to-night I also came to discuss certain matters with you. Matters which require privacy."

"No," Eve said at once. Her skin crawled at the thought of facing Joubaire alone again.

"The affairs of Commandant Saulx are not of a kind one would wish to share, surely, madame?"

"You heard what Madame said," interrupted Hugo. "I think she's mistaken to waste time with you, but if you must discuss deals, then you do it with me here."

Joubaire shrugged. "*Tant pis.* It's your funeral." He turned to Eve. "First, then. I heard the Commandant say he would arrange for you to draw what you need from the bank. I have some goods which I can deliver, without being observed, to the house you are clearing at St.-Cloud. You may purchase them from me there, for your restocking."

Eve stared at him. "You mean, you've bought. . . ." Her mind shuttered; that couldn't be right. She thought of the unsavory pair waiting outside; Joubaire seemed to have developed good contacts with the Paris underworld in a short time. "You mean, you want me to buy stolen goods and dispose of them as if they came from the house at St.-Cloud?" Joubaire was an imitator, and copied what he thought Guy had done.

Joubaire shrugged. "You may describe it so if you wish, but perhaps would prefer to think of your own profit made."

"That's receiving," said Hugo quietly.

"So, what is a word, M. le Boche? I've won a war and want to live well. Everyone in France wants to live well, so is in on a racket at the moment: the rich, politicians, everyone. It is a time to take what you can get, and I am achieving more than most. My goods at St.-Cloud, madame. I want ten thousand francs for this first consignment, but you will find you have a good bargain. These are goods which come from outside Paris, and no one knows what you bought in that mansion in St.-Cloud."

Hugo laughed disbelievingly. "You're crazy. Perhaps the first load might not be noticed with everything in uproar after the war, but you'd take Mme. Saulx behind bars with you inside six months."

"A *ma grande joie*," said Joubaire politely, staring at Eve with eyes like rivets in sheet metal.

" 'First,' you said," interposed Eve quietly. "What else?"

"I shall not allow you to refuse this, you realize, madame? But, very well. The other matter is more complicated. It concerns the murder at the Hôtel Daunay; so perhaps you would like to change your mind and not allow the Boche to stay?"

Eve shook her head, unspeaking.

"*Merde, alors.* You see, I have become very curious over M. Daunay. My time in his household was profitable, since his stable quarters were full of unexpected and useful people; he runs strange affairs from there, when one considers that he is also a financier with offices in the Rue de la Bourse."

"I would expect M. Daunay to be a man with many interests," Eve said indifferently. Anything to do with the Hôtel Daunay was of vital interest to her, but there was no need to be obvious.

"Indeed, yes. But the Bourse beds awkwardly with sending *apaches* from his stables to collect rent from pimping houses by the old fortifications, don't you think? However, let us proceed." He jerked his head in the direction of the Champs-Élysées. "He also issues tipster's sheets guaranteeing 40 percent on the investments he recommends, when the Bank of France is trying to launch loans at 8 percent. This he pays from money subscribed by the next wave of fools who send him their francs."

"He doesn't invest anything at all?" demanded Hugo, shocked to the depths of his official's soul.

"Nothing. It's good, isn't it? A woman did something similar before the war and went bankrupt eventually for twenty-eight million francs." There was only envy in Joubaire's voice. "Daunay does not appear openly of course, and if a woman could net twenty-eight million, then when it does collapse, so clever a man as he can certainly afford to spend whatever is necessary to protect himself."

"How did you find out about this?" asked Hugo curiously. "It must be carefully concealed."

"You envy me my spies, M. le Boche? But I lived in Daunay's house, and once I saw he dealt with *apaches* and their like, I made it my business to discover more. *Je suis méchant mais je ne suis pas bête, je vous assure.*"

"Why did you take so much trouble?" demanded Eve. "So he would have to bribe you, too?"

"*Mais non,* madame! M. Daunay is too dangerous a man for those kinds of games. But, you see, M. Daunay is in a difficult position. He has prospered through whatever dealings came to hand, since he is ambitious, and like me he started with nothing. Now he is rich and moves higher altogether. He sets up affairs, then moves on with his gains. *Enfin,* he is safe behind many fronts, some of them honest, and has millions of francs to sweeten inquiry. Yet he cannot break loose from his past. He has dangerous acquaintances; men to whom he owes something, and who want a share of his good fortune. Men who exist on his pickings, like collecting rents from pimps, so, *hélas*, he cannot stop collecting the rents and become altogether safe. It is sad, is it not, madame?"

Eve swallowed, unable to decide how far he was serious. "Why come to tell me this?"

"Because I am ambitious too. As I see it, M. Daunay's affairs are divided in two, with only the single dangerous string of his own interest to connect them. I mean to cut that string and take the part he does not want for myself; *en effet*, I have reached a position where I am nearly ready to cut. I have not wasted any time, you may be sure."

Both Eve and Hugo regarded his complacent pride with stupefaction, from which laughter was not far removed. "You certainly haven't," said Eve fervently, at last. "Was Michel le Loup one of M. Daunay's creatures before you took him over?"

"And the other, Tou-Tou Jean, yes. I tell you, madame, I am doing M. Daunay a service by taking such people off his hands. He is endangered by them; I can use them. He ought to be grateful to me."

"When some ambitious gangster comes along in fifteen years and juggles half your network out of your control, how will you feel?" asked Hugo suavely.

Joubaire frowned. "That is the difficulty. I should feel unsafe. But I wish M. Daunay to feel easy with me; I lack the skills to attempt his dealings with money; he has nothing to fear from me. He is an experienced man. I do not wish to fight him."

"You would lose."

"Certainly not, M. le Boche. Although I can see that you, at least, must accustom yourself to losing. But I might be forced into killing him, and that I do not want. He is well liked among people who would make it their business to discover his assassin."

"The police?"

"*Mais non*, madame. Other, more important people. So I need to come to an arrangement with M. Daunay; it is impossible to keep mouths shut for long, and someone may already be telling him how I occupied myself in his household. I was quite pleased to be posted to a military barracks at Versailles while time passed."

"So that's why you didn't come here openly?"

"Perhaps. So, madame, when you can withdraw money from your bank, I wish you to go to the Hôtel Daunay and ask to see Monsieur. You are the Commandant's wife, after all. Then you can tell him of your difficulties with banks and ask for his assistance."

"You expect me to take my hard-earned francs to the kind of man you describe, and ask him to invest them for me?"

Joubaire looked shocked. "He is honest, madame. He would not cheat someone who came to him personally in such a matter."

Eve exchanged glances with Hugo, and chuckled. "What then?"

"I want you to use the occasion to become friendly with the household again. M. Pierre thought well of you, and Mme. Benoit, too, I believe. You only need an excuse to go and they will regard you as one of themselves. Then you may tell me if M. Daunay mentions me; he knows I worked here, and if he has any interest in me at all, surely he will not resist the need to ask about me. He is clever but human, *n'est-ce pas?* I am safe if he never mentions me, a no one he scarcely noticed in his kitchen."

Eve nodded, surprised by such shrewd insight from a man of almost comic egotism.

"Then you may also listen and ask, and discover who killed old M. Saulx."

It was so totally unexpected that Eve could only gape at him. Joubaire had never shown the slightest doubt before that Guy's guilt was part of his hold over them. Her brain accelerated, her body utterly still. Tumbling, incoherent thoughts. "Why?" she said baldly.

"Because I need a hold on M. Daunay. Not for money, but so he may decide on my worth as a man of affairs instead of in the heat of anger. I thought I might find some weakness in his dealings with money, but they are too complicated. It is not my world. The happenings in his own home are easier to comprehend, and a threat there might worry him more."

"Guy . . . Commandant Saulx. *Il a être victime d'un coup monté?* He was framed?" Eve's lips slipped on the words.

"He ought not to have raped the daughter of a man like Georges Daunay," pointed out Joubaire reasonably. "It was not prudent. But afterward M. Daunay was forced to act without reflection. It was an emergency. Also, whatever was done, he himself had a part in it; it was unsafe to instruct others. I want to know what he did, and why, and then perhaps we may deal safely together, even though he has millions and I have just begun."

"You can see what God thinks of money by looking at those He permits to make it," observed Hugo dispassionately.

Eve did not even hear him, all her attention concentrated on Joubaire. "You'll have to tell me everything you know before I decide."

"Everything from what point?" Joubaire watched the Commandant's wife derisively, thinking of Eulalie.

"From the beginning," Eve said harshly. "Hugo. . . ."

He did not turn, watching Joubaire with narrowed eyes. "I've read about it, Eve. Dwyer has a file, and I suppose you can guess most of the reasons why he let me look at it. I didn't believe all of it, but it didn't make good reading."

"*Le Commandant était fou.* He was mad, monsieur." This Boche was an unexpected complication; Joubaire needed to adjust his designs in a hurry and could not see how to do it. "Mlle. Eulalie—"

Hugo's hand tightened on his gun. "We understand that part. Remember also that Guy Saulx has been a friend of mine for nearly ten years. If I take a dislike to what you say, then I can easily put a bullet in you where it doesn't kill."

"*Bien,* monsieur." Joubaire felt grudging respect for force, and a corresponding delight in exploiting weakness. "It is what didn't happen which made me suspicious, you understand. There was no inquiry, for instance. No *flics,* no newspapers sniffing for scandal; just a *médecin légiste* doing what he was told. Now, the *flics* may never have heard much, but journalists after a scandal—" He rolled his eyes. "It must have cost a million to keep them all away. Also, M. Daunay insisted that I leave the house, for no reason. There was this uproar over Mlle. Eulalie—"

"We understand that part," repeated Hugo softly.

"*Oui,* monsieur. Well, before the Commandant was punished and after Mademoiselle's affair, I was sent away. I told M. Daunay it wasn't necessary. I did not feel bound to defend the Commandant in such a matter; I could sit with a bottle of wine in the kitchen and hear nothing. But no, M. Daunay insisted that I go and gave me a hundred francs to amuse myself. I returned after they had all gone out; not really suspicious, but curious about what had happened to the Commandant. Also, a *bonne* lives there whom I prefer to back-street whores. She has a very generous disposition." He sighed sentimentally.

"What did you do when you returned?" Eve demanded. This was evidence she had desperately wanted to find but not known where to look for. She had come to believe that it simply wasn't possible that Guy could be guilty, as others thought, but Joubaire *knew.* That was the vital fact; Joubaire knew beyond all doubt or he wouldn't be here tonight. Her mind flicked back to him, every word important now.

". . . it was very late and I had to be careful, because M. Daunay had given me francs to stay out all night. But I need not have worried; the house was quiet. Even Mlle. Eulalie had gone to her evil club. I went to the Commandant's room, but he was not sensible: wild and unsafe, the way he is sometimes. So I went to fetch his drops; I wanted to lie with my *bonne,* not attend to the ravings of a maniac."

"So, for your own comfort, you forced him closer to an addiction he detested," said Eve with hatred.

"It kept him quiet, and that night above all he should have been grateful to me. But the bottle had gone. I thought he must have fetched it himself but then not taken them, because I could tell he had taken nothing. He was crazed but not dulled at all."

"So what did you do?" asked Hugo.

"I demanded what he had done with them. I was angry, thinking he had poured them away, but he did not seem to understand. He was dazed from the beating he had taken as well as all the rest, but though I forced him, he did not know anything about the drops."

"How could you force him if he wasn't sensible?"

"I filled another bottle with some lotion and pretended it was drops. He wasn't surprised by a full bottle and fought like a fiend to keep me from pouring. He had no reason to persist that he didn't know anything when I told him I would not pour if he had already taken them for himself."

"He wouldn't admit he'd put them in his father's cognac." Hugo looked sick, and Eve could not speak.

"No, but he was not capable of invention. By the time I had finished with him, he would have told me anything he had known, if only I would stop pouring."

Eve surprised herself with the thought that if she had held the gun, probably she would have pulled the trigger. The most monstrous part of Joubaire's tale was that he considered his actions entirely normal. In war he had been ordered to drug his officer if that was the only way to keep him leading men to their deaths; in peace he applied the inhumanity he had learned to serving his own interests. *Pourquoi pas?* Why not, why not, when what men sow that shall they also reap? "Then I went off to sleep with my little Suzette, and in the morning there was this great wail that M. Saulx was dead," Joubaire added. "The Commandant was gone, and when next I saw him he remembered nothing of that night, except, I think, about Mlle. Eulalie."

Except enough horror to send him into the dark behind a locked door in the Rue Férou, thought Eve in despair.

"There were other drugs in that house, from what I've read," said Hugo thoughtfully.

Joubaire nodded. "Mme. Daunay takes something to make her sleep, and there is also M. Pierre."

"Pierre!" cried Eve.

"Assuredly. For a long time, I understand, but as a prisoner of war he was deprived. Everyone knew that M. Daunay was pleased when his son was captured. Then, when he came home, he obtained morphine to speed his recovery; now it is cocaine, I am told. Drugs are chic in circles where he amuses himself."

"Whereas profits from drugs are chic in circles where you amuse yourself," said Hugo caustically.

"Why?" said Eve, disregarding this, forcing herself to disregard everything except what mattered. "Why was Anselme killed? It can't have been for money, and anyway, Guy inherited. M. Daunay would not kill for a run-down shop if he thinks in millions. When Guy— when it looked as if Guy might have done it, then that part made sense. He detested his father and with reason; he stood to gain and had a fixed idea over the furniture he had traded."

"He was crazed," repeated Joubaire.

"If you say that just once more, I will shoot you myself," snapped Eve.

"What did you mean when you said that Daunay faced an emergency that night?" asked Hugo after a pause.

Joubaire shrugged sulkily. "I'm not sure. I would not have come here to be insulted by Madame if I was. But figure for yourself. Mme. Benoit found the Commandant on the stairs with a drug bottle only minutes after I left his room. Now, that is odd. No one knew I had been with him, I was meant to be out; but I would swear he feared even to touch that bottle by the time I'd finished pouring, and he was sick besides from the lotion he had swallowed. Also, that bottle was the empty one I had fetched. Yet Mme. Benoit is a witness one must respect."

Yes, thought Eve. Gabrielle is the kind of witness courts believe. "If M. Daunay framed Guy somehow for Mme. Benoit to find, why then allow him to inherit?" she said slowly.

Joubaire shrugged again; he looked as baffled as Eve felt.

"Why did he stake a parasite like Anselme for so long, when Le Trésor never made money until recently?"

"I just can't see how it could be Daunay," said Hugo. "If he has gutter rats at his call, as you say, then he could get rid of Anselme any time he chose. Definitely not in his own house. Dammit man, people like Daunay don't kill on their own bedroom mat. From what I read, he's capable of it, but—"

"That was what I meant by an emergency," said Joubaire, looking annoyed. His plans depended on evidence against Daunay, as they had once depended on evidence against the Commandant. Guilt did not matter, only how it would serve his purposes. "There is just this one night when the Commandant is certain to be blamed, because of what he had already done to Mlle. Eulalie. Naturally, there would be talk after a death. You can bribe and keep scandal undercover, but in Paris there is always gossip. But when people heard the story of how the assassin was a demented war hero, talk died. The loss of a trifling shop did not matter to Daunay, compared with the chance to be rid of Anselme safely. A single night when it is certain the son did it, and poof! Anselme is dead."

"You don't know Daunay wanted Anselme dead."

"Who else is there? And only Daunay is capable of anything."

"Yet Guy wasn't blamed," repeated Eve. "Everyone at the Hôtel Daunay believes he did it, but if M. Daunay saw his chance and took it, why was Guy never even questioned by the police? He need not have blamed Guy at all if a natural death is so easy to arrange."

"It's as I told you," pointed out Joubaire. "It is because of what did not happen that I am suspicious, and also hopeful. A woman was raped and a man was killed, all in one of those fine mansions in the Champs-Élysées, and nothing at all came of it afterward. Nothing. I call that *tout à fait extraordinaire*, and that is why I took so much trouble to come and discuss matters with you tonight."

CHAPTER 10

Spring had come to Paris.

At last the winter was over, the cold rains gone, bleak shortages eased. The chestnuts spread their leaves, concierges and old men sat on hard chairs, watching the traffic go by; a feeling of exhilaration and freedom swept through the streets. People were liberated from dark, cold rooms and strolled tenderly arm in arm; they danced in sunlight under trees or at charming little *bosquets* in the Bois de Boulogne, shuffle-stepped to street-corner accordions and barrel organs, to the trumpet of a sad-eyed Negro sitting on the fountain edge in the Place St.-Sulpice. Overnight, Paris became beautiful and alluring, a satisfying, sensual city. A city of lovers, just as American doughboys dreamed of it, how Frenchmen had fought to keep it through four fouled years.

Gabrielle Benoit sat in the garden behind the Hôtel Daunay, a place of gravel paths and hanging greenery: the birds sang there and it was pleasant in the sun.

She saw Eve following a footman toward her and was very nearly pleased that she had returned. Georges had said that since she was American and lacked *une passion de la coeur* for Guy, she would not last long with him nor wish to see his relatives again: he had laughed when he heard that Eve had moved in with an American journalist and added that it was a pity they had not placed a bet together, because Gabrielle had not been sure; she recognized the toughness which underlay Eve's grace, and remembered how, not too long ago, she herself had considered Guy an attractive man. She liked the girl sufficiently to be disappointed when she heard about the journalist, but what was a journalist, after all?

Now Eve was here at the Champs-Élysées again, and Gabrielle thought she knew why.

She had no intention of showing it, however. "I did not expect you to find time to see us again, madame. On every side I hear about the success of Le Trésor."

"Of course I want to visit sometimes," said Eve carefully. She was wearing a lavish new hat and looked very fetching in the sun. "I'm sorry it's been so long since I came before."

Gabrielle studied her; face still, hands folded on gold thread embroidery. "I understand you are no longer living as Guy's wife."

Eve felt the blood come into her face but sat uninvited on a spindle-legged garden chair, since it was Gabrielle's invariable habit to set others at a disadvantage. "I'm glad you've heard, because it's so much easier not to have to explain things." She tilted her face to warmth and closed her eyes. "Do you know, I came to believe the winter would never end?"

"Has it ended? All I can feel is that when I sat here last, my sons were still alive."

Eve's eyes flicked open and she leaned forward, poise instantly cracked by the pain in the older woman's voice. "When I worked at Bois-Chauvert I thought I was discovering what war meant, but I didn't even begin to know until I came to Paris. There are never any words for such sorrow, everywhere; that at least I have learned. But I, too, have had my sadnesses and I have come today to ask your help. It's true that Guy and I no longer live together, but. . . ."

Gabrielle inclined her head, eyebrows expressing courteous interrogation, saying nothing.

This was more difficult than Eve had ever imagined. "I want to know," she said at last. "You told me what you believed had happened, and for a long time I couldn't see beyond it. Now I'm not satisfied."

"Why not, *ma petite?*"

Eve touched Gabrielle's hand impulsively. "Thank you."

Gabrielle did not answer, but this time her face softened. Eve thought she called her *petite* in affection, but Gabrielle knew it was sadness that she felt. This bright and valiant woman would have made a good wife for her Roger; with Guy she would know only tragedy. "First tell me why you are not satisfied; then I will answer such questions as I can," she said eventually.

"I have come to know Guy better," Eve said simply.

"*Et puis?*"

"You asked me why I wasn't satisfied and I've told you." Eve's tone was final. "Madame, when you saw him on the stairs after his father died, are you quite sure he had a drug bottle in his hand?"

"Yes. It was empty."

"Did you smell it to see what it had contained?"

"It was the bottle which contained Guy's drug."

"Yes, perhaps, but—" Eve broke off. Gabrielle seemed less formidable today and probably had no motive for lying, but certainly such information as Joubaire had offered was best kept to herself. "Who else had returned to the house by the time you came in?"

"Pierre was here, earlier than I expected, considering he had the good fortune to escort you to the Opéra ball." Gabrielle allowed herself a sarcastic smile.

"Who else?"

"Mme. Daunay only. Both Eulalie and M. Daunay came in later. You are wasting your time, Mme. Saulx. When you came before, I expressed the family's regret that we had not guarded you from an unfortunate marriage; I express it again now."

Eve shook her head, more in puzzlement than in denial. Gabrielle might be protecting someone, but it was difficult to see whom or why, when her sons were dead and her husband a nonentity: yet Gabrielle was the witness she must shake. The convenient, too-pat witness who found a murderer sitting on the stairs. I'm not skilled at this, Eve thought ruefully. I'm the naïve dope who wants to disbelieve but can't, because Gabrielle surely must be honest.

There was a crunch of gravel, and they both turned to see Pierre approaching; as usual he was elegantly dressed in dark cloth and intricately folded tie. "Eve, *chérie*, this is a most pleasant surprise."

Eve smiled at him, her green eyes glinting. "I wan't sure you'd think so."

Deliberately, she was setting out to use the arts she had learned in Paris, to tantalize and promise. Cocaine was only a word to her, but she did not think Joubaire could be right when he said Pierre was an addict: he looked pale and unwell but had done so since the first day she knew him. No matter how distasteful it might be, this time she intended to remain a welcome visitor at the Hôtel Daunay until she had discovered everything she wanted, and Pierre was a key in the door to her.

"Yes," he said pensively. "I seem to remember last time you came that you lectured me on how you were now my cousin's wife."

"How lucky you still remember, so I won't need to tell you again," said Eve cheerfully. Mouth smiling, muscles tight. He must not guess how she hated sitting with silk ankles crossed, behaving like a Bois de Boulogne *cocotte*.

Gabrielle watched her silently. She has a loveliness which comes from something deeper than skin and feature, she mused; and loveliness is a gift despised only by those who must make their way without even a pretense of it. Now me, I was not lovely, but men turned and looked when I was young, nor do they ignore me now I am old. If that was all, it would not seem much at the end of such a life. Gabrielle Benoit had not wept even when her sons were killed, but watching Eve set out to captivate Pierre with soft lips and calculation in her heart, tears burned in her throat.

Eve should have felt jubilant when she returned to Le Trésor; and instead was deeply depressed. Pierre had been his usual acid self and pressing with invitations: she had accomplished the first part of her purpose but found out nothing, and her task promised to be even more disagreeable than she expected.

Newsboys were shouting, black headlines braying at the crowds idling at café tables set out under awnings. Frantic meetings of the Peace Conference were tidying up the last remaining problems to the sound of water sprinkling from fountains and the scent of lilac drifting through long windows. Not far from where Eve hurried past on her way back to Le Trésor, Rick Dwyer was thinking about her while enduring the tedium of a press briefing at the Crillon.

Several days had passed since she had walked out on him, but he didn't believe in running after women who had gone off the boil; anyway, Eve and he had had too good a thing going together for her not to come back when she was ready. Goddam Guy Saulx to hell, some women were suckers for nursing useless bums.

In a crowded Crillon suite the heat was oppressive, the windows closed as a gesture to remind the assembled correspondents that they were a select few, privileged to hear an advance rundown on the U.S. position before the final debate of the treaty, scheduled for that afternoon. Bluebottles droned against the glass, and tobacco smoke lay like Meuse fog against the ceiling.

It was a futile exercise, Rick considered, since anything that really mattered was still confidential. Well, let's stir it up a little. He stood. "Question, Mr. Secretary. Rick Dwyer, Washington *Times*."

Secretary of State Lansing did not perform well under press interrogation, but since he disliked the President and was cordially distrusted by him in return, it was generally conceded that he seldom had a chance to know what he was talking about. "Mr. Secretary, is it true that the French will obtain the German Rhineland under the treaty?"

Lansing doodled disinterestedly. "It is not."

One or two newsmen near Rick made rude gestures; this was one point which was generally known by now.

"The French accept this position, Mr. Secretary?" Rick persisted.

Lansing drew down his mouth and grinned. The French didn't have any choice. "You may draw your own conclusions, Mr. Dwyer."

"Yes," said Rick deliberately. "My conclusion is that a deal has been made. The United States has offered to guarantee French security in return for excessive French demands against Germany being dropped."

"That is an irresponsible suggestion, Mr. Dwyer."

Rick sat down as other reporters began firing questions: a permanent U.S. involvement in European security was political dynamite in Washington.

The briefing broke up in considerable confusion soon after, and Rick went down to the bar. He wondered how he could word a dispatch so his editor would not fire him for prematurely sharing information with rivals reporting to the Democratic press: George Munro Tarbet was a strong Republican who would be outraged by any suggestion that Wilson was selling American power to the Frogs.

Rick downed three drinks in quick succession before deciding to walk to his lunch date in Montparnasse. Newsmen would not be admitted to the treaty debate at the Quai d'Orsay, so he had plenty of time before his afternoon deadline, and the sun was too good to miss.

The corner table he had booked was already occupied when he arrived, by a man whose sober suit and unmistakably East Coast Wasp features looked out of place in grubby surroundings. "You're late," said his guest agreeably.

"Yeah, sorry. I needed the air."

"Think of me, then, all afternoon at the Quai d'Orsay as well."

"You shouldn't have made such a good living at the State Department," said Rick unsympathetically. "You have to earn your bread sometimes."

"My God, how I've earned it this past six months."

"Haven't we all? You reckon the plant did any good?"

The other turned aside to order, then tossed the menu away. "God knows. Thanks, anyway."

"Yep, I've blown a good story before it was ready, and I'm not the charitable kind. My editor will be riled I didn't wait for facts to nail down Wilson good, and those Democratic hicks get all the glory."

"So long as it is printed—"

"I don't earn my living by packaging copy for my competitors," said Rick sourly. "Christ, they talk about French cuisine, but I've never eaten so much stuff that looked as if it was scraped off the sidewalk as I have this past six months."

"I think we'll all be glad to wrap this trip up and get back to the States." The other pushed his plate away and lit a cigarette. Secretary Lansing might be ham-handed in press briefings, but he would have been interested to see one of his senior delegates meeting the Washington *Times*'s correspondent in Montparnasse. "Okay, then. Here's all I can give you in return. It is confirmed that the President has given an undertaking to the French that the United States will guarantee their frontiers against German aggression. An unlimited commitment in perpetuity. The British will join, once the Senate has ratified it. That being so, the French Government have agreed to drop their claims to German ethnic territory and will cease attempting to fragment the German state."

Rick sat staring at the table, eyes screwed up against smoke from his cigarette. "Lansing knows?"

The other shrugged. "Officially, almost certainly not. Unofficially, he may guess. He's in the clear to lie at a press briefing, anyway."

Rick folded his hands and considered them carefully, as if he had never seen them before. "I pulled the last shot in this goddam war. Me and three doughboys in a shell hole with the Fritzes a hundred yards away. I believed it would be the last then."

"It could still be. You've helped a little today, even though we'd both be fired if any of our masters knew. If it goes through, this guarantee is the basis on which peace might be built again."

"If," said Rick flatly. "Wilson must be crazy to play such cards so close to his chest that not even the Secretary of State knows how much he's promised."

The other was silent; a State Department official did not criticize his President to a newsman. "He is sick," he said at last. "Sick and very tired."

"That's all it needs," said Rick bitterly. "An invalid facing Henry Cabot Lodge and the Foreign Relations Committee in full cry and saying, 'By the way, my dear old buddies, I forgot to tell you: I changed the whole foreign policy of the U.S. of A. all by myself. You just sign here and it'll be fixed up. Daddy knows best, so don't you say a word.'"

The other laughed and stood. "I must go. Between us we've started the debate and there are a great many others doing the best they can, as well. Including the President. So we must pray it isn't wasted. I'll leave you to pay for the scrapings."

Rick sat on alone, smoking and drinking morosely. He reckoned he had done everything he could at this Peace Conference, and then some. It was time he went back to being a 100 percent, no-charity reporter. Hugo had been bad enough, but today he had blown inside information which he had sweated weeks to collect.

For nothing, probably. Except that he shared the alarm felt by the very few men who were fractionally in the President's confidence, that if such a radical change in American policy was sprung unprepared on Washington just as the presidential campaign was opening, it would be rejected. Debate and softening up were essential, yet Wilson confided in no one and insulted the very Republicans whose support he needed.

Rick sighed and stubbed out his cigarette. A briefing question was the worst possible way of forcing the President's hand, but what the hell else could you do to such an arrogant sonuvabitch, who refused to read the American press? A sonuvabitch who had also three-quarters killed himself trying to negotiate a generous peace guaranteed by the power of the United States, without which it would not last.

Rick decided he would go to Germany again.

Paris was dead from a news angle; a torrent of treaty clauses were about to be churned through the printing presses, and the city jostled with newsmen looking for fresh perspectives to interest jaded readers.

Jesus Christ, Germany might be a hole in the ground, for all the interest anyone took in it now that the Germans were defeated enemies. Or threats. Or monsters. Never just people as baffled and crazed as the rest.

The old Europe had gone forever, the greatest casualty of them all from monstrous war. The mosaic of links and relationships, balances and interests which kept a populous and divided continent functioning, had been swept away; in Germany, Rick thought it would be easier to see what might grow to take their place.

That afternoon, the final full session of the Peace Conference gathered to approve the treaty even though there wasn't even a printed draft for the delegates to study, and several vital considerations, like the promise of an American and British guarantee to France, was still too secret to appear in it anyway.

The atmosphere was sullen and quarrelsome, public opinion suspicious, the less-important delegations resentful that so much had been fixed behind their backs.

The French military had the advantage of a good intelligence system and so understood the likely detail of the settlement better than most, and as practical men who had very nearly lost a war, they immediately discounted hopeful pratings about guarantees. Beyond recovering her lost provinces of Alsace and Lorraine, their country had gained nothing which would secure its future, and after an acrimonious and disorganized debate, Marshal Foch stood to make formal protest in the name of France's slaughtered sons.

Guy Saulx watched Clemenceau simmer with passion as he listened: as chairman of the session, the Tiger hammered down discussion ruthlessly, but whereas he offered short shrift to Portuguese or Poles, even he could not refuse the most famous Marshal of France a hearing before everything was over.

Short, bearded and volcanic, Foch made no secret of the fact that he believed the next war already lost, as he tore to pieces the compromises of the previous six months. "The Rhine alone is important; without a frontier we can defend, our children have died in vain, they have been betrayed. Nothing else will do. Not limitations, not guarantees from nations whose armies may arrive too late to save France, not hopes or ideals. We stay on the Rhine, and we are safe. I have at my command enough men to ensure it, so I ask why I am prevented from giving the orders? Why?" He stared at Clemenceau with eyes like black bullets until everyone in the hot room wondered what kept him from accusing his Prime Minister of high treason before them all. Then he resumed, repeating arguments for unlimited occupation of Germany, for whatever measures were necessary to ensure that France's foot remained on the throat of her mortal enemy forever.

Guy shifted his weight; he was sweating in the sun and had been standing a long time. The delegates complained about the discomfort of French official chairs, but they should see how they liked standing through half-day sessions. He turned his head and studied the high table, where the peace commissioners presided over this charade of consulting lesser mortals on the results of their labors. Everything was decided, which in itself was a kind of miracle; it was too late for change now. Clemenceau sat with his gavel poised in one gray-gloved hand, his face like that of Genghis Khan. High cheekbones and white, drooping mustache increased the impression of a Mongol regarding a world ripe for destruction.

The rest of the commissioners looked embarrassed by an ally unable to control its own Army: President Wilson a faint watercolor of the man who had come to Paris five months before, Lloyd George as alert as ever and regarding Foch with the undisguised dislike of a civilian for the military. Farther down the table Maurice Wyville stared thoughtfully at the main body of the hall—directly at him, Guy realized. For an instant, their eyes met and Guy's eyebrows lifted questioningly; then the moment passed. The British delegation deserved their reputation for efficiency, Guy reflected: Wyville certainly knew more than he ought, when he had taken the trouble to encounter an obscure French commandant personally and remained interested in him now. Worried by the kind of people the French have to use, I expect, thought Guy cynically.

Clemenceau's gavel struck as Foch sat down, at last. "Any questions? *La séance est levée.*" He never offered time for questions.

In the confusion of everyone standing at once, Guy was close to Foch when Clemenceau flung through the delegates to confront him: no attempt now at hiding fury. "*Et puis, M. le Maréchal,* for what reasons did you think fit to make such a scene in public?"

"*Pour faire aise à ma conscience,*" spat Foch; he turned his back and walked out.

Clemenceau's expression did not change, but his eyes slid to Guy. "*Eh bien, mon enfant.* We shall see whether the Marshal has a monopoly of conscience."

Who the hell knows? thought Guy. We do the best we can, but how can anyone tell whether it is possible to avert a fresh disaster, or whether time and place are already set and nothing we do can change it?

Tomorrow the Germans would be summoned to Versailles to receive a treaty which no one had yet seen in its entirety.

Once out of the building, Guy walked along the *quais,* hands clasped behind his back and *képi* under his arm, unconscious of the odd spectacle he presented, hatless in dress uniform. The sun was on his face and a slight breeze ruffled his hair. He stopped by one of the trees drooping almost to the water and closed his eyes, seeking some slight relief. His head ached and the muscles of his face cramped tight, but as soon as his eyes closed, his balance vanished and his senses swam. He sighed and opened them again, hand groping for support against the tree; if only one could know the consequences of what one tried to do, then strain might ease a fraction.

"*Ça va, mon vieux?*" said Hugo, by his side.

"*Je me défends.*" The Parisian response, which committed one to nothing.

"I have just come back from the Hôtel des Réservoirs."

"You managed to get in?" The German delegation was confined to the Hôtel des Réservoirs, in Versailles.

"Yes. They are not so closely segregated now everything is nearly finished, and permitted one escorted drive around Versailles each day." Hugo's voice was bitter.

Guy fingered bark absently, his eyes on the sunlit river. "We would have been lucky to be allowed a drive around Potsdam if you had won. You beat the Russians and dealt very harshly with them; I told you before, there is no justice after such a war."

"Then there will be another," said Hugo flatly. "We aren't a nation of weaklings, willing to accept defeat with such dishonor."

"Foch thinks so too," said Guy in the same distant voice. "But for God's sake don't talk to me of honor. We all lost that years ago in the mud."

Hugo shifted slightly, and studied him, saying nothing. God in heaven, he looked ill.

Water sloshed against stone as a tug and barges bustled past; two boys were arguing close by and swinging school books by their straps. "Is the German delegation prepared for having the treaty thrown at them without discussion?" asked Guy eventually.

"No. I've warned them in the harshest terms, but they still expect notice to be taken of their objections."

"So you've wasted your time."

"Don't we all?" said Hugo, and laughed. "Who ever takes notice of a damned thing another says, once we disagree with it?"

Guy looked at him for the first time, and Hugo felt coldness touch him, although response was there, somewhere. "How is your shoulder?"

Hugo touched the sling he wore. "Uncomfortable."

"I didn't thank you. . . . I was grateful you had thought to find out whether Eve was all right." He looked away again.

Hugo hesitated. He had debated long and hard with himself over what he should say to Guy, and reached no particular conclusion. He had come today in the hope Guy might relent and tell him more than he had been able to discover about the treaty before its formal presentation, but recognized now that this exhausted abstraction did not hide any change of mind. It might easily mark personal desperation so far beyond endurance that any meddling could bring a disaster. "Come and have a glass of something," he said at last. "There's a café on the landing stage if you're tired of stuffy rooms."

Guy rubbed at his face, Hugo's voice buzzing like machine-gun bullets when they ricocheted in flight. He decided that he wasn't sure enough of his balance to walk even to the landing stage. Perhaps if he stayed here quietly, then later he would be able to reach the Rue Franklin, where he was expected at a meeting. "What time is it?"

"Five o'clock," said Hugo, surprised.

Yes, certainly by nine o'clock he would feel better. Really, it was oppressively hot, and the machine guns firing more rapidly than before. Without thinking, he dragged at the constricting collar which French officers must wear on formal occasions for their dignity's sake. High, tight, rough with sewn braid, he tore at it now, because he could not breathe. How absurd to fight a war with soldiers who could not breathe.

He roused to feel cold sweat on his face. The sun glittered gold on water, and he thought an alarming amount of time must have passed. What infinite mercy that this time blackness was all he could remember, without the horrors which often waited for him there.

"It is ridiculous for you to attempt continuing like this," said Hugo.

"I'm all right."

"So I see."

Guy wiped his face carefully. "These attacks pass, and I have fewer than I did."

"Is it because you're no longer taking drugs?"

"That, among other things."

"What do the doctors say?"

"Nothing. I won't go near another doctor so long as I live. Which may not be long, I suppose."

"Guy, you fool. You can't just cut yourself off from whatever you've been taking without any medical help at all."

"I can. I have. It was the doctors who forced . . ." he started to shake, and carefully laced his hands around his knees. They were sitting on a low parapet at the quayside.

"Doctors, perhaps, but Sergeant Joubaire, too," said Hugo deliberately.

Guy began rebuttoning his tunic. "I shall be shot for dress unbecoming to an officer."

Warned off, thought Hugo. But at least Guy seemed collected again, and he made up his mind suddenly. "Leave that damned collar unhooked for a few more minutes and listen to me. After you had gone the other night, Joubaire broke in."

Guy became very still. "Is Eve all right?"

"At the moment, yes. But, *mon vieux*, she is not safe left there alone as she is. What are you thinking of? A girl fresh from America, married a few weeks and then thrown out to fend for herself in Paris? Thrown into a dangerous and unpleasant set of circumstances, too, some of them of your devising. You would need to be a blackguard to treat a young and inexperienced wife so."

"Do you think I don't realize it?"

"I'm certain you do, which is at least part of your trouble. Guy, I'm not the right person to condemn you, I've behaved like a fool too." Hugo told him briefly of Sarah; he did not want to, but thought it might help Guy to believe he offered sympathy, rather than accusation.

Guy had forgotten but now remembered the vivacious child he had met at the Astoria: that was the night Rick Dwyer first attempted to take Eve from him. "Dwyer," he said, not looking at Hugo. "Eve isn't alone."

"I think she is," said Hugo carefully. "She's certainly extremely concerned for you, and floundering in deep water on your behalf." He skipped everything to do with the Hôtel Daunay but described Joubaire's proposal for forcing Eve to deal in stolen goods through Le Trésor. "It wouldn't last more than weeks," he added. "But the swine is arrogant and conceited, as well as being so crooked his blood must have difficulty in circulating. He'll leave Eve to face the police when trouble comes and run, himself, with the profits. He'd soon set up again, but she'd be standing trial."

Guy stared at him. "Surely she refused? You were there, you never allowed her to accept?"

"Will you forgive me if I point out that only you possess the authority to forbid her?"

"Hugo, you couldn't have let her accept and then waited—what?— five days before coming to find me?"

"It's no good shaking me like that. Sit down, Guy, and think. We have a few days while Joubaire is with the guard at Versailles."

"Was that your price for waiting? He let you past the gates of the Hôtel des Réservoirs?"

"He helped, yes. But I didn't bargain with him and delayed only because I couldn't find you until a full session met, and I was able to follow you from the conference hall. Also, I had a great many other things to do." He had been forced into extreme and time-wasting measures to hide himself from Joubaire's *apache* followers.

"I've been back to the Rue Férou."

"Eve wouldn't tell me where you lived. She didn't want you harassed more than you already are."

"A fine husband," said Guy bitterly. "So close to the madhouse I must be spared the knowledge that without my help my wife will end in prison."

"I have told you," said Hugo quietly. "I considered you had a right to know, whatever your state. And now I've talked to you, I think that a man with enough strength to wean himself off drugs should be able to face whatever else he must, if only he will give himself the chance. Go back to Eve, Guy. It's not my business what happened between you, but you can only dig yourselves out of this mess together. Eve told Joubaire she would give her answer next time he came, which will be when the German delegation leaves. At the moment, he's kept at Versailles."

"And you allowed— you both allowed him to think the answer would be yes?"

Hugo nodded. "I was afraid for her otherwise, living there alone."

"Living there alone? She lives with—" he broke off.

"No. If you want the truth, I believe she did live for a while with Dwyer. But she certainly wasn't with him when I first came to Paris; she lived in an attic at Le Trésor, and lives there again now. Sarah told me; I thought it neither safe nor proper then, and I think it even less so now. But, as you know, hotels aren't easy for a woman alone. You have to be with her, Guy, when she is a stranger here."

"I can't. Don't you see, I can't answer for myself all the time?"

"She's your wife. You ought never to have married her, but you did. At this moment, living with her is the best of a set of bad circumstances."

"I married her for reasons which seemed unanswerable at the time. Keeping away is the only answer now."

"But whatever your reasons for marrying, you were wrong," said Hugo gently. "Perhaps you are wrong again to stay away."

What else could I have done when she told me she carried my child? Guy wondered dully. But yes, I was wrong because she lied. Also, of course, he had wanted very much to marry her.

Hugo broke into his thoughts. "Guy, I hate talking to you like this. But . . . perhaps . . . going to Dwyer wasn't all Eve's fault. Won't you forgive—"

"It isn't a question of forgiveness. I don't dare touch her for fear . . . of what I might do . . . next time the blackness comes." Face turned away, voice roughened beyond recognition.

I'm a diplomat, Hugo thought wryly, not a detective or one of those strange fellows from Vienna who believe the human mind revolves around sex with your mother; but this I simply cannot leave. "Guy, listen. Don't say anything, just listen. Joubaire wanted something else, which was another reason why I delayed finding you. On his instructions, Eve has gone today to reopen acquaintance with your relations at the Hôtel Daunay. She hopes—Joubaire hopes—this will be a first step to discovering exactly what happened the night your father died. Joubaire wants a lever against Daunay, and believes he killed your father. Can you help at all? Do you remember anything of that night?" He had not meant to speak of this at all, but if Guy feared violence in himself, then some of that fear came from what he half remembered of the past.

Guy shook his head, face still averted.

"Nothing? Think back carefully. Do you remember picking Eve up near Rheims?"

"Yes. She was beautiful even when her teeth chattered with flu."

Step by step, Hugo took him through what Eve had told him, watching agitation grow. Guy remembered Eulalie, and for a long time refused to remember her.

"Did you ever love her?"

"*Mon Dieu*, no!"

"But you love Eve?"

"Yes." No hesitation at all, and instinctive softening as he said it. He added wryly, "It's no good, Hugo. I've given my reasons why I can't live with her, and I won't change."

"So you will leave her at Joubaire's mercy, alone at Le Trésor?" said

Hugo with calculated cruelty. "Don't you think she might be less at risk with you? She survived three months of marriage, but I don't think I'd offer odds on what she'd be, after much less time alone with Joubaire."

He expected fury and was disconcerted by bleak resignation. "I know you're trying to help, Hugo, but I'd rather be alone. I'll cope somehow with it all tomorrow."

"Tomorrow you must be ordered to the formal session at Versailles, where we are at last permitted to see our treaty."

Guy's mouth twitched into the caricature of a smile, while the rest of his face remained completely empty. "I doubt whether my presence matters, though there's a meeting I must attend tonight. Joubaire is at Versailles, so probably I'll go. Once he's dead, some of Eve's problems will be solved."

Hugo gaped at him. "You mean to kill him? You'd never get away with it! The whole place is crawling with police and troops, and Joubaire— I told you, he's gathered quite a gang together. Probably they don't like him much, but—"

"Assassins of their type are out of a job if they let the boss's death go unavenged? Of course they'll cut my throat, and that would solve the rest of Eve's difficulties."

Hugo shook his head but did not speak. It would, in fact, solve nearly everything.

It was becoming dark, and jazz music floated across the water from barges tied up on the other shore, where Hugo once had danced with Sarah. Through and around splintered lives, the dance went on.

"You promised me something tomorrow, if you remember." Hugo broke the silence at last.

Guy blinked and rubbed his face, as if physically turning his understanding back to the Peace Conference and all its works. "I remember. You might like to come to the Rhineland with me."

Hugo took him by the arm and guided him along to lights where he had seen a café. Once there, he all but poured soup down Guy's throat. "How long since you ate?"

Guy shook his head; he did not know. He was fiercely thirsty, though, and drank a complete bottle of Perrier, refusing wine or cognac. "Alcohol disagrees with me at the moment."

The aftermath of drugs, Hugo supposed, and ordered more soup and bread.

They sat in silence afterward, since Guy wanted only to be alone: Hugo glanced at his watch; he had to leave soon.

Guy roused himself. "I'm not planning to throw myself in the Seine. You can go with a good conscience."

Hugo swallowed annoyance. "All right, I will. Where shall I meet you tomorrow?"

"At Versailles station. I don't know what time. After it's all over, I suppose."

"You were serious, we might really go to the Rhineland together?"

"I don't know," said Guy wearily. "Tomorrow. Somehow I'll make sense tomorrow if you'll just leave me." I'd better, he thought in dismay; suddenly there's a pile of impossible things for me to do tomorrow. Matters slithered from his grasp unless he kept each one nailed where he could see it. And there was a limit to how much he could keep nailed in sight: Foch and his continuing intrigues in the Rhineland, a meeting at Clemenceau's house tonight; these he had been managing well enough, although the effort tired him. Now there was Eve and Joubaire; the debt he owed Hugo and the fearful tangle at Le Trésor; all ebbed and flowed around his mind as he tried to think about them. "Eve had better return to America after it's all finished," he said aloud. "In a year or two she'll marry a boy from Maine she understands."

Guy's thought processes certainly take a bit of following, reflected Hugo as he stood to leave. "Take care, *mon vieux*. I'll see you tomorrow, but meanwhile I'd like you to consider very carefully if you can: that night at the Hôtel Daunay, I think you need to face it. You fear yourself because of filth you refuse to dig from your mind and consider calmly; if you would only look, I believe you'd find you don't carry too much of the blame. A little, certainly, for Eulalie, but not enough to justify such fear as you now have of yourself. I know you rather well, you see. A man changes in some ways but not in others, even with his memory slipped." He touched his shoulder and was gone.

Guy sat on in the empty café. He scarcely thought and did not doze, although he craved sleep. The proprietress watched him with alarm, distraught commandants clinking medals being quite outside her experience. Gradually, as had happened before, clear thought returned so he could use it to dredge resolution from its hiding place again.

The Rue Franklin was a longish walk, but the soup had put fresh life into him and he welcomed the simplicity of walking along deserted, tree-lined *quais*. The honk of traffic was close but not intrusive, leaves and buildings dark against lemon sky. Once, a woman came and linked her arm with his; he shook his head and quickened his pace; after half the length between one bridge and the next, she swore at him and left. He did not want a prostitute, although he reckoned they suited him best now; one took them and was not forced to stay, fearing stripped pride and blackness, when anything might happen.

There was a guard on Clemenceau's house, but Guy entered without difficulty, having been privately there before. He was also late, and Georges Clemenceau did not welcome employees who kept him waiting. He was wrapped in a shawl and still wore gray gloves, to which eccentric attire he had added a black skullcap. Clemenceau's staff had long since learned to anticipate his mood from the positioning of this cap; over his forehead and you were in trouble from an abusive, overbearing old man; rakishly over one ear and briefly you could relax.

He eyed Guy malevolently, cap well forward. "So, *mon enfant*. You have thought fit to come." He called everyone *enfant*; it meant nothing.

Guy stood at attention. "I offer my profound apologies, M. *le premier ministre*."

"*Comment?* Apologies are offered by idiots to those they despise."

Guy remained silent, since there seemed no useful answer to that, and after a moment Clemenceau grunted and turned to curse his secretary. His breath wheezed, and after a long day his back hurt where he had been shot. Notoriously short-tempered, his mood always worsened in the evening. He flicked through some papers. "Since you have come, let us dispatch business." He turned to one of the other men in the room. "Colonel Favre?"

"No further information, M. *le premier ministre*. A messenger for Mainz left G.Q.G.* at seven o'clock this evening, but he was not carrying dispatches. His message must have been verbal, or in the form of a personal letter."

"Launay?" Clemenceau might have been asleep, except for single, snapped words. The Council of Four had sometimes fallen into the error of believing their seventy-seven-year-old chairman slumbered, only to be rudely disabused if one of them ventured an opinion which might, by any stretch of the imagination, threaten the interests of France.

"No further information, M. *le premier ministre*," a civil servant said quickly.

"Why not?"

"Marshal Foch is aware that secrecy is essential if he is to succeed, M. *le premier ministre*."

"Why?"

"Because— because the risings his military staff are planning in the Rhineland—"

"My meaning was, Why has Marshal Foch been alerted to the need for secrecy? You have been indiscreet, perhaps?"

"No, indeed. We have been most careful, but excessive care makes it impossible to gather information."

* French military headquarters.

Clemenceau grunted. "Patrice?"

Patrice Fabian processed all the information uncovered about unauthorized French operations in Germany, and Guy was only one of several men he had recruited into the business of attempting to control the Army at a time when it was infinitely more popular than the Prime Minister. "Considerable quantities of small arms are being distributed in Mainz, although no method seems to have yet been perfected of placing these with German groups in other cities, or in areas occupied by the British where secrecy is essential. Secret talks are also taking place with separatist groups all over the Rhineland; the reports are before you. The Mayor of Cologne, Herr Adenauer, is the most prominent figure known to be sympathetic toward a rising directed against the central government of the German Republic, although he is prudent over what he says in public."

"Which is?"

"There was a meeting at the Hansasaal in Cologne attended by Adenauer; unofficially, but also as Mayor, you understand. Present were representatives of separatist groups as well as members of parliament from the left bank of the Rhine. He told them"—Fabian consulted a paper in his hand—"that the Rhineland was different from Prussia and if it decided to follow its own destiny then the French would be more lenient over the treaty."

"It might also give this Adenauer supreme power in such a state, instead of remaining a mere piddling mayor," interjected Clemenceau, his eyes still closed.

"Yes, M. *le premier ministre*. It is significant that such a meeting could take place in Cologne, which the British occupy, since they are opposed to anything, French-inspired or not, which would add to the disorder in Germany."

Clemenceau's eyes opened instantly to their widest extent. "Do not teach me politics."

Fabian wilted visibly. "No, M. *le premier ministre*. Certainly not."

"Commandant Saulx?"

"I was present at this meeting in Cologne, pretending to represent pro-German elements in Alsace, as M. *le premier ministre* is aware, since my report is among the rest." As Clemenceau had said, he did not need to be taught politics. "Adenauer also said that any annexation of the Rhineland by France, no matter how it was disguised, would bring another war. 'As surely as the sun rises tomorrow,' he said. The meeting passed a resolution, at the end of a day's discussion, rejecting total separation of the Rhineland from the rest of Germany."

"They set up a committee to study means of establishing their separate state," interjected Fabian.

"With Adenauer as chairman, yes. You could say he had used that method to control those who wanted it associated with France, instead of federated with Germany."

"Or one might say he sought power, simply?"

"He is not a simple man, M. *le premier ministre*. Nor is he a lover of Prussians who have brought Germany to defeat and disorder. He is angry and frustrated, like most Germans; he has also pacified Cologne, which is now completely quiet."

"Explain your meaning."

Guy hesitated; it was all in his report. "I believe he spoke one cardinal truth: association of the Rhineland with France, in any form, will bring another war 'as surely as the sun rises'. Marshal Foch sees such a plan as insurance for France, but nothing I have seen or heard in Germany has made me change my opinion that he is wrong. Adenauer is like other Germans at the moment and expresses fury against institutions which brought his country to defeat. This time will pass. It is already passing. We may perpetuate disorder by giving arms to German criminals, but France will never be able to establish a client state on German soil."

Clemenceau's inscrutable mandarin's face turned from one to another of the men in the room; none had been offered a seat. "Any questions?"

There were shuffled feet but no questions; he would have been disgusted if there had been. "*Eh bien, mes enfants.* We are agreed. My Cabinet is agreed. The information you have gathered since our last meeting confirmed my belief that officers of our Army are defying the most categorical instructions they have received, and continue to pursue policies which my government has pledged itself to terminate. You will persevere with your tasks, but time is short and information of more importance than absolute discretion. *Absolute* discretion, you understand; I do not expect you to behave like amateurs. Commandant Saulx, my secretary has your orders." He closed his eyes and folded gloved hands across his stomach.

They nodded to each other, once out in the hallway, but parted with only a handshake. Clemenceau disliked chatter in his hearing, and heard a great deal farther than seemed reasonable. Guy followed a secretary through to a littered office and signed for a sealed envelope. "Marshal Foch stirred up a hornet's nest today."

"My God, yes," agreed the secretary feelingly. "The old man was in flames all the way home."

"Perhaps he'll call Foch out, with revolvers in the Bois at dawn." Guy weighed the envelope in his hand consideringly.

The other laughed. "Ah, yes, now that would improve his temper at once! He would do it too, if it were possible. I have instructions to show you the cabinet decision taken in this matter." He flicked through some papers in a register and handed over a single sheet. "I must stay while you read."

Guy nodded, studying the rough-typed memorandum. He was far from reconciled to the spy's role forced on him, since Foch as well as Clemenceau had saved his country from defeat and was only continuing to do his duty as he saw it now. It was no oversight which made Clemenceau force Guy into publicly restating his own convictions at this time of crisis; the old man was adept at obtaining good service from the reluctant.

The official memorandum stated simply that a decision had been reached on the Rhineland and associated questions. British and American guarantees that they would come to France's aid in any future war of aggression by Germany were accepted, and in consequence, France relinquished any intention of advancing her frontier to the Rhine, nor would she add to European disorder by backing German political discontent. "*In reaching this decision, the factor considered to be of supreme importance was German national feeling in the areas concerned. A large province held down by force forever would be a source of weakness and not of strength to France. ITEM. No U.S. or British guarantees would be operative if French occupation forces stage a coup d'état in the Rhineland. ITEM. Allied occupation forces will remain in the Rhineland for fifteen years, and it should be a major aim of French policy to see that this period is extended indefinitely.*"

"Whatever that minute says, there was no possibility the British or Americans would ever agree to a French Rhineland," observed the secretary. "Foch and the press can howl as they like, but the old man has fought like a devil for French interests. In the end he had to settle for the best deal he could get. Those guarantees are worth more than French troops on the Rhine."

Guy fingered the paper thoughtfully. "I certainly hope so, or we are wasting our time."

We all waste our time, Hugo had said. When does anyone listen to what he does not want to hear?

Guy returned to the Rue Férou before reading his orders, and slept in fitful, dream-laden snatches before starting out on all the many things he now had to do.

CHAPTER 11

Before dawn on the following day, dispatch riders fanned out through Paris, bringing copies of the printed treaty to senior Allied officials. Maurice Wyville was woken at four in the morning to receive his copy, a book two hundred pages long. He dressed and shaved, being a man of meticulous habits who would not study such a document in pajamas, and walked the few paces to the Astoria, where his office was situated. It smelled stale and he went over and unbolted shutters: another perfect day was dawning. Water was racing down the gutters below to clear debris from the day before, a municipal cart spraying the road while blue-smocked men heaved at leather pumps. Otherwise everything was quiet. Just birds joyfully singing and the sound of water over stone; Wyville sighed and went inside to pick up the treaty, leaving the windows wide.

"Conditions of Peace" in French and English printed on the cover, four hundred and forty articles, seventy-five thousand words. Wyville read rapidly but with the experience which enabled him to miss nothing of importance. Of course he knew what was there, but working at high pressure over a long period, like everyone else, his mind had become yoked to whatever was causing the most trouble at the time, to the obstacles of detail, where wider perspectives disappeared.

Two hours later he took off his glasses, locked the treaty in a safe, and went out onto the balcony again. Without consciously thinking about it, he decided immediately that the balcony was too cramped, and went downstairs.

"Good morning, Sir Maurice. You're early, sir," said the messenger on duty. "Would you like me to fetch you a cup of tea?"

"No, thank you, Baines." Maurice Wyville possessed a country land-lord's memory for names. "I'm just going out for some air."

"Beautiful day, sir. Though what I say is, Paris is all very well but it'll be good to get home. I've had enough of France to last the rest of me life." Baines was a Devonshire man who had lost an arm on the Somme.

Wyville nodded and went out. A whole generation of British had had enough of France, and they trusted him and his like to make sure they never came back.

He walked fast, unseeingly, breathing sweet air. Softer and more fra-grant than Norfolk, he thought absently; perhaps Sarah would be riding out early if the weather was so splendid there, too.

He heard someone call a greeting and turned reluctantly: he was un-lucky to encounter an acquaintance walking the Paris streets at this hour. It was Herbert Hoover, the American economics expert and chief of Allied food relief to Europe, a man he liked but did not want to talk to, after weeks of endless talking.

"You've read the treaty?" demanded Hoover.

Wyville nodded.

"What do you think, eh?"

"I don't think anything particular. I knew what was in it, and so did you. I feel depressed after reading it all together."

"I certainly did not know everything that was in it!"

"I think you must realize that you did," replied Wyville, courteously but definitely. "It is the impression of the whole which is unattractive. Alone, each point can be justified, and is far less than Germany would have demanded of us if she had won."

"So the French never finish saying. As they kept shoving under our noses the terms *les Boches* extracted from Russia, as if we didn't know."

Wyville stared at the sunlit avenue; a *bonne* was beating rugs as if she were in a farmyard. "And they were right, of course. It's just that we did not come to Paris expecting to behave like Germans drunk on victory." He nodded and walked on.

At the next corner, he bumped into General Smuts talking to John Maynard Keynes, of the British delegation. Although he was the South African plenipotentiary and Prime Minister, Smuts had been in the British War Cabinet and possessed considerable influence with Lloyd George. "Good morning, sir."

"Good morning, Maurice. What brought you out at this hour?"

It occurred to Wyville that all of them had sought fresh air for the same reason. "A futile effort to outpace unpleasant thought, I imagine."

Smuts nodded. "We must change it. I shall go immediately to Mr. Lloyd George."

"It's too late. The Germans have been given only fifteen days to accept it."

"Fifteen days is the time for them to lodge objections. And they will object, so we can then renegotiate some of the more onerous clauses."

"Reparations," said Keynes. "No figure has been set, so the French will settle on something impossible and keep their troops on the Rhine until we're all paid."

"Then, we must tackle that quite different situation as it arises," said Wyville impatiently. "The monetary clauses may be unwisely drawn, but at least they are not final. It simply isn't possible to embark again on such wrangles as have already nearly split the alliance apart, when each compromise depends on some concession made before. Wilson must return for his elections, and our Army is already half demobilized."

"We'll see," said Smuts obstinately. "Lloyd George is not a hidebound man."

Wyville exchanged looks with Keynes. "No, he certainly is not."

"I shall prepare a reasoned argument and suggest he get the negotiating period with the Germans extended. They can't be left with only resentment to carry into the future."

"We've seen this coming before today and been powerless to stop it," said Wyville. "I don't think anything has changed. Mistakes have been made, and are incurable. In itself, the treaty is justifiable and will be justified. We can't go back, only try in the future to ensure that what we fear does not happen."

Smuts was a head shorter than he, impatient of European subtlety yet not an unsubtle man. "I don't accept that, Maurice. I am here today as a friend of Britain, because of British generosity after my country lost a war."

"I realize that, sir. If you recall, the generosity came somewhat after the peace was concluded."

Smuts smiled unexpectedly. "I try my way, then, and you watch out for the future."

Wyville walked back to the Astoria, his depression only increased. His judgment was . . . his judgment had been that it was unsafe for his daughter to marry a man he liked, because he was a German. He saw no reason to change it.

Although negotiations for the treaty had taken place in Paris, the presentation ceremony was to be at the Trianon Palace Hotel, in Versailles, in a room painted starkly white with windows and mirrors reflecting glare.

Only the day before had the Germans' part in the proceedings at last been made entirely clear to them. They had come expecting negotiations, and were told they would sit on *le banc des accusées*, receive a document and get out. If they refused, then the Allies had eleven million men under arms ready to march on Germany, which still barely possessed a government.

Maurice Wyville had a settled dislike of mobs, which at the moment included the whole paraphernalia of the Peace Conference. If he could have avoided it, he would not have gone to the day's ceremony: the affair was a charade, they might as well have sent the Germans the treaty by post. The crisis would come in fifteen days, if the German Republic refused to sign. Enthusiastic French banged on the roof of his official car with its Union Jack, a few women threw flowers, the police cordon at the entrance to the Trianon Palace broke. He sat, hand tight on the knob of his stick, dressed in morning coat and high collar, his expression completely unchanged and detesting them all.

"Lumme!" his driver said aloud when he caught sight of that uncompromising countenance in the mirror. "Gawd 'elp the 'Un todiy."

The Trianon Palace was a wasp's nest of scurrying, conjecturing figures, two hundred people packed into the dazzling reflections of the salon where the ceremony would be held. Wyville sat in his place and stared straight ahead, arms folded, thinking of Stoneham. A far door was thrown open, and an usher bellowed into silence, *"Messieurs les délégués allemands!"*

The Germans stood in the entry, squinting into the glare and uncertain what to do next, when the mirrors made even the size of the room difficult to grasp. They were led by their Foreign Minister, the Graf von Brockdorff-Rantzau, an aristocrat recruited for the occasion by the Socialist government, and after a moment he bowed to the assembly, which stood and bowed back.

The Germans were then led to seats facing Clemenceau, and as the French Prime Minister climbed to his feet Wyville looked at Brockdorff-Rantzau. He knew the man slightly from before the war and decided he looked quite simply ill from the task he had been called on to perform: skin yellow, eyes circled in black, face sweating. Wyville looked away again, unable to watch: it was, he thought, a humiliation similar to those staged by barbarians when they dragged defeated enemies through the streets in chains. The old Europe indeed was dead.

Clemenceau clearly felt no such scruple. He was wearing the same baggy clothes he always wore and stared at the Germans unblinkingly. "Messieurs, the hour has struck for the settlement of our account. You have asked for peace, and we are disposed to give it to you. I am compelled to add that this treaty has been too dearly bought by the peoples

represented here for us not to be resolved to secure by every means possible the satisfactions which are our due. You have fifteen days to make
written observations, following which we will communicate final terms
and set the date for signature of the treaty." He looked around perfunc-
torily. "Does anyone wish to speak?"

"Yes," said Brockdorff-Rantzau, shuffling paper. "*Messieurs les
délégués alliés—*"

"Translators!" snapped Clemenceau. "Each phrase must be translated!" He glowered at the German for daring to speak.

Without fainting, Brockdorff-Rantzau could not have looked worse
than he already did, but the faces of the rest of the German delegation
showed clearly the stupefied horror they felt at being so summarily
dealt with, when in spite of every warning they had expected something
very different.

"Arrogant swine!" spat a Frenchman sitting behind Wyville. "They
trample France underfoot and kill our sons, yet still expect to be treated
as though they ruled the earth."

By the time translators had been set to their task, Brockdorff-Rantzau
was trembling visibly, whether with rage or humiliation it was impossible to tell. It remained impossible to tell as he spoke. His voice hesitated between an aggressive shout and a menacing hiss, his manner expressing outrage, agitation, accusation, and unrepentant German pride,
sometimes within a single sentence. Wyville remembered ruefully that
Brockdorff had always been an abysmal public speaker; he was certainly
succeeding in making the worst possible impression on his enemies.

"Speak up!" shouted Clemenceau at intervals, interrupting everything. "I can't hear such words!"

". . . The demand is made for us to acknowledge that we alone are
guilty of having caused the war. Such a confession in my mouth would
be a lie." Brockdorff-Rantzau finished against a rising buzz of sound;
President Wilson muttered something angrily to Lloyd George, who
expressively snapped the paper knife he was holding.

Clemenceau stood again. "Has anyone else any further observations
to make? No? *La séance est levée.*" He jerked his head and the Germans were hustled from the room.

"*Quelle insolence!* Where was repentance in such a speech? So what
do you think of such conduct, monsieur?" The Frenchman who had exclaimed before mopped his face as if preparing to have a seizure.

"What conduct?" asked Wyville coldly.

"Such incredible conduct as not even to stand when he replied to
Clemenceau! *Ces allemands!* I tell you, monsieur, they never change."

"Didn't he stand up? I failed to notice. I make it a rule never to stare
at people when they are in obvious distress." Wyville nodded distantly

to one or two acquaintances but did not speak again until he was out in the courtyard, and then only to order his chauffeur to drive back to Paris immediately. He had no stomach for the triumphal meal which was scheduled to follow next.

Charles, he thought, staring at frolicking crowds. My God, boy, there must be some few million of all our sons under French grass who are ashamed of us today.

CHAPTER 12

Versailles station clock was showing twenty past five before Hugo saw
Guy coming toward him: he had begun to think he would not come,
and feared some disaster.

They clasped hands briefly and neither thought it odd, on this day
above all.

"What now?" demanded Hugo, eyeing Guy's field-service uniform.

"I have a truck with me; we'll talk as we go."

But Guy did not talk as he threaded the old Renault through people
thronging the roadway. A few carried flags, others shouted nothing in
particular, the cafés did a roaring trade. He turned right by the closed
entry to the Palace of Versailles, and pulled up farther along the street.
"You know where you are?"

Hugo nodded. "The Hôtel des Réservoirs, where our delegation is
staying, is just along the street."

"Listen, then. Once they've recovered from shock, because among
other things Brockdorff-Rantzau was so hysterical with nerves he made
a very unwise speech, the German delegation will realize they can't do
much more here. They've only fifteen days, and the place to decide
such matters is Berlin. I can get you in there, but it's for you to decide
whether to go with them or come with me. You'll be useful in the
Rhineland and will approve of my orders, but the choice must be
yours."

"I'll come with you," said Hugo without hesitation. "I'm too junior
for anyone in Berlin to listen to me on such matters. Even here, they
didn't take notice of a word I said."

Guy smiled. "Try just once more, then. Here's a pass; you won't have any difficulty. Go in there now and offer a final word of advice. Tell them not to publish the treaty, now they have it. The details haven't been released here, and will not be. Germany will lose any chance of changing anything once the world knows what's in it. Public opinion will prevent the statesmen from yielding any gain at all."

"Who told you?"

"It's common sense, *mon vieux*. It was also an opinion put to me in another context, and I agree with it enough to offer you this chance today."

Hugo took the pass from his hand. "I won't be long."

Half an hour later he came back, walking very fast. He was white around the cheekbones and carried himself as if it was an effort to coordinate his movements.

Guy turned the truck out of the town without speaking.

"Where are we going?" asked Hugo eventually.

"Vaucresson. It's on the military loop line around Paris." It was also a place Guy Saulx disliked intensely.

"And then?"

"We go by train to Mainz. G.Q.G. of the French Army of Occupation in the Rhineland. There is a coup d'état being set up from there, designed to establish a separate Rhineland state under the protection of France. I have orders to obtain sufficient detail on illicit arms shipments by our military to blow the whole thing wide open, so Clemenceau may then act to prevent it."

Hugo stared at him. "If Clemenceau wants to act, why not charge every officer he suspects? If ever a man had power, it is Georges Clemenceau today."

"No. The mainspring of the plot is Foch; its executor Charles Mangin, commander of occupation forces. Butcher Mangin, Hero of France. A killer who might tear the Army, and the Rhineland, apart for what he believes is patriotism. We need the plot to fail and then sweep up the bits discreetly: this isn't the time for scandals or for a mutiny in the French Army."

"I should have thought Clemenceau only too happy to dismember the Reich," said Hugo bitterly. "Are you sure you aren't expendable, while he double-crosses you?"

"Quite sure."

They hardly spoke again throughout a hideously uncomfortable journey in a train which gasped steam and recovered from every slackening of speed with a pounce that hurled the unwary on the floor. It was packed with troops returning to bases in Germany and eastern France, bulky equipment filling every space.

"There's no sign of demobilization," said Hugo once.

Guy turned his head on the railed seat back; rest was impossible. "The Army may yet be needed."

Fifteen days. Fifteen days before it might march to war again.

If this train was any evidence, then troops were already being moved forward, in case Germany refused to sign.

Senlis, Soissons, Rheims, Verdun.

It was mercifully dark by then, the soldiers morose and silent as if even the air of Verdun was cursed. Hugo stole a look at Guy, ready to hold him if he broke. At the far end of the carriage, a man kept telling anyone who would listen how he had lost all his comrades here. Guy's eyes were clamped shut, face rictus-tight, body strung like wire. He did not move and Hugo kept silent; at least among these men Guy would find sympathy if he screamed.

The train clanked roughly over temporary line, mile after mile of it, stopping often. The moon rose over the fearful landscape of nothing anyone who had not been here could recognize, and Hugo discovered that he himself was shivering: a year in the trenches left him with memories too.

Metz, once in German Lorraine and now French again.

Saarbrucken. Hugo woke with a jolt to realize there had been no frontier. He was back in Germany and it was all French, the station platforms full of horizon-bleus.

Kaiserlautern; then, for some reason, Mannheim and a loop down the Rhine to Mainz. No Germans anywhere, streetlights off, the countryside dead.

Fresh air was very welcome after the stink of the train.

"Tell me about Eve," said Hugo as they stood on the Rhein Promenade at Mainz and watched the sun rise over the river. He did not want to talk about what he saw here, when Guy was a French officer in his homeland.

"I saw her only briefly. I said I must be away for a few days, but she was not to worry or commit herself to anything. I would tell Joubaire to deal only through me. I found her a room with a widow in the Rue Tronchet." He might have been making a military report to a superior.

"And you saw Joubaire."

"Yes."

"You didn't kill him?" inquired Hugo sarcastically, the desire to hurt most unexpectedly born. Even old and valued friendships would not long survive the pressures of Mainz under French occupation.

"I have a job to do here first; so have you, since you agreed to help. Afterward you may quarrel with me for being French."

There was a long silence. "My home is to become Polish, did you know?" said Hugo at last. "All West Prussia, and Posen, too. I read the clauses in the Hôtel des Réservoirs."

"I knew, yes. It's better we don't talk about it."

"It needs shouting to the world! All those Prussian towns given to people like the Poles! What will become of our culture, how safe do you suppose our women will be when the Poles take over?" He thought about Sarah then, in her home which was a little like West Prussia, yearning for her with sharp and sudden pain. But there was no doubt how right her father had been proved, when among other things the Von Kobis family would be penniless unless they chose to live in Poland.

"What became of their culture when you held the land they share? Hugo, we mustn't talk about it, or we'll be so busy quarreling, the Rhineland will go the same way."

"Why should you care?"

"Because France has been offered guarantees of British and American help if Germany threatens her in the future. The American Senate would refuse to ratify the agreement if we broke the undertaking we have given in return, and seized the Rhineland for ourselves, the British be delighted by any excuse to retreat to their island. The guarantees are only against German aggression, Hugo."

A platoon of French soldiers marched past, rifles slung, while Germans took off their hats to the officer, as was the regulation. Hugo's eyes narrowed. "I feel aggressive right now."

Guy shrugged. "I'll meet you here at seven tonight. I'm best on my own at G.Q.G. anyway, and if you don't choose to be here, I shall understand."

"It's always the conquerors who can afford to be generous," said Hugo disagreeably.

"Then, you should wonder whether anything would be changed if the treaty were less harsh, when you find even generosity intolerable. You told me to face the night when I lost much I value at the Hôtel Daunay; perhaps I must say the same to you. You were defeated, Hugo. You have to face it and stop pretending that something different happened."

He left Hugo seething with anger, his temper further inflamed by a day in Mainz under the eyes of French soldiers, who behaved as occupation troops always do. Complacently, noisily, possessively; offering provocation and flaring into violence if offense was taken.

Seven o'clock.

Reluctantly, Hugo went back to the Rhein Promenade and waited, smoking sulkily while he watched horizon-bleus flirt with a nursemaid. He was being childish, knew it, and could not help himself.

In Paris it was possible to believe that friendship owed nothing to nationality; when Hugo saw his own land occupied, primitive hatred slipped its leash.

He waited a long time, sitting in dust with his back to a tree. He could have sat on a bench, but most had French soldiers on them, and he preferred the dust. He was very tired after two days of strain in Versailles and divided Mainz, with only a night of stiff-backed dozing in between: he drowsed while he waited and woke when someone tripped over his legs. He swore most undiplomatically, realizing it was nearly dark.

"Follow me if you want to," said Guy quietly. "Wait a few minutes and I'll let you catch up." He broke into loud apologies for clumsiness and then walked off, hands in his pockets. He was dressed like most younger German males in Mainz, in a mixture of threadbare army and civilian clothing.

Hugo fought his desire to depart in the opposite direction and stood, dusting himself carefully. Two French soldiers passed; one said something to his companion and they laughed, staring at Hugo. Although disheveled, he still looked an obvious aristocrat.

Hugo followed Guy; if he had stayed, he would have flattened those sneering faces and been shot in the morning.

Guy was waiting in shadow just beyond the corner; when Hugo fell into step at his side, his furies boiled over. "God blast you all to hell! If I see you masquerading ever again in German uniform, I'll tell the first crowd I see that you're a Frenchman. There must be plenty of murders in the back streets of Mainz at night." Somehow the defeated remnants of a proud uniform made the insult worse.

Guy did not alter his pace and replied in German. "I'm sure there are. But I think you should wait until morning before deciding whether to go your own way, and come with me tonight."

Hugo stopped dead. "No. I'm not falling for any more French double-dealing with Germany as the stake. I meant it, Guy. I'll set a mob on you if I see you dressed like that again."

"Then, you will have your opportunity tonight. We're going to watch a mob, and at the end of it you may tell them all about me if you wish."

"You think I'm bluffing, don't you?"

"I think you're behaving like an uncivilized clod, but as it happens these are uncivilized and cloddish times."

Hugo's breath caught in an unwilling grunt of amusement. "Damn you, Guy."

"And damn you, too, *mon vieux*."

There didn't seem anything more to say after that, and they walked together in silence through twilit streets. Curfew was close and the few people still out were hurrying, heads down and adding to the impression of grimy desolation. French patrols had fixed bayonets and were blowing whistles in warning.

Guy hesitated at an intersection of streets, this area full of warehouses and rusting railway sidings. "It's somewhere off to the left here."

"Where are we going?"

"To a separatist meeting. You will find it divided between adventurers, glassy-eyed idealists and criminals. I hope you may have a chance to convince the idealists at least that they are backing a loser. The criminals simply need to be put behind bars again, as soon as I know how they are distributing the arms our military supply to them."

Hugo could see other figures slipping across deserted tracks and converging on a derelict warehouse ahead. "It'll be curfew when the meeting ends."

"I hope we shall find somewhere to bed down quite close." Guy's voice was flat, but Hugo looked at him sharply. He had not had time even to doze in the dust and must be exhausted, although for this kind of thing he seemed to remain both alert and shrewd.

There were thugs standing by the warehouse door, but Guy's German was fluent and had barrack-room intonations learned in the Prussian Jaegers. He also possessed various papers stamped with the devices of an independent Rhineland, hid any shortcomings behind aggression, and squeezed a way in for himself and Hugo without difficulty. Ill-natured jostling continued behind them, and when the meeting started, speakers needed to shout to make themselves heard.

Only one man, with an eyeglass and dressed in a black suit, held attention, using an odd mixture of claptrap on Rhineland civilization and hardheaded explanation of the benefits of separation from the rest of Germany. Most of his listeners cheered when he mentioned that the national police would be disbanded when separatists took over.

"Dr. Dorten," whispered Guy. "You won't be surprised to hear that in any separatist riot, police criminal records are the first thing his followers try to destroy. Instructive, isn't it?"

Hugo stared at the faces around him in the gloom. As a Prussian diplomat, he had little experience of scum but recognized the type without difficulty. He had seen similar countenances in Freikorps uniform, and supposed he would find them in antiseparatist meetings too.

Dorten was saying something about a march on Cologne. "We have arms, my friends. I expect more large deliveries soon, and then we can free our beloved Rhineland. Within days, I propose to send flying columns through the countryside to gather money for our cause."

Most of the gathering shouted approval at such an obvious license to loot; the more official-looking supporters on the platform looked apprehensive, but only one had the courage to protest. "We are setting up a free state, not anarchy, Herr Doktor."

"A free state, yes! A great state, yes! We are the pioneers, eh, my friends?" A howl shook the rafters, and the protester sat abruptly.

Another man spoke and said what great patriots they all were; once the Rhineland was separate, the French would withdraw their troops and also allow Alsace and Lorraine to join their new state, instead of tying them to France.

Hugo swallowed, heart beating. He knew now why Guy had brought him here, but surely he would be torn apart if he attempted to inject sense into such a gathering. He felt Guy's hand on his arm, and turned to see his lips frame a single word: later.

Fighting spread soon after; the speakers were forced to yell louder and even then they went unheard. A gang of toughs who had been recruited as bodyguards began to punch and kick indiscriminately at those they could reach.

"This way," said Guy, and began to force his way through brawling people.

Wedged together and using force when they had to—jokes, abuse or their own weight when they would serve—Guy and Hugo eventually reached the space cleared by the bodyguards for their bosses. Once there, Guy began a shouted altercation with the nearest guard, who automatically swung a truncheon at them. Guy ducked and seized his wrist. "Take me to Herr Dorten. I have brought a messenger with important news for the cause."

The guard kicked out and shouted: immediately, two others came to his aid and Hugo leaped forward as Guy fell under a tangle of bodies. He swore and kicked with the rest, confusion complete. He tripped, and pain flared as a boot crunched into his ribs; then an enormous report sounded in his ear and there was room to stand again.

"Keep back," said Guy, his voice odd in Hugo's ringing ears. "We have a message for Herr Dorten and I'll shoot the legs off anyone who tries to keep me from delivering it."

The warehouse was stilled for an instant by the shot, scuffles breaking out again when nothing else happened. The guards fell back and left them facing one of the ugliest men Hugo had ever seen, a revolver almost lost in his fist. It was pointing directly at Guy. "State your business, offal. Then I decide whether you see the Herr Doktor or whether your body is dredged from the Rhine tomorrow."

Guy nodded and put his gun back in a holster hidden under his tunic. "Herr Dorten knows me. Tell him it is Felix, the emissary from his friends in Elsass."

The other hesitated and then gestured with his revolver. "You tell him, but keep your hands behind your back until he recognizes you."

Guy shrugged and crossed his wrists behind his back. "This is Hugo Kobis, the messenger I spoke of." A von would not be an advantage in such company.

The man spat. "He can stay here."

Hugo waited for what seemed a long time, thinking in a bemused way about Guy claiming to represent German-speaking Alsace separatists, and trying to ignore the guards still watching him. One held his jaw from a punch which it gave Hugo satisfaction to remember, and they discussed loudly among themselves what they would do to two spies if Herr Dorten had no use for them.

The brute with the gun returned, and jerked his head grudgingly. "Go over there."

Hugo went, and heard anger flare behind him. We'll need to watch our backs when we leave here, he reflected.

Dorten was less impressive when met face to face than he had been as an orator. Pale skin and fanatical eyes simply gave Hugo an uneasy impression of abnormality. The men around him were more ordinary, and only the obvious thugs looked satisfied by their company.

Guy was leaning against the table, arms folded, talking earnestly. He turned. "Herr Doktor, may I present Hugo Kobis? He was an acquaintance of mine in Elsass before the war and until yesterday was in Paris, gathering information under orders from our Foreign Ministry."

"Their Foreign Ministry, not ours. I do not acknowledge Prussian authority in the Rhineland."

"We must face facts, Herr Doktor. At the moment, the Rhineland is part of the Reich, as Elsass is part of France."

"By brigandage! The French have no rights in Elsass."

"They won a war, as we won the last when Elsass became the trophy of our victory. Tell Herr Dorten what you know, Hugo."

Hugo von Kobis despised mobs exactly as Maurice Wyville did; his orderly mind and natural humanity were offended by hysteria, while proletarian pressures snapped his hackles into protective arrogance. But he told them clearly and persuasively, a diplomat trained to a job, however disagreeable the circumstances. "The French may only have rights of conquest over Alsace," he concluded, "but the treaty our delegation received yesterday required Germany to give up all future claim to the area and the French will never shift on this, no matter what happens in the Rhineland."

"You lie," said Dorten flatly. "The French High Command in Mainz promises us differently, and gives us arms to prove it."

"So what does General Mangin promise?" inquired Hugo sarcastically.

"Once the Rhineland is separated from the Reich, German Alsace shall be ours, to rule as we please. France will not feel threatened by our small state, as they are by a Reich led by Prussians."

"Their army of occupation will withdraw?"

"Certainly."

Hugo laughed contemptuously. "More than a million Frenchmen died in war against us, yet Herr Doktor Dorten has only to ask and the French will give him whatever he wants? You delude yourself and your followers, I assure you. The French may laugh as they watch you helping them to dismember Germany, but they will give you nothing, only take."

The dark-suited men whom Hugo guessed were officials, teachers and the like exchanged uneasy glances.

"You're wrong, Herr Kobis." Dorten's pince-nez misted with annoyance. "As I told you before, they have already given a great many arms as well as assistance to our cause."

Hugo wanted to smash his complacent, greedy stupidity, his own temper now thoroughly lost. "How does it feel to be a puppet of French power? I could forgive you if you were simply paid, but no; you want to strut as a ruler and let others sweep up the pieces of disorder. Our countryside terrorized by gangs pretending to collect for party funds, the cities ruined because anyone not besotted by ambition will know that a separate Rhineland state cannot last. Even if Alsace were given the choice, which it won't be, it would vote to stay French." His eyes swept over each listening face. "With you as their alternative, I don't blame them."

For an instant they all stared back at him with dropped jaws, disorderly uproar a frame to utter stillness, Dorten deathly pale, fogged glasses giving him the look of a fish floating belly up.

His head turned at last on a scrawny neck, skin scraping audibly on high, stiff collar. "Take him, Hansi."

The coarse, prizefighter's face of their escort slackened into a satisfied grin. "*Jawohl*, Herr Doktor."

"You can't just kill him, Josef!" said the official who had protested before.

"Why not? He will betray us."

"Who to? The French? They know everything already." His eyes swiveled to a man Hugo had not noticed, a man in civilian clothes but with the bearing of a soldier, still seated and tilting his chair negligently with one highly polished shoe, while the rest stood.

Dorten said nothing but continued to watch Hugo malevolently. The seated man said nothing either, chair creaking as he tilted it slowly back and forth.

Hugo smiled, turned to him in mock courtesy and spoke French. "You enjoy watching executions, I expect."

"Of my enemies, monsieur? I neither enjoy nor dislike them. Sometimes they serve a purpose."

"In this case, Germany's purpose, don't you think?"

He considered, chair rhythmically creaking. "Possibly."

Hugo turned back to Dorten, still smiling. "You see? The puppet master is wondering whether he should stop you from enjoying your treat. The French wouldn't want your more scrupulous colleagues to learn too early that their snug Rhineland will be ruled by scum who murder whenever their ruler nods. Good evening to you, *meine Herren.*" He turned his back on Hansi's gun, and kicked the nearest man out of his way.

The flat report of a shot made him leap, expecting agony.

"*Au revoir, monsieur,*" said the Frenchman politely. "Next time you enjoy a bottle of good French wine, I suggest you give thanks that your kidneys are still intact." A service automatic was in his hand, and Hansi stared disbelievingly at his wrist, where a blue hole spurted blood.

Hugo smiled tightly. "An awkward choice for you, when at least some of those here may remember how it was the French who decided whether a murder was advisable or not. Dance well on your strings, Herr Doktor." He sidestepped a guard and jumped blindly off the platform into the crowd below. Few of them knew what was happening and some surged forward while others recoiled from the shot, hiding Hugo in scuffling. The bodyguards knew, though, and after an instant of stupefaction surged in pursuit: the Frenchman would not stop them from trampling any German they chose into the cobbles; he simply objected to Dorten's imperiling his usefulness by prematurely thrusting butchery on squeamish followers.

"This way!" said Guy urgently.

Hugo felt himself drawn aside into darkness, half his mind wondering whether in this situation Guy was entirely trustworthy, when he worked for yet another section of French interests. A steep, unlit stair twisted down ahead of him into darkness, Guy's voice warning against excessive speed; he must have been here before. Boots clattering in pursuit, the ring of metal quite distinct where some had reinforced toes and cleats for kicking.

Air damp on his face but still no light. Hugo drove hard into Guy's back and both nearly fell. "Up," said Guy, his hand urging Hugo against a wall. Metal rungs bolted to bricks, heavy with rust under Hugo's fingers; he climbed swiftly as boots and swearing voices hurtled down the stairway at his back. Two shots, deafening in a confined space, and a flash of light too brief for anyone to see their quarry silhouetted against the wall only ten feet up.

More people came flooding into what must be some kind of basement, broiling together in the confined space. Hugo thought what a strange position he had landed in, stuck to wet wall instead of dealing in overheated rooms with the world's diplomats. Wars make fools of us all, he reflected wryly, but in reality his temper was very much inflamed. He had come with Guy but unforgivingly, and now there was the added humiliation of watching his countrymen behave like rats in a byre while the French stepped in to preserve his life for purposes of their own.

Very carefully, he continued to climb, the noise below hiding any sound he made. The steps led up to some elevator Hugo could not see, the looped cable awkward to negotiate in the dark; he was certain Guy wasn't following but could not safely wait for him on rusty metal rungs. Oddly, he felt no fear, only anger burning in the slow fire of pride and anguish.

He reached a grating at last and hauled himself over the edge while, below, the search continued to eddy aimlessly about. A shout as someone came down the stairs with a lamp, its light illuminating open mouths and surrealist figures.

Someone yelled when Hugo moved—he had not thought they could see forty feet up in such feeble light—and there was a concerted rush for the bottom rung. The first man took the lamp and began to climb slowly, hampered by its weight and heat: halfway up, Hugo recognized Guy. He must get off that grating and away into the roof space, but immediately he stood, those with guns fired, bullets spanging off metal and ricocheting around brick walls. Yells followed from the climbers, terrified of being shot.

Hugo was untouched in such deceptive light and scrambled hastily up into darkness. He had thought of waiting at the top of the ladder, where it would be easy to prevent anyone from coming up, but that would invite a marksman's shot, although there was no further firing for the moment, everyone waiting for the climbers to reach him.

The bobbing lantern was quite close. What the hell did Guy expect him to do now? Hugo discovered he was on the control platform of the elevator, its massive steel beam poking out through the wall ahead, roof timbers dimly seen in moonlight coming through the opening.

Hugo swung himself up again, onto the loft floor this time. Nowhere else to go, everything black except for the paler square where the elevator poked out.

A great many cases were packed into the loft, most of the storage space solidly taken up, so there were few places left where he might hide. Nor did he want to hide; he wanted very much to fight and win, since he was fed to vomiting point on defeat.

The elevator was thick with grease, which stuck to his hands and clothes. This place was frequently and recently used, and Hugo had seen too many ammunition and small-arms cases not to recognize the type when he felt and saw them.

Screams and leaping light flared unexpectedly behind: Hugo saw his own shadow sharply black and his flesh crawled from the shots which must find him now. More screeches, shouts, bellowed orders.

He craned around, hands on the cases he must climb to reach the farther spaces of the roof, and saw that Guy had smashed his lamp as he gained the top of the ladder. It could look like an accident but was not. Blazing oil poured over dry timber and ran in flickering trails down the iron ladder, searing hands and panicking climbers as its timber fixings began to burn. One or two men jumped and landed on the mob milling in the cellar below, the rest trampled savagely on their fellows' fingers.

Guy did not appear, and Hugo fell heavily off stacked crates in his haste to find him. The floor was also burning, and with the ladder gone they hadn't long to find another way down before flame illuminated everything.

He found Guy standing completely still in shadow, his hands over his face. "Are you hurt?"

"I hate fire." His voice was high and unnatural, body shaking.

"Christ!" exploded Hugo. "You brought me here for your own bloody purposes, which I expect included arson if you saw your chance, so you can damned well get me out now you've succeeded." He tore aside protective hands and slapped his face, hard.

He had acted instinctively, as temper which had smoldered dangerously all day finally ignited. Guy managed well enough when he had to; a jerk back to urgency was what he needed now. But Hugo's blow was more than a carefully measured shock; Guy was French, and this evening he had contrived for Hugo to witness German gutter scum add shame to the other horrors of defeat.

Hugo felt only satisfaction when Guy's head cracked back with the force of his blow. He stumbled, arms flung up, and Hugo hauled him forward and slapped again, palm and knuckles. Held him two-handed and shook, savagely, filled with primitive triumph that this time he was winning over Frenchmen. "Do you hear me? Pull yourself together and get me out of here."

The flames were bright yellow and leaping for the roof, iron platform glowing with heat. At least some of those cases must contain ammunition, which would soon explode.

It had been dark and now there was too much light. Hugo had thought he might be able to release the brake on the elevator and swing down on the cable, but the yard was filling with people, staring and shouting at the fire.

Only Guy's eyes remained dead when flame illuminated everything else; no change of expression, nothing. He was no longer a friend, scarcely a person; instead, an enemy who dared to wear German uniform after years spent killing Germans. Hugo's hands moved without any wish of his to make them move, from his enemy's shoulders to his throat, his fingers curving into sinew. So had he yearned all day to choke the arrogant horizon-bleus swaggering on the streets of Mainz.

Thirty-six hours before, Hugo had been in Paris, where living remained an art and people danced all day: there, even defeat became unreal. Mainz was brutal fact, and humanity crumbled under so monstrous a shock. He was no longer thinking of the fire at all. "*Alors, mon commandant.* I suggest you remember how victors should behave. I am not an unsuspecting girl like Eve, to be left in the lurch whenever the fancy takes you."

Something flickered behind the mask of Guy's face, and was gone.

"You hear me?" said Hugo almost conversationally, and closed his hand like a trap, thumb under jawbone and palm against Adam's apple. Fingers avoiding the artery where compression brought unconsciousness. Hugo von Kobis might be a Junker and a gentleman but he had learned some unpleasant tricks in the barrack room; as a cadet, he had once suffered the split-nerve pain this pressure carried to lungs and ear and eye.

And as he tightened his grip, for the first time he consciously experienced the luxury of inflicting agony on another; power like a god and blood cresting, singing in his mind. For an instant, his hand clenched into savagery and then was snatched back as he cried out against the horror of his own enjoyment.

At the same moment, a ripping crackle of flame was immediately followed by heavy smoke, then a booming roar as part of the roof over the fire collapsed. Both Hugo and Guy jerked around instinctively to stare at it, eyes and mouths gaping, sweat drying in the heat.

"This way," Guy croaked, hand to his throat but sense in his face again, although whether danger or rough handling had restored it, Hugo could not tell. He hoped very much that it was danger, so Guy would never remember the cancer of violence which a moment's aberration had set into the bone of friendship.

Hugo followed without a word, smoke becoming denser every moment. He tripped over unseen obstacles, the floor cracking sharply as flames ate away its support.

Guy turned once when he fell, then stood without offering help before leading the way into spark-filled darkness again. He remembered, and remembering, he could not be deceived: Guy Saulx already knew too much about the pleasures others gained from ruling the defenseless.

The warehouse was perhaps two hundred feet long and a hundred feet wide, well alight among the upper timbers at one end and beginning to catch elsewhere from sparks and collapsing joists. There was no sign of Mainz Fire Brigade, although the alarm must have been raised by now.

The upper floor where Guy and Hugo were trapped was divided into compartments, the one nearest the elevator stacked with French guns and cut off from the others by a brick dividing wall, a design intended to contain exactly such a fire as this.

"No way through there," shouted Hugo, the fire drowning other sounds. It was becoming very hot, their lungs laboring for air.

Guy gestured, hand to his throat again. The roof was in two spans and formed a central gutter where the slopes met in the downward point of an M. "Stand on my shoulders and break into the gutter. There's a weak place."

There certainly was, lead loosely held by wire clips. Guy had been this way before, searching for arms probably. Hugo clawed at clips and slats, his nails ripping as he struggled to disentangle wire. Then he was through, gulping night air as coolness flowed against his face.

A great deal more than coolness flowing; a tearing gale, in fact, blustering past his shoulders as the fire sucked air through the hole he had made, flames crackling joyfully from this fresh life. Rapidly, he widened the hole until he could wriggle through and then leaned back to offer Guy support.

Both found the other's touch unexpectedly repulsive, the moment of struggle until Guy had heaved himself through the narrow gap almost obscene with unwanted intimacy. The gutter was a catwalk between two slopes of roof; they were completely hidden, yet could not stay there long. One end was closed by fire, and escape from the other meant a climb down exposed wall to the yard below. When Guy had been here before, he would have come secretly and been able to choose his time to scale drainpipe or brickwork to reach the roof. Now every move they made would be brightly lit.

Orders and counterorders blew on the wind; there was a great deal of amateur blundering in the absence of the fire brigade, but far too many people were in the yard for them ever to make that climb in safety.

Guy dropped to his knees, and for an instant Hugo felt the same furious irritation, the sense of betrayal through the weakness of another. *Dolchstoss.* The stab in the back which lost wars and lives alike. Blood rushed to his face, eyes blurred and his heart beat loudly: this time he would tear the bastard apart and not be to blame.

Then the moment passed, was gone, outlived, his mind rational again in bitter air. Barbaric impulse overthrown by shame, though the reckoning remained.

Guy looked up and indicated a square with his hand; he had not slipped into confusion again and was peeling guttering from slate and timber. In strange and scarlet light their eyes locked, and Hugo moved too late. Instinctive menace remained in how he stood, the wish to hurt in outstretched hand and sweating, shock-filled face: Guy stood quickly and moved back out of reach.

"I'm sorry," said Hugo. "I am ashamed. My God, I'm sorry, Guy."

Behind them, the ammunition cases began to explode, ripping bullets into brickwork.

Guy turned his back and crouched to lever up slate. "We can break into a different section of warehouse here, and later mingle with the crowd. Our military command prefers their arms to be burned rather than risk spreading rumor by letting firemen see what's here. There'll be plenty of confusion to cover us."

Voice rough, and unforgiving.

The most brutal irony was that their friendship should have been broken by a man who despised excess. Hugo von Kobis had respected his nation but ordered his life by the mixture of pride and conscience which men call honor; yet, within a day of returning to his occupied homeland, hysterical patriotism had swept everything else aside, and the price was nothing ever the same between himself and Guy.

It was as if war became angered when anything escaped destruction, and found its own ways of smashing what remained.

CHAPTER 13

Two hundred and fifty miles to the east, dawn was already a faint line on the horizon. The printing presses of the German Admiralty had been working all night, and several thousand copies of the draft treaty of peace were stacked, ready for distribution. Weary workers were yawning and smoking, waiting for the last checks to be completed, so they could go home; no one spoke. While they worked, each had absorbed the sense of the hundreds of articles, watched them swirl through rollers, chopped and bound into thick, accusing blocks of print. Germany renounces. . . . Germany renounces. . . . Germany accepts responsibility for all the loss. . . . Germany renounces. . . . Peter Lehr, late of Hauptmann von Kobis's company, spat on inked metal type. "*Schmachparagraphen!* Shame paragraphs! We should fight again, rather than sign." He forgot that all he had wanted to do only months before was sell his rifle, beat up a few officers, and go home.

No one answered him.

Outside, the streets of Berlin were empty. Revolution had been swept from the center of the city, and for the moment the Freikorps were supreme, revolutionary leaders murdered, the impression of order increased by troops lounging on street corners. Only a closer look revealed unfamiliar symbols on collar and sleeve, and chance flaring incidents easily split the fragile crust of calm. A new government had been elected, but in the streets the louts still ruled: more discreetly, but they ruled.

By midday, it was hot. Lehr had slept seven hours and went out for a beer; newsboys were scurrying, placards screaming. Beer-garden tables were filled by people reading the terms Lehr had printed through the night. He belched, and dragged a fistful of paper marks out of his pocket. Complete copies of the treaty were selling for less than the price of three beers. He thought he would buy one to show little Rudi, his son aged four, as a joke when he was older, when the Reich would be strong again, and treaties something the Germans used to wipe themselves.

By the corner of the Tiergarten, a drunken Freikorps trooper fired at a pigeon and sent passersby scurrying; elsewhere women stood in line for food, men argued in the sun. Work was scarce and prices rising every day, but at least it was peace.

Peter Lehr spat.

Next day, the treaty was on sale as far away as Magdeburg and Frankfurt, the day after in Hamburg, Cologne and Mainz. Scarcely a German had not read or heard the tally of defeat, and for the first time the German Government began to discuss seriously what they should do.

Eleven days of the Allied ultimatum time remained.

President Wilson's promise of justice had easily become an excuse for a Cabinet inexperienced in diplomacy to pay very little attention to what was going on in Paris, to overlook unpalatable facts and believe all would be well. Now ministers came from Weimar, and a public debate took place in the Great Hall of Berlin University, as if they knew that such a momentous decision could only be taken in the old imperial capital.

The debate was vitriolic, the speakers almost unanimous: the treaty must be rejected. As hysteria mounted, anyone who attempted a rational discussion was howled down.

Chancellor Scheidemann both led and followed the mood of the hall: such losses, such injustice could not be accepted. Under the treaty as it stood, all the Reich's colonies were lost; all her Navy; all her merchant fleet; all her Air Force. Nearly all of the Army, three quarters of her iron, a third of her coal. Lost: West Prussia. Lost: Lorraine. Lost: Alsace. Severed from the Fatherland: East Prussia. Lost: North Schleswig, Eupen, Posen, Silesia. Lost. Lost. Lost. Where is the peace of justice Wilson told us to expect?

Germany cannot sign.

Ten days of the ultimatum now remained.

The sun blazed down from a cloudless sky everywhere in Europe. The first summer of peace had begun, and the Gräfin von Kobis watched dust devils blowing across the lands her husband had left in her care when he went off to war. He was with the Supreme Command,

and privileged in being able to send private letters by military messenger. She looked at the paper in her fingers, tears slipping unnoticed down lined cheeks.

"... *as usual the politicians make a great noise but leave the decision to the Army. Even our pitiful Socialist Republic wants to fight, apparently, now they have read the treaty. Liebchen, you must pack everything you can, and leave within a week. We gain honor by fighting again, but nothing else. We cannot win, and our beloved West Prussia will be opened at once to the Polish hordes. God have mercy on us; either way, we lose everything except your dear self. I understand Hugo is safe and in Paris with our delegation ... at least one child has been spared to us."*

One child. Lotte von Kobis looked across the plains through misted eyes. Rupprecht, Willi, and handsome, dashing Rudolf: she had been so proud of her sons. Loved them and this place so much, never known real anxiety since the day she married, until the war came. Dear Otto, such a good husband. Such a lovely, happy, laughing family together. Dear God, why did You not send me daughters instead of sons? Christ of all mercy, why give me such happiness, only to take it all away?

She wiped her eyes carefully; she must not weep yet. Otto said she had a week to get clear, and in this countryside populated by the young and old, by women and men maimed in the war, she must continue as guide and guardian of them all. Those who wanted to come must be helped to come; the animals and crops and stores brought too, if possible. She bit her lip; the Army had long since taken most of their draft animals.

She went toward the stables briskly, calling to old Putzi, the sole survivor from twenty-two grooms kept four years before.

First Quartermaster General Wilhelm Groener was gathering information from his officer corps. He had no doubts about what he would discover, but being a man of provident mind, took care not to lose battles for lack of information. He despised his new socialist masters in Weimar and detested the rabble which defeat had loosed into the streets of the Reich: he had walked through Berlin in the full uniform of his high office simply to throw his contempt in the face of the mob, and neither calculation nor bravado had entered into it at all.

He regarded all politicians as indecisive and probably criminal as well; he had, on the other hand, been disconcerted to discover that his supreme commander, Field Marshal von Hindenburg, showed no signs of making any decision either. The Allies had reluctantly extended the deadline for acceptance of their treaty, but within days Germany must decide whether to sign or, for honor's sake, at least offer token resistance.

General Groener picked up his cap, thereby starting a chain reaction of clicked heels all the way to the front door of his headquarters. He could see what was coming already, but his duty was clear. If the German Army could offer reasonable resistance, then he must recommend refusal. If not, Germany must sign.

Either way, First Quartermaster General Groener would be left with the blame, while Hindenburg slumbered in the gallery of heroes. So be it. The German people were going to need someone on a pedestal in the years ahead. If it was his duty to be hated, then he accepted that as well.

Meanwhile, he required information.

In Paris, another general sat at his desk in the sun, writing. Heat did not worry him; in South Africa it was often a great deal hotter than this.

General Jan Christiaan Smuts wrote carefully, pausing often for thought. He had talked only yesterday with Lloyd George and discovered that the British Premier, too, thought that the treaty as it stood threatened the future peace of Europe; but mere verbal agreement was not enough.

He stroked his beard reflectively and wrote again. He had commanded brave men who lost a war not very long before, and that, too, sharpened the nag of conscience.

". . . *the reparations demands are ridiculous, since it is unlikely that German industry will have sufficient coal on which to operate, once the Silesian and Saarland fields are lost . . . the huge extent of Poland, with frontiers extending far into German-speaking territory, is a cardinal error which history will avenge. . . .*"

Some redrafting needed there. Never mind, it was best to write from the heart. Passion might save the world, when legal drafting only brought disaster closer. He stared out the window at leaves trembling against a summer sky: he had watched so many young men die under the sun. ". . . *We shall not be forgiven if Germany is forced to sign a treaty at the point of a bayonet which they will in due course repudiate with the bayonet. The final sanction for our labours must be the approval of mankind, not just the approval of our allies.*"

He read through what he had written and began swiftly to redraft while preserving his sense: the case he argued must be conclusive.

It was not yet too late.

George Munro Tarbet sat with his feet on his editorial desk and read Rick Dwyer's latest dispatch from Paris. The Washington *Times* was strongly Republican, and he had warned Dwyer that feeling on Capitol

Hill was disenchanted with the President's Paris caperings. Senator Henry Cabot Lodge, chairman of the Foreign Relations Committee, had declared that the proposed treaty ran counter to the Monroe Doctrine, while Senator Brandegee likened Wilson's activities to the Mad Hatter's tea party.

George Munro Tarbet lit a cigar and read on, grinning. His name made him sensitive to attacks on the Monroe Doctrine, and he liked the sarcastic touches to Dwyer's writing. The United States was exasperated with Europe, as well as with a President who ignored American affairs for foreign wranglings. Goddammit, the dried-up prude wasn't even producing any entertaining scandal, in Paris of all places.

Tarbet chipped off a couple of dull paragraphs about guarantees: Lodge could be trusted to make good use of such dangerous nonsense in his campaign speeches and wouldn't thank the *Times* if it spoiled his pitch by screaming premature headlines. The rest of the dispatch was a witty exposure of wheeling and dealing among the diplomats, and he marked it for the following day's edition. Washington would laugh to hear that Wilson considered his League of Nations a lesson to Jesus Christ, since He had omitted enforcement machinery from the Sermon on the Mount.

Tarbet glanced at a flimsy in his tray: Dwyer thought Paris washed up for news until the ultimatum expired, and was off to Germany. Fine; he could report the Allied invasion when it came.

He rang for a messenger.

David Lloyd George summoned the entire British Cabinet for an unprecedented meeting in Paris, and when it finished, he possessed authority to demand a far-reaching revision of the treaty.

Immediately, he called for a meeting with Clemenceau, Wilson and Orlando, before briefing the other British peace commissioners.

"The French won't hear of it, sir," said Wyville.

"The French don't matter. The Americans never wanted the treaty in this shape, and with them on our side we can force the French into satisfactory compromise." Lloyd George positively sparkled at the idea of reversing the entire British position on a negotiation which had taken six months.

"It's too late. Most of the German objections have been answered already, and rejected. The date for their final acceptance or rejection of the treaty is less than a week away."

"Nonsense!" Lloyd George detested rigid attitudes. "There's always time for reason to prevail."

Wyville restrained his desire to lay a handsome wager on the outcome with his Prime Minister, reflecting that Lloyd George probably wouldn't pay up when he lost.

At a Council of Four meeting held that evening Clemenceau rejected every one of the British proposals for revision, acidly pointing out that Britain was not proposing to restore either Germany's Navy or her colonies. "This does not surprise us; the British are always happy to make concessions on French interests. I am not. France understands and has suffered from the greed and arrogance of Germans, and will concede nothing. We do not need to apologize for our victory."

Lloyd George did not reply: he would fix Clemenceau, once Wilson added American power to the British position. Their promise of a joint guarantee of France's future security already made it impossible for the French to withstand concerted pressure.

Wilson stirred; he looked like the mummified remains of the man who had come to Paris, except for the nervous twitching of his face. "Gentlemen, I feel sick at heart. You overrode the counsel offered by the American delegation and now are frightened by what you have done. You are afraid the Germans will not sign. You should have thought of that before. This makes me very tired; if you had been reasonable months ago, you would not need to funk out at the end." He stared at the British, almost spitting the words. "Every clause in the treaty rests on compromise in another clause; we cannot alter it now, simply to get it signed. The Lord be with us, gentlemen." His head sank between his shoulders, and it was clear that he was praying.

Clemenceau looked at Lloyd George derisively. "Did you expect the Germans to like our treaty, monsieur? We are not here to please *les Boches* but to prevent them from attacking us again, as well as to force them into paying for the damage they have caused. It is a matter of practical arrangement, purchased with our children's blood. The position of the French Government is simple: we will not accept revision."

Wilson did not speak again, but there was no mistaking his position either. He could not endure more negotiations, and since the quickest way home lay through enforcement of the treaty, then he intended to enforce it.

Lloyd George spun his web of words and overdue reason to no avail, and in the end flexibility saved him.

He bent with the rest.

Eve Saulx sat in her box of an office, open account books in front of her. The past month had been punishingly hard work, with every spare moment spent out at St.-Cloud. She had decided to clear the house contents she had bought before Joubaire returned with his grotesquely dangerous idea of placing stolen property there, and had finished the night before.

It had all been highly profitable, but at the moment she scarcely cared. Today was an ordinary sort of day, yet she did not know how to fit in all the matters clamoring for attention: there were the usual batch of letters to write, accounts to keep up to date, and last month's balance, too. A session with Marguerite over pay, because prices were still rising, followed by complaints from Paul and the two men who now assisted him in the workshop about the quality of postwar timber. A Faubourg furnishing house had left a message about fabrics for display. Then she had an appointment with a buyer from the Ritz, who demanded special discounts for such a prestigious order. Two society women wasted an hour of her time and bought nothing. The wife of the Swedish ambassador, with an unhousebroken dog on a ribbon, likewise wasted her time. An attractive young couple, blissfully happy and spending freely to furnish their apartment: Eve enjoyed them, but by the time they left it was nearly eight in the evening.

She went back to her office and flopped into the hard chair, feeling utterly wrung out.

Alone, making money just wasn't worth such enormous efforts.

She gouged thick black strokes into blotting paper. Guy had been gone nearly a month, and she pretended to herself that she wasn't worried; when she remembered to pretend, that is. But she worried all the time, a growing ache of worry which told her he had not been well enough to go. She realized that for military routine he probably seemed competent enough, but strain was deadly: and each time crisis struck he found recovery more difficult. He had been harassed and preoccupied during the last, short time he had come to Le Trésor, said his mission to Germany should be brief and meanwhile she was not to worry about Joubaire. He knew how alone she was, how dread must increase now Joubaire would soon be released from duty at Versailles; surely he could not stay away much longer.

But what did Guy really know when everything about him was so uncertain? And what could she possibly say or do to release them both from an intolerable situation, when eventually he did return?

Eve contracted her stomach muscles experimentally; no doubts any longer. Next Christmas, she would give birth to a child. Christmas 1919. What a truly horrific year this had become, and with no sign of improvement either. Idly, she picked up a letter from her mother. It was an exact description of how matters were in New Moose on the day Elizabeth Ottoway wrote; there was a prayer for her well-being but no touch of the warmth Eve craved. Maine and its certainties seemed infinitely remote from postwar Paris.

She sighed and stood, looking at her watch. She wanted to go to the lodging Guy had found for her in the Rue Tronchet, take a bath and sleep forever, but tonight Pierre had asked her out again. Her muscles tightened once more, but for a different reason: she feared going alone with him again to a party of his choosing.

He was amusing and, beneath his cynicism, not unkind; he had also become derisively impatient when she refused to sleep with him, irritated by prudishness she could not—did not want—to outlive. He idled the day away and roused only in the evening, most of his friends raffish and their entertainments shockingly irregular; for the first time, Eve had felt consciously grateful for her own principled upbringing and did not mind admitting to herself that she enjoyed Gabrielle's sedately witty gatherings far better.

But, so far, she had gained a few unexpected insights into life at the Hôtel Daunay and confirmed some guesswork, without apparently coming much nearer to solving the mystery of Anselme's death. So she must go again tonight, because this she owed to Guy: the peace would soon be signed, and afterward, if he should somehow fight his way to recovery, then she did not intend squalid, half-true, untrue accusations to be waiting for him at the end of it.

Yet the peace was very far from being signed. As Eve hesitated over which dress to wear for a night which would not end before dawn, the Graf von Brockdorff-Rantzau decided that he could accomplish nothing more by staying in Versailles. He was German Foreign Minister and must return to offer his opinion to a chicken-gutted Cabinet: the treaty could not be signed, and if that meant war again, then war must be accepted.

The cars taking the German delegation to the railhead were swamped by a hostile crowd in the streets of Versailles. Pavé was levered up and thrown, car windows broken and the Germans inside cut by flying glass. A pace at a time, police cleared a path for them through hooting, jeering people, while Brockdorff-Rantzau clenched his hands to stop their trembling and his shirt stuck to his ribs.

A woman spat through the splintered windshield at him, her face contorted. "Assassins! Butcher of my husband! May you be castrated so your sons do not murder mine."

Eight days now remained before the armies would march again.

The French troops on guard laughed and let the police get on with it. Their job had been to keep the Boches confined to the Hôtel des Réservoirs, not to protect them from a little sport. They cursed instead of laughing, though, when the cars finally disappeared and they found they had fresh orders, now there was nothing left to guard.

"*Mes enfants,* you are posted to the 95th Chasseurs," said the elderly captain who arrived to take charge of them. "The unit entrains tomorrow from Vaucresson, and a truck will arrive to take you there."

"Where after Vaucresson, *mon capitaine?*" asked Sergeant Joubaire; he had not bargained for this.

The captain looked at them with compassion. "The frontier; where else? If the Boches refuse to sign, then it is war again."

War. *Jésus Christ, non. Pas possible.* A hostile, foot-shuffling silence fell while men who had enjoyed seven months of peace thought about war again.

The Boches. The dirty, fucking Boches wanted to drown them in mud again.

They'd won, hadn't they?

Mon Dieu, hadn't they won, after all?

Sarah Wyville was attempting to control unruly hair and stomach. When the Channel packet left Dover, the weather had been fine, although sultry ramparts of cloud piled above the horizon. These swiftly advanced up-Channel, and the storm broke before the short crossing was complete. If she went below she would be sick; if she stayed on deck she would arrive in France looking like a hunting accident, and quite possibly be sick as well.

Sarah swallowed, and decided to stay on deck: she would always accept a gamble if the stake was worthwhile. Like the gamble of returning to Paris. It was probably no more than a hoyden's trick, which would result in embarrassment for everyone, but she had not been able to refuse the chance when it came.

The ferry plunged into a wrenching corkscrew of a roll, and Sarah Wyville forgot everything except the distance in to port.

CHAPTER 14

Hugo von Kobis lay on planking and stared at light filtering through broken beams. He could see stars, hear military footsteps in the street outside, feel the lassitude brought by hunger. He fought the desire to curl up somewhere safe and sleep forever; in occupied Germany it was a constant struggle to prevent defeatism seeping into nerve and will. He might have felt different if he could have repaired his failure with Guy after they escaped from the fire at the warehouse, but though he tried, the link was gone.

Hugo understood now why Eve found this man impossible to live with. He pitied her, and wondered how she could have endured even a few months' intimacy with someone so unstable and exhausting. Especially Eve, a girl fresh from a nation untouched by war, when Guy Saulx was the result of war personified.

Guy lay beside Hugo now, hands linked behind his head, staring wide-eyed into darkness. Hugo admired him at the same time as he resented who he was: the man who had provoked him into behaving like a savage. He feared his stamina, which forced their pace night after punishing night, valued his judgment, and dreaded the times it vanished. He was also worn out by days and nights of sweating to make amends to someone who seldom slept or spoke and was often too sick to eat, driven by nerves and demons beyond the normal habitations of the mind.

Gallant, generous, uncomplicated Eve married to this man. It did not bear thinking about.

"Soon," said Guy quietly, and rolled over to peer through torn boarding.

Soon. Another hour, two perhaps; what the hell difference did it make? Then they would be off again, tracking another consignment of French arms through dark and secret streets. Hugo gritted his teeth; he felt too limp to move. Because this time, if all went well, they would bring nearly a month of raspingly uncongenial work to some kind of conclusion. Dorten had proclaimed his Rhineland state at Wiesbaden two weeks before, and Clemenceau had acted instantly, forewarned by Guy's reports. Disconcerted by how much their Prime Minister knew, sulkily Dorten's French supporters dissociated themselves from the rising and the attempt was routed by outraged German workers, Dorten himself being forced to scuttle into hiding.

He was not beaten, though, nor were the French military who wanted him as their puppet. Until they were, Guy was forced to stay on in Mainz, most of the threads of conspiracy already in his hands, secret hiding places known, friends at French G.Q.G. taking him for one of themselves. And since Hugo did not want the Rhineland to be at the mercy of marauding gangs, and also because of his bad conscience over Guy, he stayed too. They had watched French staff officers confer with Dorten, heard promises and encouragement, waited until shipments of arms covertly began again.

The dilemma still remained. If Clemenceau ordered the arrest of highly placed, patriotic officers for what would be widely regarded in France as a praiseworthy attempt to incite German disaffection, then he would simply inflame popular opinion against his government. If he announced that French security was to rest not on a weakened Germany but on the permanent guarantee of the United States and Britain, then he risked losing that guarantee. Wilson's promise, on which everything else hung, needed to be ratified by the Senate, and senators of both parties would be outraged if they heard of it first from the French. And Wilson himself might easily abandon the fight for ratification if Clemenceau betrayed his given word and allowed French plottings to sputter on unchecked in the Rhineland.

"I ought to report to my own government." Hugo broke the next long silence, and failed to keep exasperation from his voice.

"So should I, when I've been out of touch for three days now."

"Well, do it, then!" snapped Hugo. "If your politicians controlled their generals, we should never have needed to come to Mainz at all."

"If yours controlled theirs, we should not have fought a war," replied Guy dryly.

"So our enemies say, but Germany did not start the war singlehanded. The only difference is, we pay the whole price and get called criminals because we lost."

"There is no whole price."

"I see it plain enough." Hugo wished his emotions did not tear so easily in Mainz, and added: "My mother is probably trapped in her own home by Poles, without either husband or sons to defend her. I ought to be there, not here."

"Yes, I think perhaps you should. I wouldn't try to keep you."

Hugo was completely taken by surprise. "I must finish here first."

Guy turned back to his observation of the street. "I'm sure you're right."

"But you would go?"

"In your position, loving your mother, yes. Unless your father has gone. But I can't judge these things, you see."

Hugo realized that this was the confession of a man distrustful of his own reactions because he had never known the normal ties of family affection. Yet who said that he himself would go . . . if he loved. "What are you going to do about Eve?" he asked abruptly. "If anyone should be elsewhere, it is you."

For a long time he thought Guy would not answer, then the breath of it reached him. "For that . . . she would need to love me."

They lay in silence then, June night turning chill.

The sounds they were waiting for came about two o'clock in the morning: the rattle of tires over cobbles.

Hugo tensed and began to count. Six trucks without lights, escorted by two armored cars with French troops perched on top. A staff car. Ten more trucks. Another armored car.

"That's them. It must be."

Guy nodded, eyes on his wristwatch reflecting starlight. "Three and a quarter minutes to pass; they're loaded heavily, by the speed they're going. As we expected, they must have picked up every arms cache in Mainz."

"You'll risk it, then?"

Guy stood and began to change swiftly out of dirty overalls and into his own French uniform. "This time, I must. It's the right moment and there probably won't be another. By tomorrow those arms will be on their way down the Rhine; the day after, God knows where. If anything goes wrong, you know who to contact."

Hugo nodded; Guy had not noticed how he had listened but promised nothing. He intended to wait in case his help was needed tonight, but had decided that from then on, their interests had ceased to be the same: he had trusted the future of the Rhineland to untrustworthy French for long enough, when he wasn't even sure that all Clemenceau's intrigues had been explained to him. So he meant to go to the British. Guy believed that the bulk of the arms were to be shipped down the Rhine tomorrow; the British occupied the lower Rhineland

and would not consult the feelings of French generals before arresting everyone concerned in such a deal.

Commandant Saulx's first priority might be to avoid any crisis between his country and her allies; Hugo von Kobis was happy to encourage friction between Germany's enemies. If by judiciously fueling Allied animosities he could also help keep the Rhineland within the Reich, then his time in Mainz certainly would not have been wasted.

Even on parting, they did not touch. After years of friendship and now working closely together for nearly a month, the casual gestures of parting, possibly forever, remained out of reach.

Guy had a small car concealed quite close, and Hugo waited until the sound of its engine faded before following circumspectly on foot. Mainz at night was full of French who shot at sight. He was sure that he ought to return to Paris, where Sir Maurice Wyville would be his best contact with the British; he was also relieved by his decision, having become very tired of dodging gun-happy poilus and their German clients.

Hugo calculated carefully and decided that three days of the extended Allied ultimatum time must remain. In Paris they would be dancing still, a self-absorbed carrousel whirling the world out of sight; the statesmen would be waiting, though, with their millions of armed men already moving toward the frontiers of the Reich. In Berlin . . . he shook his head. Christ knew what they were doing in Berlin. If he went back to Paris to see Wyville now, he could easily find himself trapped in enemy territory when he ought to be committing suicide with the remnants of the Wehrmacht. How absurd, really, to be caught in a place like Mainz at such a time.

The Rhine was quite close to where they had been hiding, the dock lights switched on along the stretch of quayside requisitioned for French military use, the whole area bustling with activity. Hugo felt horribly exposed, when this particular cargo was being loaded at night precisely because curious Germans would be confined indoors.

He slipped across the road and crawled through undergrowth where neat walks had been before the war: there was no need to risk himself unnecessarily when he could see what he needed from a distance.

Lights reflected off black water, bridge girders curling upward not far above his head. Hugo began to climb, ignoring the insubstantial feel of his muscles, the fluttering in his belly. After tonight, he hoped to heaven he could return to diplomacy for good.

He disliked heights, and the steel was so massive he never seemed to achieve a secure grip. After a few minutes, he glanced back over his shoulder; he must not reach out so far that the scene inshore became indistinct.

The French had guarded themselves from watchers in the streets but not from someone perched on girders thirty feet below the bridge parapet. On the dock, Hugo could see cases of the pattern which had become so familiar over the past month and a group of officers watching some soldiers carry yet more cases onto four moored barges. No sign of Guy yet, although the time they'd agreed on was past. Then Hugo heard the engine coming, snarling through the gears, rattling loosely over cobbles.

The French officers heard it too, and looked up curiously, not in the least alarmed. Only the French drove in the streets of Mainz at night.

The car struck the barrier set across the entry to the dock squarely; Hugo saw the sentries leap for safety and felt his hands tighten on rust-coated steel. That must have been a hell of an impact. The car slewed wildly, he heard tires screech, shouting from the men along the quay, a splash as someone jumped unwisely and tripped into water.

It was like the magic-lantern shows of his childhood, posturing figures in black cutout whirled by a handle he couldn't see. The officers jumped and raged, Guy out of sight inside the car but shouting back. Which was a relief: if he had been stunned in the crash, this part of his intention would have collapsed.

Hugo watched as everything wound down to a halt, the hand on the handle stilled. The soldiers stopped loading to watch; the officers stood with their heads together, talking earnestly, the luxury of rage forgotten. Guy had said that he expected to find at least four colonels there, one to go with each barge, when each was to be slipped off at a different place down the Rhine. Hugo could see Guy now, leaning against the radiator of his car, a revolver in his back.

He said something and was jabbed for his pains, took off his *képi* and wiped his face. Hugo breathed out in relief; *képi* off meant everyone was as worried as hell, close to panic.

The next few minutes were the vital ones, designed to bring overwhelming pressure on sensitive military nerves. Guy calculated that four colonels gathered on a quayside in the dark, under secret orders to hand over arms and then lead Germans into a coup against their allies, would be sufficiently disconcerted, when he hurtled into their midst, for the whole operation to lurch out of sequence. They were operating clandestinely; he could show them orders signed by the Prime Minister for their arrest, yet was himself an officer. They had guns hidden in barges full of grain; he would tell them that they were not to be arrested for political schemings but for theft of property from the French Republic. They accepted orders and believed they served France; he would spell out the ignominy of cashiering and criminal charges which would follow from arrest, now that the arms were loaded and difficult to dispose of in a hurry.

At the least, he thought, they would take him direct to General Mangin while the barges stayed tied up, and though Mangin was capable of ignoring any hazard, at G.Q.G., Guy had a colleague waiting with a box full of documents forged by the Deuxiéme Bureau to substantiate his charges of corruption.

A pack of unpolitical colonels ought to be horrified by proof that their superiors were simply making dishonest francs, and though Mangin and Foch would know exactly what trick had been played on them, their denials would lack force when both accusation and documents were totally unexpected. Guy expected to use the consequent recriminations to break the conspiracy into quarreling fragments, and Hugo agreed it was possible but not certain.

The plan was risky, though. Risky to confront officers chancing court-martial single-handed; risky because the reactions of men who discovered with shattering suddenness that they might be trapped and ruined in an unworthy cause were unpredictable; risky because Guy's bluff might be called. If he was shot and his body thrown in an alley, tomorrow the Germans could be blamed. Skillfully used, forged evidence might prize conspiracy apart; alone, it would not stop an operation due to spark within days.

Risky, too risky, surely, and the purpose suspiciously imprecise. Hugo swore under his breath; he was certain Guy had not told him everything he intended to do. They had worked together from necessity, but since the night of the warehouse fire neither completely confided in the other. Which was another reason why Hugo now intended to follow his own instinct and go to Maurice Wyville in Paris, whatever happened here tonight.

Down on the quay the figures began to scurry aimlessly, sergeants bawling; then a shot echoed across the water. Hugo exclaimed aloud, expecting Guy to fall. Surely they could not kill a fellow officer on an open dock, in front of fifty poilus.

No, apparently not. He was still standing with a gun in his back, hands now above his head. Figures frozen by the shot moved again, and Hugo began to shiver with reaction. For a moment, he had thought . . . he wanted time to pass in peace so one day he could put things right again with Guy.

The whole group of officers were climbing into cars. Hugo watched, heart thumping with excitement as engines revved and men tripped over each other trying to squeeze into open seats, Guy roughly shoved in among them. He had made them afraid, and fear showed in how they handled him. A good sign, Hugo supposed, unless you gagged on it.

He strained his eyes; they'd known that from here it would be difficult for him to see. In fact, he couldn't see.

One of the cars stopped by the smashed barrier and someone came pelting back to burrow in Guy's car. Hugo couldn't grasp what he was doing, since there wasn't anything for him to find. The officer evidently thought so too; he slammed the door in fury and sprinted back: Hugo laughed aloud. He did not know what story Guy had devised to make the man look in his car, but a rear door slammed meant so far, so good. Guy thought he could carry through what he'd planned, so Hugo was free to go to the rendezvous and wait. I hope to God he's right, thought Hugo as he began to work his way off the bridge, because this time he wasn't waiting anywhere.

Four hours to pass before curfew lifted and the first train left Mainz for Paris. Whether Guy thought he could succeed or not, Hugo saw no reason to change his decision: the French could sort out their own quarrels; his concern was with the Rhineland.

Guy Saulx sat back in the staff car, outwardly relaxed. He did not want to offer any excuse for the fear he felt around him to curdle into violence, when he was alone among men who had been thrown into extremes of confusion and alarm only minutes before. Once violence was unleashed, it could only turn on him, and he was very weary of quarrels not his own. His chest and arms ached from the impact of his crash, his back from the gun jammed there, his head from the effort of keeping so many complex dealings in their right order. During these last, terrible weeks there had been so much he had to accomplish and remember, when he was so tired each thought needed to be separately shaped. And then somehow kept in its place. It helped a little that he believed any anguish was worthwhile when France's security was the stake: the guarantees of strong friends were infinitely more valuable than the laying waste of enemies. He struggled to remember . . . he did not think he had forgotten anything. Please God. Please God, too, that this time it would truly be the end. He feared pain and the darkness, but if they would just kill him, surely it would be welcome. The best and only way for Eve. He closed his eyes, and immediately the jolting roughness of their ride fragmented balance, shock and snapped strain sweeping him into a vortex of twisting, sucking space.

He fought to free himself, but savage currents tore at his grip and he was lost in the gut-shriveling terror of what happened when he failed to free himself. Heart bursting, bone clamped on lungs and blood, panic sinking into throat and belly.

And suddenly it was the worst time he had known. He was engulfed by fear until only fear was real. So cold the world was ice. So alone there was no word to measure how much alone he was, in a place he had seen before and screamed when he saw it. Now he was there, and drowned in its depths.

He's crazy, someone said. *Mon Dieu,* here we've been sweating blood and he's no more than a maniac escaped from his keepers. If he was an animal it would be merciful to shoot him. A different voice and Guy curled around the place where they shot animals like him. They laughed then: pealing, shrieking, mocking voices hysterical with relief, crimson throats a tunnel to the darkness where he lay.

Each breath became a sweated, knife-edged gasp through mud, but light, when it came, was worst of all. Shafts of it driving at his eyeballs, of color unimaginable. He scrabbled to escape more deeply into his pit, but he was bound to mighty batteries of artillery pouring fire into the darkness where he went, steel muzzles locked above his head.

Men were nothing.

Flame, and spirals of retching dark remained, where he was bound to the barrel of a gun. The brazen fury of guns, a sword in his brain.

Rick Dwyer decided that before going to Berlin or Weimar, he would stop off among ordinary Germans and try to discover whether they would even attempt to fight again if their government refused to sign the treaty. His journey from Paris to the German frontier had been slow, the sidings full of Allied soldiers, everywhere a bustle of military traffic. He visited the American Expeditionary Force Field H.Q. and found few doubts there, just hundreds of thousands of fit young men anxious to prove themselves and then go home. The U. S. Army would invade Germany with enthusiasm, tomorrow if possible.

Rick did not expect qualms among the French, and found none. They were not enthusiastic, like the Americans; rather, apprehensive that so long as Germans were left alive they could and would fight, but convinced that safety for France came from German noses in the dirt. Rick did not find them friendly, either. The American guarantee of French security was still secret, the United States regarded as a gullible infant nation which had used its power unjustly to deprive France of the fruits of victory.

Depressed, he traveled on to Mainz. He intended to journey down the Rhine to the British in Cologne, and travel to Berlin from there. Without knowing it, he passed Hugo rattling over the points outside Mainz Hauptbahnhof on the first stage of his journey back to Paris.

Rick's train had been crammed to the racks with French; any invasion of this area would take place with the advantage of an inflated occupation force already in position. He checked his bag in at the station, since he intended to stay only hours in Mainz, and then followed his normal habit of wandering the streets alone to sense the pulse of a new assignment. There were groups of workmen on street corners, long lines of people outside the few shops open; the women looked exhausted, the men surly. The sky was free of smoke, and Rick reckoned few factories were at work. Would these people fight? Could they fight? He was unable to judge any more clearly here than in Paris. Outside the occupation areas perhaps it would be easier.

He walked down toward the Rhine, past a knot of men with red armbands who were holding a meeting in the middle of the road. If the French withdrew, Mainz would be Communist by morning. Or Freikorps. Or Separatist. Everywhere, Rick sensed stealthy intrigue: he might not speak German, but he recognized the feel of this place. Chicago in the strikebreaking years had been like this, and in the slums probably still was—voided of authority and waiting for the next rabble-rouser to happen along. Dark figures scurried down alleys, groups broke up and casually drifted together again in plotting coveys; echoing, frightened footsteps in the shadows. If he had also made this trip to discover what kind of Germany would one day be reborn, then, half an hour out of Mainz Hauptbahnhof, Rick wasn't reassured.

French patrols tramped past, bayonets fixed even in daylight. They did not care what the Germans plotted among themselves, whether they starved or killed each other in the dark. This was enemy country, and to them only their own interests mattered.

There was a great furor going on near the Strassen Bridge. People were hanging over the parapet, standing several deep, chatting and animated in contrast with morose gloom elsewhere. Rick shouldered his way through the crowd hopefully; any incident would be welcome, so he could make the bleak reality of Mainz more comprehensible for readers of the Washington *Times*.

A tug had sunk against the quayside. A tug and a string of four barges. Well, whaddaya know? thought Rick, staring. A tug and all four barges sunk together; now, he would call that odd.

"When did it happen?" he asked the people nearest him.

There was hesitation before a man answered in English, and Rick had the impression that if he had spoken French he would have encountered only silence. "Early this morning. A— A *sprengladung*." He gestured with his hands. "Boom!"

"An explosive charge? Four of them?"

"Five. The tug, too, *mein Herr*." He grinned. "The French . . . the tug was used by the French."

"You mean your people blew it up and sank the whole string of them? Whatever for? The French Command will be—"

"Very angry, *mein Herr, ja.* They haf— they have taken people all morning, but I think a little anger is worth much to find ourselves. You agree, not?"

"Perhaps," said Rick, declining to commit himself to confusions of grammar and loyalties. "What will the French do to the people they have arrested?"

"Shoot, perhaps, to make sure. But there is a hear— *es geht das Gerucht,* you understand? A whisper?"

"A rumor?"

"*Ja.* A rumor that a French officer did it. He was—" The German crossed his eyes, pulled at his lips and bubbled spittle; everyone nearby laughed. Two children copied him, then clasped each other, giggling.

"Some French officer went nuts and scuttled a tug and a string of barges?" demanded Rick incredulously.

"Nuts." He savored the word. "I think, yes. So they say. So they cannot easily shoot us when we hang over the bars and—" He bubbled through his lips again.

Rick looked around and saw that a great many Germans were enjoying themselves at the expense of the French. Horizon-bleus were splashing and cursing to no obvious purpose with hawsers just below, and every time one of them looked up, dozens of grinning faces lolled tongues and gibbered.

Perhaps the Germans would fight, after all, reflected Rick. The spectacle was unattractive but certainly defiant.

He walked to the nearest French district headquarters and showed his press card to a clerk. "Take me to the officer in charge, will you, son?"

"Capitaine Bloch is on patrol." The boy eyed Rick's American cigarettes enviously.

"Perhaps he'll be back soon?" Rick lit a cigarette and pushed over the pack.

"Thank you, monsieur. You may wait here if you wish; the Boches are not in a good mood today."

"I noticed. So what happened down by the Rhine?"

"Well, it is very strange. A friend of mine, he was on patrol last night and he told me our troops were loading those barges. I have never known such work done at night when most days in Mainz we have too little to occupy us."

"What were they loading?" Rick hoped now that Captain Bloch would lose himself on patrol; a bored clerk was a likelier source of information than an officer mindful of French honor.

"Cases, monsieur." The clerk fiddled with bottles of ink.

Rick slid his press card back into his billfold, exposing the wad of notes he had brought for his journey to Berlin. "Cases may contain many things."

"Yes, indeed. Expensive things, monsieur."

"Shall we say five hundred francs' worth? Two-fifty for what was in the cases, the rest if there's a story worth printing."

The boy licked his lips. Such a sum was several weeks' pay for a French soldier. "Arms, monsieur. Cases of army rifles and ammunition. A few machine guns and grenades, not many. They had come in *camions* secretly earlier in the evening."

Rick slid two hundred and fifty francs under blotting paper. "Then the barges sank?"

"About five o'clock in the morning. There were thuds, not loud, we did not hear them here but a patrol on the bridge was very close. The barges sank rapidly, dragging each other down, but men on the quay cut the tug loose. Then there was an explosion there, too. General Mangin came himself to look. He was very angry."

"And he is a dangerous man when angered."

The clerk looked as if he wanted to cross himself; he was very young and spoke with a strong Languedoc twang. "*D'accord, monsieur.* Very dangerous."

"So he ordered some Germans to be arrested?"

The boy looked uncomfortable. "They will be released soon. General Mangin is a formidable man but not unjust."

Rick fingered the remaining notes idly. "A great deal of damage has been done. I'm not surprised if Germans were arrested. France and her allies cannot afford to be made objects of scorn."

"Naturally, we must be strict, monsieur. But not unjust; that is for Boches. You see, those barges were sunk by a Frenchman, which is why the Boches mock us today."

"Tell me about it," said Rick quietly. "The Germans may be laughing but I'm not. I think perhaps this story could be nearer tragedy than farce."

"Yes, monsieur. It is sad. Me, I did not fight; I was very happy when the armistice came, and I was still training in the barrack square. But I have heard terrible things in my battalion; I am not surprised by anything I am told any more. This man, he was an officer, brave, much decorated, but kept in the Army when they should have sent him instead to breathe the good air of the Pyrenees. It is not right, monsieur, that a man four years in the trenches should be told there is still more he must do."

"No," said Rick soberly. "It was not right."

"He crashed through the barrier last night on the quay, so naturally he was arrested. He seemed normal although odd, my friend said. Then, I do not know why, the officers on the quay decided to take him directly to General Mangin. The driver of the car in which they traveled said the change in this commandant was quite sudden; one moment he looked asleep, the next he went wild." The clerk could not help smiling. "Of course, a carload of colonels did not like a madman scrabbling at their breeches. They were annoyed, too, I think, by wasting time over someone who proved a lunatic. So they ordered him tied in the guardroom here until an ambulance could come, and then went off themselves."

"But the barges?" persisted Rick, puzzled.

"We were ashamed," said the clerk frankly. "This man with medals and *brisques* from four years in the trenches blubbering in a corner, and we ordered to tie him like a criminal while those colonels sniggered. When they went, we loosed him and offered wine; some who had been in the trenches and understood these things talked to him. After a while he seemed better, quiet, *vous savez?* Ill and frightened but not dangerous any more. We thought he would sleep."

"And he didn't?"

"No. He— I think he was too much afraid, monsieur. He broke out and went down to the quay again, as if it was on his mind. Much later he was found there begging the men to leave the barges before they sank. When they blew up, of course he was blamed, although if he did it he must have set the charges earlier. He was too dazed for such a task after he left here."

"Will anyone testify that he was not capable of it?"

"It is our opinion only, you understand, and we are in a great deal of trouble already for letting him escape. Undoubtedly this commandant knew something, or why would he go back to the quay again, when all he really desired was to hide under the table here? And if one of us speaks, and anyone listens, then what would happen? The Germans arrested by General Mangin will be shot. After all, someone sank those barges. We are tired of blood, monsieur. Let us return to *la belle France* and leave the Boches to jeer from their bridges."

"Now, that's the most sensible comment on the international situation I've heard in a long time," observed Rick, pushing over the remainder of the notes.

The boy flushed. "I am probably mistaken, monsieur. I do not understand these things, only that as for me, I should like to return home to Albi." He touched the notes and then drew back his hand. "Keep these, monsieur. For the cases, yes. I am content to take payment for telling about the cases. Why not, when it is peace? But I should be ashamed to profit from the afflictions of a man like Commandant Saulx."

"*What?*"

The clerk jumped at Rick's tone. "I— I did not wish to be rude, it is just—"

"Saulx. You said his name was Saulx?" Of course, it had to be that screwball Saulx. Everything fitted, except there were so many shell-shocked men wandering the camps and streets of France. Eve had told him Saulx had been sent on a mission to Germany, Rick remembered now.

"*Mais oui, monsieur.* He was a commandant of chasseurs; our adjutant was in his sector once in the war."

Rick stared at him, thinking hard. Christ, what a mess!

He had called twice at Le Trésor to see Eve, ignoring his own rule about not running after women who had gone off the boil. But Eve wasn't just any woman, and although Rick resented possessions which might prevent him from leaving whenever he chose, he'd been annoyed when she turned him down flat.

"When Guy comes back; I know I must settle my life then. I promise, Rick. Until then I want to be alone; I need time to think and I surely don't find spare minutes in the day." And she had smiled at him, lips softly curving, but unhappy.

"That's crazy, honey. Alone in Paris, for God's sake. We had fun together, didn't we?"

"We had fun, but that's the way I want it. I'm sorry, Rick."

He recognized finality in her voice; she could be as obstinate as a Missouri mule when she chose. All the same, he had tried very hard to change her mind, and seeing her so obviously overwhelmed by the problems of Le Trésor, he'd expected to succeed. She listened straight through all his arguments and said, quite simply, no.

"Goddammit, what the hell does it matter to Saulx!" Rick had exclaimed, exasperated. "He isn't here, and hasn't done a damn thing to help while you've slaved to turn a third-rate store into something Paris notices. You walked out on him, didn't you, or have I made a mistake along the line?"

She shrugged, an oddly French gesture. "I'm not arguing, but I don't want Guy to come back this time and find me living with you. Later . . . I don't know. I must straighten myself out, and soon. Not now. Not until he's back."

Well, thought Rick, staring at duty rosters in a French guardroom, Saulx wouldn't be coming back. Rick had not admitted his own nagging worry that Eve actually might be quixotic enough to live with the bastard again if he asked her, but he felt real relief now.

"Was Saulx killed when the tug blew up?" he asked abruptly.

"No, monsieur. It was a scuttling charge only, and no one was hurt. The Commandant only thought he should warn people because his senses were confused."

"Where is he now?"

The boy shrugged. "I suppose he will be sent back to France. We have no suitable hospitals here. They couldn't court-martial a man in his condition, although to shoot him might be a mercy."

The French had taken over a hospital in Mainz for the inevitable accidents of an army, but eventually Rick satisfied himself that Saulx was definitely not there. At G.Q.G., all his questions were met by urbane incomprehension; he was offered a briefing on the general situation in the French area of occupation, and nothing else.

Frustrated and angry, he walked through hostile streets, wondering what to do next. A professional newsman to the bone, he knew he must leave that evening for Cologne and Berlin, yet wanted to sew up the affair of Guy Saulx first. Then, when he returned to Paris, he could tell Eve exactly why she need not wait any longer before making up her mind.

Where the hell would the French put an inconvenient maniac before shipping him back to a trash can in France?

As soon as he had put the question logically to himself, he knew the answer. Military men might skimp on hospitals or straitjackets, but they always provided a pen for prisoners. He went to the barracks used by the French and asked for the provost section.

Even so, it took a great deal of time. Rick chafed and fretted as minutes became half an hour and then an hour, while he was passed from one unwilling hand to another, progressed from blank refusal by underlings to a one-armed provost colonel who looked as if his sole purpose was to officiate at executions, with a monocle like a shell splinter stuck in his eye.

He brushed aside Rick's offer of cigarettes, tapping polished boots impatiently with a riding crop. "I am on duty, monsieur. You wished to see me on official business, I understand."

"Not exactly. I hoped to enlist your sympathy."

"Indeed?" He looked as if the word was unfamiliar.

Rick had already decided that his press card would be worse than useless here; unless he could reach a humane impulse, then he was wasting his time. "M. *le colonel*, you have here a prisoner called Guy Saulx—" Rick wasn't certain of it, but nothing would be gained by hedging bets "—who I know is ill, rather than criminal. His wife is American and a friend of mine; we come from the same place in the States. She is desperately anxious about him and begged me to see him if I could."

"Any wife of Commandant Saulx would be French, monsieur."

"By marriage, of course. But I'm sure you understand why I should wish to help in such a sad case, if I could." Just let Saulx be good and crazy so there's no hope for him, and then watch how I help his wife get over the shock, thought Rick.

The colonel swished at a fly with his crop. "What makes you think Commandant Saulx might be here?"

"I've heard things. Whatever he has done, there are plenty of people in the French Army who do not condemn a man because he has shell shock after four years in the trenches, and wish to help his wife if they can," replied Rick blandly.

The colonel nodded slowly. "*Moi aussi, monsieur.* This life after the war, it is very hard, *n'est-ce pas?* If I allow you to see him, I shall require your word of honor that you will tell only Mme. Saulx what you have heard and seen in Mainz today."

An obscure French fracas in the Rhineland would not be news in Washington, at least until he had discovered more of what lay behind it. "Of course not," said Rick easily. "I really appreciate this, Colonel."

"Perhaps I am glad to ease my conscience. It is not my habit to lock up men who have served their country beyond the limits of their strength."

It was not right, the depot clerk had said; it was not right for a man like him to be told there was still more he must do.

Rick Dwyer had disliked everything he had previously heard and discovered about Guy Saulx; as he followed a corporal down grimy passages, the shadow of this man he thought he knew reached out to fill his senses with unease.

The barracks detention wing stank, and even in June the walls were wet. During the months of revolution in Germany, no one had been responsible for cleaning it, and the French had made only a perfunctory effort since. The corporal unlocked a door. "Here, monsieur. It is the best we could find for him. I will be outside; call when you wish to be let out."

The door shut with a clank, and Rick stood not knowing what to expect. The cell was constructed to house a dozen or more; there was a barred window, a table, and a reasonably comfortable camp bed in a great deal of empty space.

At first Rick thought the corporal must have made a mistake and the cell was empty; then he saw movement in the darkest corner and the shape of a man standing there.

"Commandant Saulx?" His mouth was annoyingly dry; whichever way you looked at it, this was an awkward meeting. When the colonel agreed to it, he had not realized he was confronting his prisoner with his wife's lover.

"Yes, who is it?" The voice was low but unexpectedly firm.

Christ, why had he come? "I was in Mainz, and wished to— It's Rick Dwyer, if you remember."

"I remember." Flat, unexpressive, calm. He had not moved out of his corner.

"I thought there might be something I could do to help."

"No."

Rick was finding it unnerving to talk to a shadow pinned against a wall. "For God's sake, man, don't you want to get out of here?"

"Is that what you came for, M. Dwyer?"

"I haven't much influence with the French, but. . . ." His voice trailed away. Of course it wasn't what he'd come for.

There was so long a silence that Rick began to wonder whether Saulx had forgotten he was there. He moved over to the table and sat on its edge, where he couldn't be missed, and where he, too, might be able to see more clearly.

As his eyes adjusted to dimness, Rick was jolted by the man's appearance; he had expected a disheveled nut, but Saulx was scrupulously neat: in uniform, collar hooked, shaved. Only, he was so rigid it was clear he could not move from where he stood, face sweating, eyes in pits so deep that shadow was complete.

Rick's compunction stirred. "Why don't you let me help you to bed, so you can sleep?"

"Why don't you go, M. Dwyer? I exist if I can keep from sleep."

"But you can't! No one could. Good God, man, that's crazy."

Somewhere in that shell of a face, there was a flicker of amusement. "I know. I can't believe no one told you."

Rick grinned, taken by surprise. "Yeah. It doesn't seem to me so true in here. Look, if all the guns of hell are in your head, why not scream? If you want to jump from the roof, then let me tell you that half the human race feels much the same at the moment. Relax. If you just stand there you'll faint eventually, and have a hell of a bruise to add to the rest."

"Yes. But if I screamed . . . you wouldn't like it. And I am too much of a coward to drop before I must. When I do . . . in the darkness. . . ." He began to shake, and with a convulsive effort turned and grasped at the wall behind. ". . . Get out. All you can do to help is go."

Without thinking, Rick grasped at him and felt knotted muscles under cloth. After a long time, Saulx spoke again, his voice shuddering as well now. "Don't tell Eve."

"I must. Christ, she has a right to know."

"No. She has a right . . . to live. You said . . . you came to help. If there was any truth in that . . . at all . . . say nothing. Lie. Anything. I don't want her to know."

Rick dropped his hands. "You selfish swine. You can't just disappear. How long then before French law would cut her loose?"

Saulx stayed facing the wall, forehead on wet brick. "Do as I say . . . and don't come here again."

Rick banged on the door for the corporal. "I'll think about it. Someone around here sure needs to think of her first for a change."

Saulx did not reply or move again, torn breath the only sound cut off when the corporal bolted the door behind them.

CHAPTER 15

Although Eve went to the Hôtel Daunay as often as she was invited or could find an excuse to go, she found that the personality of Georges Daunay remained oddly incalculable. He was courteous, detached, hardworking, a cynical wit the only similarity between him and Pierre. Like his son, he also wore expensive clothes well and was practiced in the art of pleasing women, but being infinitely more virile, he was better at both than ever Pierre would be.

Eve hated him, which made judgment even more difficult.

After nearly a month of encountering him whenever she could, she admitted to herself that if she hadn't hated him, probably she would have responded to such a dominating presence. Whenever he entered his house the atmosphere changed: the footmen stood straighter; Gabrielle's nondescript husband stopped smoking; Pierre lounged as elegantly as ever, but Eve saw how tense he became, as though he expected his father to take his mind by storm. Only Eulalie reacted differently, and pity replaced revulsion once Eve realized that her outrageous clothes were flaunted as a signal of defiance, how dreamy she became after provoking quarrels in which she was the one most hurt. At some of the disreputable gatherings where Pierre took her, Eve had seen Eulalie coiled on cushions half asleep and absently caressing some soft and stupid female while festive crowds almost trampled on her: she fought her father all the time and only felt able to relax with fluffy silliness. Yet Daunay actually spoke very little and was not often in his house; it was just that he filled any space he touched, and everyone accepted that even when he wasn't there he knew exactly what they did.

Which meant that he certainly knew who had killed Anselme Saulx.

Obliquely, Eve tried to question Pierre about his father but discovered that he knew surprisingly little about him.

"My mother, Anselme, and Tante Gabrielle often used to talk about their childhood in Alsace," he remarked one day. "But I've never heard my father mention the time before he became successful. My mother said once that when she married him she loved the southern twang in his voice, but you'd never think he'd been born anywhere except Paris now, would you?"

Eve agreed that Daunay looked and spoke like a true Parisian. "He doesn't move like one, though," she added; Daunay walked like a big-game hunter who knew a wounded tiger lay nearby. "It's the only characteristic you really notice, which marks him out at once from everyone in a room."

Pierre laughed, envy in the sound. "Except that he is marked always and all the time. I remember as a child how he seemed a god to me, who scarcely needed to speak. You had to watch for signs like the thunderbolts of Zeus. A twitch of muscle was all there was to tell you that somehow you hadn't pleased him."

"He never spoke?" demanded Eve incredulously. Daunay chatted easily enough with her.

"Oh, of course he said all kinds of things. I never listened, I suppose. I knew it didn't matter. He judged what you were, so when he asked where you'd been, or whether you could repeat your lesson of Racine, they were no more than the politenesses of a mind made up."

"Poor little boy," said Eve, and touched his hand impulsively.

Pierre covered her hand with his and then bent to kiss her fingers. They were walking together in bright sunlight after a *thé dansant* in the Bois de Boulogne. "Poor Papa, too. He was successful, you see. From nothing to the Champs-Élysées in thirty years. By then he expected to be able to change anything to the way he wanted, and people, too, of course. He couldn't accept that our both wanting me to please him made no difference. Eulalie never tried to please him, but that wasn't any better."

Eve shook her head. "You're wrong. I guess she wanted to, once."

"Well, she certainly didn't succeed. Papa hides it well but he detests knowing how Paris sniggers at her antics."

"You admire him," said Eve flatly.

"Don't you?"

"No."

"Why not? He likes you; I can always tell."

"You've all forgotten, haven't you?" said Eve softly. "He ordered a couple of thugs to beat a sick man senseless, after he couldn't fit into the Daunay scheme of things any longer. That sick man became my husband."

"Guy deserved everything he got."

"Gabrielle said very much the same, and I didn't agree with her, either. I'm not arguing, but you asked me why I hate M. Daunay, so I just told you."

Pierre waved his cane at a *taximètre*, head averted, silent all the way back to her lodging in the Rue Tronchet. "Are you coming tonight?" he asked when he handed her out. His voice was expressionless, but his hand stayed on the taxi door, as if he could not wait to get away.

Eve nodded. "It isn't often I get asked to such a grand affair." She also had plans of her own for making use of tonight.

He stared at the pavement. "It would be better if you didn't come."

"Why ever not? Anyway, I accepted Gabrielle's invitation. It would be shockingly rude not to come." Mme. Daunay never stirred herself sufficiently to act as hostess in her own establishment.

"I doubt whether anyone would notice whether you did or not. Just sometimes, Papa becomes bored with respectability, and tonight is to be one of his jokes on Paris."

In that case she was certainly going, thought Eve with a kind of grim anticipation. Georges Daunay was the key to everything in that household, though she agreed with Hugo that he almost certainly would not kill in his own home. "I'm coming," she repeated.

Pierre shrugged; he had withdrawn from her suddenly. Was thinking of something else, longing to go, fingers twitching, eyes straying to the taxi driver. He hesitated a moment, then jumped back inside without another word and was driven off, leaving Eve staring.

She had watched him carefully these past weeks, and decided coldly that Rick was probably right when he said he took drugs, but until today had only occasionally glimpsed what she imagined might be craving. She had seen it now. Despite her inexperience, Eve had no doubts at all, since he had forgotten her because of haste he could no longer hide.

Why?

Because she had said she hated his father?

No, that must be absurd. Because he realized for the first time precisely why she continued to go out with him; that though the death of Anselme Saulx was long forgotten by Paris gossip, she still remembered it?

She traveled up in the wheezing, clashing elevator thoughtfully. *Pierre?* She had never seriously considered him, since he had been out at the Opéra ball with her that night. Because she liked and felt sorry for him. She shivered involuntarily as she thought about Pierre now. It had been he who told her that his father returned to the Hôtel Daunay very late on the night that Anselme died; after himself, and after Anselme. And she had sighed, and checked with Gabrielle, and simply thought how it confirmed that Daunay could not be the killer.

And yet . . . and yet . . . Pierre didn't fit either.

Eve dressed abstractedly, but carefully. Three hundred guests had been invited to *un bar dansant des Daunay*, and sharp Tout-Paris eyes would be scrutinizing everyone's toilette tonight.

When she arrived at the Hôtel Daunay, it was seething with more people than it could conveniently hold, the garden strung with fairy lights, the roadway a solid block of autos. Windows were flung wide to sultry air, and the blare of ragtime drew crowds to gape at the scene within: women in the fastest of fast new fashions, women who lacked bosoms and behinds but showed a great deal of everything else; men becoming incapable from the lunatic inventiveness of the drinks. The disapproval of the elderly had already been crushed by the hectic atmosphere, the servants demented by the impossibility of it all as relays of bands played louder and louder.

Eve had never dreamed, had never encountered the kind of party this evening promised to be, and in spite of Pierre's warning found it difficult not to gape like a yokel at the frolickings around her, the noise beyond description. As soon as M. Daunay welcomed his guests, they launched into fevered gaiety, the sweet and sickly breeze of degeneracy blowing through packed salons. Pierre's face was flushed, although Eve had never seen him drunk before; everyone roared incoherently against the sound of the bands, against the shouts of others drunker than themselves. The cocktails might have been shaken by a mad painter: flaming pinks and yellows layered with green liqueur; concoctions of ink and absinthe; of Savoie black currant and sardines in gin.

Eve could not swallow the brew Pierre brought her, and touched it with her lips, pretending to drink. "Whatever is it?"

"Egg, cocaine and port. Drink up, *mignonne*, and I'll fetch you something different. There's two hundred different kinds. What do you say to whisky and gunpowder?" He kissed her, lips drooling, eyeballs rolled up. He was barely conscious; M. Daunay's joke on Paris was to turn his barman into a sorcerer's apprentice, shaking concoctions which were close to poison. Pierre knew something had been planned, but, mesmerized, still walked into his father's snare.

Soon, every flat surface was occupied, people holding each other and anything else which offered while they drank, and losing balance very soon after. In the splendid salons perhaps three dozen persons retained their senses, a few dancing solemnly in corners to such instruments as were left from wrecked bands, the occasional sober survivor regarding the scene with incredulous scorn.

Pierre was holding his head on a couch, his weak stomach incapable of digesting sufficient of such horrors to make him completely insensible. In one way the party was not quite as frightful as some Eve had gone to since she accepted hospitality with the extravagant set Pierre patronized; such dizzying concoctions made the state of everyone's head and stomach his prime concern. Boredom, sophisticated spite and seduction—all disappeared in such a maelstrom.

Eve watched Pierre, calculating. He was beyond noticing anything, surely. The time had come to do what she had planned, and under far more favorable circumstances than she could have hoped for. A few guests were leaving, though it was still early, good-naturedly exclaiming about the fiendish contrivances of barmen. They would have done better to blame their host, who had ordered such a contemptuous trick on fashionable Paris.

Eve went upstairs. She had swallowed almost nothing, but even so the taste in her mouth was foul, and she went first to find water. There were people stretched out on beds and moaning in corners, but the family rooms were at the back of the house, sensibly locked off by a wrought-iron gate when entertainment was offered on this scale. Eve did not hesitate but went up to the next floor, remembering a back staircase which served the whole house. As she went higher, there was a smell of emptiness: the servants lived under the roof, the second floor having been designed as a separate suite if the son of the house married. It was unlit and stuffily hot.

Eve held her breath and listened. Indistinguishable noise from downstairs, up here only the creak of woodwork and scuttle of mice. She wrapped her skirts close before moving softly to look for the servants' stair. She was wearing a new silver lamé gown, and without allowing her mind to linger on it, thought she would like someone besides Pierre to admire her in it.

In a glow reflected from outside, she very soon found what she had expected to be there: steep stairs designed without elegance in mind and leading to the family floor below. Leading up, too, of course, to the servants' rooms, above. Eve reflected that they would probably be drunk as well by now, and went down, heart hammering. There were lights below, glowing on carpet and marble; she stood in shadow and studied the layout of this part of the house.

The Hôtel Daunay was planned in a kind of H, the right-hand bar of it facing the Champs-Élysées and set aside for guests—she had slept there when she came with flu. The stairs and a wide double landing filled the central part, the linking gallery between the two sections of the house barred by the wrought-iron gates she had seen from the other side. This other passage was a duplicate of the one she knew, and ran the full length of the house, the family rooms looking out over the garden. Eve was uncertain who slept where but had determined to search this floor while everyone was occupied below. Although any evidence of Anselme's killing was long since obscured, she felt unable to make sense of all she had learned this past month until she had seen the setting where everything had happened. The pieces surely must be in her hands; the pattern lay somewhere in the hidden life of this strange house.

Softly, she went down to one end of the passage: Gabrielle was the danger, Eve was sure. She would disapprove of the debauch downstairs and was quite tough-minded enough to retire when it suited her, having drunk nothing.

A door either side of the passage end confronted Eve. She opened the left-hand one and slipped inside: she would have to pretend she felt unwell if anyone came. It wasn't entirely untrue, either. Even up here the reek of obscure liquids was nauseating, and her stomach had been none too certain of late. Whatever she found here made no difference to other decisions she must make, very soon. When Guy returned; when Rick came back; and they both must be told of the child she carried.

The room felt empty.

She flicked the switch by the door and the room flooded with light. A man's dressing room; clothes neatly folded, change piled symmetrically on a washstand. Eve went over to it, feeling horribly guilty, and touched letters lying there as well. *M. Benoit, aux bons soins de M. Daunay.* Gabrielle's husband. It wasn't a surprise to find him obsessively neat; Gabrielle would eliminate any sloppiness in maids or occupants at her end of the passage.

Aux bons soins de M. Daunay. Under the care of M. Daunay. Yes, whatever happened here, Marcel Benoit would keep quiet, a lifetime sponger on the bounty of another. The door opposite was almost certainly Gabrielle's, so Eve decided to leave it for the moment. The next door was carelessly ajar, the light left on, clothes strewn everywhere, their gaudy colors like upset buckets of paint. Eulalie's room. Eve closed the door behind her and stood looking, memorizing, wondering just what she had hoped to achieve by coming; thinking of Guy, who had been driven by despair to come and see Eulalie here, and so triggered a disastrous sequence of events.

This was where it had all begun, this, surely, where she must begin too. Eve went over to the gaping cupboards; either Eulalie had forbidden her maid to tidy up or was too much despised to receive even reasonable service.

Racks and racks of clothes; Eve blinked at their profusion. She bought expensively herself now, but sparingly, each outfit judged for adaptability and style. She couldn't begin to guess how much of everything Eulalie owned, most of it hardly worn and badly hung; un-French, since Parisiennes prided themselves on elegant grooming. One cupboard was shut and Eve eased it open, the click loud in stillness. She stood, breath held, and listened. If Gabrielle was next door, she could have heard that click. No, surely not. This house was very different from the clapboard-built Ottoway homestead. Eve swung the door wide and stood staring. It was full of male clothes, from tails to poilu's uniform. Coarse back-streets shirts and trousers smelling of garlic; leather belts and boots. Eve understood the kind of woman Eulalie was, nor did she even feel critical any longer; but it had never occurred to her that Georges Daunay's daughter roamed the streets of Paris dressed as a man.

It must be awkward getting in and out of the house dressed in these, she thought wryly. In fact, it wasn't the kind of thing you could keep secret, which meant that everybody knew. Eve riffled through socks and underwear distastefully, then stopped in surprise. Several belts with knives in the kind of sheath she had seen on the two *apaches* Joubaire had brought to Le Trésor. No attempt at concealment, as if carrying a knife when one went out was nothing out of the ordinary.

Eve shut the cupboard thoughtfully and looked around the room again. Most drawers gaped slightly, jammed on handkerchiefs and scarves and gloves: there was no hope of making a proper search, especially when she did not know what to look for.

But Joubaire had said that no matter how respectable he wanted to be, Daunay could not shake off his past, and here was his daughter dressing the part of an *apache*, presumably for the thrill of it. Daunay wanted his daughter safely married, yet knew that not even the fastest member of Tout-Paris would accept her as a wife, no matter what the dowry. In France, a man under twenty-five needed his father's permission before he married, and over that age would surely have the sense to fight clear of Eulalie. So Guy had been chosen, and hustled by pressures on Le Trésor while still too dazed to think very clearly about the price he would have to pay.

Eve eased open the door into the passage. No movement, nothing. Not much from below any more, either, which wasn't surprising. Sardines and ink, cocaine and formic acid would defeat anyone and without much delay. Pierre's room next; Eve recognized the jacket he'd been wearing in the Bois that afternoon. An invalid's room, and she felt a fresh surge of pity for him; shame, too, that she should have been half convinced that somewhere here she would find evidence of his guilt. When everyone was suspect it wasn't easy to keep absurdity at bay. After a few minutes she changed her mind, astonished by what she found. It was a hypochondriac's room. The washstand and dresser were laden with pillboxes and bottles, the bedside table, the drawers she opened. Handkerchiefs and socks mixed carelessly with spilled pills, broken syringes, and enough drugs to poison a herd of buffalo. If anyone wanted to kill Anselme Saulx, then the only motive for going up two flights of stairs to fetch Guy's drops from Joubaire's room was to incriminate him. Nothing was locked, the windows tightly shut, the atmosphere unpleasantly sweet. Eve shivered as she had when she first wondered about Pierre's guilt. She would never be able to look at him again without seeing this room, too. Though she had come to accept that he might take drugs, she had never visualized such a profusion of experimental pill-swallowing. Astonishing how a façade of face and manners could hide so much.

How much had Guy, estranged from his father, really known of his relations?

She picked up a few pillboxes at random and put them down again. It must be illegal for doctors to prescribe such a quantity and variety of medicine: the Daunay physician summoned to look at Anselme Saulx's corpse would have little choice but to see what he was told to see.

There was no point searching this room. Any drug she could name, and a great many she could not, would be here somewhere. More medicaments in the cupboard, and more vast quantities of clothes. A familiar, unexpected smell as well. Eve wrinkled her nose, sniffing.

Garlic, and the sourness of bad wine.

She felt among smooth cloth and found what she had known must be there: the kind of outfit she had also found in Eulalie's wardrobe. The same mixture of cheap material and almost Gypsy decoration that *apaches* wore. Somewhere would be punched leather belts and sheathed knives: they took a little while to find, because, unlike Eulalie, Pierre had made some effort at concealment. Thrown on top of a cupboard, and all except one thick with dust; Pierre had probably grown out of eating *moules cocaïne* in the Café des Assassins now he was capable of finding whatever he wanted in the comfort of Tout-Paris.

The next room was empty and the furniture sheeted. Anselme's presumably. Guy came here so seldom that he must have slept in the guest wing. Eve thought back to her visit and was almost sure he had been at the far end of the same passage as herself.

She switched on Anselme's light. The shutters and windows were closed, cupboards swept bare, drawers empty. Nothing here. She lifted the corners of dust sheets and discovered unexpectedly splendid antiques. The other rooms had been solidly furnished with nineteenth-century pieces: Anselme had bought only the very best and furnished his room himself. Eve touched a Louis Quinze escritoire admiringly; the inlay was exquisite. Some Sèvres lay in a box, and between the bed and the wall she discovered a couple of trunks. She was becoming nervous by now; she had been up here far too long. Even on this exceptional night, luck could not last forever. She unstrapped a trunk hastily and discovered packed clothes, which must be Anselme's ready for disposal. Again, to Eve there seemed an enormous quantity of everything. She remembered Guy's two uniforms at the Rue Férou, his single canvas roll of underwear; even Rick didn't possess a tenth of this amount, although he had a variety of clothes for the many purposes of a reporter.

Anselme Saulx, who had said he must sell what was left of Guy's inheritance in order to purchase himself an annuity, and certainly Le Trésor had not sold furniture profitably under his management; yet these were the possessions of a rich man, every suit nearly new, no sign that anything was kept once it was a few times worn.

Eve did not know what to think. She wanted to sit quietly and work her way through what she had seen, but there wasn't time. She supposed the annuity was straightforward: Daunay wanted Guy for Eulalie, and in some way compelled Anselme to sell, so as to gain the hold he wanted. But if Anselme was rich, and Eve had discovered in the books of Le Trésor illicit dealings whose nature she now could guess, how had Daunay pressured him?

She dared not linger any longer, yet knew she was missing a great deal; once she had left, she would think of a dozen things she ought to have looked for. Whatever would the police have made of the Hôtel Daunay? No wonder the household made sure the *flics* lacked any excuse to poke their noses here.

Two rooms remained at the end of the passage, matching the pair inhabited by Gabrielle and her husband. Eve hesitated, wondering whether to go back and listen for movement in Gabrielle's room. But she could not believe there was much to discover from Gabrielle, although tight-knit French family loyalties would continue to keep her silent, especially now her own sons were dead.

Eve stood a long time in the passage, listening to blood beating in her ears. It was uncanny to be up here spying on her hosts while a debauch, spectacular even by Tout-Paris standards, gave her an unexpectedly easy chance. Uncanny but not shameful any longer: she had seen enough for shame to become something one left outside the Hôtel Daunay.

There was soft light inside the next door when she opened it, and the same smell as in Pierre's room, only much stronger. Eve stood paralyzed, waiting for someone to call out.

No sound, nothing.

A pink-shaded night-light burned just inside the door, and the room was insanely hot. Hortense Daunay lay on an immense bed, mouth sagging open, hair straggling limply over her shoulders.

Eve gasped, expecting her to wake, but nothing happened. Rattling snorts came from that open mouth, sprawled body like discarded rubbish; rucked, unbuttoned nightdress wet with sweat.

Eve felt nausea sharp in her throat, and when she went over to the bed this time, she recognized the name on the pill bottle. Codeine. Her mother had suffered from sick headaches one summer, and young Dr. Thorp had prescribed the new drug codeine—to be taken when the pain was worst. Her mother had taken four altogether, because other days the pain wasn't quite bad enough.

Hortense Daunay had a bottle of two hundred by her bed, another spilled across the counterpane; she was quite clearly stunned for hours.

Eve had thought her torpid but nothing more: she was beginning to doubt the value of her own judgment now she saw how far outside her experience these people were. She remembered vividly how Guy had lain wakeful night after night, refusing the help of drugs. Once, she had feared that so strong a recoil might be rooted in subconscious guilt; now she realized he must have been determined never to follow the way his aunt and cousin took. What must he then have felt when an army doctor and Joubaire, between them, forced him into dependence so he could stay sane enough to lead his men?

Eve felt tears wet on her cheeks; that part was right, she was certain. It fitted with everything she had seen Guy suffer and only partly understood.

Surely, this must confirm her own convictions. A man who thought like that, who was fighting desperately to free himself from something which horrified him, might throttle an enemy in fury but never kill coldly with those same drops.

Eve looked around the room cursorily, head swimming. She could not stay here, had never breathed such fetid air in her life. On the chest of drawers were some framed photographs, and she picked one up. It was a yellowed wedding group, and with difficulty Eve recognized the flaccid body sprawled on the bed behind her: as a young woman, Hortense Daunay had been plumply pretty, and smiled in smug pleasure beside her handsome husband. Eve could not take her eyes from Daunay. A vital, swaggering personality fairly leaped from the photograph, without the camouflage of respectability. Tough, determined, hand on hip but not in gentlemanlike ease; rather, as if he touched a hidden knife. A man to dazzle any girl, and suck her dry afterward.

Eve put it down and picked up the next: a boy and a girl in a field, making a daisy chain and laughing together. Innocent and charming, the kind of picture mothers treasured; only, this was of Eulalie and Pierre, whose rooms she had just visited. What spoiled hopes lay between that sunlit day and this night, between a pair of laughing children and these two as she had come to know them.

The last photograph was larger, a family group taken on some special occasion. Daunay stood in the center, white-haired and well fleshed as he was today and arrogantly dominating the rest. Hortense was muffled in black silk by his side and smiled drowsily up at him, one hand on his arm. Quite probably she still loved him, and sleep was her escape from his contempt. Eve looked among the unfamiliar faces also there: those two boys must be Gabrielle's. Anselme Saulx looked well pleased with himself and contemplated a fat cigar, but Guy wasn't there. Away in Alsace, as usual, no doubt.

Eve put it down with a snap, and turned. Gabrielle was standing just inside the door, watching her.

Eve felt blood drain from her face with shock. A moment before, she had felt faint from heat and fumes; now she was clammy cold.

Excuses seemed quite futile. "I was looking at these photographs."

"So I see. Would you like me to show you one of your husband as he was before the war?"

Eve nodded, bemused by Gabrielle's acceptance of her presence here, and followed her from the room. Everything seemed infinitely removed from her, and at the same time oddly detailed: the grain of marble and pattern of carpet printed on her brain, while the fact of being caught ransacking her host's premises remained unreal.

The house was quiet, and there was no movement from the guest wing as they passed the linking passage. Gabrielle walked ahead without looking around, and Eve thought foolishly about how there was nothing to stop her scrambling over the wrought-iron gate and running away down the Champs-Élysées in her silver lamé gown.

Gabrielle's room was surprisingly comfortable. A prie-dieu in one corner, but otherwise it was furnished more as a sitting room than a bedroom, and a coal fire burned in the grate.

She saw Eve looking. "I usually prefer my own company during the day."

Eve nodded. She could not think of anything to say, afraid that excuses would slither out the moment she opened her mouth.

Gabrielle stood watching her, hands folded quietly together. Soon

Eve found herself wishing she would do or say something, anything, if only she would stop watching her.

She swallowed. "You said you had a photograph of Guy."

Gabrielle lifted her eyebrows. "Was that what you were looking for?"

Eve tried to smile and could not, held by Gabrielle's eyes, dark and somber in a white face, instilling an intense feeling of foreboding. "No, it wasn't. Pierre was unwell and wanted some pills, so I came up to get them and went into the wrong room when I saw the light on."

Gabrielle inclined her head, expressing polite interest. "How unfortunate! You passed Pierre's room on your way to Mme. Daunay's."

Eve was certain that Gabrielle knew she had been into all the other rooms. "How stupid of me! Perhaps you would be kind enough to show me the pills Pierre wants."

A scornful smile touched Gabrielle's lips. "I am sure it will not be possible to choose correctly. You realize you have been fortunate? You had only M. Daunay's room left to enter and he is within, and not a man who cares for intruders."

There was a change in her manner, subtle but complete, so Eve was startled by how unmistakable it was. Alone of all this household, Gabrielle had never altered at all in the presence of Georges Daunay; now Eve understood at once that she had loved him for a long time. Her voice gained life and color when she spoke his name; there was blotched color over her cheekbones and softness to her lips.

She must have been thinking, thinking, thinking alone upstairs while the house around her shook to the corrupt malice of the man married to her sister, and just this once her guard was down, tragedy showing in the bones and courage of her face.

Rick had said, months ago, half joking, that Gabrielle perhaps once slept with Daunay. Eve had felt faint disgust but not thought of it again, since Gabrielle possessed the kind of presence which made such thoughts seem ludicrous; but of course she had and, even in her sixties, quite possibly still did.

The silence became intolerably long again as Eve tried feverishly to see where this fitted into all the rest. "I wouldn't have gone into M. Daunay's room. I made a mistake over which one Pierre said was his," she repeated at last, innocuous words shuffling over dangerous moments in the hope of learning more.

"You certainly would have, and caused a pretty scandal, I don't doubt. Georges likes attractive women and would have treated you as you deserve." Her eyes never left Eve; she had been almost kind this past month; now she watched her with positive dislike. Jealous anger had made her keep Eve from opening that last door, certainly not fear that there was anything she might discover.

So this, too, was part of the chance which must be seized if she was to discover more, no matter what the risk. "That photograph I saw. . . . M. Daunay was a fine-looking man on his wedding day."

Gabrielle smiled. "He is a man to dwarf others. Too much of a man to live one life: can you imagine how much he has achieved? In his time he has come from a hilltop village in the Creuse to a mansion on the Champs-Élysées."

Eve murmured something, it didn't matter what, because Gabrielle wasn't listening.

"He needs to trick Paris sometimes. To show them what fools they are, compared to him. Three hundred of those who most fancy themselves as Le Tout-Paris came here tonight, and only a handful had the sense to refuse drinks any peasant would throw into a ditch. Georges told them it was the lastest mode, and because they were offered pretty colors and a new sensation they feared they'd look foolish if they didn't drink. Georges told me only a dozen or so would refuse, and he was quite right."

Gabrielle had already argued herself out of grief and into derisive pride: this impartial witness whose word Eve had thought must be accepted when she said she saw Guy on the stairs with a drug bottle on the night her brother died.

Fragments fitting, falling apart, shuttling into newly shifting patterns, so much remaining tantalizingly obscure. But keep talking; pick each word carefully, very carefully now. "It's a pity M. Daunay did not warn Pierre to keep off the drinks tonight, if he intended such a joke."

"He did, and in such matters Pierre can usually be trusted, although in precious little else." Derision back in Gabrielle's voice again. "Drugs and alcohol do not mix, but I suppose the fool . . . was a fool. Attracted by color and strangeness, like the rest." She picked up a paired frame from the mantelpiece and thrust it at Eve. "The war took the best and left the rubbish behind."

Eve looked at two faces which bore a remarkable resemblance to that of Georges Daunay on his wedding day. Dark, arrogant, acquisitive faces lacking any trace of decadence. "Your sons were very good-looking," she said gently.

"They took after their father."

Eve thought of insignificant Marcel Benoit. "I am so sorry, madame. Everywhere there is so much sadness."

Animation faded from Gabrielle's face. "Merci. You live with your sadness too, and have nothing to show for it except a shop, which is something, I suppose. I at least have a grandchild. My Roger was not at all a good boy, I fear, but bien amusant, and he left me this son by a shopgirl. I do not know why I tell you, except you are sympathique and just sometimes one requires a little pity, *hein?* I keep him well away from here, since I do not want anyone to know. He will not grow up like Eulalie and Pierre."

She picked up an album, riffling through pages before picking out a piece of pasteboard. "Keep this, if you wish, and let me offer you my advice. Stay away from here. I wept for you when you came back."

Eve ought to have been enraged; instead she felt desperately sorry for this proud woman who had only a ruined life to remember. "Why weep for me, madame?"

"It's a little late to pretend you might be stupid," said Gabrielle with a flash of her old tartness. "A woman of your breeding would never have returned here unless love laid the task on her, and you know very well why I should weep for any woman who loves Guy. If you no longer wish to run back to America with your journalist, then you must allow your husband to forget the past instead of wasting time searching for something you will not find. Bring up your children as I brought up mine, in ignorance of this place. Guy's mother was a German, but simple and loving, a good woman. It is a pity she died when he was so young, but at least he grew up away from here. If you can give him peace, perhaps you might be happy."

"And Guy's father, was he a good man?"

Her face became a mask. "Stop looking, as I have warned you. There is nothing to find."

"No, Mme. Benoit. You said I wouldn't find what I sought, not that there was nothing to discover," Eve said levelly. "I should like you to go and ask M. Daunay whether I may see him, please."

"Georges is not to be disturbed by impudent girls, nor am I a servant to run with messages."

Eve smiled. "Your servants are all drunk, madame. Very well, I will announce myself."

She walked along the passage, anger burning so brightly now that she felt nothing else. She would most certainly accept Gabrielle's advice, and after tonight never come back to the Hôtel Daunay. She felt Gabrielle following her but did not look around: of course, she first had to get out of the Hôtel Daunay before such advice was of any use.

She knocked on the heavy mahogany door at the end of the passage and went in at once. "*Bonsoir,* monsieur."

Although by now it was surely very late, Daunay was sitting behind a desk, writing; completely sober and immaculately dressed, in contempt for his disheveled, vomiting guests. He looked across at her meditatively before standing to greet her; no sign of surprise, his control complete. "*Bonsoir,* Mme. Saulx. This is an unexpected pleasure."

He pulled out a chair for her, and she thanked him as she sat. He seemed unperturbed to find her in his room, an unscrupulous and supremely capable man whom nothing surprised any longer. Urbane manners disguised aggression, agile brain replacing a knife as his chosen weapon.

"She insisted on coming," said Gabrielle from the door. "I found her in Hortense's room, but she had looked through the rest as well."

He bowed ironically. "Would you like to search my room too while you are here?"

Eve lifted her chin. "Very much."

He laughed, but did not renew his offer. "Have you come to apologize for such unusual behavior? Seat yourself and shut the door, Gabrielle, I beg you."

Eve studied his white, square face. The change of coloring and extra jowl since his youth made an enormous difference, as did the veneer of culture. But beneath lay the same drive and ruthlessness she had seen portrayed in his wedding photograph, the same swagger and certainty of himself. "No, I haven't come to do that, monsieur. I've come to ask whether Mme. Benoit has told you that you have a grandson."

It was as if the flesh of his face set into concrete. Eve felt her own breath stop in sympathy with his, the choking gasp from Gabrielle thrown into utter silence.

"No," he said, and Eve admired him in that moment, although she had come in hate. The shock had been immense, and within seconds he had himself in hand again.

Gabrielle sat graven, staring at the floor.

"Your son Roger," said Eve, almost gently. "Not a good boy, as Madame said to me. You must ask her where she keeps the child."

His eyes flickered. "I will."

"You know why I've told you? Why it makes a difference?"

He stood and went to bring over a bottle of cognac. "You needn't fear to find sardines in this. Yes, now I think about it, I know why. What a pity that your talents are wasted in a shop, Mme. Saulx. I understand perfectly now why you have been so successful in intriguing Paris within so short a time."

Eve pushed away the glass he offered her. "I also happen to be particular about who I drink with."

"So very American. Such lack of finesse," he observed suavely, but Eve watched his fingers tighten on the stem of his glass and knew she had angered him, however well he hid it. He is a dangerous man when angered, Joubaire had said, but she needed him angry at the moment.

"I would have told you," said Gabrielle suddenly.

"Eventually, perhaps."

"Yes. This house— I want him to grow up a man and not a weakling spilling his life into the gutters."

"No," said Eve softly. "Not this house, but you, M. Daunay. She loves you, and love is not often blind, whatever the adage says. She knows it is you who have ruined everyone here. You are too much of everything; too much feared, too much the ruler, a destructive force loose in too small a compass. A child would be crushed as everyone else has been. Your wife and legitimate children; M. Benoit, who is a name for his wife and nothing else at all. Anselme Saulx, who was Gabrielle's brother and lived here knowing everything, and sold his soul for comfort. Illegitimacy saved her sons; she means to use it to save your grandson, too."

He poured cognac for himself, hand completely steady. "So you have come to settle everything, like President Wilson with his points and principles? How fortunate for us all that the Atlantic is so wide."

"I came to discover who killed Anselme Saulx. Unfortunately, there is nothing I can do about justice afterward."

He was staring at Gabrielle, only half listening, fingers drumming on the edge of the desk. "How old is the boy?"

"Four years old. He also is called Roger."

Daunay's mouth twisted. "A chip off the old block, then, since his father cannot have been seventeen when he sired him. We will talk of it later." He turned to Eve. "I never give anything free, but will offer you a bargain you don't deserve. In return for your assistance in the matter of a certain Bertrand Joubaire, I will tell you of the matters you desire to know."

"What kind of assistance?"

"A kind which will set your mind at rest. Forever. He is a clumsy and greedy fool, but annoying. I intend to be rid of him soon, and have seen how he has been pestering you, too. I am only asking you to bait a trap in your own interests." He threw back his head, and suddenly he was as she had seen him in the photograph, the lava of vitality and ambition flowing hotly from well-stoked fires.

Joubaire's craving for petty power, his plots and cruelties which had made Eve's life such a misery, were immediately reduced to the level of minor irritants which could be swatted whenever this man chose. Like the inhabitants of the Hôtel Daunay, Joubaire did not stand a chance.

Eve shook her head.

"*Comment?*" Daunay thrust his face close, calm broken for once.

"I told you why I came tonight, and it wasn't so I could fit into your plans as scapegoat for another murder." Eve needed every particle of control forged through the past, appalling months to hold her voice steady and keep her eyes on his. In the folds of her skirt, her hands and legs were trembling, not from fear but from temptation she had only just survived.

The temptation to assist in trapping a man whose death would free her from several crushing burdens.

"I see I was mistaken in your intelligence," said Daunay in a cool, reasonable voice, although he no longer looked either. "Perhaps I did not make myself clear. I do not permit small-time crooks to disturb my peace of mind, nor to profit at my expense. The choice isn't yours but mine, even though on this occasion I offered to discuss the death of Anselme Saulx in return for your cooperation. That is all. If you decide not to collaborate with me, then I am very well able to use you and your shop for my purposes and make no return at all."

Eve stood and shook out her skirts. "You made yourself clear, but I'm stupid, I guess. Nor do I want to discuss a thing, because I've found what I came to look for and that's all I wanted: to know, not prosecute. So you should remember sometimes just how lucky you were that I don't bait traps, no matter how richly deserved they may be. Because the trap I'd enjoy to set would have you howling in its teeth, for what you did to Guy."

There was no warning in his face or eyes, only the bite of his hands as he seized and shook her until her senses spun. Vaguely, Eve heard Gabrielle cry out; she stumbled and fell as Daunay's grip relaxed.

He leaned over her, his face revolving with the room. "As Gabrielle says, we cannot afford another Saulx dead in this house. It's unimportant anyway, when all I need to do is wait. Enjoy yourself, madame, while I stand back and watch how Joubaire ruins you. Then I will arrange for his removal, and not before."

CHAPTER 16

Eve left Daunay's room and then the house, conscious only of relief that her task was over, but once outside, this faded, to be replaced by desolation. Hot-eyed and oddly dizzy, she stood on the wide marble steps of the Hôtel Daunay and thought how little the night had really solved. She knew what she had wanted to know, and it made no difference to any of the problems that mattered. Absurdly, she wished she had apologized to Gabrielle for betraying her confidence, been kinder to people caught as she was, in traps of their own devising.

A few *fiacres* were drawn up under the trees of the Champs-Élysées, drivers and horses dozing: autos were tucked away in garages at such an hour, while *cochers* still touted for the remnants of a living.

She called one over and, on impulse, directed him to St.-Sulpice; he was old and looked as if nothing could astonish him about the human race, not even a woman unescorted on the streets of Paris at four in the morning, driving around the left bank in a silver evening gown.

The mist of a summer dawn curled off the Seine as their horse trotted over the Alexandre III bridge, leaves and buildings etched against a tranquil sky. A few early lights showed in shuttered buildings, one or two cafés were sweeping out the last of the night's revelers. Dance, drink and sing, because tomorrow you must do it all over again. Buckets of melted ice, yawning waiters, faded flowers. A solitary drinker swilling champagne between deserted trolley tracks.

Yet around it all remained the grace of Paris, untouched by barbarism. One or two figures trudged to early shift with last night's bread thriftily tucked under an arm, passing women in felt-soled cleaning shoes. The waft of hot bread was woven into the air, the first trolley car boomed past, a tug hooted on the river: along the quays, Eve's *fiacre* overtook some country carts full of vegetables, the horses finding their own way while the drivers slept.

Eve looked at it all, and understood why she had not wanted to drive straight home. In spite of everything, she had come to love Paris, and needed to share the hardheaded reality of its citizens after such a night as she had spent. She did not stop in the Rue Férou, since Guy had said he would come to see her when he returned, which meant he wasn't back.

Eve sighed, and stared at gray buildings rolling past, wishing she had been happy here. She could have been happy in shabby, unaffected St.-Sulpice, with its cobbles and pavé, its pigeons and lion-faced fountain in the square.

Goats, too. Eve smiled as a goatherd came up the street toward them, playing his pipes as if he were Pan alone in a wood. A woman came out of a house holding a bowl, and the goatherd began to milk a big-bagged black goat in the middle of the road. The *cocher* drew up with a shout, and stayed to gossip until the goat was milked. The rest of the flock took advantage of the pause to stand on their hind legs and peer up the lampposts as if they were searching for mysteriously absent leaves.

Eve watched, feeling rested and less alone than before. Here she was with people she understood, and soon she must face the other kind again.

The *fiacre* clip-clopped back across the Seine, sun golden but buildings still in shadow. Street vendors were making early sales to cafés, their calls echoing as if the twentieth century were not yet born. "*A la barque! Les huitres à la barque!*" "*A la crevette, à la bonne crevette, j'ai de la raie toute en vie, toute en vie!*" "*Huit sous mon oignon, voilà des carottes à deux ronds la botte!*"

Her *fiacre* turned into the Rue Tronchet and stopped to allow a regiment of infantry to pass. The men were marching heavy-footed, heads down and silent, while women drew aside and watched, their faces set in sadness.

The Germans had not agreed to sign the treaty, and two days now remained before their time ran out. The twentieth century was most lethally alive.

Hugo found the Hôtel Astoria easier to enter than he expected. The messengers were unarmed, the atmosphere civilian, hall and passages almost deserted, as if the mornings were a time when the British gave undivided attention to their cooked breakfasts. In fact, he realized, there was little more for peace delegations to do. They waited like everyone else now the flash point of decision had moved from Paris to Berlin. No more hectic compromises and whispered deals, no more tracings of obscure parts of the globe whisked through the streets to waiting statesmen: the diplomatic task was complete, and only time would show who had truly won and lost.

Hugo leafed through the London *Times* while he waited for his name to be taken up to Maurice Wyville; the British press was as relentless as ever in its attitude to Germany.

"Will you come this way, sir?" A gray-haired messenger led him up a wide staircase and knocked on a cream-and-gold-painted door. "Mr. Kobis, Sir Maurice."

Wyville sat back, hands folded on his desk. He was alone, a secretary's table vacant, his expression the unrevealing façade which upperclass Englishmen managed to perfection.

"I'm very grateful to you for seeing me, sir," said Hugo.

"Yes, it might look a trifle questionable to the uninitiated," Wyville agreed. He had not stood or moved.

Hugo flushed. "I know it seems as if I am taking advantage of Sarah's affections again."

"And you are not?"

"To come here, I suppose. But I think your government will agree that we have some common interest in the news I bring. I have just come from Mainz. It is the French headquarters—"

"I am reasonably well informed, Mr. Kobis."

"I'm sorry, sir. Then, I expect you know that the French occupation command is actively encouraging Rhineland separatism, in defiance of their government. Clemenceau—"

"Clemenceau wants an Anglo-American guarantee on future French security, and knows perfectly well it will not be forthcoming if France plays ducks and drakes with the terms of the treaty. Proceed, Mr. Kobis."

Training rescued Hugo from a flurry of half sentences. In this room he was a representative of the Wilhelmstrasse in negotiation with His Britannic Majesty's rather annoying government, and it helped to steady him. "Yes, Sir Maurice. But the French High Command is not reconciled to, and still has not accepted, this policy. I have been engaged in tracing the destination of arms which have been released from French magazines for the use of separatist and criminal gangs, and have documents which show the names of both these gang leaders and the French officers attached to them. The entire French command in Mainz is deeply involved, and they intend to ship these arms down the Rhine, probably today. Which means into the British as well as the French zone. They know that if their plans are to succeed they must attempt a major *Putsch*; skirmishes in places like Wiesbaden have become a dangerous waste of time. So they intend to declare their state in Cologne, where your government would find it difficult not to become involved and where Mayor Adenauer is sympathetic to their cause. To the French command this is a first step toward dissolving the Reich into separate, petty states."

"Yes, I know."

Hugo's jaw dropped. "You know?"

"Britain possesses a nonpolitical Army. When Colonel André, of the French command, unwisely approached our commander in Cologne for support, he came immediately to Paris and reported this rather remarkable conversation. Mr. Lloyd George discussed the matter with M. Clemenceau, whose efforts to defuse the situation were considerably helped by our information, I believe."

Hugo felt deflated and uncommonly foolish. How like the *verdammt* British to look thoroughly supine yet know far more than they ought to all along. "In that case I am sorry to have troubled, and perhaps embarrassed you, by coming here."

"Not at all, my dear boy. Information about arms and intrigues in our zone of control is always useful, and the French neglected to inform us fully on that aspect of the matter. Were you responsible for sinking the shipments before you left Mainz?"

"Sinking the shipments! No! At least, I suppose that . . . perhaps I'd better tell you everything now."

Wyville regarded him thoughtfully. "I should think that might be best. Sit down, Hugo."

Hugo sat, trying to arrange his thoughts and wondering where to begin. "You remember where Sarah used to work sometimes? Le Trésor, a shop kept by Mme. Saulx?"

"In the Rue Daunou? Yes, perfectly."

He would, thought Hugo with resignation, although to his knowledge Wyville had never been near the place. He plunged into an intricate description of why he and Guy had gone to Mainz together, and how a patriotic German and a serving French officer had found both hatred and a common purpose there. "So you see, I thought that perhaps by telling the British I would make quite sure nothing went wrong at the last moment, when I wasn't completely sure. . . . Guy— Commandant Saulx thought that if he broke in on the conspiracy at such a sensitive time it would panic them a bit, but—"

"I should think it might," said Wyville dryly.

"Yes; well, he thought that at the very least it would throw everything out of gear, and it did. Although the shipment was due to sail the night before last, they all stood a long time arguing, then took him away with them. To see General Mangin, he hoped."

"Taken away with whom?"

"The colonels who were due to leave with the arms; so that part was in confusion immediately. I thought then that there was something Guy hadn't told me, and I see now how he must have set charges among the arms, or in the barges more likely, if you say they all sank. With the whole French command in Mainz squabbling about how much Clemenceau knew, they'd be even more alarmed when news came that the whole lot had sunk where it couldn't be shifted before investigators from Paris came. I see now that Guy had it carefully fixed, instead of the risk I thought it at the time."

"I wonder whether he also realized you would come to us? I expect he will have made his own arrangements to keep M. Clemenceau informed, but I will make sure the French Government is aware of this favorable moment to whip in its generals." Wyville reflected that he had been impressed by Saulx when he made it his business to encounter him, once he learned that this was the officer being used as agent provocateur with Foch.

"And Köln, Sir Maurice? Germany has suffered enough without having more blood spilled there."

"Cologne is quiet. Herr Adenauer was permitted to come and visit your delegation before they left Versailles for Berlin. Herr von Brockdorff-Rantzau informed him that, in his opinion, there was no possibility that the Allies might relent over such matters as attaching Alsace to an independent Rhineland state. Herr Adenauer's enthusiasm for Rhineland separatism did not survive the interview." Wyville's hands moved among the papers on his desk and then folded again. "Adenauer was just another loyal German who found himself in doubtful company while trying to do the best he could by his responsibilities."

Hugo grinned. "I'm sure you could never be regarded as doubtful company, sir."

Wyville looked mildly interested. "Do you intend to tell your masters at the Wilhelmstrasse that you came here today? I really would advise against it."

Hugo had not reflected on that aspect of the matter, but now that he did, explanations appeared singularly unattractive. "I shall have to think about it."

"How wise! You should perhaps request your friend Saulx to hold his tongue about your dealings together also. You may rest assured that the British Government protects the sources of its information, even from its allies." He paused, and then added deliberately, "A future German Government might be even less indulgent than your present masters if it should ever discover that one of its officials once had secret dealings with us. Think about it if you must, but do not be tempted into deciding that honesty might be the best policy. Be discreet, and save your life."

"How is Sarah?" Hugo had not meant to ask.

"She is well. I explained to her the conversation we had together, perhaps more clearly than you were able to do. She remembers you with affection rather than resentment, if that helps at all. Nothing else has changed."

"No, nothing else has changed," said Hugo somberly. "I did not enjoy my time in Mainz, nor was I reassured by the scum set loose on the streets of Germany nowadays. I leave this evening for the east; when I heard last, my mother was alone at our home near Posen, and whether we accept or reject the treaty, the Poles will be in West Prussia then."

"I will instruct my secretary to make out a press pass for you as far as the British zone. From Cologne onwards you should not have any difficulty until you reach the east. Destroy the pass immediately you have used it; keep nothing which might in the future connect you either with us or the French. Good luck." Wyville stood and offered his hand.

Hugo shook it, then clicked his heels and bowed. "Thank you, but I hope you take too gloomy a view of the future."

"No one hopes it more than I, but one cannot be too careful." He rang for a secretary and, in the few remaining minutes of their meeting, spoke only of trivialities.

Hugo walked out into the street, under the dark green leaves of summer. The stone flags were hot under his feet and he wondered under what circumstances he would see Paris again. He glanced at his watch: it was only just after ten, some twenty-seven hours since he had left Mainz. The thought of another interminable journey, this time into the chaos of the east, was hideously unattractive. He must see Eve first. Give her news of Guy and tell her he ought to be back soon. However furious General Mangin might be, he could not long detain an officer of French intelligence working under the Prime Minister's orders. In fact, Guy might be back already, since as a supposed Swiss journalist, Hugo had encountered endless delays. In which case, he would tell him of Wyville's advice to keep his mouth shut, advice which seemed better each time Hugo thought about it. Poor Guy, with Joubaire and the devil knew what else to deal with now.

Hugo sighed. It wasn't his affair, and he could transact business but nothing else with Guy until these murderous times had been outlived. He owed a different duty now, and remembered Guy saying that in his place he would have left before for West Prussia. *Adieu* Paris; *Will-kommen* to the stirred dregs of defeated Germany.

Lost in his thoughts, he practically walked into Sarah coming around a corner with her usual impetuous speed. He grabbed at her to keep her from falling, and they stood in each other's hold, laughing with unself-conscious delight.

"Hugo!"

"My dear, how beautiful you are."

"I never kissed anyone on the pavement before."

"Neither have I." They turned to walk with their arms twined, heads close together.

"It's nice, though. What about going out on the Pont d'Iéna and kissing right in the middle, just in case someone missed it here?"

"What a splendid idea! I thought you were still in Norfolk."

"Oh, no! My mother's sister came to visit; she is quite dreadfully dull, but she and Mother are happy all day long, remembering how they flirted at Henley in 1897, or some such thing. I went to stay with a school friend, and Mother didn't even notice me going."

"A school friend living in Paris?"

"Of course not! I mean, it wasn't a school friend at all. I came here instead, and once I was here, Father let me stay, because he is going back himself in a day or two. Dear Hugo, do you know I was quite dreadfully sick crossing the Channel?"

"Why did you come?" He knew why she had come.

She brushed his cheek with her lips, laughing. "Don't be conceited. I came to see you, and all you wanted was to hear me admit it."

Hugo held her tightly. "*Ja*, I wanted to hear you admit it."

"And then when I reached here feeling quite horribly green, Father said you had gone." She frowned. "It isn't like him to lie."

"He didn't. I returned this morning." Hugo wondered how the devil Maurice Wyville knew he had gone.

Sarah smiled impishly. "How wretched for him! He would have packed me back across the Channel at once if he'd known you might come back."

They kissed, heedless of indulgent Parisians, who thought it a very proper thing to do, right in the middle of the Pont d'Iéna, sun hot on their shoulders and glinting off the Seine, a scented breeze blowing from quayside trees.

With derision, Hugo realized that at the age of twenty-eight he was behaving like a romantic adolescent. Derision did not matter, though, since nothing changed what he felt for Sarah except that with the years it would have strengthened. Unfortunately, a great deal else mattered, and this meeting was a disaster.

He leaned on the bridge balustrade and gazed at silver water, thinking of her by his side, her hand in his and a smile on her lips. "I love you, Sarah."

"Oh, Hugo, yes, I know. Me, too. I mean, I don't intend to make a habit of kissing men on the Pont d'Iéna."

He turned to face her. "I find it hard to believe that people really behave like this. It is like a bad play. Sarah, I have to return to Germany today, and this time I shall not be coming back."

"I've already told you that I'm not one of those women who has to be fenced off from every trifling difficulty. I understand why you left Stoneham and I'm not as angry as I was, but why do you think I came to Paris again?"

"Braving seasickness on the way," said Hugo, smiling.

"Not braving it at all; I hated every minute! Don't change the subject; do you remember you once remarked on how I held to an awkward question?"

"Then, let me answer it. I am sure you are not a woman who needs to be sheltered from difficulty. I love you because of it. But I must return to Germany, and after this recent time I have spent there, I know an Englishwoman would be unhappy living there. I did not entirely agree with your father before, but you were so young I had to accept his judgment and hope matters might improve in the future. Now . . . I'm afraid he could be right."

"And if I don't care?"

"You would, and so would I. I haven't asked you to marry me, Sarah, and I don't intend to."

Her face tightened and her eyes were very bright. "Then, this is Paris, Hugo. What about one of those left-bank hotels I've heard ladies whisper about behind their gloves?"

He gave a gasp of laughter. "*Liebchen* . . . you are seventeen. Of course I would like it very much, but no."

"There is something magic about being old, which makes left-bank hotels perfectly respectable?"

"There is nothing right about them now with you."

Sarah was not a fool and recognized defeat when she saw it. She was also somewhat consoled by the reflection that if she accepted his decision, then Hugo might continue to feel obligation toward her for some time afterward. When peace was only a few fragile months old, she needed to gain more time during which the prejudices of war could be swept from underfoot. He may find he can't dismiss left-bank hotels so easily when he remembers me then, she thought optimistically. It would be educational for him, being in love with her. She had always thought that diplomats had some very stuffy notions, left to themselves.

"I would like it very much if you would kiss me again, then," she said. "Think of me and the Pont d'Iéna sometimes."

They kissed to the sound of footsteps tapping by, a sound like their own lives passing. Sarah's confidence vanished, and they clung together wordlessly.

"I will remember the Pont d'Iéna," said Hugo.

"And come here in twenty years' time as a portly Prussian, remembering a foolish fling?"

"Remembering his love, yes."

"Hugo . . . I think I shall visit Paris again in less than twenty years."

He freed himself gently. "No, *Liebchen*. Visit London instead."

She came with him to the Gare de l'Est, which was a mistake: their parting far worse than either could have believed possible so long as they remained together in sunshine on the Pont d'Iéna.

CHAPTER 17

In Weimar, everyone was exhausted and close to hysteria. Cabinet ministers screamed at each other, the National Assembly broke up in disorder and the second government in three days was on the point of collapse. There were only hours to go before the Allied armies would invade Germany if she refused to sign the treaty, and decision seemed as impossible to reach as ever.

Fritz Ebert, recently elected President of the German Republic, would have liked to join the Cabinet in their imminent scuttle from responsibility, but he was a stolid man, with a rigid sense of duty, who considered he had no right at this moment to escape from the burdens of his position. Leaving Chancellor and Cabinet to their recriminations, he put through a telephone call to Supreme Headquarters; he was entitled to a military judgment, which he, as an ex-trade-union leader, could not possibly make.

He glanced at his watch; 3:30 P.M. At seven o'clock the armistice would expire and the Allied troops would march, German ports be blockaded again. He spoke briefly into the telephone; he would ring back in one hour for the answer to a single stark question: under the present chaotic circumstances, could or could not the Army fight?

In Paris, too, calm had disappeared. The boulevards were swept clear of soldiers as regiments filled up their ranks again and deserters hid from steel-helmeted patrols. The Council of Four was in continuous session in President Wilson's study, an anxious crowd in the street outside kept back by police.

It couldn't happen; it simply wasn't possible that war would come again tonight.

Five o'clock, and still no word from the German Government.

The Supreme Command of the German armed forces was quartered in the bleak Baltic town of Kolberg, and in his office there, General Groener faced Field Marshal von Hindenburg. Both knew that resistance was impossible, when what remained of the Army was deployed to keep Bolsheviks and Poles out of the east. The telephone rang and they stared at it, then at each other.

"*Der Reichspräsident, Herr Feldmarschall*," said an aide.

Hindenburg stood. "I have an appointment. There is no need for me to speak. You give the President his answer, Groener."

Groener shrugged as the door shut behind his chief. He had not expected Hindenburg to bear the shame of speaking words which finally sealed Germany's defeat.

He lit a cigarette and picked up the telephone. "Groener here."

"The Army's answer?" Ebert was horribly aware of time vanishing while his Cabinet wrote letters of resignation.

"We cannot fight, *Herr Reichspräsident*. Resistance is hopeless and will bring the very severe risk of further revolution if we try."

"You understand the significance of such advice at this moment from the Supreme Command?"

"*Ja, Herr Reichspräsident*. If the treaty cannot be resisted, then it must be signed. The Army recognizes this, and I personally pledge that the officer corps will accept orders to that effect."

First Quartermaster General Groener was a man of precise mind, who also accepted the responsibilities of his high office.

"Thank you, General Groener." Ebert hung up. Now for the Cabinet, and his frightened, useless Chancellor.

In ninety minutes the troops would march.

Really, there was nothing to discuss which would keep the minutes from ticking away. Silence had fallen in President Wilson's study, and the four leaders avoided each other's eyes, wondering who was to blame for the position in which they found themselves.

Only Clemenceau looked impassive, eyes closed, mustache drooping. The French press accused him of betraying his country's interests, so, unlike the British and the Americans, he would be well content if Germany had to be invaded. Then, when the treaty was eventually signed and ratified, France would have its Anglo-American guarantee of security, and his policy would be vindicated as well. The Germans deserved everything they suffered and a great deal more besides; he would have enjoyed joining a plot to take the Rhineland from them instead of having to suppress it, but one must be practical, after all. And one must win: wars, security, as well as authority over generals grown arrogant in their power. He was satisfied he had taken what he could of each. The Tiger grunted, hearing footsteps hurrying.

An officer came into the room, a paper in his hand. "The German Government has accepted. They agree to sign."

Wilson seemed to sigh. "Thank God. Thank God."

Thanks to the blood of two million Frenchmen, thought Clemenceau the atheist.

Lloyd George read the bitter, vengeful phrasing of the German message, his expressive face blank for once. "*Yielding to overwhelming force, but without on that account abandoning their view in regard to the unheard-of injustice of the conditions of peace, the Government of the German Republic declares that it is prepared to sign. . . .*"

He flicked the paper over to Wilson; he could thank God for it if he liked.

Eve heard guns like summer thunder in the air. The glass of her window vibrated from the sound, and she went out into the Rue Daunou, her face lifted questioningly to the east.

It could not be guns so close to Paris.

Everyone in the street had stopped, staring at each other, frozen like figures in a print. Dread clutched at hearts and thoughts, dread they had all lived with these past few days. Then movement started; shouts, running footsteps, and smiles breaking out on anxious, thankful faces.

A woman crossed herself and turned to Eve. "It's all right, the guns salute peace at last. Soon my husband will be home."

"My son," said an old man, tears running down his cheeks. "One boy killed and another blinded by the Boches, but at least the youngest will be spared."

Eve felt her own throat knot, for herself and for so many others who had suffered more than they could bear. The war was truly over at last.

Never, never again.

This very night, Guy might be home.

Bertrand Joubaire felt as relieved as anybody that the Boches had finally given up. Military patrols did not often search for deserters in the maze of streets below the Butte of Montmartre, but it was inconvenient to be forced to exercise care whenever he wanted to visit the center of Paris. He had enough to do without worrying about the Army as well as *flics*.

He couldn't say quite what had alerted his instinct for danger, but he was aware that his plans were going less smoothly; Tou-Tou Jean and his like were less respectful, and several coups had proved unprofitable or even downright dangerous lately. Consequently, he had less money than before to satisfy his followers, which might account for their insolence. One had actually betrayed a cache of stolen goods to the *flics*, which was the kind of thing *apaches* never, never did.

Joubaire scowled and threw a handful of sous on the bar to pay for his wine. If he had not known that Daunay no longer concerned himself with petty criminality, he would have suspected that he was to blame. Joubaire had heard about Georges Daunay's capricious and unforgiving sense of humor, and admired the stories he was told. He did not find them amusing now.

He wished he could be absolutely sure that nowadays Daunay was too grand to worry about such minor matters as Sergeant Joubaire using part of his network for his own profit. Meantime, he needed money. A great deal of money, immediately, so he could cement doubtful loyalties and launch himself into success again.

He set out for the Rue Daunou; at least there wouldn't be any more military patrols to dodge.

Eve stayed quite late at Le Trésor. She had nothing particular to do, and though there were a dozen celebratory parties where she would be welcome if she went, she could not shake off the idea that Guy might come tonight.

There couldn't be anything more for him to do in Germany, no reason why he shouldn't return to Paris. She eyed the telephone, trying not to feel resentful, since Europeans did not seem to regard it as something you used in the normal course of living.

Yet if Guy had walked in through the door, she would have been panic-stricken. Each day, she noticed the changes in her body more and still could not imagine how she would tell him—or Rick, either. Nor what she would do after she had, when she felt quite unable to estimate their reactions. Well, yes, she was afraid she knew exactly how Guy would feel, but could not bear to think about it.

She decided to sketch a new design for the window which she planned to celebrate the peace, an occupation she usually found soothing. As summer dusk fell, she stared at Le Trésor's frontage from across the road and realized she did not have a single interesting idea to put on paper. She could draw a patriotic setting easily enough, but knew the whole conception had lost its freshness. Buyers came because she took trouble with her stock, but the shop in the Rue Daunou was no longer a novelty, a source of speculation as to what her next extravaganza would be. She needed to change and expand, add a consulting service on American lines, stock carpets and materials, and tuck little bowers for refreshment among her displays, so bored clients could arrange assignations between the fatigues of spending money. Or change again so Le Trésor was the only functional, totally modern store in Paris.

She sketched hastily, in careless black slashes of her pencil. She enjoyed thinking and planning, ideas usually springing easily from her mind, but the sheer fatigue of realizing them was more than she could manage at the moment.

Surely Guy must be out of the Army soon, and able to help.

But even supposing he could bear her near him, she could not visualize him at Le Trésor at all. It had been a way of defeating his father, an idea of normality in his mind, not a place where he had ever really worked.

Fat drops of summer rain began to fall and she went back inside, sketch pad in hand.

"*Bonsoir*, madame," said Bertrand Joubaire, arms folded, waiting for her with a grin of pleasure on his face.

Rick Dwyer decided that it would be easier to send his dispatches direct from Paris, rather than risk having them lost by uncooperative, sullen operatives in Berlin. Officially, the city was working normally and the troops were off the streets, bloodshed confined to faction fights in the provinces. He gathered that Munich and Hamburg were both in a bad way, but had no desire to visit either.

He would come back, but had seen as much as he could take for the moment. Everything was in short supply: food, manners, self-respect, order, work. Also water and electricity, which only sometimes came from tap or switch. Rick supposed that those who should be producing it were standing on street corners along with most of the population, eyeing him with hatred as he passed.

There was a train leaving Berlin for the west at nine-thirty in the evening, and he decided to take it; he wanted to see Eve again, and filing copy was a good excuse for his editor.

The night was turning chilly, leaves fluttering in the Unter den Linden. People trudged past, not speaking, shoulders hunched. Soon rain began to fall, and the sky clamped low, as if hatred and bitterness soaked into the earth itself.

Rick drank three watered beers in quick succession, thankful he had decided to leave tonight.

Joubaire moved into Le Trésor, and within a single day disrupted everything. He was in a hurry and felt he had already waited too long.

Eve did not know what to do, and thought how Georges Daunay would enjoy watching her being crushed, how he would wait until it was all over before moving in himself.

She tried to tell Joubaire that she had less to fear from the police than he had, but he took no notice at all. "You see, madame, I know you are wrong. *Certainement,* I do not want the *flics* to come here, but you, too, would be in for an unpleasant time if they did. You may say that the Comtesse de Saint Luc is a useful ally in the matter of furniture the Commandant stole—"

"Bought."

"It doesn't matter. Once the *flics* came here, they would close you down for investigation, no matter what the rights and wrongs of anything may be. Then they would discover that some of the goods you brought from St.-Cloud were stolen too."

"What!"

He regarded her dismay with satisfaction. "Did you think I would tamely accept it when the Commandant forbade me to come here again? I placed whatever I wanted in the house at St.-Cloud when you weren't there, so now you have several things in your showroom which the *flics* would recognize."

She had made an inventory. It couldn't be true. But of course she had been so busy that the inventory had been fitted into odd moments, and she remembered how pleasantly surprised she had been by one or two pieces unearthed from back rooms, how she had congratulated herself on buying so cleverly and well. He could have done it, not for money but for the hold it gave him, when he saw how Nathalie de Saint Luc's soirée destroyed the other hold he'd thought he had.

Worry clamped tight, desperate, nagging worry, when she couldn't think how to discover whether he was bluffing.

It was terrifying to have Joubaire back in the shop each moment of the day, when she had thought her discoveries at the Hôtel Daunay had broken his last hold over her and Guy. He no longer dressed smartly or addressed her respectfully; she was forced to beg him to keep out of the way while she dealt with customers, her mind flurried, cool manner disintegrating when spoiled women became capricious.

By the end of that first day, she was exhausted, and no nearer deciding what to do. Daunay would enjoy his cognac tonight.

Eve was thankful when closing time came at last, and also apprehensive that Joubaire might not let her go. She had to keep calm, had to, when panic would deliver her, bound, to his schemings. She was nearly sure that most of what he said was bluff, and two could play that game if only she could find time to think.

Marguerite came in with the shutter key, as she always did. "That evil one is still upstairs, madame."

Eve put her fingers to her face; she could feel her skin trembling. "He is lodging tonight in the upstairs room."

Marguerite sniffed. "*Il n'est pas un garçon bien aimable.*"

An understatement of classic proportions, Eve thought. "I hope he won't stay more than a day or two. Perhaps tomorrow Commandant Saulx will be home." She needed desperately to share this whole appalling mess with someone; she could not manage alone any longer.

Marguerite shrugged. "*Monsieur le Commandant* did not rid us of the wicked one before."

Eve put her head in her hands after Marguerite had gone. She had been fooling herself; because he was not here, it was dangerously easy to pretend that Guy could help, for no better reason than her certain knowledge that he had had nothing to do with his father's death. Which in this situation made no difference at all.

She pulled on a summer coat and went softly to the door. Joubaire was standing in the shop and turned as she came. "Where are you going?"

"Back to my lodging. Mme. Riquart will be expecting me."

"I thought you lived here?"

Thank God she didn't. "I have lodged in the Rue Tronchet for several weeks. Mme. Riquart will be worried if I'm not back for supper." Which wasn't true; she was often late.

He pulled at his lip, then shrugged. "*Bien.* A night for reflection will not be bad, but tell her you are going away for a few days. Tomorrow we shall visit your bank together, and afterward you stay here, under my eye, until I've done."

"I haven't authority with the bank—"

"Certainly you have." He glanced at glowing furniture and smart paint. "Commandant Saulx made arrangements, and I can see you are not in the same difficulties as before. You have been buying for yourself, so beyond doubt may withdraw whatever francs you require."

He took her keys and locked the door behind her, his face puckered in contempt that she should be so stupid as to imagine she might fool him, Bertrand Joubaire, one of the rising brains of the Paris underworld.

Eve sat on the edge of her bed, hour after hour, through the night, thought twisting and turning among the fragments of her life. She had to fight back before it was too late, useless to wait in hope that the burden would somehow be taken from her, when Joubaire had spent the day wrapping his tentacles around everything in Le Trésor. He was no longer interested in preserving profit, only in breakup value.

But Daunay would kill him soon . . . too late to make any difference to her. Unless she went back to the Hôtel Daunay and agreed to help. She stood by the window and watched dawn grow over the gray roofs of Paris: whatever Joubaire did, she could not help to contrive his death. She smiled wryly to herself; it was a decision of self-interest, too. Daunay could kill Joubaire any time he chose, and wanted her help only because then she would be meshed into his schemes. That was how such men worked; they netted everyone they touched, building empires life by life, knowing that each eventually would serve some purpose. If she yielded to Daunay's pressures now, one day, perhaps years ahead, his underlings would be there, presenting his bill for payment.

She stripped, and washed in cold water, body aching from a sleepless night. She looked at herself in the mirror: breasts fuller than they had been, but her belly still nearly flat; slim hips and strong legs surprising in their grace when she felt so frowsy. She made a moue of distaste and dressed hastily in the elegant clothes she wore nowadays, then paused and slipped the photograph Gabrielle had given her from a drawer. It had been taken in some Metz studio and was dated 1911. Guy in German Army uniform; she supposed Anselme had kept it in case he needed to discredit his son in the future. Eve did not look at the coarse conscript's tunic but at the face above: she had told herself many times that she would not have recognized her husband as he had been only eight years before.

And yet she would.

Superficially the change was staggering, from this smooth-skinned boy to gaunt man, from open, considering stare to bloodshot eyes with their expression completely hidden, but there was also much which was the same: the shape of head and stiff, thick hair; defensive mouth and the sense of endurance. This boy had encountered little mercy in his life. Today perhaps he would be back; she must not immediately pile more burdens on him when there was quite enough bad news to break, without adding Joubaire to the rest.

She walked briskly to Le Trésor, where Joubaire was waiting for her in the doorway, vindictive because she was late. "We will go at once to the bank."

"Later," said Eve. "There are a couple of dealers I must telephone first." She pushed past him before he could argue, but found it almost impossible to talk sense when he watched her unblinkingly throughout both conversations.

"Now," he said immediately she hung up.

Eve laced her fingers together and rested her chin on them. "I've been thinking things over during the night."

His lip lifted. "I thought you might."

"It occurred to me you might not know that Georges Daunay is only waiting for you to ruin me before he kills you."

He came over in a single stride and seized her hands. "You're lying!"

"No," she said calmly. "He asked me to become part of his plans, and I refused."

"*Merde!* When?"

"Three days ago. I went to the Hôtel Daunay to try and prove some ideas I had over Anselme Saulx's death. My ideas, not yours, as it happens."

He tossed her hands aside and straightened. He looked half stupefied. "Daunay knows? You're sure? *Merde*, he knows what I am— what I am doing?"

She nodded. "He's a frightening man, isn't he? I wonder why you ever thought he might not know, or that if he did, he would not care."

He babbled out about how Daunay would not risk such great prosperity by dabbling again in the *apache* crookery of his past, but Eve did not reply. Joubaire must have been crazy to take so great a risk, however tempting the possibilities might seem. She had spent half an hour in Daunay's company and would never have made the mistake of thinking he might yield anything that was his. She remembered then how she had met him before, fleetingly as his guest; only because she had been determined to discover the secrets of his family had she reached behind his dignified façade to something far more elemental. If Joubaire had never dealt with Daunay face to face, then it was perhaps possible to make such a mistake.

"What are you going to do?" she asked. Cool detachment was her only chance.

He rasped stubble on his chin, then shook his head. Eve read his thoughts easily: his instinct was to kill, but he feared to move in case that was what Daunay wanted.

"Perhaps you should think about it, as I did last night," she said maliciously.

"None of this makes any difference to you. I need all the money I can get, even quicker than before."

"And the moment my last sou is in your hands, it'll be the end for you, too."

"You're mighty close to Daunay's plans," he said, suspicion flaring.

How odd! She felt almost sorry for him, as a solitary prisoner might be for his jailer. "I was able to take advantage of a moment's weakness, when Daunay learned something he didn't know which mattered very much to him. Pierre killed Anselme Saulx, because Daunay had forbidden Anselme to supply his son with drugs as he had done before the war. He used Anselme to collect a rakeoff from such trafficking in drugs as he no longer wanted to do himself; Eulalie and Pierre both make money on it too; I've watched them with their smart set very closely this past month."

Joubaire slammed his hand on the desk. "You're talking riddles. Daunay would never permit scum like Anselme Saulx to corrupt his son. Make money for him, yes, why not? But the moment he sold drugs to Daunay's only son, he'd have had his throat cut and he must have realized it."

"That's where I stuck too," agreed Eve. "Then I saw photographs of Mme. Benoit's sons who were both killed. They could only have been Daunay's. He did not care what happened to a runt of his litter called Pierre, until he was the only one left alive. Daunay retains some peasant reactions, I guess, like setting a high value on family ties but none at all on degenerates. Pierre came back from Germany half cured, yet could hardly wait for drugs again. I think— I can't prove it, but I think Daunay may have calculated it was safer to use Anselme to make sure Pierre was supplied with something innocuous. Then Pierre reckoned Anselme was double-crossing him when whatever he received didn't have the effect he'd hoped for."

"Daunay put Anselme up to it?" said Joubaire, puzzled.

"When he realized Pierre would find what he wanted elsewhere, otherwise. There's a great deal of drug-taking at the moment in the Tout-Paris set." Eve had missed the signs before, knowing nothing of what they were. "Daunay despises Pierre, yet now he is his only son. He's a man used to molding others to his will; perhaps he thought he could change Pierre, although he must have feared it was too late."

Joubaire showed his teeth. "Of course it is too late. He has the children he deserves."

Eve nodded. She detested Daunay but did not intend to tell Joubaire that somewhere was a boy aged four who possessed his enemy's blood, a source of weakness if he was found. "He has the underlings he deserves too. I discovered that Anselme had begun to milk off profits from his dealings in drugs, through Le Trésor. I found some old account books here, and once I knew what I was looking for, it wasn't difficult to find. I suppose furniture was a good cover if carefully used, but I wouldn't think Anselme Saulx a careful or a painstaking man; in peacetime he probably would have been caught. So Daunay wanted Le Trésor out of his control, which suited his plans for Guy, too."

Eve remembered how she had left the Opéra ball early with Pierre, who had not been unwell as she had thought, but jangle-nerved with craving. He must already have seen his chance to blame Guy, and waited to see how events had moved by the time he reached home. It didn't fit any other way, although Eve could still scarcely believe it when she remembered how he had been with her . . . how he had kissed her in an alcove of the Opéra. She shivered and looked across at Joubaire, loathing him again for what he had also done that night: when Pierre returned home, a cursory look at his cousin must have revealed that he would never be able to defend himself from any accusation the Daunays chose to make.

Yet Guy had not killed his father, and Daunay was too astute to spill blood on his own carpet, so he had not done it either. Only when Eve realized that Gabrielle might be lying, and Daunay the only person she would lie for, had supposition fallen into place. Because he would protect his only surviving son, which Pierre certainly realized. After the years of being disregarded, he probably found some caustic amusement in presenting his father with such havoc to clear up when he returned very late that night.

So Guy had become an explanation held in reserve, although Daunay neither wanted nor expected him to be arrested unless his plans went badly wrong: police in his house were the last thing he desired. A compliant doctor had done what was necessary, those who felt skeptical about a natural death fed with suggestions that shell shock was to blame. In the aftermath of war, pity stifled gossip more easily than money. Most outsiders apparently accepted that Anselme's own intemperance had killed him.

Joubaire broke in on Eve's reverie. "I can't see why— if it was Pierre, then why did Daunay make sure I was out of the house immediately after the attack on Mlle. Eulalie? If you are right, then until Anselme was found dead, he couldn't have known anything about it."

Eve nodded. She believed that even Pierre had thought of what he possibly might do, but had not decided to do it until after he left her. She visualized him returning from the ball, coughing with exhaustion, stripped nerves spilling into violence when he took whatever Anselme provided and it did not help at all. An impulse killing, but in a bizarre way also rancor against his father. "I said before that Daunay retains some peasant reactions: he expected you to feel loyalty toward a man who had led you bravely through war and hardship. You understood how little the Commandant was to blame for what he did to Mlle. Eulalie, yet were prepared to leave him to be beaten up in ritual revenge. I always understood that part because of how I felt myself; and for the same reason, to you it remained a mystery. Daunay is a dangerous man but not contemptible. He couldn't believe you would be rat enough just to sit in the kitchen and drink wine. He was wrong, that's all."

But Joubaire was scarcely listening any more. As his hopes of any hold on Daunay vanished, he had become so much afraid that he thought only of himself. "The bank. We must go to the bank at once. I shall need a great deal of money if I am to get away." He looked accusingly at Eve. "Your trade is quiet today."

"Le Trésor isn't a bakery," she retorted tartly. "We have clients who occasionally spend heavily, not a crowd putting sous on the counter. At this season Le Tout-Paris enjoys the Mediterranean sun, and even if we'd been at war again today they wouldn't have changed their plans."

"I can't wait—"

"Many of them return to Paris about mid-September, or so I'm told." Eve was enjoying herself for the first time in weeks, calm no longer assumed.

He gnawed at his lips. "How much have you in the bank?"

She selected a sheet from among some papers. "Seventeen thousand francs."

He grabbed at her again. "You must have more than that!"

"It seems a great deal of money to me, and I can't draw more than five thousand at a time anyway."

His hand tightened viciously. "Bitch. You're lying to me."

Eve flinched; she could not help it. "Ask the bank to show you the documents. When Commandant Saulx signed a *bon pour autorisation maritale* so I could draw on our joint account, that was the limitation made. Frenchmen don't trust their wives unnecessarily." Certainly Joubaire would never trust anyone, and the bank wouldn't show him the papers even if he dared to ask. In fact, Guy had trusted her with everything they possessed, and the figures she showed Joubaire came from an account for current expenditure.

"Very well, madame," he said savagely. "We will go immediately to collect five thousand, and then I will make my plans to dispose of the goods you have here."

Eve felt oddly unprotected in the street with Joubaire at her side, although it was infinitely worse when they returned again to Le Trésor and he began heaving furniture carelessly into piles. She stared out the double window she knew so well, feeling as if she had the scrap dealers in; Joubaire was becoming dangerously uncontrolled in his fear, and she dreaded the moment when his temper would explode. Soon, very soon, and probably over some unimportant trifle. He had nothing to gain from hurting her and a great deal to lose but was already close to panic, and panic triggered violence.

Somewhere out there, Daunay had people watching her. She shivered and turned away as a crash sounded from upstairs, as if Joubaire had booted something fragile out of his way.

Eve opened the door and walked out. She ought to have gone as soon as there was nothing more she could do. Instead, as Joubaire had expected, all her instinct had been to remain and try to protect what she had slaved to build, but in this mood he would ransack and spoil, sell through dealers, anything, and there wasn't a damned thing she could do to stop him. But, dear God, how it hurt to go, and add Le Trésor to the failures of her life, even though failure this time was not her fault.

One day, she intended to be back.

It wouldn't be safe to return to the Rue Tronchet, she realized, because Joubaire had insisted on knowing where she lodged, nor to the Rue Férou. She nearly turned back then, because how would Guy find her if she disappeared?

But she couldn't go back; she had to leave Joubaire to destroy everything, knowing that when he had finished he would himself be killed. The police couldn't help, no one could help, any attempt at explanation ruinous so long as Daunay remained impregnable behind his millions. Nor would it save Joubaire's life; there was never likely to be anything to connect an anonymous corpse in a gutter with the Champs-Élysées.

Eve decided to go to the Crillon, where the American delegation was packing to leave. Probably Guy would try there if he really wanted to find her, and Joubaire most certainly would not.

The first person she saw in the foyer was Rick Dwyer.

CHAPTER 18

"Why, Rick!" Eve exclaimed joyfully. "I never guessed you would be back in Paris yet."

"I wasn't. I arrived this morning, and after a damned uncomfortable journey, too." He kissed her hungrily. "Worth it, though, when before I went away you looked at me as if I was something scraped off the sidewalk. I suppose it's too much to hope you came here looking for me?"

Eve flushed. "I didn't know you were back."

"So you didn't. Come and have a drink instead; then you can tell me what trouble you're in this time."

"What makes you think I'm in trouble?"

"I'm a newsman, remember? Trained to notice agitated women and other portents of disaster." He steered her toward the bar, half empty because most members of the American delegation were taking a hard-earned holiday before returning to the States.

Eve sighed and looked around her; suddenly life seemed set in its course again. Familiar American voices close by, highballs and disinfectant smells, blueberries on the menu and casual friendliness from the marine waiter. She simply couldn't worry about Joubaire ransacking Le Trésor any longer: at least the interest of Le Tout-Paris should be reawakened when Nathalie de Saint Luc next visited and found the place swept bare.

Rick was watching her. "Frogs gotten you licked at last?"

Eve smiled. "It isn't easy to set aside twenty-one out of twenty-two years of your life inside six months. I enjoy relaxing sometimes."

"Regrets?"

Her eyes narrowed; it was too early to force decision yet. She still needed to see Guy first. "Over some things; not others, though. I like Paris, for instance—if just a few of its inhabitants would swim away down the Seine."

He laughed. "I'd enjoy to ditch a few from Washington in the Potomac after I've been back a few days."

"You're going back?"

"A message was waiting in the office. Once the Germans have signed, my editor wants me to cover the politicking that will be needed on Capitol Hill if the treaty's ever to be ratified. He reckons that having seen things at this end, I'll write an extra dimension into reporting there."

"I expect he's right."

His eyes flickered at her tone. "Could be. Wilson's got a hell of a fight on his hands if he's ever to force it down the Senate's throat. If you want my opinion, he won't succeed, but the dogfight should be interesting while it lasts. The Washington *Times* likes its reporters to do a stint at home from time to time anyway, and I'll enjoy going back for a while."

Eve nodded, unexpectedly swept by homesickness. She could no longer imagine herself back in Maine, but in the Crillon and surrounded by Americans delighted to be going home, she, too, ached for America. "Good luck," she said at last.

"Why don't you come with me?" His eyes were on the glass between his hands.

"I'd like to," she said candidly, and smiled. "But for all the wrong reasons, I'm afraid."

"Tell me a few, and let me decide whether they're so wrong," he suggested.

"To get away, and live in the States again. To let you do the worrying for a while."

"You sure believe in being frank," he said wryly.

"I've grown up, Rick. I think now that some things are better laid on the line."

"All right," he said slowly. "Then, there's something else you have to face. Saulx won't be coming back. There's nothing here for you to stay for, except perhaps another war." If the Senate did refuse to ratify the treaty, and Rick was willing to bet on it, then no matter what promises Clemenceau had received from President Wilson, the guarantee of French security was dead as well. America would turn her back on her former allies and think it good riddance. Rick Dwyer was not a sentimental man, but admitted to himself that at the moment he could scarcely wait to get out of Europe.

Eve sat paralyzed with shock. Lips dry, words out of reach.

He watched her steadily. "Come with me, Eve. You deserve a good time, and I'd enjoy taking the worry from you for a while. Later, we'll see how we feel. I'll be frank too; I always thought I'd hate to be tied; now I'm not sure."

"What happened to him?" She had not grasped anything Rick had said since he told her Guy wasn't coming back.

"I'm sorry, Eve, I can't. It was one of those secret government deals, and I'm not sure about the details. Nor will anyone else tell you; take my word on that. But I didn't make any mistake; Saulx won't be coming back." He wondered what the poor bastard would think if he knew that everything he'd done would be wasted—perhaps worse than wasted —once American promises on French security were made worthless by Washington resentments. He sighed; luckily, Saulx was incapable of thinking anything.

"You know something," said Eve levelly.

"A little. Not much. There's been some arms smuggling in the Rhineland and he was caught in the middle of it. He wasn't fit enough for fancy footwork, I guess."

Eve stared at the crisp linen of her dress, frowning when she saw it was wet. Then she realized she was tipping her highball so it ran over her fingers as well, and set it on the table. "Where is he?"

"What do you mean?"

"He was a French officer. They won't— he'll be buried in France, surely."

"Does it matter?"

"To me it does."

"There was an explosion," said Rick, thinking hastily. "I reckon they won't worry too much about formalities when the whole deal was secret. You'll hear officially soon. Eve, for God's sake face facts, as you said you must only a few minutes ago. The guy was brave, but a disaster as a husband. You're well rid of him."

"I'm going to have a child," she said, and straightened in her chair.

"Jesus! Eve . . . ?"

She looked at him. "I don't know, Rick. Probably it's yours, but the night I left him he— just possibly it could be his." Her voice choked; for a long time it had not occurred to her that though she conceived during the time she lived with Rick, there was this one chance that Guy could be the father.

"When?"

"About Christmas, I suppose."

Without speaking, he picked up her glass and his and went for another drink. "You're quite certain it could be either of us?" he demanded when he came back.

She nodded. "Which answers another kind of question too. You see, I know now how very much I hope it is Guy's."

"You're a goddam fool if that's true!" he retorted, anger flaring. "At least my kid would have a father who didn't gibber in a cell."

Eve's eyes widened. She opened her lips to speak, and then closed them again.

"I guess Saulx was okay once; it was just the war," Rick added awkwardly. "I'm sorry, Eve."

He wasn't, but could not shake off a feeling of guilt even though Saulx, too, had wanted it done this way.

"How much do you know of French law, Rick?"

He blinked. "Some, I guess."

"Way back, oh, months ago, one day I felt whipped by everything and went to book my passage back to the States. Probably I wouldn't have gone, but do you know what the steamship company told me? A married Frenchwoman needs her husband's consent before she can leave the country, a written chit before she can so much as buy a ticket or obtain a passport. If you want me to come with you to Washington, you'll need to wheedle Guy's death certificate out of the French Army first."

"You mean you'd come?"

"If you could fix it, yes." She was watching him intently.

"Why, Eve—" He broke off, disconcerted by the white, set face across the table. "Give me a few days, honey, and I'll see what I can do." That French provost colonel in Mainz had said that if it was what Saulx wanted, they'd put through next-of-kin documentation eventually.

In Paris, Rick simply didn't know where to start.

She smiled then, color flowing into her face again. "He isn't dead, is he? You'll have to tell me everything now."

"I told you everything."

"You never said he was dead, and he isn't. For a newsman you're a damn bad liar, Rick." She drank her highball in a gulp.

He sighed. "Okay, you win, but none of it was my idea. Saulx told me not to let you think he was still alive."

Color drained from her face again. "Why?"

If he lived to be a hundred and covered mayhem all over the world every year until then, Rick reckoned he would never be landed with a more unpleasant task than telling Eve Saulx just how far her husband was, and was not, still alive.

Rick had been uncertain before, but loved her when he had finished.

As he had surely loved her a long time now, for her courage, among other things.

Eve listened quietly, fingers pleating folds in her skirt, and stayed silent a long time after he had finished. "Where is he now?" she asked eventually.

"I don't know. In a trash can— in a hospital back in France, I suppose."

"Could you find out?"

"He doesn't want to see you, Eve. Sometimes he's clear enough and realizes just what he's done to you; you'd only make matters worse if you go to him now."

"I'm his wife, Rick. And if you say that sometimes he's clear, then that is a place to start." She looked out through the open doors of the Crillon at pigeons pecking in the Place de la Concorde. "It's peace at last, and he can rest. With me he can rest; I know he can. Once, he slept through a whole night without waking, in my arms; with me he has a chance. Alone, he'll have none at all."

"How about you, Eve? It'll be one goddam hell of a life for you."

"What would you expect me to do? Dance, drink and be merry with Le Tout-Paris, while he's locked away in the dark?"

"He's much worse than he was, Eve," Rick said gently. "And you know the kind of thing he did before. How will you bring up a kid—my kid, dammit—believing such a man is its father?"

"With pride and love. You can burn that file you keep hinting at, when so far as he's concerned, most of it isn't true." She took the photograph out of her bag, where she had put it earlier without quite knowing why. "That's what he looked like once; now, will you find him for me?"

Rick sat frowning heavily at the Bourbon held between his hands. He had lost. She wouldn't come with him to Washington now; later, if he still wanted it, he might have another chance with her. "Only after you've made me a promise."

"Which is?"

"If ever in your heart you know you are defeated, you will send me word of it."

She stood and kissed him on the cheek. "Dear Rick. Yes, of course." All the marvelous warmth he had sometimes seen in her was there, a breath away. "I don't mean to be defeated this time, though. Which is as well when you think how much explaining you might have to do to a future Mrs. Dwyer, just when you least expected it."

"I want your promise, and the devil take Mrs. Dwyer."

"You have it. Shall I wait here while you go out drinking with your contacts?"

Eve took a train to Lisieux and then traveled by branch line deep into the Calvados country of Normandy. The land was ripening toward harvest, the timbered villages huddled into winding valleys and surrounded by orchards and rich, sloping meadows. When she climbed the leg-stretching distance down to the wayside halt of Hautbec, stillness closed about her as soon as the engine and high carriages disappeared. The air was soft after Paris heat, and high hedgerows made tunnels of the dusty roads.

"You are a visitor to Calvados, madame?" asked the blue-smocked railwayman who took her ticket. He had been weeding onions, cap and jacket slung on palings.

Eve nodded. "It's lovely to be in the country after Paris. I want to reach the Château Erquy."

The old man's expression altered, and he wiped his hands carefully on the seat of his breeches. "Ah, *les pauvres garçons là*. We must pray that the good air of Normandy will heal them."

"How far is it to walk?"

"*Tiens, madame, je vous demande pardon!* I will harness my good Clothilde and drive you there myself."

Eve laughed; this was a life she understood. "What about your rail-road station?"

"A station like this is not exacting, madame. Perhaps two people may alight here in a day, and today Madame is the second. Wait for me but a moment."

So Eve sat beside M. Marchand in his pony trap and drove the three kilometers down green valleys to the Château Erquy, her face lifted to the scents of the countryside. In Paris she had ceased to think of places like this; now she no longer thought of Joubaire, Le Trésor, or Georges Daunay. Almost consciously, she was allowing herself this short time without strain, as preparation for what was to come.

"A train leaves for Lisieux at twenty hours, madame. It is the last of the day." M. Marchand broke in on her thoughts.

Eve stared at the great iron gates they were passing through, apple orchards almost hiding the conical towers of a small château. It seemed less forbidding than she had feared. "I don't know when I shall be returning to Lisieux."

"*Entendu*. But if I can be of any assistance, then Madame has only to ask. My Clothilde can reach the château from the station in a very short time."

"Thank you, monsieur. Kindness helps so much," said Eve, and meant it.

The Château Erquy was partly staffed by nuns, which was reassuring, although there were also some tough-looking orderlies about and extra doors had been set at the entry to each passage. The interior was cool and smelled of flowers.

"Mme. Saulx?" said a sister doubtfully when Eve explained who she was. "The Commandant is marked as unmarried on his dossier."

"How is he?"

The nun crossed herself. "Alone with the devil, madame."

Eve lifted her chin. "Then, he is not alone any longer."

Guy was lodged in one of the thick brick towers, and on the way up Eve passed other doors and heard sobs and cries; outside his, it was very quiet.

She went in alone; he was over by the barred window, standing, his face to the wall. Her heart changed beat and slammed painfully against her ribs; she had not known what to expect, but he was standing as she had seen him so often stand before, sustaining somehow the only defense he knew. Like her, he was not beaten yet.

She spoke, but he did not hear, so she went over and stood beside him, looking out through bars at green fields and peace.

After a while, she moved and touched him. "My love, how dared you tell them you had no wife?"

Slowly his head turned and she saw a face stripped down to bone. "Eve. I was afraid— I knew that if Dwyer told you, you would come."

"He tried not to," she said smiling.

"I begged him. . . ." He stood unseeing for quite a long time; then, with an effort she could feel, caught himself again. He was wearing only a shirt and army breeches; unshaven, and with everything wet from the sweat of terror. "Eve, I don't want you here."

"You haven't the choice, my dear, since I need you quite as much as you need me." She kissed the stretched skin of his face. "I'll tell you about it one day soon. How would you like it if we went together and lived in your old home in Alsace? I thought today that I should like quite simply to walk out on Paris."

Eve continued to talk to him through what remained of the day, and on into the dark. Occasionally, he answered. Often, he was not there at all. Sometimes breath died in his throat and he crouched with his hands locked above his head, a fragile shield from mud and steel. Then her voice or touch would reach him, his own determination burn through anguish, and between them they would rebuild courage piece by piece until he stood again, although he was so tired he could no longer speak. So tired it was a madness in itself and, nerves unstrung, he shuddered from the slope split open at his feet.

Eve held him then as she had not done before, while outside the birds sang before another dawn. "Come and sleep now, my love. With me you can rest. We shall do well together."

She had been right: alone, he no longer had a chance.

Eve lay holding him and thought of the years ahead when patience and pity would not be—as they never had been—sufficient. Only love could weather such a storm, and at the end of it find grace enough in both of them to achieve acceptance for a child unlikely to be his.

And love is, or is not; nor would it long endure on the wish for it alone.